The third book of Robinson's trilogy, **Death by Paradox**, stands alone as a rare and balanced blend of science and fiction, fulfilling the imaginative potential of the author's earlier novels. In this epic, based on a fine understanding of his characters and the clear intricacies of the plot, he challenges Einstein and develops the field of planetary psychology as well.

Death BY Paradox

R.M. ROBINSON

firefall™

First Edition: October 1, 2014

Cover Design & Illustration:
Marcia Repaci, North Creek Design
Editor: Elihu Blotnick

hardcover: 9781939434142
paperback: 9781939434159

FIREFALL EDITIONS
Canyon, California 94516-0189
www.firefallmedia.com
Printed in the USA

Library of Congress Cataloging-in-Publication Data

Robinson, R. M.
  Death by paradox / by R.M. Robinson. -- First edition.
    pages cm
  "Science Fiction by Scientists."
  Summary: Follows a family of planetary explorers through their experiences
pleasantly coexisting with friendly aliens known as the Tattoo People, but when
giant aliens hostile to all life but their own invade, humans turn to strategies as
diverse as nuclear weapons and music to stop them.
  ISBN 978-1-939434-14-2 (hardcover) -- ISBN 978-1-939434-15-9 (pbk)
  [1. Science fiction. 2. Interplanetary voyages--Fiction. 3. Life on other planets--
Fiction.] I. Title.
  PZ7.R567547De 2014
  [Fic]--dc23
                              2014010856

SCIENCE FICTION BY SCIENTISTS-tm

RM Robinson

THE SEEDS OF ARIL
Earth reborn, 20,000 CE,
8,000 light years away.

A PLANET CALLED HAPPINESS
The sequel to SEEDS

DEATH BY PARADOX
The third book in the trilogy

Larry J Friesen

BETRAYAL / BATTLE / STORM
Space mirrors Earth in the warp
of love and weave of war.

"Life did not take over the globe by combat,
but by networking."

Lynn Margulis and Dorion Sagan,
on the endosymbiotic theory.

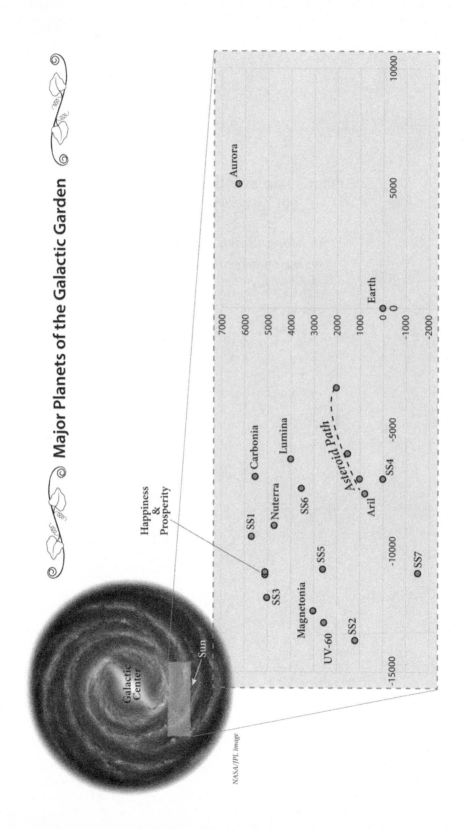

Major Planets of the Galactic Garden

NASA/JPL image

Mizello Family Tree

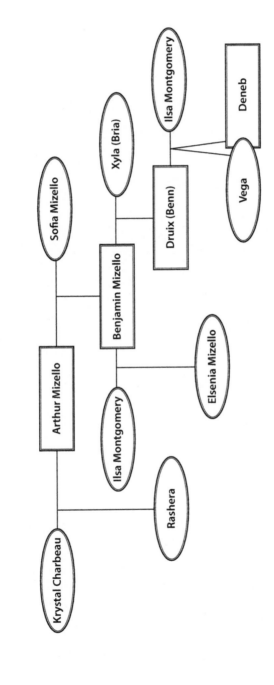

Death BY Paradox

PROLOGUE

139,769 CE
Century 1400

Risto Jalonen was nearly delirious when Arilian physicians pulled him from the magnetocryogenic chamber of his space capsule. They weren't particularly shocked by his condition, having received information of his illness many years earlier, transmitted on radio frequencies while the capsule was still several light years away. Risto suffered from cancer caused by exposure to high-energy particles. He'd been traveling the galaxy for 140,000 years.

Every galactic explorer understood and accepted the risks of prolonged exposure to cosmic radiation during space travel. Back in the 22nd Century, the Galactic Space Explorers Union laid the foundation for voyaging to destinations taking thousands of years by developing the necessary technology: propulsion, life support, magnetocryogenics, and other complex systems upon which success would hinge. Yet the most challenging obstacle had never been completely overcome. Damage to human tissue from cosmic rays over long periods of time eventually destroyed human cells, creating malignant cancers resulting in illness and inevitably death. The imperfect solution was to line the capsules with a uniquely designed composite material, lighter than lead, yet offering comparable protection from energetic particles. Only the highest-energy cosmic rays could penetrate the barrier. The Union also commissioned studies to model the flux of radiation throughout galactic space. As the motion of cosmic rays is influenced by the magnetic fields of celestial objects, the models revealed otherwise invisible pathways where the flux was lowest. When calculating the trajectories between galactic destinations, computers on space capsules automatically selected paths to minimize the travelers' exposure.

During the 22nd Century, the Union both organized and financed the launch of more than 1200 galactic explorers, each occupying a single vehicle. Half the explorers still traversed the galaxy now—in the same capsules that had survived thousands of years in space, as well as landings on alien planets too numerous to count. That the capsules had survived the ravages of time and the risks of interstellar travel and planetary exploration was a testimony to superb engineering, but it was also evidence that space is by and large a fairly benign environment. Once humans found ways to protect themselves from radiation hazards, there was little else to fear from empty space other than the extremely rare collision with another object, or even rarer circumstance of encountering hostile aliens. Other than the Tattoo People, who weren't in the least bit dangerous, the part of the galaxy explored by humans was largely devoid of other intelligent life forms.

Survival during long duration space travel was enabled by magnetocryogenic technology, in which intense magnetic fields provided instantaneous immobilization of the living cells in organic tissue, allowing freezing and unfreezing of humans without death or injury. Once frozen, the absolute zero temperatures of interstellar space ensured that travelers could remain safely in suspended animation for thousands of years, as immutable as petrified rocks. Magnetocryogenics freed humans from the time constraints of interstellar exploration. Their space capsules employed propulsion systems that gradually accelerated the vehicles to velocities nearly half the speed of light. Even with that, it typically took thousands of years to travel from one star system to another. But it didn't matter to the frozen explorers. They grew accustomed to dealing with the unimaginable lengths of time that passed from one conscious moment to the next, in the same way that humans on Earth weren't surprised when they went to sleep at night and woke hours later to find the sky no longer dark. For the galactic explorers, each time they were unfrozen, it wasn't a new day, nor even a new year, but a new millennium—a new age.

To support the galactic exploration enterprise, the Union designed, constructed and deployed seven large supply ships. They too had survived the millennia, still fully functioning, cared for by custodians, kept alive by the same magnetocryogenic technology that gave the galactic explorers almost unlimited life-spans. The supply ships were safe havens for wandering explorers, miniature Earths, complete with sustainable and reproducible supplies of food, fuel, air, and water.

Still, no one really knew how long it would be before the explorers started showing the signs of radiation illnesses. It was only after the first reports surfaced among the messages being transmitted through the Union communication network that explorers realized an epidemic had started. Those who developed symptoms were instructed to come to Sparil, a smaller planet established as the spaceport for its neighbor Aril, the first extra-terrestrial planet to be inhabited by humans. Aril and Sparil were eight thousand light years from Earth. The only other planets with human populations in Century 1000 were Prosperity and Happiness, another pair of planetary siblings four thousand light years from Aril and twelve thousand light years from Earth.

Human expansion into the galaxy had been facilitated by two unexpected and extraordinary discoveries. One was that a supernova explosion had sprinkled the raw materials for life-sustaining planets into a sector of the Milky Way galaxy which came to be known as the Galactic Garden. It contained thousands of planets with abundant varieties of life forms, both plants and animals, providing endless destinations for the members of the original explorer fleet. The planets of the Galactic Garden also provided countless possibilities for humans seeking to establish new colonies on distant worlds.

The other discovery was that humans were not the only intelligent life forms populating the Galactic Garden. Many of the new worlds were inhabited by aliens called Tattoo People, who literally sprouted from a prolific vine, introduced on barren planets by asteroid-like objects. The hardy vine from which the Tattoo People originated had been genetically engineered by an alien race to take hold in even the harshest planetary conditions. Once established, the vine transformed the planet's atmosphere to support the alien civilization. Over the course of thousands of years, the vine spread and matured until conditions were right for the birth of the first batch of Tattoo People from pod-like structures that sprouted from the branches. The cloned aliens emerged to an oxygen-rich atmosphere that was ideally suited for the new civilization. Once the first population of Tattoo People dropped from the vine, subsequent generations reproduced in much the same way as humans. Fortuitously, the same biosphere that sustained the aliens was also conducive to human habitation. For many thousands of years, humans and the Tattoo People lived parallel existences in the Galactic Garden.

Risto Jalonen was brought to a special clinic on Sparil, staffed with skilled physicians and caregivers, specially trained to handle the unique ailments that radiation exposure produced. He was placed in an intensive care facility and treated to the extent possible, given the advanced stage of the cancers that infused his body. Eventually, he was moved to a special ward that housed other explorers also suffering from radiation exposure. They were kept in absolute zero temperature confinement, frozen before succumbing to the illness, taking advantage of the same technology used on the space capsules. The primary difference between the magnetocryogenic chambers on Sparil and those on the space vehicles was that in space, explorers could remain permanently frozen simply by being exposed to the cold emptiness about them. In the clinic on Sparil, freezing temperatures were maintained through refrigeration, which consumed large amounts of energy. Arilians disdained the dependence on any such technology because they knew how precious and dear the cost of producing that energy was, especially on Sparil. However, exceptions were made for freezing the explorers who were among the original group that ventured from Earth in the 22nd Century, particularly Risto Jalonen, who had been instrumental in saving Aril from invasion back in the 650th Century.

Patients in the cryogenic ward were unfrozen occasionally and given updates on the progress being made to cure them of their illness. None of the explorers really wanted to be kept alive in storage, but the Arilian physicians convinced them that by doing so they'd provide a means to test various new remedies for radiation damage to human tissue. The cure, when it was eventually developed, would save the lives of many space travelers. The noble explorers suffered the indignations of being no more than laboratory animals, knowing that by doing so they might be of great help to other space travelers.

Prior to undergoing the freezing process, Risto became barely coherent, long enough though to speak with the physicians. They listened to his erratic words, wondering how much credibility to place on the ramblings of a 22nd Century explorer from Earth, dying of radiation-induced cancers.

"Asteroid," Risto mumbled. "Find the asteroid."

"Which asteroid?" one of the doctors asked.

"In space. The asteroid. It shouldn't be there. Find it."

"Where is it? Where is the asteroid?" a second physician insisted.

Risto lifted a trembling hand and pointed skyward. "It is there. You must find it."

The doctors exchanged glances. There was little more to be said.

"We will find the asteroid, Mr. Jalonen. Don't worry. You must rest now. Are you ready to be frozen?"

Risto turned his head slightly to look at the doctor who'd spoken, as if confirming his reality, or veracity. Then he lowered his hand and nodded his consent. The physician pressed a button and Risto slid into the circular opening of the chamber where he'd remain until the Arilians unfroze him again. The physicians made a note of Risto's words and entered it into the record. None of them felt it warranted any attention. Risto would be oblivious soon to all such concerns.

CHAPTER 1
— Century 1416 —

ELSENIA MIZELLO'S life trajectory was unlike any other human in the galaxy. She was conceived on the amusement park planet called Happiness and then transported, frozen in utero, to Aril, where her mother, Ilsa, first learned of the child she was carrying. Ilsa remained on Aril to raise Elsenia while her husband, Benjamin Mizello, left with two other explorers to investigate the source of strange radio transmissions coming from Happiness, inexplicable because it was widely believed the planet had been evacuated in advance of an impending asteroid impact.

When Elsenia was ten years old, she and her mother departed Aril to reunite with Benjamin on the Union supply ship commanded by his father, Arthur Mizello. Instead of meeting Ilsa and Elsenia on the supply ship, Benjamin decided to remain on Happiness with Xyla, the woman who'd traveled with him to explore the planet. By the time Ilsa learned of his decision, Benjamin was dead. Abandoned and dejected, she departed from the supply ship with Elsenia and traveled back to Happiness—for no other reason than her desire to see the world once more to which she'd lost her husband. Benjamin and Xyla's son, Druix, found Ilsa and Elsenia and befriended them. Because freezing and unfreezing allowed galactic travelers to start and stop the aging process at will, Druix and Ilsa were the same age when they met. In a strange twist of fate, they fell in love and married. Several months later, they returned with Elsenia to Aril. Thus, before she'd even reached the true age of twenty, Elsenia had logged more than forty thousand light-years of space travel.

Being the daughter of parents who hailed from 22nd Century Earth made Elsenia an outcast on Aril. She neither looked nor acted like her native-born Arilian schoolmates. Rather than having fair skin with light-colored hair, Elsenia had olive skin and hair that was almost black. She was shapely, not as delicately as her mother Ilsa, but exotically, in a way that would have turned heads on 22nd Century Earth. On Aril though, her appearance more often drew stares, which she returned with expressions of defiance. The strong contours of her face and the fire in her eyes were ample warning to mischievous Arilian children that she was not one to be teased.

Although attending schools on Aril wasn't easy, Elsenia quietly accepted her fate, exhibiting remarkable stoicism for one so young. She'd grown used to being an outsider, and if she resented the life her parents had burdened her with, she never showed it. The zeal with which a young girl her age might have directed toward social interactions, Elsenia channeled into her studies and she excelled in Arilian academic institutions.

For a family that had traveled so far, the lives they adopted on Aril were unusually restrained. Ilsa and Elsenia dwelled in a small house on the campus of the university where Druix taught history. Ilsa, who'd been politically active during her years on Earth, quickly became an elected official in the town where the university was located. She had started out writing for the local news agency, but when her views grew in popularity, she was drawn into political circles.

Elsenia often wondered how it would be to live on a world where there were so many others just like her. Ilsa and Druix were the only other adult humans of her race. Ilsa and Elsenia were as close as a mother and daughter could be, in spite of the volatility in their relationship born of the suffering they'd endured when Benjamin chose to abandon them. Ilsa could be distant and short-tempered at times, which either resulted from or fueled Elsenia's stubbornness and strong will.

Druix had always been more like a brother to Elsenia than a father. He was both, or neither, depending on how she chose to look at it at any particular moment. In any case, he seemed more comfortable playing the role of an older brother. Thus, Elsenia never really knew what it was like to have a father. She couldn't honestly say this had any impact on her. When needed, Ilsa gave her all the love and attention she needed, maybe even more than she needed. Elsenia should not have lacked self-confidence. She'd handled herself extremely well considering the trauma of leaving Aril at the age of ten and being forced to live thousands of years on a Union supply ship.

When Ilsa announced she was pregnant, Elsenia was just as delighted as her parents. If nothing else, she wouldn't feel the same isolation and alienation she'd long endured. Because of the many years Ilsa had spent in space, her doctors recommended she spend the last trimester of her pregnancy on Sparil, where physicians were more experienced at dealing with complications that might arise due to her previous exposure to cosmic radiation. Druix accompanied her, leaving Elsenia feeling even more alone than ever.

Four months later, Druix and Ilsa returned with twins, a boy and a girl, named Vega and Deneb. Not surprisingly, the infants forced Elsenia's family into a new routine that made galactic exploration seem unimaginable. As she helped with the mundane tasks of caring for the babies, Elsenia's memory of her time in space took on dreamlike qualities. She worried that the twins would ground Ilsa and Druix in the challenges of parenting to such an extent that they'd lose their commitment to return to space. After some discussion, Ilsa and Druix reassured Elsenia that they'd remain on Aril only until the twins completed their college education. A pause of ten to twenty years to raise the twins wouldn't prevent them from resuming their exploration of the galaxy. Ilsa and Druix were in their late thirties and Elsenia was sixteen. They'd all still be young and healthy enough to take to the skies again when the twins were ready.

Observing the twins growing up on Aril strengthened Elsenia's abiding fascination with the Tattoo People, those alien beings who sprouted from a prolific vine whose seeds were carried by mysterious asteroids. They were called Tattoo People because of the complex patterns of pigmentation covering their bodies, patterns they could alter through mental manipulation. Tattoo People also possessed the unique ability to communicate via radio waves. The speed at which they shared information made the entire population of a planet act and think as a single entity. The

Tattoo People displayed a unity of purpose that gave them strength, security, and permanence. These were the very traits Elsenia's unpredictable childhood had stripped from her.

Upon graduation from high school, Elsenia attended the university, concentrating in academic areas that might expand her knowledge of the enigmatic aliens. Their origins from the vine demanded courses in biology and genetics, while their ability to communicate via radio waves required knowledge of electrical engineering and radio science. Their unique mental abilities and the way they used their minds to control the pigmentation of their skin led to courses in neural science, physiology, and anatomy. She also attended classes in social psychology also, with the goal of gaining insight into the group dynamics by which the Tattoo People lived.

With her parents' busy schedule, it often fell upon Elsenia to care for the twins. She resented the intrusion on her studies, but didn't complain. Watching the twins develop reinforced her interest in how children learn—the neuropsychological under-pinnings of behavior and personality. Granted the twins repre-sented an extremely limited sample, but Elsenia became skilled at extrapolating from her observations. In particular, she applied what she learned from the twins to the Tattoo People, who in many ways were like children, except with the uncanny and pow-erful ability to communicate so effectively among themselves.

From the time Vega and Deneb were old enough to un-derstand, Elsenia made up stories for them. The most popular were those she told of "the Family". The matriarch was a shriveled old hag, grumpy and mean, prone to forgetfulness, rudeness, and hysteria. She had two children, who were as different as night from day—not like the two of you, Elsenia would tell them—not like twins at all. One was bright, precocious, and curious—em-bracing the beauty of the universe, basking in its wonder and elated by the diversity and contrasts it offered. The other was ob-sessed with its own virtues, intent on overcoming the physical world for its own benefit and success. The first found fulfillment from within, while the second used vast amounts of energy and resources in ambitious pursuits. Each of the siblings gave birth to offspring that were different still from their parents. That made five in all—a Family of five—just like theirs. Soon, those five gave birth to others, and the Family grew. Each member of the Family was unique, with different personalities and different strengths and weaknesses. They tried to work together and cooperate, but it was difficult because they didn't communicate well. It wasn't just that they spoke different languages—language differences were easy to overcome. It was mostly because they were far apart.

Elsenia made up many stories about the Family, putting them in absurd situations that engaged and delighted the twins. They were captivated by these tales, even though they knew how every story would end. They'd wait breathlessly for the punch line, when Elsenia would ask the inevitable question that closed each story: "And do you know why the Family did this?"

Their eyes would light up and they'd gleefully mimic the answer, which Elsenia would say in the sing-song voice they loved, "Because all five in the Family were planets!"

The twins would laugh and clap their hands in delight. They knew they lived on the bright, creative planet, Aril, whose sibling was the self-absorbed planet called Prosperity. Aril created the futuristic spaceport called Sparil, while Prosperity created the amusement park planet called Happiness. The old, grumpy matriarch of the Family was Earth.

Elsenia's tales of the Family were fueled by the twins' natural curiosity. They often asked questions that challenged Elsenia to create new circumstances and situations among the characters of her stories.

"Are there male planets and female planets?" Deneb asked one day.

"Not really, but planets can fall in love," Elsenia answered.

"How?"

Elsenia invented a story about how two planets fell in love. One was a planet that was so strange, no other planet paid any attention to it. It was a very lonely world for a long time, until finally a planet that didn't mind its strangeness discovered it—a planet looking for true companionship. The planets didn't fall in love right away, but their love grew as they learned more about each other.

"Are there shy planets?" asked Vega.

"Yes, there are," said Elsenia, and she told the story of a planet that orbited a star nested in a cloud of interstellar gas. Other planets tried to observe it, but the light from its star winked on and off through the surrounding shroud of dust. Most galactic explorers passed it by, anxious to experience the excitement and adventure of planets that had more to offer. But those whose curiosity drove them to visit the planet were rewarded with a unique kind of beauty unmatched in the galaxy.

Elsenia couldn't make up stories fast enough to keep up with the twins' inquisitive imaginations.

"Can a planet commit suicide?" the twins wanted to know.

Elsenia wondered how they'd heard the ancient term. "Yes, a planet will occasionally destroy itself," she said solemnly.

"Why?"

"For many reasons, but usually it's because the civilization becomes too self-absorbed. It allows its self-interest to dictate its actions. Without a collective agreement that the planet is more important than the life forms that inhabit it, the gradual erosion of the biosphere is inevitable. Earth nearly committed suicide many thousands of years ago. Its population introduced chemicals into the atmosphere that slowly poisoned the air. No one would stop because by doing so they'd be unable to maintain the quality of life they'd grown accustomed to."

"That isn't suicide," the twins said, their voices expressing youthful indignation. "That's stupidity."

Elsenia laughed. "You're right. Sort of. It depends on how you look at it. All suicides stem from the failure to view one's existence in the proper context. Typically, this leads to a despair that can't be overcome—a despair that leads to self-destructive behavior."

The twins were only ten, but they were bright enough to understand what Elsenia was saying. They both nodded, seemingly satisfied with the explanation.

"How about crazy planets? Are there any crazy planets in the Galactic Garden?"

"Almost certainly," Elsenia answered. "Happily, humans haven't yet encountered one of them. A crazy planet would be the scariest and most dangerous of all."

CHAPTER 2

— Century 1416 —

GIVEN THEIR ANCESTRY, no one should have been surprised by the strangeness of the twins. Ilsa Montgomery was a 22nd Century human, doubtless of Anglo-Saxon heritage. Druix was descended from Benjamin Mizello of Italian-American heritage and Xyla, a Malanite of the planet Aurora. The humans who had colonized Aurora were from 80th Century Earth, most probably from the continent of Asia, but at that time all resemblance between them and their ancient Asian counterparts had disappeared.

In appearance, Vega had Ilsa's flawless complexion and Druix's ebony hair. Like Elsenia, she was easy to spot among the Arilian children, who sported tresses of blond, yellow or red. Deneb had Druix's tall, gaunt physique, but with his mother's piercing eyes. He had the same sharp features as his father, but like his mother, he had a delicate nose and prominent mouth that could issue a delightful smile, and often did.

It was the Malanite blood that probably contributed most to the unusual abilities Vega and Deneb manifested, even when very young. Malanites had an innate capacity to reengineer their genetic make-up in response to environmental or social stresses. Xyla had been born a fur-covered Malanite on Aurora, but shed her coat completely after she escaped the frozen planet. Whatever adaptation Malanites developed as a result of environmental stresses was passed on to their children. This accelerated adaptability of the species was unprecedented in the normal course of evolution, but shouldn't have been unexpected. After all, what better trait could a species possess to give it an edge over others in the game of natural selection? How many species had gone extinct because the one chance mutation that would enable it to survive never took place? Any species that could reconfigure its genetic make-up in real time, so to speak, would have a huge advantage over others.

Druix should have had the same unique capabilities as the

twins, but it never manifested itself in any obvious way. Perhaps the old adage about traits skipping a generation was true because what was manifested spectacularly in the twins was not apparent in Druix at all. This is not to say they were chameleon-like in their ability to adapt to their environment over the course of minutes or hours. Their adaptations were much more subtle. The changes weren't noticeable from one day to the next, but over several years they were unmistakable.

During one extremely cold Arilian winter, both Vega and Deneb grew a coating of very fine, pale fur, hardly noticeable to most. Ilsa and Druix wondered whether they might grow a full coat, like their maternal grandmother had on the icy planet Aurora. But when the weather warmed, they both shed their coats completely.

Arilian schools emphasized the importance of running, and subjected all students to rigorous drills. After several years, the twins developed phenomenal stamina, and they easily outpaced their Arilian classmates. They were excellent swimmers, too, particularly Vega. Although they started out equal to their peers in early exposure to the sport, after two or three years they were far superior. Deneb excelled in speed, while Vega exhibited an endurance that was almost superhuman. She could swim underwater for long periods of time, causing extreme distress in her parents, who waited nervously on the Arilian beaches waiting for her to emerge safely from the surf. Ilsa checked Vega periodically to see if she was developing webbed feet.

Through the years, the twins perfected their memories because it was a skill that aided their performance in the Arilian schools. They learned new languages with ease, and often practiced their talents on each other, confounding family and friends with conversations only the two of them could understand.

Not surprisingly, the twins also had an uncanny ability to communicate with each other telepathically. Their teachers tried to separate them when they took exams, but even in different rooms, they could share answers. Arilian instructors soon adopted the attitude that it didn't matter if the twins helped each other because they would undoubtedly live their lives that way anyway.

Though Ilsa was obsessively protective of the twins, she allowed Arilian physicians to study them, subjecting them to carefully prepared and sufficiently benign experiments. In one of the experiments, Arilian researchers separated the twins by long distances to see if their abilities were compromised, or delayed, in any way. To their amazement, it didn't matter how far apart on the planet the twins were displaced. They could each accurately read the thoughts of the other. It was as if they shared a common brain that spanned any gulf the Arilian researchers introduced.

There was speculation that the twins communicated via radio waves, a skill their paternal grandmother had developed after spending years teaching the Tattoo children on Happiness, the amusement park planet. But efforts to detect radio waves failed. Researchers suggested an experiment to determine the time it took for the twins to transfer a thought or image from one to the other. It required them to be separated by a sufficiently large distance. Relativity theory, which had proven just as valid on Aril as on Earth, was based on the assumption that nothing could travel faster than light speed. The assumption always had to be qualified, however, because one could easily imagine something that must certainly exceed light speed, the classic example being the intersection of two flashlight beams. That point can travel infinitely distant in the time it takes to rotate the flashlight beams till they are parallel. Thus, the relativistic limit is that nothing *carrying information* can travel faster than the speed of light. If the twins could simultaneously share the same thought, even when far apart, the theory of relativity would need to be questioned. Unfortunately, Ilsa never agreed to allow the twins to be separated by a distance large enough for the test to be made. To make the experiment definitive, they'd have to be several million kilometers apart, by putting one twin on Sparil, for example, but it would never happen as long as Ilsa was in control.

Ilsa's overprotection of the twins went hand in hand with

her certainty that dangers lurked in the universe, and that the whole family traveled a delicate path through space and time that might steer them toward calamity at any moment. It had happened at least three times in her life: when her first husband was arrested and imprisoned by federal authorities eons ago on Earth, when she was kidnapped by Carl Stormer, and when she lost Benjamin to the Malanite woman on Happiness. The years she and Druix spent on Aril were almost certainly the most carefree ones Ilsa had ever known, but that only heightened the dread she routinely succumbed to. Even though her fears appeared irrational at the time, they were to prove insightful in the end.

Ilsa wasn't the only one to have these dark imaginings. At times, both Vega and Deneb were burdened by ominous thoughts. It was unclear whether the twins were simply reflecting Ilsa's misgivings or independently receiving subtle hints of some pervasive evil. Given their uncanny abilities, it was easy to believe the twins could perceive what others could not. Their eerie skill at reading each other's minds was inexplicable, even to Aril's advanced researchers. It wasn't a stretch to imagine that the twins were hypersensitive to subtle disturbances in the psyche of human civilization.

This is not to say they were unhappy children. On the contrary, their ability to adapt to the inevitable changes of childhood gave them security and confidence. The two got along remarkably well and were almost always together. They found strength from each other, even through adolescence when interaction with peers threatened to come between them.

Ilsa worried incessantly over whether the twins would be social outcasts in the Arilian schools they attended. She knew that whatever maladjustment they had as children would be exacerbated during adolescence, and this could inevitably lead to depression and bitterness, as she had learned a long time ago with Elsenia. Ilsa's concern simultaneously amused and irritated Elsenia because her mother hadn't thought twice about whisking her daughter away from Aril at the age of ten to embark on a long space voyage, only to end up on a Union supply ship. Where were the misgivings back then?

While the twins, Druix, and Elsenia all found fulfillment in various academic pursuits at fine Arilian institutions, Ilsa spent her time at the Central Data Archive and Library that contained the knowledge carried from 22nd Century Earth. Here, she entertained her obsession by reading ancient texts, hoping to find some insight and enlightenment to better fathom the root of evil in humankind. Even after hundreds of thousands of years of evolution, Ilsa believed that human civilization still carried a curse, a suppressed capacity for unspeakable malevolence. Though the rest of the family had been fortunate enough never to have confronted that aspect of human nature, Ilsa was convinced that it still existed and might manifest itself at any time.

Ilsa, Druix, Elsenia and the twins constituted a family of outcasts on Aril, but their options were few. They'd be aliens wherever they went in the galaxy. They'd long since come to grips with the reality and inevitability of their isolation from societies. There were five of them—a society of their own, and they made the best of it—at least for a while.

Elsenia worried that Ilsa and Druix might lose their resolve to recommence galactic exploration, but her concerns were unfounded. There was no disagreement within the family, that sooner or later they'd all leave Aril. It was in their nature, imbued by the events that prevented them from feeling at home at any location in the galaxy. The only question was when their travels would begin. For Elsenia, it couldn't be too soon, but she'd agreed to hold off until the twins were old enough.

At the age of 23, after she received her doctorate in biomedicine, Elsenia landed a job on Aril's neighboring planet Sparil, working at a hospital established specifically to treat the illnesses that space exploration brought upon space travelers. When she announced that she'd accepted the position, the news didn't sit well with Ilsa. She'd suffered the loss of Benjamin after he departed on a space journey, leaving her on Aril to raise Elsenia alone. She never saw him again. She had an abiding fear that if Elsenia left the planet, she'd never see her daughter again either.

Elsenia sympathized with her mother, having witnessed how the loss of her husband had devastated her, but Elsenia reassured her that she'd remain on Sparil until the twins finished their schooling and they were all ready to resume galactic exploration together. Ilsa finally relented, and Elsenia departed on a shuttle to Sparil to start her new job. She hadn't realized how deeply she'd miss her family until she disembarked at the spaceport and found herself readjusting to an entirely new society.

The spaceport attracted the most inquisitive, adventurous, and creative young people Arilian universities produced. Sparil was the magnet that drew all Arilians with wanderlust and unimpeded imaginations. It was also the gathering point for galactic explorers, many of whom were from the original group that first left Earth in the 22nd Century. Thus, Elsenia was exposed to humans of the race most similar to her and her family. Though these visits were transient, it excited her to know that on a galactic scale she was not as alien as she'd felt on Aril.

CHAPTER 3

— Century 1416 —

ELSENIA WAS ASSIGNED to the research institute attached to the medical facility on Sparil. With her training in both biology and medicine, she'd been tasked to study the reams of data received from life support sensors onboard the space capsules. She had to analyze the physiological data to determine when explorers were approaching the limit of their exposure. Sensors on the capsules kept track of the cumulative dose of energetic particle radiation, but it was common knowledge that the cumulative dose was poorly correlated with the onset of symptoms. Arilian physicians looked for physiological precursors to the malignant cancers, as it was usually too late to help explorers if treatment started after symptoms appeared.

Of course, other tantalizing data crossed Elsenia's desk as well. Each of the space capsules carried instrumentation that analyzed the organic material explorers had collected during their excursions to planets in the Galactic Garden. The information on the nature of extraterrestrial organisms was a humbling experience to those who worked at the research facility. It showed how little they understood about life—and death.

Still, even inundated with this rich and absorbing data, Elsenia maintained her obsessive fascination with the Tattoo People. The number of planets with their population continued to grow. Elsenia knew she'd never be satisfied until she could visit one of them. Even when the first victims of radiation exposure succumbed in the most horrible ways imaginable, she was steadfast in her desire to return to space. Nevertheless, she adhered to her promise and waited patiently for the twins to complete their training, after which they could all set off to explore the galaxy together.

While working at the institute, Elsenia learned that one of the patients held in frozen suspension at the hospital was Risto Jalonen. Elsenia owed her existence to Risto, the explorer who'd rescued her mother from a space capsule on an uncontrolled path toward destruction at the galactic center. Risto had also been instrumental in neutralizing the opposing forces during the invasion of Aril. Her father Benjamin was recognized as the hero of that war, but the outcome may've been very different had Risto not intercepted the reinforcements on route to aid the invading army.

When Elsenia learned Risto would be unfrozen for a periodic examination, she asked to visit him. Even though the Arilian physicians asserted that Risto was responding to treatment, it broke her heart to see the state the cancer had reduced him to. She'd read about his many exploits and found it hard to believe this patient was the same stalwart adventurer. Risto was about 45 years old in unfrozen time, but he looked much older. Elsenia could only see the outline of his emaciated frame beneath the bed covers. His face, the only visible part of him, was pale and lined with wrinkles, adorned by a stubble of blond beard, coarse and uneven. His piercing blue eyes were the only remnants of the spirit residing within his failing physiology. When Elsenia introduced herself as Benjamin Mizello's daughter, his eyes lit up as if illuminated from within by hazy daylight.

"I never met your father, but I'm a great admirer," he said, speaking slowly and deliberately. "Our paths and destinies crossed several times."

"I hope you don't mind that I came to see you. I told your doctors I wanted to meet you. It's a great honor to meet the man who saved my mother's life."

At this, Risto smiled. He extracted a trembling hand from beneath the covers and reached out to touch Elsenia's face. "I see the resemblance. You are beautiful like your mother."

"Thank you." It was the first time anyone had told her she was beautiful. On Aril, her appearance was considered anything but attractive.

Elsenia visited Risto frequently over the next several days while physicians continued his treatments. They discussed many things, but the one topic that energized him most was the Tattoo People and how they originated from an alien vine. Risto had been intrigued by the mysterious origin of the aliens since his capture by the pirate gang led by Stella. He'd given up the opportunity to visit the planet Happiness, allowing the game warden Theonius to land in his space capsule while he left in Theonius' vehicle with barely enough fuel and life support to reach the nearest supply ship. By the time he reached Supply Ship 6, Risto learned from Benjamin's father, Arthur Mizello, of the Tattoo People and all that was known at the time. Upon leaving the supply ship, Risto embarked on a self-imposed mission to search for one of those asteroid-like objects that carried the seeds of the alien vine. He believed this would provide unambiguous clues as to where the objects came from. Once the asteroid had impacted a planet, all evidence that it might have carried was obliterated. Only by exploring one of these asteroids en route to its destination would the secret of the Tattoo People be revealed.

"You realize how unlikely it'd be for you to encounter one of these objects," Elsenia pointed out.

"Yes, of course, which is why I devised an automated technique to search for them. It was very simple. Any object in space that's close enough to a space capsule will, for a brief instant, eclipse the light from the distant stars it occults. I programmed the telescopes on my capsule, which are always observing the surrounding stars for navigational purposes, to identify any stellar eclipse. In interstellar space, there should be no reason for the light from a star to turn off, even momentarily. If the telescope detected such an event, the computer was programmed to track the object responsible, making more detailed observations of its size and speed."

Risto spoke slowly and with great effort. He closed his eyes. Elsenia thought he'd fallen asleep. It was pitiful to see the famed adventurer reduced to this feeble condition. Soon, without opening his eyes, he continued, his mouth dry and his voice raspy. Elsenia offered him water, but he declined.

"It was a shot in the dark, so to speak. A very unlikely experiment that had little chance of success, but given sufficient time, it might succeed. Sure enough, after only a few thousand

31

years, my search routine had discovered an object drifting in interstellar space. It was an elongated, oval-shaped form, about 40 km long and half again as wide, spinning and tumbling randomly. As far as I could tell from observations, it was very much like the asteroids that exist in all planetary systems, but its presence, drifting by itself in the void of space, not even distantly associated with a star or planet, bothered me.

"Naturally, I wondered if it could be the transportation system that carried the alien vine, but my observations revealed it to be nothing more than a very large, cold rock. I considered landing on it, but with such weak gravity, that would have been too risky. I, or the capsule itself, might drift off into space. Plus, with the object tumbling and spinning, I'd use up huge amounts of fuel positioning the capsule near enough to the surface to venture outside. Instead, I kept my vehicle close, collecting high resolution imagery of the object. That data, I hope, has been archived for future analysis. Once I was satisfied I'd made every observation possible, I returned to my magnetocryogenic chamber. Before doing so, I programmed my navigation system to follow the object, and continue taking pictures of it moving through space. For the observations I already made, I had illuminated the object with the exterior flood lights of the space capsule. Otherwise, it would've been completely invisible. I knew I'd use far too much energy imaging the object continuously because of the drain the illumination had on the vehicle's battery power. So I programmed the computer to only take an image every year, lighting it up for that limited time to conserve the capsule's electric power. Still, this technique provided hundreds more images. The Arilians are also in possession of that data."

"Have they looked at it?" Elsenia asked.

"I am sure they have." Risto managed a weak smile. "But the Arilians are very secretive, in general. They won't tell me one way or the other whether the data have been useful. Probably they feel that in some way it'll stress me and compromise my health. If I was worried about such things, I'd never have become an explorer in the first place. Perhaps the Arilians will be more forthcoming with you."

Elsenia touched Risto's hand, the one he'd used to caress her face. The skin seemed paper thin.

"I'll see what I can do. You're right. The Arilians are very taciturn, but they owe my family a great deal."

"As do we all," said Risto. With that he dropped off to sleep, or pretended to.

CHAPTER 4

— Century 1416 —

EVERYONE CALLED HIM LEMMY, but his full name was Lemanuel Von Sigma, purportedly a descendant of the famous Arilian radio astronomer Sigma de Anthony. The Arilians were adamant about keeping track of genealogy. No one questioned Lemmy's heritage. He worked on Sparil as a senior science advisor, a title that carried much recognition, but little responsibility. On Sparil, he was well known for his extensive analysis of the data received from explorers of the Galactic Garden. As the data included many different types of observations and measurements, Lemmy was equally adept at biology, geology, oceanography, meteorology, and space science, and whatever other discipline his quest for knowledge led him to. Lemmy was the logical person for Elsenia to consult for information about the asteroid observed by Risto Jalonen. She found Lemmy in his office, which also served as a storage room for the devices and equipment he'd collected through the years.

Lemmy was a short, rotund fellow, with thinning yellow hair, accentuated by an orange dress with a scarlet belt. Arilian men and women alike wore dresses, the extra material needed to close a garment around one's legs seemed wasteful to the frugal Arilians. Lemmy bustled when he walked and shrieked when he talked. Every sentence he spoke was highly animated, whether he was discoursing on the diversity of life forms in the Galactic Garden or remarking on being late for a committee meeting. Elsenia had no idea what color his eyes were. He never looked at her directly. He acted as though his mind had many more things to do than waste time worrying about social interactions. He remained still for only brief instants, and Elsenia found herself scurrying to and fro with him as he moved about the laboratory.

"Yes, I have looked at the data from Mr. Jalonen's capsule," he pronounced. He sat at a computer console which projected a holographic display of fractal complexity. Intertwining vortices of multi-colored filaments filled the space before him, shifting and rotating in response to subtle hand gestures from Lemmy, the creator of the display.

"These are the paths of state variables," he explained. "Each point in this volume represents a possible configuration of the system I'm studying."

"Which system is that?" Elsenia asked.

He glanced at her with a look that was first anger, then sympathy. "It doesn't matter. It can be any system. The more degrees of freedom there are, the more tangled will be the interconnecting strands. The point is, once a system is in a given state, it must follow a path along the filament upon which the state is situated. Here," and he gestured toward the spaghetti filled space, "The paths are squeezed tightly together, so it is relatively easy for the system to jump to a different state."

"I thought you said it has to stay on the same path."

"Yes, I did say that, but that's in the absence of outside forces. An external influence can move the state from one path to the next more easily here where the filaments are bunched than over here where the filaments are far apart."

"I see. Makes sense." Elsenia paused. "Still, it would be nice to know what system this is depicting."

With that, the display dissolved. Lemmy rose and moved across the room to an upholstered chair, offering Elsenia one next to him. He had calibrated her intellect and decided she'd be more effectively talked to on a lounge chair than in front of a holographic display of system state variables. He knew Elsenia was a biologist, but apparently there was as big a gulf between them as the filaments in his display at their most rarefied location. It would take a great deal of external influence to move Elsenia from her path to his.

"How can I help you?" he asked.

"I'd like to know whether you learned anything from the analysis of the data from Risto Jalonen's space capsule."

"Mr. Jalonen brought back a tremendous amount of data. Can you be more specific?"

"He took pictures of an asteroid-like object in interstellar space. Have you studied those images?"

Lemmy seemed to grow more attentive. "Yes. Extensively."

"Can you tell me what you found?"

In the next instant, Lemmy's rotund form was out of the chair and back at the computer. By the time Elsenia caught up with him, a three-dimensional image of the asteroid had appeared in front of them.

"At first, I considered the asteroid rather unremarkable. It required a great deal of analysis to deduce why it was so unusual. Mr. Jalonen's instincts were right, although I'm amazed by what he was able to discern using intuition alone."

"Instincts are extremely valuable," Elsenia said. "You should try them sometime."

"Yes," replied Lemmy, missing the irony in her voice.

He continued. "I probably wouldn't have paid such close attention to the asteroid at all had it not been so odd for it to be in interstellar space. Asteroids and similar objects are found in association with planetary systems, gravitationally bound to a central star. The only way an object can escape the planetary system is by an explosion or collision that imparts sufficient momentum to overcome the gravitational confinement."

"That doesn't seem so unusual," Elsenia said. "The galaxy is filled with colliding objects."

"True, but in any such explosion or collision, the debris produced comes in a broad range of sizes. Most of the debris products are small particles. The abundance of objects decreases with their size. It's a universal principle. If there is one object in interstellar space the size of the one Mr. Jalonen encountered, where are all the smaller ones?"

"Perhaps they're there, but we haven't observed them. You said yourself how difficult it is to find objects that have no intrinsic luminosity."

"Ahh, but you forget. Galactic explorer capsules have been crisscrossing the galaxy for thousands of years. If they encounter even the tiniest particles in their path, their weapon systems activate to neutralize the objects before a devastating collision occurs. We compile statistics on how often the collision avoidance weapons have been used in interstellar space. We would know if space is strewn with small particles."

"How often are they encountered?"

"Almost never."

Elsenia nodded. "Then Risto's object is an anomaly."

"Very much so, but that's not its only strange aspect."

Lemmy waved his hand and two thin filaments, one red and the other blue, appeared within the holographic display.

"Mr. Jalonen programmed his capsule to follow the object for several hundred years. When I analyzed the trajectory of the asteroid, I found that it didn't follow its expected path."

"What was its expected path?"

"Exactly what Isaac Newton would have predicted 140 thousand years ago. With no forces on it—and in interstellar space the gravitational force from distant stars is infinitesimal—the object should move in a straight line. Mr. Jalonen's object did not."

"How could that be?"

"I'm not sure, but the question made me continue my analysis. I pored over the thousands of images Mr. Jalonen brought back."

Lemmy was waving his hands again, and now the holographic display showed the asteroid tumbling through space with a disconnected, jerky motion.

"The jerkiness is the result of the long time gaps between images. Each photo caught the object at a different phase in its tumbling motion."

Elsenia stared at the jumping image, trying to see anything out of the ordinary.

"Did you see that?" Lemmy asked.

"See what?"

"I'll play it again."

Elsenia watched intently.

"Did you see it that time?"

"Something sparkled."

"Yes! What you saw was an image during a time when the

camera caught something highly reflective—perhaps metallic. It's only one image. I'll freeze the video on that frame."

Lemmy moved his hands and the movie stopped on a single frame. The entire asteroid appeared in three dimensions, an irregular object with pockmarked surface, like a miniature moon. Within one of the larger craters were bright shapes, some circular, some rectangular, some linear.

"What are they?"

"We don't know, but we can say for certain they're not natural features."

"Who made them?"

"Can't say. All we know is that those objects are probably manufactured from metallic or ceramic materials."

"Could this be one of the asteroids carrying the alien vine?"

"It very well could be, except it's not obvious why it'd be so large given that it just has to carry the material necessary to initiate the growth of a weed. An asteroid this big might easily blast a planet to pieces before it seeded a new garden. We've estimated the size of the vehicles carrying the alien vines. For all the known planets that have been struck, the estimated size is several times smaller than this."

Lemmy brought the video to life again. The object resumed its jumpy tumbling.

"We need to find out what this object is," Elsenia said.

"Yes, we've alerted Admiral Chase and the galactic explorer fleet and provided our best guess as to the object's trajectory. Hopefully, an explorer can intercept it. It'd be extremely helpful if someone were to land on the asteroid, but that's much too dangerous given the way it's tumbling. In any case, it will be many thousands of years before we receive any further information. You and I will be long dead by then."

Elsenia was thoughtful. "Where is the asteroid going?"

"What?" said Lemmy.

"You said you calculated its trajectory. Which way is the asteroid going?"

Lemmy looked momentarily confused. "There are no directions in space," he said, finally.

"Of course, there are. Can you show me the path of the asteroid?"

"Very well."

Grudgingly, Lemmy entered commands to the computer. Moments later a map of the Galactic Garden appeared. Superposed on the image was an arc, a yellow streak against the star-filled background.

"This is my best estimate of the asteroid's track."

"Hmm," said Elsenia, trying to orient herself to the image. "Where is Aril on this map?"

"It's right here." Lemmy pointed to an inconspicuous spot on the display.

"So the asteroid's moving toward Aril," Elsenia remarked.

Lemmy sighed impatiently. "Ms. Mizello, I'm sure it's just a coincidence that the asteroid's trajectory points approximately toward Aril. You must understand, the galaxy is very large. The odds that this object is on a course toward Aril are negligible."

"Unless…"

"Unless what?"

"Unless the asteroid is not moving in a random direction."

"Why would it not be moving in a random direction? It's an asteroid."

"I don't know. Call it intuition."

"There is no place for intuition in science, Ms. Mizello."

Elsenia moved toward the door. "It's Dr. Mizello, actually. And you're wrong. Science is all about intuition. Thank you for your time."

Elsenia's fascination with the asteroid and Tattoo People fueled her desire to begin her own explorations. She became increasingly impatient waiting until the rest of the family was ready. Finally, she heard from Ilsa that Vega and Deneb had completed their university coursework and signed up to become galactic explorers. Given their family background, they were easily accepted into the program. It meant they too would be transported to Sparil to receive the practice and training required to explore space in vehicles that had changed little since the time they'd first been developed on 22nd Century Earth. For the two years they were attending the academy, the twins were close to Elsenia again. She was relieved of the isolation she'd endured during her years on Sparil. Ilsa felt more comfortable knowing the twins weren't alone during their training.

Whatever the twins learned in the Arilian school for galactic exploration reinforced their will to embark on a life of adventure. Both knew and accepted the fact that after thousands of years voyaging in space there'd be no return to the life they were accustomed to on Aril. Elsenia, who well knew the distress and anguish this might cause to a young person, had long conversations with Vega and Deneb, to make sure they understood the irreversible decision they'd be making. Not surprisingly, the twins were undeterred by these admonitions. The attraction of the unknown, the call of unexplored worlds, and the thrill of adventure, collectively gave the twins a commitment and dedication that was imperturbable. The two reinforced this desire in each other as well. Together, the twins exhibited courage and resolution far beyond what either could achieve alone, and that was already quite impressive.

During their last year in the training academy, Elsenia received word from her parents that they'd begun preparations, divesting all their personal possessions and cutting the ties they'd made to Arilian society. As they were oddballs from the start there, the prospect of embarking on a journey with no return was only a slight impediment. Druix, the historian, was fully prepared to step out of the time frame of planetary life and into the reference frame of galactic exploration, where thousands of years were like minutes. Ilsa, who'd been whisked from her home on Earth unwillingly, had developed a wanderlust born from trauma. She was seeking a new beginning somewhere in the galaxy, or perhaps an end to whatever had begun 140 thousands years ago. How could local politics be fulfilling after being in space, witnessing the rise and fall of planets and civilizations, alien life forms, and the mysteries of the Galactic Garden?

Ilsa and Druix showed up on Sparil in time for the twins' graduation from the academy, a celebration of an end of their time on Aril and the beginning of their lives as galactic explorers. Of course, the twins had excelled at the academy. They'd breezed through all the formal instruction, both practical and in the classroom. The training they received was intense. Galactic explorers had to be prepared for the hazards of interstellar travel, as well as the broad range of conditions they might find on the planets they visited. It was a far more intensive course than Druix had received back in the 700th Century. Elsenia and Ilsa were now the only ones in the family without formal training. However, both had experienced interstellar travel, landed on and departed from planets, knew the procedures for resupply of space capsules at Union ships, and, most importantly, understood the navigation and communication systems of their vehicles.

In the weeks following the ceremony, the family prepared for their departure. For long hours they debated destinations, but could reach no agreement. It was Ilsa who finally settled on the compromise. They'd all go to the same destination first, one that she and Druix had selected. It was a planet called Lumina, with a thriving civilization of Tattoo People, but no human presence. Ilsa and Druix felt that Lumina was alien enough to give everyone a realistic exploration experience that wasn't particularly dangerous. After that, they'd reconvene to decide the next destination. The twins, in particular, didn't have the basis for making meaningful choices on where in the galaxy they might want to go.

CHAPTER 5

— Century 1483 —

ALMOST SEVEN THOUSAND YEARS LATER, the five space capsules carrying Elsenia and her family landed in a clearing on the planet Lumina. Lumina had been visited by explorers in the past, but many thousands of years separated consecutive encounters between aliens and humans. The clearing in the midst of the alien vine where they landed was the same one used by previous explorers. This was a good sign, as it suggested the aliens of Lumina had purposely preserved the space for future human visitors.

Elsenia was excited to see Tattoo People again. Her first encounter with them had occurred when she and her mother visited Happiness. Her fascination with the aliens began during that visit. Although they weren't human, their physiology was so much like humans it astounded her. The similarity between the two species inspired Arilian scientists to argue for a common origin. However, it was well known from the fossil record on Earth that humans had evolved from apes over millions of years. The two disparate origins could not be reconciled in any plausible way. The debate was particularly heated among the science community of Aril because there were no apes on the planet, or any other kind of mammal other than humans. The fossil record was information solely contained within the data archive brought to the planet many tens of thousands of years earlier. It was so old and so impossible to confirm that some dismissed it as folklore. Even the occasional communication Aril received from Earth didn't help quiet the skeptics, who doubted the people of Aril descended from an animal species on a planet thousands of light-years away.

The explorers who had visited Lumina previously carried with them the customized translating devices used so successfully to communicate with Tattoo People of other planets. These translators, which were contained in medallions small enough to be worn on lanyards about the neck, converted the audible speech of humans to a pattern of radio waves detectable by the Tattoo

People, and vice versa. It took only a short time for the translators to learn the unique conversion between the audible and radio wave equivalents of the language. Unfortunately, although Tattoo People of different planets had been born from the same alien vine and were anatomically alike, they didn't share the same language, or perhaps they'd started out with the same language but then evolved distinctly through the years. The radio waves used by the people of Lumina were transformed by the translating devices into audible sounds that were pure gibberish to the explorers. Similarly, when the humans spoke into the devices, the radio waves produced must have been equally incomprehensible to the aliens because they responded with helpless gestures and confused looks.

Previous explorers of Lumina showed the aliens video images of their cousins on Happiness co-mingling with the humans there, but this confounded the aliens even more. Many humans who visited Lumina and tried to establish a rapport with the aliens left disappointed and frustrated. Elsenia and her family were prepared for the challenges of their arrival and planned accordingly.

Elsenia, Druix, and Ilsa were not unfamiliar with the alien vine. They'd seen it on Happiness and even walked through one of the corridors carved through the dense foliage. On Lumina, the density of the vegetation was an order of magnitude greater. The forest was completely impenetrable except for those narrow pathways designed for the aliens' slim anatomy. The landing site was one of the few open areas. The advice the family had received from previous explorers was to land and wait because there was no way to enter the surrounding forest. Eventually the Tattoo people would show up. They did.

Calling the aliens of Lumina Tattoo People was even more of a misnomer on that planet than it had been on Happiness. What were originally thought to be tattoos were variably pigmented skin patterns. The aliens were able to control the pigmentation mentally, an adaptation allowing them to blend in better with their surroundings. It was undoubtedly a defense mechanism built into their genetic make-up to protect them from predators or other enemies. But on Lumina there were no predators. On Happiness, the aliens used the skill as an art form, manipulating their pigmentation to produce beautifully intricate images, which bore some resemblance to the tattoos humans created in a much more painful way. On Lumina, however, the aliens made no attempt to produce anything visually appealing. The art form did not exist for them. Previous explorers reported that, when the aliens were shown pictures of their counterparts on Happiness, they manifested expressions of annoyance and disgust.

The absence of distinguishable body markings made it difficult to tell one alien from another. This would have been terribly inconvenient had it not been for the fact that it didn't really matter who the humans were communicating with. The aliens all exhibited the same personality, a collective one. The aliens of Lumina were so well connected, they manifested similar behavioral and social traits that defined their civilization. The collective personality of the planet was one of sternness and strength, a persona that might've been born from experiencing and overcoming great challenges and hardships. This intrigued the visitors because none of them could fathom the aliens of Lumina undergoing any significant strife or suffering in the safe confines of the nurturing vine. Still though, the visitors drew their impressions from very limited knowledge and insight. The civilization must have been thousands of years old. It was hasty to presume the aliens had lived carefree existences for so long. Elsenia and her parents found themselves wanting to understand more, but none of them were trained to perform that type of analysis. With the Tattoo People, one had to build on the assumption that the progress of the civilization was heavily dependent on their ability to communicate and share knowledge completely and instantaneously. It gave them strength that Elsenia envied, a strength she had not personally experienced.

The Tattoo People of Lumina weren't rude or antagonistic toward Elsenia and her family, but they possessed an attitude of aloof detachment the visitors weren't prepared for. Druix had been with Benjamin when they'd first established a means of communication with the Tattoo People on Happiness. Their response had been extremely welcoming. They were delighted to be finally able to speak with the humans who shared their planet. On Lumina, no such jubilation was evident, and having to host human visitors seemed more a chore to them. Perhaps it was the centuries that passed between visits by space travelers. It was too much to expect that Tattoo People several generations removed would feel affinity to humans.

In any case, the aliens were civil upon greeting their new visitors, and were patient as they tried to reestablish a means of communication. As soon as they understood the translating instruments and how they'd been tested on their cousins on another planet, they grudgingly treated their visitors with more respect. All this took place very soon after their arrival in the clearing where the capsule landed. When the introductions concluded, the twins wandered off, curious to explore the surrounding forest. Ilsa protested, but the Tattoo People reassured her they were fine. The aliens who had greeted the humans so reluctantly had somehow embraced the twins and whisked them away on a private tour.

Elsenia, confronted with the serious, reserved demeanor of the aliens on Lumina, felt intimidated by them, as though at the mercy of an authority figure. Oddly enough, she found herself drawn to the aliens in a way she couldn't explain. Not that she was physically attracted to them—their biology and physiology were worlds apart, so to speak. It was that the aliens presented a persona Elsenia found dark, mysterious, and unreachable.

The family set up a camp in the clearing where they'd landed and settled into a routine that quickly became carefree and easy. Occasionally, the aliens brought them food and water, and sometimes lingered, sitting on chairs they carried with them—made from the branches of the vine, of course. Elsenia, Druix, and Ilsa became more proficient at the alien language, and the Arilian translating devices rapidly accumulated the extended vocabulary necessary for seamless communication with the aliens.

It was well known that all civilizations of Tattoo People thus far encountered by humans designated elders as historians.

Druix lost no time in seeking out one of them to learn about their history and folklore. It was a frustrating endeavor, ultimately, because the Tattoo People on Lumina were innately secretive and suspicious of strangers. Nevertheless, Druix persisted and soon gained their trust, but only after sharing with them all he knew about human history, which was truely extensive. They took particular interest in his account of how humans and Tattoo People of other planets lived together. This went contrary to their instincts, which was to live in isolation and maintain their independence and self-sufficiency.

On her part, Ilsa took interest in the many ways the Tattoo People made use of the vine. Her curiosity was entertained in a grand way by the Tattoo People. Flattered by her reactions to these works, they proudly escorted her on tours, showing her how the various parts of the vine were harvested and fashioned into remarkably useful and beautiful objects. The only parts of the plant never used were the tendrils that extended from the vine's branches into the ground. The Tattoo People seemed extremely protective of these tendrils and would not disturb them in any obvious way.

Of the three adults, Elsenia was the least successful in her interactions with the Tattoo People. Their realm was to remain a mystery to her. No matter how many times they escorted her through the tangled and twisted trails carved through the dense foliage, she still had the feeling she was only seeing a small part of their vast domain. She learned, that the Tattoo People occupied their time turning the fast-growing plant into homes, furnishings, and utensils, while harvesting its berries to make an amazingly diverse array of foods. Yet somehow Elsenia sensed there was more to their endeavors. They seemed to have a deeper purpose—one that they'd never reveal or even hint at.

Their fascination with Vega and Deneb should have been a clue, but Elsenia interpreted that as stemming from a pseudo-kinship they felt with the twins. All Tattoo People were connected because they communicated so well. Unity of purpose and harmony came easily to them. Did they see the same potential in the twins? Vega and Deneb were as closely linked as two humans could possibly be, which must have intrigued the Tattoo People and created a fellowship that the rest of the family wasn't privy to.

CHAPTER 6

— Century 1483 —

THE TWINS' GRANDMOTHER on their father's side was Xyla, the Malanite woman who had traveled from the planet Aurora in search of Benjamin Mizello. Eventually, she and Benjamin were married on Happiness, an event celebrated by the humans and Tattoo People of that amusement park planet. Xyla devoted her life on Happiness to teaching the Tattoo children, and in doing so became loved and respected by young and old alike. The ease with which she established a rapport with the youth of Happiness must have been passed to the twins, as the Tattoo children on Lumina also gravitated to Deneb and Vega. The twins enjoyed the attention and grew accustomed to the procession that accompanied them wherever they went exploring.

The twins learned to play a game with the Tattoo children, a kind of relay race. Two groups of five to ten players constituted the competing teams. They all agreed on the starting and ending points of the race several kilometers apart. With so many circuitous pathways through the intervening foliage, multiple routes from start to finish were possible. One person, usually a willing adult, gave the team members specific locations to go to and wait. Players didn't know where their teammates were. When the game began, one runner from each team left the starting line. Teammates, scattered throughout the forest, used their radio telepathic abilities to let the runners know where they were. When the runner found a teammate, he or she transferred the baton to the new runner. Each player carried a wooden ring to slip on the baton on receiving it. This ensured that all team members carried the baton during the race. In the thicket, there was no other way to tell if they had. The race was not a spectator sport.

The game was developmentally beneficial to the Tattoo children because it taught them how to communicate with one another using the radio transmission and reception abilities they all possessed. It also trained them to control their transmissions, because there was a catch to the game. If a member of one team intercepted the signal from an opposing team member and located that player first, then he took that player's ring. When that happened, the team would have to replace the lost ring, either by going back to the starting line, or finding an opposing team member. The games could become wildly chaotic after a while and often lasted a good part of the day.

At first, Vega and Deneb participated by being the adults who assigned locations to the team members. Later, they actually joined as team members, although they weren't particularly good players because they couldn't broadcast information as to where they were. Interestingly though, Vega and Deneb knew where each other were and, when one was found by a teammate, would tell exactly where the other one was, whether on the same team or not. This delighted the children and offered an additional degree of chaos to an already frenzied sport.

The first team to send a player across the finish line with all the rings from their team was the winner. It didn't matter which player crossed the finish line with the baton as long as he or she had the right number of rings on the baton.

The adult Tattoo People of Lumina observed these shenanigans with patient indulgence. They tolerated the twins' participation in the children's games because their ability to communicate mimicked their own telepathic skills, but they couldn't understand how Vega and Deneb did it. They appeared to be no different from other humans who, as far as the Tattoo People could tell, communicated by reading the very complex motions of each other's lips. Tattoo People had lips, but they were only used for eating, and occasionally kissing. They had nothing to do with communication. The only way humans could communicate with them was by speaking into the strange boxes they all carried on lanyards wrapped around their necks.

Then one day while the entire family was having a meal at the campsite, three Tattoo People appeared. Druix rose from the table and turned his translating device on.

"Welcome." His arms parted in a gesture of hospitality,

even though he knew he had nothing to offer that the Tattoo People might want.

"We wish to speak to the two young humans," came the response. Druix looked to where the twins sat, their meal interrupted. "They're here," replied Druix, as Vega and Deneb stood simultaneously.

"They must come with us," one of the Tattoo People said.

This caused Ilsa to rise from her seat and move next to Druix. It was late in the day, an odd time for the twins to go in the forest.

"What do you want with them?" she asked.

"We wish to speak to them." The Arilian translating device used the word "speak" instead of the more general term "communicate".

"Why can't you speak with them here?" asked Ilsa, concern in her voice.

"There are others who wish to participate." The words came out haltingly, as if the alien was choosing them carefully.

Now Elsenia joined Druix and Ilsa. The sides were even. Vega and Deneb remained at the table.

"You won't harm them," said Elsenia. She had studied the mentality of the Tattoo People extensively. She spoke the words as a statement. Tattoo People didn't understand questions. She knew also that they appreciated frankness and honesty. It was best to come to the point quickly.

"We will not hurt your children. They are friends with our children. We only wish to speak with them."

At this, Ilsa nodded her approval. Vega and Deneb left the table and joined the group, stopping before the Tattoo People.

"Follow us," said the Tattoo man.

The three Tattoo men turned as one and disappeared into the thicket by the same way they'd entered. A moment later, the twins followed, each offering a slight reassuring wave to the rest of their family, who stood numbly watching.

"It will be okay," said Elsenia.

"I know," said Ilsa. "Otherwise, I wouldn't have let them

go. I just wonder what they want to talk about."

"We'll find out when they return," said Druix.

In fact, they didn't find out when the twins returned several hours later. Both were deep in thought, looking far more exhausted than when they'd spent the day chasing Tattoo children through the forest. When Elsenia, Druix, and Ilsa probed them for what the Tattoo People wanted, they said they'd explain later.

That explanation never came, however, because the next morning Vega and Deneb disappeared into the forest again. It was clear to the other family members that something had changed in the twins since they'd been whisked away, as if they'd suddenly become adults. The playful and upbeat way they approached life had been altered. Ilsa, Druix, and Elsenia discussed the change, but none could explain it. Ilsa decided one night that she would have to talk to the twins in the way only mothers can, but that opportunity never presented itself because of the unexpected arrival the next day of Admiral Julian Chase.

CHAPTER 7

— Century 1483 —

ADMIRAL CHASE, hearing that Elsenia and her family were on route to Lumina, had decided to join them during their visit. He traveled on his command ship with a crew of fifteen, all from 550th Century Earth. Three of them boarded space capsules and descended to the surface of Lumina, landing in the same clearing where the family had set up camp. Even for Elsenia, who'd been exposed to the miracles of space travel from a young age, it was a tremendous thrill to see the three vehicles descend, slowed by billowing parachutes above and fiery rocket jets below. She hadn't many opportunities to encounter the members of the Earth fleet that had helped save Aril back in the 650th Century. She was surprised when they emerged from the capsules.

Although all three were equally imposing in stature, Admiral Chase was easy to distinguish. He strode with confidence and authority, one step ahead of the others. They all had the fierce amber eyes that were so characteristic of that race of humans. To Elsenia though, it was the texture of their skin that made it most difficult for her to believe they were humans at all. When Admiral Chase shook her hand in greeting, she struggled not to recoil in shock at feeling the coarseness of his leathery skin. She tried to imagine the environmental conditions on Earth that had produced this genetic adaptation.

"You must be Elsenia," he said, addressing her first.

"Yes, and you're Admiral Chase."

"Call me Julian."

Elsenia hesitated. "I'll try."

He smiled. All the fierceness in his countenance faded away, as if it had never been there to begin with.

Later, after he'd spoken with Ilsa and Druix, he found Elsenia working at her desk. It was a crude structure she had assembled with help from the Tattoo People. It was twilight. The temperature on Lumina was so mild no one needed shelter. Sometimes in the early morning, Elsenia was cold and had to retreat to the confines of her capsule, but other than that the family lived in the open.

"May I sit here?" asked the Admiral, pointing to a chair.

"Sure." Elsenia said, wondering if it might break under his weight.

"I knew your father," he started.

"So I understand. You were one of the last to see him on Happiness before he died."

"Yes. He gave me something."

"I know. He gave you his memoirs."

"Yes, but also something else."

Elsenia was confused. Neither her mother nor Druix had told her about any other gift from her father. The Admiral seemed to notice her confusion. "This was not a gift for you."

"Oh," she said, embarrassed. She looked to Ilsa and Druix, who were speaking with Admiral Chase's troops. The first stars were just starting to appear in the darkening sky.

"But I'd like you to have it," the Admiral said.

"What is it?" Elsenia asked, genuinely curious.

Admiral Chase reached behind his back and produced an EMP weapon—sleek, white, compact, and light.

"He gave you an EMP weapon? What the hell for?"

"It's not just any EMP weapon. It's Stella's."

Elsenia was puzzled. Why had her father given the Admiral an EMP weapon that once belonged to a notorious galactic space pirate?

Admiral Chase summoned one of the men who'd landed with him. When the man approached, the Admiral handed him the weapon.

"Captain Stenzel, if you'd be so kind as to shoot me with this weapon."

The man examined the weapon briefly, then raised it and nonchalantly fired it at the Admiral.

Elsenia's jaw dropped in panic and surprise as a flash of blue electric light shot from the gun and engulfed the Earth Fleet

Commander, who shuddered momentarily as if he'd felt a chill. Then, unharmed, he reached up to take the weapon back from his shipmate.

"Thank you, Captain."

The man turned and walked away.

"What just happened?" Elsenia stammered.

The admiral smiled. "This is a smart weapon. It senses the intent of the person holding it. If it senses no fear, panic, or desperation in the shooter, it emits a harmless pulse of electricity. It's not lethal unless the person holding it feels genuinely threatened by the target. Fortunately, Captain Stenzel doesn't view me as a threat. Otherwise, the demonstration would have gone badly."

Elsenia shook her head, still confused. "I don't want it," she said.

"It might come in handy."

"For what?"

Admiral Chase looked down at the gun, turning it over in his hand. "For protection. If you're going to travel the galaxy, you have to be prepared."

Elsenia took the weapon from the Admiral. It was amazingly light, especially given its potential destructiveness. Although reassuring to hold, Elsenia couldn't help feeling uneasy. She'd never held any weapon before. Every galactic explorer carried weapons, but Elsenia had never taken formal training or had the opportunity to own or use a weapon.

"Your tour of the galaxy will take thousands of years, from one destination to the next. You can't always be confident that a planet hasn't become dangerous over time. This will protect you from most threats and you won't have to worry about accidental harm to you or a loved one."

Elsenia thought about the twins.

"The sensors in this weapon make it like an extension of yourself. You couldn't accidentally injure someone with it any more than you could accidentally strike someone."

Elsenia nodded. It made sense. She looked over to where Ilsa and Druix were still talking. The Admiral read her thoughts.

"I'll explain it to your parents," he said.

Admiral Chase remained on Aril for several weeks. Elsenia saw him often. They had many more conversations, with the Admiral expressing genuine interest in her study of the Tattoo People. They both felt a common sense of privilege, living at a time in human history when not only space travel was possible, but contact with alien civilization had been established. It was a unique era. When Elsenia expressed this thought, Admiral Chase agreed, but with some reservation. When she questioned his hesitation, he said, "One of the supply ships I visited was Supply Ship 2. The custodian is Alphons Demetriano. Perhaps you remember the role he played in helping Xyla meet up with your dad."

Elsenia had read her father's chronicles many times. She was well aware of how the old physicist had guided Xyla to Sparil at the time of the First Galactic Exploration Conference. He'd known that Benjamin would be there, too, and it was inevitable they'd run into each other. Demetriano's efforts to bring the two together had been successful beyond anything he could have imagined.

"Yes, I remember. He was very old at the time. I can't believe he's still a custodian. How is he doing?"

"He doesn't shave," Admiral Chase said. "He has a long, white beard. When I asked him how old he was in real years, he told me he'd stopped counting long ago. I'm not sure how he keeps up with the tasks of running a supply ship, but somehow he manages. His greenhouse garden is thriving and the ship's functions are operating normally. There seemed to be a deliberate slowness in his movements, because he seemed capable of greater speed. It was as if he was able to retard the passage of time, solely by adjusting the pace of his own movements—as if he were in control—not the laws of biology or physics. At first, I was impatient with him, but then soon came to realize that I just wasn't accustomed to his time frame. Once I understood and accepted this, watching him fascinated me."

"Is he still collecting data on every space explorer?" Elsenia asked. Her father's journal had described Xyla's visit to Supply Ship 2, where Alphons had shown her three-dimensional, lifelike renditions of Benjamin and her step-dad, Druix.

"He's gone beyond that," said Admiral Chase. "His curiosity and analytic skills are remarkable. He uses every piece of data acquired by the ship's radio. I had the feeling he possessed unlimited knowledge about the entire galactic enterprise, but teasing information out of him was a tedious task. The more I questioned him, the more amused he was by the cat and mouse game we played. I was the cat, and his knowledge of the universe was the mouse."

"He sounds like somewhat of an imp."

"Very much so, but in the sly, mischievous sense of the word. There was no evil or malice in his manner or his purpose. Plus, you and he share a common interest."

Elsenia already knew what Admiral Chase was going to say before he said it. "The Tattoo People, you mean?"

"Right, except that you're fascinated by what the Tattoo People have become , whereas he's more interested in their origin than their evolution on each planet."

"The two are not unrelated," Elsenia said.

"Perhaps not, but certainly Alphons shows little interest in how their society evolves on different planets."

"So does he have a theory about where the Tattoo People come from?"

"Not really, or at least not that he revealed to me. He showed me a sketch, a map of the galaxy highlighting the planets inhabited by Tattoo People. Next to each was the year the planet had been struck by the asteroid carrying the seeds of the alien vine. These were only estimates, to be sure, because he had to extrapolate backward in time based on assumptions about the extent of the vine's growth, the atmospheric conditions of the planet, its size and physical features, distance from its sun, and other factors way beyond my understanding, but Alphons was extremely methodical and meticulous in his analysis. In any case, the data revealed an unmistakable pattern. It was consistent with a scenario where all the objects carrying the vine were launched from a location near the center of the galaxy."

"Very nice," Elsenia said, nodding. "That's a plausible way of locating their origin. Planets located close to the galactic center would be struck earlier than those farther away, assuming all the objects were launched about the same time, but that doesn't explain why. Did Alphons have any theories about that?"

"None that he'd reveal to me, but if you find yourself in the vicinity of Supply Ship 2 during your travels, you should stop by and talk to him—if he's still around."

"Maybe I'll do that," said Elsenia, thoughtfully.

Elsenia told Admiral Chase about her conversations with Risto and Lemmy on Sparil. The Admiral told her that no independent sighting of Risto's asteroid had been reported, but he cautioned about the difficulty of finding a dark object in space with only an approximate determination of its trajectory. Elsenia and Admiral Chase speculated about possible connections between the large asteroid Risto had discovered and the smaller ones that carried the alien vine with the DNA for a new population of Tattoo People. With so little in the way of observational evidence, the possibilities were endless.

ELSENIA ENJOYED her conversations with Admiral Chase during his visit to Lumina. For someone who'd traveled a large sector of the galaxy and figured so prominently in the defeat of an invading army of Aril and in the pursuit of Stella, the space pirate, Julian Chase was a man of great introspection and humility.

"My role in those events was peripheral," he told Elsenia. "My troops defeated the invaders of Aril, but it was your father who orchestrated the strategy that won the day, and it was Benjamin and the Tattoo People who ultimately defeated Stella. I showed up on Happiness forty years too late."

"You shouldn't underestimate the influence you and the Earth fleet have had in determining the outcome of events, even though you weren't present at the moment of victory."

"True, but remember, leaving Earth in the 550th Century

was an incredibly dubious endeavor back then. I had to do an impressive amount of soul searching to convince myself it was a cause important enough to undertake, and that I had the unique skills that the task required. Now, I have to admit to myself that anyone could've played the marginal role I did in determining the course of events."

Elsenia touched his arm. "You're being too hard on yourself. Your name is known throughout all the human-inhabited worlds of the galaxy and among the Union explorer fleet also. You're the steadfast law enforcer. Your presence in the galaxy is comforting to the rest of us in a very profound way."

"And then there are my failures," he continued, ignoring her comment. "We've still been unable to find Max and Sadie, whose supply ship was hijacked by Stella. They were shoved into their capsules and set adrift to an unknown destination. We have no idea even where to begin to start looking for them."

Before departing from Lumina, Admiral Chase gave Elsenia one more gift, a rendezvous plan. She was stunned. Rendezvous plans were encoded in ceramic medallions that were virtually indestructible. They held the coordinates in space and time where the owner of the medallion committed to be thousands of years in the future. Sharing of rendezvous plans was usually only done among relatives and very close friends.

"Here's my rendezvous plan," Admiral Chase said. "Please feel free to make use of it. I'd like to tell you that I'll always be around to help you if you need me, but I know that's impossible. It distresses me that should you find yourself in danger during your space travels, I'll be too far away to be of any aid. The best I can do is promise you I will be in these places." He held the medallion aloft.

Elsenia was taken aback. The offering of a rendezvous plan was one of the most intimate gestures a galactic explorer might make, almost equivalent to a marriage proposal of ancient times.

"I couldn't," She stammered.

"Please." His voice was weak, incongruous to his size, and certainly unusual for the commander of the Earth fleet.

"What if I don't show up?"

He smiled. "There are destinations programmed in here out to the 3000th Century. It'll make me very happy just thinking you might appear at one of them."

"Admiral Chase. Julian…" Elsenia started.

"Don't worry, Elsenia. If you don't show up, then it was never meant to be. It's enough for me to know that you have the medallion. I expect nothing beyond that."

Elsenia looked down and cupped her hands together. He placed the medallion in her palm. She was surprised by its weight. She grasped it, eyes closed. Then she heard a movement. When she looked up, Admiral Chase was walking away.

As a child of two 22nd Century humans, Elsenia was a rare breed in the galaxy. She'd grown up on Aril among a humanoid race that had changed over more than 100 thousand years from her kind. The closest living humans to her were the galactic explorers, who were much older than she was, even after discounting the many millennia they'd been frozen. Plus, the ones she encountered were invariably diseased, showing up on Sparil to be treated for radiation damage or to die.

Admiral Chase and members of the Earth fleet came from an Earth 50,000 years farther in the future than Elsenia's parents. Though their appearance was markedly different from hers, they were still Homo sapiens, and there was no biological hurdle to a physical union between Elsenia and one of them.

Nevertheless Elsenia had suppressed romantic inclinations for so long, she had difficulty accommodating the notion that she might have a sexual relationship yet. The feeling discomforted her a great deal, though she didn't understand why. Was she afraid? This was unknown territory—like landing on an unexplored planet. Anything could happen.

Elsenia examined the medallion, tempted to view its contents on a computer. Where was the first rendezvous location? How many years in the future? How old would she be when and if she met Admiral Chase there? How old would he be? If she chose to, she could take off now in her capsule and program the vehicle to go to the first rendezvous point. She'd meet Admiral Chase in just a few short hours of unfrozen time. Then what?

AN UNSETTLING SILENCE fell over the camp after Admiral Chase's departure. Elsenia and her family had overstayed their welcome on Lumina, it seemed. After the twins secretive meeting with the Tattoo People, the family grew impatient with the daily routine that had been reassuring and acceptable previously. They came to the simultaneous conclusion that it was time to leave. According to the plan they'd agreed on before their departure from Sparil, now was the time to decide their next destination. However, Ilsa preempted the discussion with the announcement that she and Druix wanted to visit Earth next. Because the two parents had unilaterally decided their next destination, it thereby left the same option open to the three siblings. Ilsa couldn't force all of them to follow her and Druix. Instead, she allowed them to go their own way provided they all agreed to meet at a prearranged time on the planet Happiness. She set the reunion date far enough in the future that it gave her children forty thousand years to explore elsewhere, the amount of time that she and Druix would need to travel to Earth and back to Happiness.

Pleasantly surprised to be able to decide for themselves, Elsenia and the twins discussed their options. Although the twins readily agreed on where they wanted to go, Elsenia's preference differed and she decided to set off on her own to the part of the Galactic Garden where the heaviest concentration of Tattoo People lived. For reasons they wouldn't explain, Vega and Deneb wanted to start their exploration by visiting Supply Ship 2, the one occupied by the eccentric physicist Alphons Demetriano. Ilsa's decision to let the members of her family make their own decision was a sound one. Had they tried to find one destination agreeable to all, they'd have remained on Lumina a long time.

Elsenia received another rendezvous plan before she and her family departed. It was from Ilsa. Elsenia expected it, but was surprised that her mother would give it to her attached to the same iridescent necklace her father had given Ilsa before they left

Earth in 2149. Then, Benjamin had purchased two from an old lady at the International Galactic Explorers Conference in Washington DC. Druix had the other one, given to him by Benjamin on his departure, when he left Benjamin and Druix's mother, Xyla, to live out the remainder of their lives among the Tattoo People and their human friends.

Elsenia knew how much the iridescent strand meant to her mother, and she was deeply moved that she'd been entrusted with it. She and Ilsa had never been apart. Soon, they'd both lift off, and be separated by an unimaginable gulf of space and time. The only link they'd have was the information frozen into the crystalline structure of that small ceramic medallion.

CHAPTER 8

— Century 1502 —

MAX AND SADIE VAN DER SCHAFT WERE FINALLY UNFROZEN after seventy thousand years. They'd been set adrift in separate space capsules by a band of intergalactic pirates who'd hijacked their supply ship on route to its new post in the Galactic Garden. Up to that time, their duties as custodians of a Union ship had been largely uneventful. They made sure the greenhouse gardens and fuel and oxygen manufacturing systems were operating and ready to provide the needs of an occasional galactic explorer. Visiting space travelers looked forward to their stops at Max and Sadie's ship, knowing they'd be resupplied with the best food products and highest quality fuel and oxygen, plus the couple was quite simply the happiest of all the custodians. When Max and Sadie disappeared, it was a great loss to the Union fleet.

Fortunately, the pirates had been merciful enough to put Max and Sadie in their magnetocryogenic chambers, which meant they'd remain permanently frozen during their long voyage. To the great amusement of the pirates, they programmed the navigation systems to take the custodians to a neighboring galaxy, a trip that would have taken millions of years. The pirates never expected that the course they'd doomed the couple to follow would bring them very close to the center of the galaxy. There they were found by aliens developing plans for galactic colonization.

Though the aliens were technologically advanced, the two wandering space capsules baffled them. The capsules moved incredibly fast—at speeds much greater than the alien spacecraft were capable of. The aliens tracked the vehicles for several years while puzzling over how to capture them without destruction. Only after the alien engineers developed a much faster vehicle were they able to overtake them. Moving at the same velocity, they affixed rocket engines to the hulls of the capsules, to decelerate and steer them to the alien home planet. It was an ambitious undertaking that took decades to complete but the aliens' curiosity was unwavering. The aliens were, after all, descended from a race determined to colonize other parts of the galaxy millions of years earlier. They'd never been successful in getting beyond their own solar system, though the knowledge and technology that resulted even from their failure was a lasting legacy of their endeavors.

Max and Sadie's capsules were brought onto an orbiting space station and observed and studied by dozens of scientists and engineers who were quite deliberate in their examination. Though they could easily have broken open the hull to see what was inside, they refrained from taking any damaging action. Little did they know that by delaying, they might cause Max and Sadie's death. The magnetocryogenic chambers were designed to maintain absolute zero temperatures in interstellar space. Onboard the alien spacecraft, ambient heat from the vehicle and air within it might cause Max and Sadie to defrost. The magnetocryogenic chambers, surrounded by magnetic coils, meant to be activated prior to defrosting, protected vital organs until normal body temperature had been reached. Defrosting without the magnetic field would have meant certain death for Max and Sadie.

But luck was with the human couple. The aliens were able to remove the external bolts to access the manual controls and open each vehicle's hatch. Once inside, they spent several days examining the interior before venturing to press the large red button that initiated the defrosting cycle. A few hours later, Max and Sadie emerged from their chambers in fear and bewilderment. The creatures they encountered were giants, with bluish-green skin and huge hands that were more dexterous and far stronger than those of humans. Apart from those differences, the aliens could have been human. They had all the other features of Homo sapien anatomy. Their mouths made no sounds though, and Max and Sadie's efforts to communicate with the aliens were completely futile.

When the couple found each other under the wondering gazes of the aliens, they embraced, sobbing with joy and relief. The last memory both of them had was being shoved through the corridors of the supply ship by the pirates. The overwhelming fear and doubts from seventy thousand years earlier were still with them. Now they experienced the rising panic and terror of totally unfamiliar surroundings.

"I was so worried about you!" cried Sadie.

"I'm okay," said Max.

"Who are these people?" asked Sadie, looking about at the giants watching them.

"I'm not sure they're people—unless they're some evolved form of humans. How long were we frozen?"

"I've no idea."

The alien space station had artificial gravity, but much reduced from that of the Union supply ships. Max took Sadie's hand and they backed slowly toward the open hatch of a capsule. The aliens watched them. It was impossible to read their emotions. As Max and Sadie reentered the capsule, they moved toward them, then stopped. The hatch opening was too small for the large beings to enter easily.

"What are you going to do?" asked Sadie.

"Turn on the computer. We need to find out where and when we are."

Max sat at the control console and Sadie stood behind him. She looked about the cabin to see if it was intact. Everything appeared untouched. The weapons were gone, but she assumed that was the work of the pirates who'd hijacked the supply ship.

Max activated the computer and display monitor. With shock he saw the year was 150,155. He and Sadie had been frozen and traveling through space for more than seventy thousand years. The map display showed them within a few light-years of the galactic center. If they were dead, they could hardly be more displaced from human civilization. Sadie laid her hand on Max's shoulder to comfort him and steady herself. What would become of them now?

Sensing movement behind them, they turned to see one of the aliens peering curiously at the computer monitor. Sadie stood to one side to give the alien a better view of the display.

"Show him Earth," Sadie said to Max. He brought up an

image of Earth. The alien watched in quiet amazement.

Before long, more aliens had squeezed into the small space of the capsule. Max continued to display images of human civilization—images of Earth, humans, Union exploration vehicles, and the planets visited by galactic space explorers. The aliens watched without interruption for as long as Max continued to show new images. When he grew tired, Sadie took over. More aliens entered the capsule to watch, replacing those who'd seen enough and left. After several hours, Sadie rose and moved away from the computer. To her astonishment, one of the aliens took her seat, barely able to fit into it, and with no hesitation brought the computer to life. In observing Max and Sadie manipulate the controls of the computer, the alien had already learned how to operate the device.

From that moment on, Max and Sadie were denied access to the control consoles of the two capsules. The aliens largely ignored them, allowing them to move about the space station, enter the capsules for food and water, and sleep on metal mesh hammocks set up nearby. Max and Sadie wondered, if they would ever get to visit the planet from which the aliens came? Would they be ignored completely until their food and water were consumed and they died? The doubt and uncertainty was unbearable. Max finally decided to activate the radio beacon of his capsule. It was highly unlikely that there was another Union space vehicle in the vicinity, but trying to reach out couldn't hurt. While in the capsule pretending to get food from a supply cabinet, he slipped into the control room and activated the distress beacon. Within seconds, two aliens appeared. They grabbed him with their incredibly huge hands and threw him from the capsule. In the near weightless environment of the space station, Max's body flew fifty meters before impacting a wall. Sadie rushed to help him, but was pursued by four aliens. They reached her before she could get to Max. With one swing, the alien closest to Sadie struck her, and she tumbled unconscious to the floor.

Max and Sadie regained consciousness bound to their metal mesh hammocks. They lay in pain, trying to gather their thoughts and understand what had happened. Before long the aliens returned, lifted them roughly from their confinement, and dragged them through the corridors of the ship to a room filled with aliens sitting at control consoles, each an almost identical duplicate of those in the space capsules. On a platform above them was an alien, much larger than the rest, and with an air of unmistakable authority and strength. Next to him, in a conical container was a single plant under a bright lamp. In the dark, colorless surroundings of the alien space station, the green hue of the plant shone as if lit from within. Brilliant red berries hung from its branches.

The alien turned to face Max and Sadie. Towering over them, he peered down, his expression unreadable. His eyes were so dark and deeply inset they could have been empty sockets. Gazing into these voids, Sadie imagined she was looking into the depths of hell. Instinctively, Max moved between the alien and Sadie, a gesture that had no meaning to the alien, other than to determine which human would first suffer his wrath.

Max and Sadie's luck was still with them though. After several moments, the large alien decided that the two humans were worthy of no more of his time. They were dragged away. This time, instead of being brought to their hammocks, they were taken back to their capsules and rudely shoved into the magneto-cryogenic chambers. Before they could wonder as to what was happening, they heard the loud bang indicating the onset of the magnetic field prior to freezing. With that, Max and Sadie were frozen and their capsules ejected from the alien space station.

Once again they were helplessly at the mercy of external events over which they had little control.

CHAPTER 9

— Century 1542 —

UNDER THE MINISTRATIONS of advanced Arilian medical science, Risto Jalonen recovered from the cancers spread through his body. The Arilians urged him to remain on Sparil, where physicians could continue to monitor any remaining malignancies. They offered him a variety of positions. Given his experience as a galactic explorer, he could teach courses at the space academy and serve as an advisor to new recruits. But Risto refused all opportunities. He was determined to track down the asteroid he'd discovered and find out its origin and purpose. He spent many hours with Lemmy discussing the asteroid and reviewing the limited data they possessed. Lemmy could only give Risto a very approximate estimate of where the asteroid might be currently. The brilliant scientist was even more indefinite about where it might be when Risto reached it. This didn't deter the ancient explorer. He lost no time in arranging for his space capsule to be refurbished and prepared for galactic space travel. No one on Sparil could have dissuaded Risto from his self-imposed mission.

Lemmy's calculations and the advanced instrumentation of Risto's space vehicle served him well. Six thousand years after leaving Aril, Risto was unfrozen automatically from his magnetocryogenic chamber when the long-range radar on the capsule detected a hard target, just a fraction of a light-year away and with the same general properties as the asteroid Risto had previously observed. Risto exited the chamber and took his seat at the control console to program a rendezvous course with the object. As he was still some distance away, he refroze himself for the trip remaining—about six Earth months.

The next time he unfroze, only a few hundred kilometers from the asteroid, he used the manual controls to travel the remaining distance. As Risto's capsule approached the asteroid, he realized the true difficulty of the task he'd undertaken. The massive object was both rotating about its long axis and tumbling about its center of mass. Though large, its gravitational field was negligible—not large enough to draw his capsule in, which would've made things easier. His propulsion could have slowed his rate of descent. Without gravity, he had to use precious fuel to approach the asteroid's surface at a slow enough speed to avoid being damaged by the tumbling mass. To make matters worse, the asteroid's surface was irregular. If Risto wasn't able to match the capsule's speed to the motion of the asteroid, it might be struck by a protrusion rotating into his vehicle. When and if his capsule contacted the surface, he'd have to use more fuel to make sure he didn't bounce away, like a baseball bat hitting a ball. The only way to complete the landing maneuver safely was to go in extremely slowly, checking constantly the relative distances and motion of his capsule and the asteroid. In fact, "landing" was an inaccurate description of his closing maneuver. Without significant gravitational attraction, it was more a docking maneuver than a landing. By coupling his vehicle to the object, Risto could then be sure that its motion in space matched the asteroid's. If he didn't attach his craft in some way, he might not find his capsule there after any extravehicular exploration.

He felt the capsule's gentle impact on the asteroid surface, but waited for several minutes to make sure there was no residual motion between the two objects. Then, he exited the capsule through the airlock.

In his many planetary explorations, Risto had visited some of the most frightening and inhospitable planets one could imagine. Yet, he'd found none that challenged his courage and resolve more than this diminutive, drifting rock. It had no atmosphere, of course, which meant that brilliant stars spun about him in dizzying pirouettes as the asteroid tumbled. The planets he had visited all had suns, which somehow made them seem less foreboding. Even outside his capsule, empty space wasn't as desolate as the surface of the asteroid. As he moved away from his vehicle, its presence was a stark reminder of how alone and helpless he was. Adding to the sense of bleakness was the asteroid's surface, which was a solid mass of black rock, as black as space itself. There wasn't a speck of dirt or dust on the surface. Without gravity, those small particles had been gradually swept away, not by wind, for there is no wind in interstellar space, but by the pressure from radiation that, though feeble, was sufficient over many thousands of years to impart the necessary momentum to any loose material, casting it off from the parent body. What remained was as barren and lifeless as any object could possibly be.

Risto traversed the surface by pulling himself along, his hands grasping at any rocky crag that offered itself. He was trying to preserve the fuel in his jet suit in case he needed it later for a hasty return. He knew where he was going. A few hundred meters away from where he'd left the capsule was the large crater within which Arilian scientists suspected there were metallic objects. Risto had examined the single image his capsule had obtained during his last visit to the asteroid. The presence of metallic objects was unmistakable, but now, moving across the rocky surface, it was difficult for him to believe there could be anything here but cold, hard, stone. The blackness of the surface seemed to swallowed up the light from his helmet lantern.

The ground sloped upward as he neared the edge of a large crater that must have been formed in a collision with another object millions of years earlier while the asteroid drifted among its neighboring planetesimals, all part of the primordial stew left over from the formation of a star. Where was that star now, and how had this object been separated from its siblings?

Reaching the edge of the crater, Risto steadied himself by hooking his hand into a narrow fissure in the rock. He peered down into it, directing his helmet light toward its center. There, just as he had imagined from the single image, was an array of metallic structures. He wished his light were bright enough to illuminate the entire interior of the crater. He was sure it'd reveal that the metal structures, in varying shapes and sizes, filled the entire cavity. Most were single posts protruding from the ground approximately one meter in length. Atop each was a circular ring, a cross, or a single line with a set of perpendicular bars, all made of the same material, not shiny as new metal, but dull, with the grayish sheen of aluminum or tin.

Even in the feeble illumination of Risto's helmet light, the metallic objects were unmistakable. The laws of physics are the same everywhere in the universe. If a civilization, human or otherwise, endeavors to detect radio waves, it must build antennas. The antenna metal provides the pathway by which electrons respond to the time-varying fields of the waves. Just as objects floating in water or beads on a string move in response to wave-like motions, electrons in a metal oscillate with the passage of radio waves. That motion gets transmitted to whatever detector system the antenna is connected to.

The shape and size of the antenna are also constrained by the laws of physics. The size must be comparable to the wavelength of the radio wave for optimum response to the disturbance. If one wants to detect radio waves over a broad range of wavelengths, then antennas of many different sizes are needed. This explained the variety of sizes Risto observed within the confines of the crater. Radio waves can be polarized; the direction of the disturbance they create may have a preferred orientation that might change in a regular way. Indeed, the preferred direction may rotate like the hands of a clock. Circular antennas, or two linear antennas oriented at right angles to each other, help with the detection of these types of waves. Even the spacing between adjacent antennas is important because it helps determine the direction from which the radio wave is coming.

Risto gazed at the field of antennas before him, contemplating the implications. Whatever race of beings constructed this created an array to maximize the amount of information resident in the received transmissions.

Moving across the floor of the crater was easy because he could grab the protruding metal structures and propel himself from one to another. He worried only vaguely that the antennas might be transmitting, which meant he'd be bathed in a sea of potentially damaging radiation, but something told him these cold metal appendages were as lifeless as the asteroid itself. He looked about carefully as he moved along, hoping to find some clue to what manner of beings constructed the array, perhaps an inscription, a serial number or some other text written in an alien alphabet, but there was nothing.

Then he spotted a clearing—a circular area void of antennas. When he approached, he saw the ground in that space was covered by a large, circular plate made of black metal. In the center of the plate was a hole, perhaps a meter in diameter. Risto moved over the plate slowly. Here there were no protrusions to hold. He propelled himself along by paddling his hands over the metal surface, careful not to push too hard lest he drift away.

Finally he reached the edge of the hole and peered in. It was deep—impossible to tell how far into the interior of the asteroid it extended. He stared down for some time, and after a while saw, or imagined seeing, a light emanating from the bottom —a very pale, faint, green glow.

Risto positioned his body over the center of the hole, and with one short burst from his jet pack, propelled himself downward, head first. It was all the impulse he needed to initiate a slow, continuous descent into the blackness. His helmet lamp illuminated the walls of the cylindrical hole about him, but ahead of him all he could see was the faint, green glow. After several bumps against the wall of the cylinder, his descent slowed, and he used his hands against the smooth, metal walls to continue his motion. Fortunately, the diameter of the hole didn't vary. Nonetheless, thinking about the great distance he'd come from the surface gave him a growing sensation of claustrophobia. There was hardly enough room for him to turn around should he panic and need to return to the surface. It didn't matter. He knew he had only to fire his jet pack once or twice in the opposite direction and he'd be propelled back out of the cylinder, like a bullet shot from the barrel of a rifle.

The glow at the bottom of the hole grew larger, as he approached it, and he saw that the green light emanated from an opening in the side wall where the hole terminated. He moved through the opening and found himself in a large room suffused with light coming from a large, shed-like structure about thirty meters away. The metallic shed was completely closed except for a single window, the source of the green radiation. He moved to it for a closer look. Below the window was a symbol, etched into the metal, a "V", with a horizontal line across the upper part of the letter. As he puzzled over it, he noticed in panic and despair the radiation detector built into the sleeve of his space suit, showing the level of radiation about him at critically dangerous levels. He'd exposed himself to radioactive emissions from some type of nuclear reactor. He cursed his fortune that after escaping death from cosmic radiation, he now found himself bathed in more of the lethal rays emanating from a device in the bowels of an enigmatic, interstellar asteroid.

Risto knew he should leave, but was too intrigued by the other objects surrounding him, hundreds of black metal cylinders, standing erect like soldiers in a phalanx, each as wide around as the cylindrical hole he had just descended through. They were arrayed along a single, continuous track that circled the room in concentric rings spiraling inward. He moved to the nearest cylinder and grasped it with both hands. Bracing his feet against the track, he attempted to move it, but the cylinder didn't budge. Had it been sitting freely on the track, it should have been moveable in the gravity-free space of the asteroid. Risto glanced at the other display built into the sleeve of his spacesuit, showing the strength of the magnetic field about him. He wasn't surprised to see that the intensity of the field was thousands of times stronger than it had been on the asteroid's surface. The closer to the cylinder he was, the more intense the field. The cylinders were magnetic, with a force field strong enough to bind them tightly to the metal track beneath them.

Risto used the video camera built into his spacesuit to record the scene about him. Eventually, dozens of Arilian scientists would puzzle over the images interminably before concluding what Risto already knew. He was in the ammunition cartridge of a magnetically-based weapon. Each cylinder was a bullet ready to move along the track into position at the base of the barrel, the long shaft he had passed through. The force that propelled the cylinders through the barrel was in all likelihood electromagnetic, powered by the nuclear reactor burning steadily and dependably for thousands of years. Electromagnetic weapons were used on Earth long ago, and perhaps still were. Each magnetized cylinder had a north and south pole. A magnetic field would be generated in the barrel of the weapon, probably via coils of wire wrapped around the circumference along its entire length. The initial direction of the field at the base of the barrel produced a repulsive force to impel the bullet upward. The displacement would result in a change of polarity of the magnetic field via the currents in the coiled wire, giving the cylinder another impulse upward. The process would be repeated as the bullet accelerated through the barrel. On Earth, the magnetic force would have to overcome the gravitational force, but in space, acceleration was unimpeded, the bullet gaining velocity with extreme efficiency until finally shooting out from the gun with incredible speed. Risto was thankful it hadn't fired while he was in the barrel. Being struck by one of the magnetic cylinders meant instant death. He could only hope the weapon wouldn't fire during his return trip. He'd already decided to use the jet pack to make his exit as quickly as possible.

The realization humbled Risto, that although he was intelligent enough to view the evidence about him and deduce that he was in the guts of a magnetic weapon system, he was completely unable to fathom the intent of any civilization, human or alien, to construct such a device. What purpose would compel any engineers to design an electromagnetic gun that propelled metal cylinders from the interior of an asteroid in interstellar space? Perhaps there were warring planets somewhere in the galaxy, waging battles that featured duels between missile-firing asteroids. Was this a weapon of war gone astray?

And then there were the antennas. Why have antennas on the asteroid? Why receive radio waves if there were no sentient beings on the asteroid to listen to them? Perhaps the asteroid was supposed to carry an alien crew, now gone. Gone where? He didn't think the asteroid was ever meant to carry a crew. It was autonomous, and if that was the case, then the antennas must be part of the targeting system, gathering information used to aim the weapon. But what or who was the target?

That was the most important question of all.

CHAPTER 10
— Century 1583 —

ELSENIA'S FIRST STOP after leaving Lumina was Supply Ship 5, once occupied by Andrew Harding, then taken over by Benjamin Mizello after Admiral Chase and the rescue fleet from Earth defeated Harding and his cohort Carl Stormer.

Benjamin had traveled on the supply ship to rendezvous with Ilsa, and stayed on the ship until replacement custodians arrived, an Arilian couple named Hespera and Johanis. One of Johanis' first tasks as custodian was to perform the marriage ceremony that joined Benjamin and Ilsa.

Ironically, Hespera and Johanis also unwittingly helped guide Xyla in her effort to find Benjamin. They advised her to attend the first space-based Galactic Exploration Conference on Sparil. Benjamin was certain to be there. The couple was aware of the part they'd played in Elsenia losing her father and couldn't do enough for her during her visit to the supply ship. Very quickly, they learned what Elsenia wanted most—information about the Tattoo People—they worked tirelessly to help her. The news explorers transmitted about the expansion of the Tattoo People's empire excited and intrigued Elsenia. The race of beings that had launched the space vehicles carrying the alien vine must have been intent on establishing its dominance by sheer numbers. But the mystery of their ultimate purpose remained unknown, as the Tattoo People on different planets made no attempt to communicate with each other and remained as disconnected as they could possibly be. And the extent of the disconnection was great, given the vast distances that separated them. Paradoxically, the Tattoo People virtually thrived on the effectiveness of their internal communication on any one planet, yet on a galactic scale, each planet was an island in a vast ocean.

Evidence of their isolation was the disparity among the various planets. Visiting explorers reported encountering Tattoo People of markedly distinct personalities. On one planet, they were reserved and suspicious of strangers, as on Lumina, while on another, they were outgoing and gregarious. Some Tattoo People were openly hostile to visitors, while others were warm and inviting. It wasn't clear at all how their societies diverged so drastically when all started out essentially the same. Elsenia found herself increasingly intrigued by the puzzle and strove to learn as much as possible. Delving into the pasts of these planets was like peeling away the layers of their psyches, and Elsenia soon thought of herself more a psychologist than a biologist.

Thanks to sugestions from Hespera and Johanis, however, the next planet Elsenia traveled to didn't have a population of Tattoo People. Named Magnetonia, it was unique among those of the Galactic Garden because the alien vine had grown there for thousands of years, but a new civilization of Tattoo People had never emerged. Furthermore, the planet had been settled by humans, who for unknown reasons lived for hundreds of years. Elsenia departed the supply ship anticipating how much she might learn from humans blessed with such longevity.

CHAPTER 11

— Century 1620 —

Eᴌsᴇɴɪᴀ ʜᴀᴅ ʟɪᴛᴛʟᴇ ᴇxᴘᴏsᴜʀᴇ to robots and cyborgs. They were certainly not a big part of Arilian culture. Humans on Earth had been infatuated with the technology for several millennia and then lost interest, like a child with a new toy. Thus, when Elsenia landed on Magnetonia and a robotic receptionist greeted her, she was ready to abandon her visit and return to the reality of galactic space travel. The robot sensed her discomfort and explained that Magnetonia was such a popular destination for galactic travelers the people decided to delegate the task of escorting visitors to a robot corps. They had the advantage of lasting thousands of years, long even by the standards of Magnetonians. The robot memories retained data from all previous visits to the planet. Many galactic travelers returned, sometimes after thousands of years, and were greeted by a robotic tour guide who remembered them.

Elsenia grudgingly allowed herself to be guided through the spaceport by her assigned robotic escort.

Magnetonia was given its name by the first explorers who visited the planet because of its tremendous magnetic field— thousands of times stronger than Earth's. Not only was the field more intense, it was more complex and structured as well. On Earth, the lines of magnetic force wrapped neatly around the planet from one pole to the other. On Magnetonia, magnetic force lines emerged from all over the planet's surface, extending upward to heights of several hundred kilometers, then looping back to the surface again. The planet was covered with so many loops that if they could be seen, the planet would've looked like it had been threaded everywhere by loosely stitched filaments. Amazingly enough, even though the magnetic field couldn't be seen, the alien vine had grown unimpeded for thousands of years, preferentially along the field lines, making visible the twisted loops, allowing Magnetonians the privilege of visualizing magnetic lines of force.

Though the alien vine thrived on Magnetonia, issuing abundant berries every season just like the mature vines of other planets, the pods from which the Tattoo People normally emerged never blossomed. Interestingly, the humans of Magnetonia learned to care for the vine with the same dedication and diligence as the Tattoo People would have.

While Elsenia waited for a shuttle outside the spaceport, the robot recounted the history of Magnetonia. It had been colonized by a fleet of emigrants from Prosperity. After landing on the planet, they hacked away at the vegetation creating a clearing to establish a new colony. Unlike Carl Stormer's attempt, fifty thousand years earlier, they succeeded, by growing crops and using the lumber from the alien vine to build homes. Their civilization was fully integrated with the hardy plant, which covered much of the planet's surface.

A vehicle that moved along roads so smooth they might have been made of plastic transported Elsenia with other tourists. Peering out of the vehicle at the spectacularly beautiful landscape, she understood why Magnetonia was such a popular destination. The loops and arcades of the planet's magnetic field entrained the vine to grow naturally in ways that produced magnificent bridges, covered roadways, and shaded tunnels, and the Magnetonians made use of the vine in bizarre and clever ways. Thus, everything Elsenia saw had the same gentle curves characteristic of magnetic fields, without a sharp edge or angled wall anywhere.

Stopping, Elsenia was shown to another reception area, where she and the other travelers waited for instructions, as part of a carefully choreographed process for greeting new tourists. She was the only tourist traveling alone. The others stood in groups of two to four people, waiting expectantly. A diverse collection of humans from different planets, they were distinct in their appearance, language, and manners. Though curious about each other, there was little interaction among the groups.

Elsenia's personalized robotic guide offered her a choice of Magnetonian adventures. She could take a nature tour, concentrating on the natural wonders of the planet, with options ranging from mildly strenuous and safe to extremely demanding and possibly dangerous. Another tour visited prominent historical sites. Still another featured a variety of thrill rides, taking advantage of the rolling curves of the alien vine to provide the dips and turns to entertain the happy tourists. There was a transportation tour also, which allowed visitors to experience unique walkways, elevators, cars, trains, trolleys, boats and aerial tramways, all based on advanced magnetic technology.

The robot then invited Elsenia to browse the reception area, where three-dimensional displays showed the tourists what they might expect from each Magnetonian adventure. Not seeing any that appealed to her, she asked the robot guide if there were others to choose from.

The robot paused for several seconds, processing this request, then said, "Perhaps you'll be interested in the science tour."

Intrigued, Elsenia replied, "Yes. That sounds better."

The robot led her to an empty room. There stood a single kiosk. He activated a display monitor. A list of names appeared. "Here are the most famous scientists in human history. You may choose from any on this list to be your guide on a tour of the planet. Most of those interested in the science tours choose Einstein. Some prefer Gauss, the master of magnetism. A few pick famous astronomers. The scientists on this list come from different planets and times in human history. Please, make your selection."

The list of names was impressive, but not surprising, as thousands of years of human history had produced many distinguished scientists. Elsenia had difficulty deciding, till one name caught her eye: Lemanuel Von Sigma, the famous scientist of Aril whom she'd spoken to about Risto's asteroid.

Several minutes later, she found herself standing before a robot with an incredible likeness to the eccentric scientist. She was about to ask if he remembered her, but didn't get a chance.

"Hello, Elsenia. It's good to see you again," Lemmy said.

"How can you possibly remember me?" she asked.

"The Lemmy you met on Sparil was extremely diligent at keeping records of everything he did and all the people he met.

He wrote about your visit. Your conversation with him, and other information about Lemmy, is programmed into my memory bank. Follow me, please."

Lemmy led Elsenia through a series of corridors to a room that looked exactly like the laboratory she'd visited on Sparil. It brought back memories of her conversation with Lemmy and his attempt to teach her about the trajectories of state functions. Now, the same monitor showed images of exotic landscapes on Magnetonia. The robotic Lemmy was as animated and expressive as the real Lemmy she remembered, except now he directed his enthusiasm at the marvels of Magnetonia. Gesticulating excitedly toward the images, he expounded on the planet's features.

"Scientifically, Magnetonia is unique and fascinating, distinguished by its complex and structured magnetic field, the result of the motion of material within the planet's molten core, where dense masses of liquid magma churn and bubble. The mixing, rotation, and upheaval of this molten matter produce electrical currents, violently random in direction, intensity, and vorticity, but giving rise in an impossibly complex way to the magnetic forces that wind with paradoxical grace and smoothness through the planet's mantle, giving Magnetonia's biosphere magical powers, which I will say more about later.

"These same dynamic interior forces also produce other marvelous features of Magnetonia's topology. Volcanic peaks are sprinkled about the planet, erupting frequently, spewing incandescent lava over land that will never be habitable. In other areas, powerful geysers shoot streams of steaming water thousands of meters skyward. Earthquakes are frequent occurrences as well. Fortunately, the people have learned to construct their homes using the same structural principle as the alien vine. There is so much flexibility in the buildings that they are virtually indestructible. The occupants of the dwellings hardly pay any attention when the ground shakes.

"Another consequence of the planet's chaotic magnetic field structure is the spectacular aurora that occurs all over. On Earth, auroras are largely confined to the polar regions because

Earth's magnetic field guides the incoming particles from the Sun to high latitudes. On Magnetonia, the magnetic field funnels the particles all over the globe. The appearance of the aurora at any particular place and time depends on when the particles arrive, the orientation of the field that carries the particles, and the angle of the field at the point of impact. From space, Magnetonia appears as an electrically charged sphere, upon which brilliant and colorful discharges bounce and skitter across the surface in ghostly patterns, like a planet-sized display of ball lightning in space.

"Not surprisingly, the Magnetonians have become extremely clever at harvesting the powers of magnetism. Their technology makes good use of the pervasive magnetic fields. Still, the Magnetonians have only scratched the surface. I believe there are many more undiscovered ways magnetic fields may be harnessed.

"Are you looking for masters of the galaxy?" the Lemmy robot asked. "There may not be such a race of beings—certainly not humans, though they may think they are. No. The masters of the universe will be the race that has learned how to confine plasmas with magnetic fields, allowing for the controlled fusion of atoms, to produce an endless supply of energy. They will survive when and where other humans cannot because they will know how to create magnetic shields to protect their bodies as they travel through space for thousands of years from one stellar destination to the next. Your ability to be frozen for thousands of years is based on magnetocryogenics, where strong magnetic fields make possible the freezing of human tissue rapidly enough to avoid damage. It's the magnetic field that bestows this power.

"Magnetic fields are invisible lines in space that confine and guide the motion of charged particles, providing mysterious linkages that connect celestial objects, making an event occurring in one location manifest itself in bizarre and unpredictable ways at another location impossibly far away.

"Magnetic fields are the invisible forces that permit the formation of galaxies in the universe. True, it is gravity that pulls the primordial matter together, but by itself, the material falling in toward the center of mass would acquire angular momentum during its descent. As matter falls toward the center, its rotational motion grows faster. Eventually, the centrifugal force from its angular speed would overcome the pull of gravity, and the material would be ejected outward. However, in the presence of a magnetic field, those forces bind the falling masses together. Thus, it's the magnetic field that permits the concentration of material in the universe. Without it, masses would be flying about randomly through space, never acquiring the accretive properties needed to form larger, discrete masses, the ubiquitous stars and planets.

"Have you thought about how your computers select the routes the galactic explorers take when traveling from one location to another? It's not just the shortest distance between the two points. The Galactic Explorers Union constructed a model of the magnetic field in space. In three-dimensional space, there are places with strong and weak magnetic force, a result of the combined strength of the fields from all nearby stars. The map takes on three-dimensional contours, as with the topography of land surfaces. Galactic explorers use routes through regions where the magnetic fields are weakest, just as someone might traverse the land by walking through the valleys. Weak magnetic field regions are places with the lowest cosmic ray fluxes. These highways in the heavens are the most benign routes the explorers may take. Without them, they would succumb to the ravages of cosmic ray exposure in only a few hundred years of space travel, even with all the sophisticated shielding of their capsules.

"People of Magnetonia have grown to worship magnetic fields. They believe the source of all life is magnetism. By far the most incredible feature of the planet, one unforeseen by those who colonized it, is that intense magnetic fields have miraculous healing effects. The people seldom suffer from illness or disease, and they age more slowly than their human counterparts on other planets. The average life expectancy of the people here is about 300 years."

"What's it like to live such a long time?" Elsenia asked.

"It is not so different," Lemmy explained.

Elsenia laughed. "Of course, it has to be different. People

here live practically forever."

"They don't live forever. They live a long time—longer than other humans. But they don't act any different because they've grown accustomed to their longevity. They don't even notice it."

"But certainly the extended lifespans create challenges? Who takes care of all the elderly people? How do they occupy their time? What do they do to keep from being bored?"

"The elderly take care of themselves. Many of them teach and care for the children. Others engage in various artistic pursuits, finding ways to express their emotions and experiences. Many visitors are frightened by the thought of living so long, but they don't understand Magnetonian civilization. The people don't live one life for hundreds of years. They live many lives. They reinvent themselves whenever they wish. When a person transitions from one life to another, it's a cause for celebration. Magnetonians are always celebrating, because each time a person decides to start a new life, they host a big party to commemorate the event.

"As for boredom, Magnetonians are never bored. Boredom arises from unrealistic expectations of what being alive offers. Magnetonians thrive on time itself because there is so much of it, or perhaps there is so much time because they thrive on it. They consume the minutes and the hours and the days, taking them in and being nourished by them. Time strengthens them. They build their lives on the accumulation of days."

"But they die eventually."

"Yes. It is usually a very quick death—like the collapse of a building that has been built too tall, or a bridge that is carrying too much weight."

"That seems very strange to those of us who live according to a different biological clock."

"You, of all people, should understand how poorly defined is the concept of time. Galactic explorers live for thousands of years, yet you can't understand how Magnetonians live for a few hundred."

Elsenia smiled. "Good point."

"If I was to remain on Magnetonia, do you think I would live hundreds of years?" Elsenia asked.

"Perhaps. Are you happy?"

Elsenia hesitated. "I don't know."

"It's important," Lemmy said. "Unless you're an inherently unhappy person, everyone eventually reaches a point in their lives when they are reasonably happy—not ecstatically happy, like when one falls in love, achieves great success, or discovers something new—but just comfortable with the present state of affairs for you and your loved ones. People on Magnetonia eventually reach and remain at that point, living every day with the awareness and appreciation of true happiness."

"What about those who are inherently unhappy?"

"Yes, there are those. They never appreciate the simple joy of living. They have been damaged, or perhaps their ambition and pride prevent them from ever feeling completely fulfilled. These are the people who despise and resent others who have been successful, or have something they don't have. These people can draw the life and spirit not only out of a room, but out of the entire planet. They judge without basis, they suppress without reason, they hate for the sake of hating. These people, strangely enough, do not live long on Magnetonia. They destroy themselves from the inside, although they blame others for their destruction. Magnetonia is not the right place for people of that ilk. Magnetonia is like a magnet of the human spirit, attracting those with the right polarity and repelling those possessing negative forces. People with positive attitudes are reinforced by the rewards and beauty of the planet. People who aren't open to that beauty, or who choose to steer the world toward their own private versions of hell, are repulsed."

Elsenia had been wise in her choice of tours. The science tour led by Lemmy allowed her to experience all other adventures. In each case, Lemmy explained the scientific principles behind the thrill rides, the modes of transportation, and natural beauty of the planet. At the historical sites, Lemmy described how scientific breakthroughs influenced the course of political and social events.

Elsenia and Lemmy compared Magnetonian society with those of other planets. She insisted that the long lifespan of the people should result in profound differences.

"The biggest difference," the Lemmy robot responded, "is not how people behave individually, but what they accomplish collectively. Magnetonians carry out projects that take decades to complete—projects that those with shorter lifespans would never begin because they couldn't be completed in a single lifetime. The infrastructure of the planet is painstakingly constructed with incredible care and precision. If a mistake is made, or something doesn't turn out as planned, the people tear it apart and start over. Do you think it's a coincidence that everything humans create is completed in a time scale that is less than the average lifespan of a person? It's because this is what humans do. Naturally, if humans lived hundreds of years, they'd initiate activities that take longer. Not all animals do this. Consider bees or ants. It takes many generations of ants to build an anthill."

"We build cities," Elsenia interjected. "They're the human analogies to hives and anthills."

"Yes, but a city is hardly a single project. It's a combination of many smaller projects. On Magnetonia, almost all projects take a very long time. Even a painting might take several decades to complete. It doesn't matter."

"What about the population?" Elsenia asked. "Wouldn't such long lifespans make the population grow too quickly?"

"Not necessarily. It's the number of offspring that are born that makes the population grow—not longevity. Did you know that the total number of humans in the galaxy right now is about 10 percent of the total number that lived through all of time? That means if all the dead humans came back to life, the population would only grow by a factor of ten. But if everyone who has ever lived had one more child, then the human population of the galaxy would be orders of magnitude greater."

Before her departure from Magnetonia, Elsenia said good-bye to Lemmy. She'd all but forgotten that he was a robot. He'd become a friend. But she couldn't leave until she asked the obvious question—the one she'd been wanting to ask since her arrival. "So what's the secret? Why do people on Magnetonia live so long?" she asked.

"No one really knows," Lemmy answered. "Many scientists visit the planet, intent on learning the secret. Countless theories have been proposed. All, in some way, involve the planet's intense magnetic field because that feature distinguishes Magnetonia from others in the Galactic Garden. Some claim that the magnetic field has magical regenerative powers on human tissue, an idea that has been around for eons, but has never been proven by physiological studies. It's true that strong magnetic fields can affect the electrochemical processes of human organs, but how that translates to longer life is a huge leap.

"Others favor the idea that the strong magnetic fields deflect cosmic rays so effectively that the people of Magnetonia are not exposed to the cell-damaging radiation that everyone else in the galaxy has to endure. They believe the greatest threat to living organisms is radiation due to cosmic rays. A planet upon which life struggles for a foothold will soon become lifeless because of the relentless onslaught of energetic particles from space. Without magnetic fields, planets would be bombarded by lethal radiation tearing its destructive path through living tissue, producing tunnels of atomic devastation in its wake, and causing cancerous growths and species-altering mutations. Were it not for Earth's magnetic shield, its doubtful life would have evolved beyond the simplest organisms that slithered through the primordial slime. Absent the impact on cells from penetrating radiation, there's no reason why human cells should age in any way. Cells reproduce new cells. Why should the new ones be different from the parent cells?"

Elsenia's favorite theory among those Lemmy described was one even less grounded in evidence than the others. It was the idea that the aurora, which danced ceaselessly in the skies of

Magnetonia, had mystical powers that graced its people with long life. The silent undulations of light were like vibrant haloes, gifts from the gods, who bestow their blessings on the mortals below—blessings in the form of freedom from disease and the debilitation of age. Elsenia knew it was a silly notion, but the people of Magnetonia spent every night watching the luminous displays. When the sun rose in the morning and saturated the sky with its own brilliance, they talked about the previous evening's aurora, and anticipated the setting sun so that they might see the celestial lights again. Perhaps longevity was as simple as that, Elsenia thought. It was ending each day with the fervent desire and anticipation to be alive to see another miracle unfold on the next.

Elsenia departed Magnetonia feeling satisfied that her visit to the planet had altered her view of the universe. She had a greater appreciation for the power of magnetic fields, the benefits of human integration with the alien vine, the accomplishments that can be achieved over long time scales, and the usefulness of robotic beings, at least as tour guides.

CHAPTER 12

— Century 1646 —

FROM THE OUTSET, Ilsa's return to Earth was not the homecoming she imagined it would be. A sudden squall erupted, producing chaotic winds and driving rain that buffeted the two tiny capsules as she and Druix descended. Fortunately, the parachutes remained intact to slow their landing, but that also meant they were even more at the mercy of the strong air currents swirling about them. The capsules struck ground at an angle, rolling over several times before coming to a stop.

Druix emerged first and struggled through torrential rain to where Ilsa's capsule lay on its side, wedged beneath a large tree that had absorbed the momentum of the tumbling vehicle. He managed to open the capsule's hatch and climbed into the control deck where the twisted remains of Ilsa's landing seat filled him with dread. She was unconscious, pinned beneath a section of electronic equipment that had broken off from the console.

There was little Druix could do but remain with his wife, ready to comfort her should she awaken. He saw no excessive bleeding, but in the darkness of the damaged capsule, he wasn't sure what other signs of injury he might be missing. The minutes he waited passed with agonizing slowness, until emergency teams from the Earth spaceport arrived.

Druix sat beside Ilsa's mangled body in her hospital room. During the ten years he'd spent on Earth with his mother, Druix had the occasion to visit hospitals, particularly when Xyla's first husband lay dying. He couldn't help being intrigued that the appearance of a hospital room had scarcely changed in many thousands of years. Ilsa's bed was surrounded by instruments and equipment of various sorts that were probably far more advanced, but on the outside, one black box is much like another. The subdued lighting and neutral coloring of the room were universal standards, it seemed. Druix had no idea what kind of fantastic marvels 1646th Century Earth might await them outside, but here in Ilsa's recovery room he could convince himself he'd never left the planet with his mother so many years ago.

Attendants entered and left, checking the equipment, performing cursory examinations of Ilsa, occasionally moving her or adjusting her limbs, which had been wrapped in a plastic-like material that kept them immobilized and perhaps had healing properties. The confidence and casualness with which they went about their business reassured Druix. There seemed to be no panic or urgency in their ministrations. Whatever modern medical procedures were being applied to Ilsa must certainly have a high likelihood of success. Whenever he asked them a question or engaged them in conversation, they just smiled, with fingers to their mouths in the age-old gesture that indicated the need for silence. For all Druix knew, none of them spoke Union English. His attempts to speak to them in other languages produced no better response.

Druix considered the fact that 175,000 years earlier, humans of Earth were little more than apes on the planet. Were he and Ilsa as primitive as apes to these futuristic earthlings? Was their medical science good enough to accommodate the anatomical differences between ancient humans and those they were accustomed to treating? In appearance, the modern earthlings were not that different. The leathery skin that was characteristic of Admiral Chase's race had softened. Though light tan in color, the texture was more like that of 22nd Century humans. Hair had softened as well. Most of the hospital staff, both male and female, had long, wavy, golden-brown hair, more rich and luxurious than any Druix had ever seen.

After a while, an elderly woman entered. She approached Druix and offered her hand, introducing herself in precise but accented Union English.

"I am Petyuba. I'm your wife's doctor."

Petyuba was ancient. The lines and wrinkles that covered her face and hands were evidence of many decades of exposure to the elements. She'd made no attempt to mask or ameliorate the ravages of time. Druix began to doubt the worthiness of a medical professional endowed with knowledge of healing, yet apparently unable to defend her own anatomy from physiological decay. Maybe the woman was a thousand years old, but by Earth standards still looked young for her age. It was impossible to tell.

Belying her ancient appearance though were her eyes, which were now locked on Druix. He struggled to calibrate the thoughts and emotions that fueled their fire. They were blue, but so faintly so that they might have been clear crystals simply reflecting errant skylight slanting through the windows.

"Your wife has suffered serious injuries. The healing process will be very long."

"Will she be okay?"

Petyuba turned to look at Ilsa before answering. "Yes, of course. It's just a matter of regeneration of the damaged tissue. You understand. Don't you?"

Druix was confused. He remembered the sight of Ilsa's body crushed beneath the wreckage of the capsule. "I'm worried if she'll recover completely."

"Do you have a place to stay?"

It was an odd question. Druix hesitated before answering. "No. We just arrived."

Petyuba seemed deep in thought. Still looking toward her patient, she said absently, "Perhaps you should stay with me." Then, after a pause, "Both of you. That way I can look after your wife during her recovery."

"I couldn't impose on you. I'll find a hotel. My wife can remain here. Can't she?"

The tinge of blue in Petyuba's eyes turned gray. "Nonsense. This is not the Earth you remember. Things are not done the way they used to be."

Druix recalled the cool detachment of the nurses and attendants as they looked after Ilsa. Truth be told, he'd be uneasy leaving Ilsa alone at the hospital. He glanced to where she lay wrapped in plastic, unconscious and immobilized. She could be near death, for all he knew.

"I'll arrange to have her moved," said Petyuba.

"Is she in pain?" Druix asked.

"Of course not. She's in a state once referred to as a coma. She feels nothing and knows nothing. She will remain that way until the regeneration process is complete."

Druix nodded. He believed the ancient doctor, but for some odd reason didn't completely trust her.

"How long will that be?"

"I can't say for sure," Petyuba answered. "Remember that you and your wife have physiology that is more than 160,000 years older than present day humans. I have no experience upon which to base an estimate. It could be several weeks or a few months."

"But less than a year?"

Petyuba frowned. In words of ice, she said, "If she doesn't recover in a year, she will never recover."

Druix felt a knot in the pit of his stomach. "Very well," he said. "We'll do as you suggest."

Transportation on 1646th Century Earth was via individual bullet-shaped cylinders that traveled through underground tubes. The intersecting network of conduits beneath the ground was like a jumble of spaghetti. Travelers stepped into the cylinder, the doors closed, and then the missile was sucked into the frictionless, evacuated network of tubes. The speed and direction were controlled automatically to move passengers head-first to their destinations. They were protected, as the cylinder sped through the tubes, by contoured cushions that insulated them from the buffeting g-forces of acceleration, deceleration and turns. Music played through speakers built into the headrests and was the only sound Druix heard during his twenty-minute journey. He could see nothing. He'd been on Earth twelve hours and still had no idea what the planet looked like. He wondered how Ilsa would be transported. With sudden panic, he regretted that he'd left her alone. He had put all his trust in Petyuba, a woman he'd only met an hour earlier.

When the cylinder stopped, it rotated into a vertical position, then dropped, like the piston of an engine. Then the walls rotated, revealing an opening through which Druix exited. He found himself in a dome-shaped room, suffused with blue-green light. The transparent surface of the dome revealed that he was underwater, surrounded by murky liquid, dimly lit from above. At the opposite side of the dome was the entrance to a corridor, also constructed of clear walls. He walked through the passageway, gazing uneasily at the water pressing upon its exterior surface. The corridor led to a larger domed enclosure. There, he found Petyuba waiting for him, sitting in a chair upon a raised platform near the center of the hemispherical dome. Druix saw that the chair was able to tilt and rotate, affording the occupant the ability to easily pivot about. It would be the natural inclination because outside the dome the sea was no longer murky. Instead, the clear water revealed a spectacular vista of marine plants and animals.

Druix looked about in stunned silence. The room was filled with objects he couldn't identify. He wasn't sure whether they were furnishings or artwork. Each was constructed from brilliantly colored glass and crystal, held together with gently contoured metal work, seeming to capture and blend with the surrounding marine biota. The variety of shapes and sizes defied any attempts he might make to understand their function.

"Where's Ilsa?" he asked.

"She'll be arriving shortly. She'll be brought through the airlock at the back of the house." Petyuba gestured in a direction that helped Druix orient himself as to what was considered the front and back of the hemispherical volume.

"I've had a meal prepared for you. Let's have something to eat first and by the time we're done, your wife will be situated in her room."

The two of them ate together—a meal brought by stony-faced attendants served on a table that unfolded like the petals of a flower. Druix was struck by the absolute silence within the dome. Not only were they insulated from exterior sounds of any kind, but the weight of all that water upon the enclosure seemed to stifle any errant sonic vibration. It was like the opposite of an echo. Sounds impinging on the material of the dome were swallowed up by the surrounding sea.

"It's really safer living here at the bottom of the sea than any place on Earth," Petyuba said, sensing his uneasiness. "We're totally free from the influences of atmospheric elements, whether they be heat, rain, wind, tornadoes, hurricanes, or floods. Even the occasional tsunami is hardly felt at this depth below the surface. We have no freezing winters, no blazing summers, no ice or fog or blizzard or hailstorm. No lightning or thunder either. The temperature of the water around the dome hardly ever changes, even with the passing of the seasons up above. We don't worry about earthquakes or volcanic eruptions or those crazy storms in space that light up the skies and play havoc on our technology."

"Do many people live in the ocean?"

"There are millions now. The number is growing rapidly."

"You'd never know it. It feels so isolated here."

"They're out there," said Petyuba, in disgust. "You will see them. We had to be very discreet in transporting your wife."

"Why is that?"

"Because you and your wife have created quite a stir on Earth. There is great interest, especially in her."

"We can't be the first travelers from space who have visited Earth."

"Of course not, but you, and particularly your wife, are from a more distant time than any of the previous visitors."

"Ilsa left Earth in 2149."

"Yes, and they're anxious to get a sample of her DNA."

"Why?"

Petyuba set her elbows on the table and brought her hands together. "You might find this difficult to understand, but people of Earth are experiencing great uncertainty. Many feel depressed and alienated because they've lost track of their ancestry. In our society, worth is dependent on how far back one's lineage can be traced. In this hierarchy, those who can connect their lineage back to the earliest times on Earth yield great power over others. Ilsa's DNA would be the new standard by which people might compare their mitochondrial DNA."

"Have you given them Ilsa's DNA?"

"No. Not yet. I'm only allowed to do it with her permission. Even you, her husband, can't grant that permission."

"But certainly it's not that hard to get a DNA sample. Why would you need permission?"

Petyuba shook her head in disappointment. "Yes, it's easy enough to get, but it's considered an invasion of privacy. If you know a person's DNA, you know everything there is to know about him or her."

"How can people possibly protect themselves from having their DNA lifted? Even a strand of hair carries their DNA."

"Yes, but one would have to know who the strand came from. That's the key. It's impossible to associate any particular DNA with a specific person. Without that, the DNA is worthless. That's how we protect ourselves. There's what you might call a black market in DNA. It's a very valuable commodity, the more so because of how tightly authorities attempt to control it."

"What would someone do with a DNA sample anyway? Doesn't it take sophisticated equipment and technology to decipher it?"

"Yes, but there are illegal entities offering those services as well. It's a continuing battle trying to control the illicit transfer of information resident in stray DNA samples. Your DNA, and your wife's, would be extremely valuable. I had to use great caution in transporting you both to my home. Only a very few people know where you are."

Druix looked about the room. Would it be that difficult to extract his DNA from the others that might be lingering about? How many other people had visited Petyuba's lair? What had become of their DNA?

An attendant approached the table and said something to Petyuba in a language Druix couldn't understand.

"Your wife is here."

Petyuba rose and Druix followed her to a corridor leading from the dome. It was made from the same transparent material as the rest of the house. Along the corridor were doors that led to other smaller, dome-shaped enclosures. Druix peered into the first one. It was empty except for a bed and several odd pieces of furniture. Unlike the other parts of Petyuba's undersea domain, the enclosure of the smaller room was opaque. It made sense, Druix supposed. It was better not to see the sea creatures that might be swimming about while half awake attempting to sleep.

Druix passed several other similarly furnished rooms before finally arriving at the one where Ilsa lay. He wondered what transport system had been used to convey her. As the doctor had promised, Ilsa was surrounded by much of the same equipment she had in the hospital. An attendant sat in a chair next to the bed, looking absently at Druix.

"In many ways, she's better here," Petyuba said. "The air is carefully controlled to maintain the optimum balance of chemicals, including negative ions to deter harmful agents."

Druix approached the bed and stroked Ilsa's cheek, as if confirming her presence. Even comatose, she retained the perfect beauty that made her unique. There'd been many studies about what physical features constituted pure and universal beauty. Symmetry, clarity of complexion, gentle contours of skin and bone structure—Ilsa had them all, even with her eyes closed, which served to sharpen and focus those features. More importantly, Ilsa always behaved as though she were oblivious to her own beauty. Now, unconscious and expressionless, her physical attractiveness was even more understated. It was difficult to believe that anyone could exhibit such perfection in the absence of movement.

"She's beautiful," said Petyuba, as if reading his thoughts.

"I just want her back," said Druix, choking away tears.

"She will recover," said Petyuba confidently. "An attendant will be here all the time, and I'll check on her as often as I can."

"Thank you," said Druix. "You're too kind."

Druix couldn't sleep that night, not because noises kept him awake. There were none. And there were no intrusive sources of light. The blackness within the dome of his bedroom was absolute. Not since he'd departed from Lumina had he gotten a full night's sleep. It was adrenalin that kept him awake—adrenalin produced by his panic-filled thoughts, imagining the many threats that endangered him and Ilsa. What threats? The unknown ones: the mysterious Petyuba and her inexplicable hospitality; the blank-faced attendants, who, in their indifference, projected contempt; the enigmatic people of planet Earth, who protected their DNA as if it were the only aspect of their identities not shared; or the weight of thousands of tons of water on the dome that surrounded him, and the strange sea creatures that floated invisibly about. And, of course, he wondered if Ilsa would ever be the same? Would she have any memory of what had happened?

Druix rose and felt his way to the doorway of the room. Moving cautiously down the corridor, he entered Ilsa's room, dimly lit by the faint pinpricks of light from the medical equipment. There was a chair next to her bed, where the attendant had sat earlier. Druix slumped into it, looking at Ilsa, her pale complexion reflecting the ghostly light from the nearby instruments. What an unfortunate life she'd led. She'd been married on Earth to a man who was convicted of cyber-crimes and sentenced to federal prison. After meeting Benjamin Mizello, he left to begin his exploration of the galaxy with thousands of other young, idealistic adventurers. Then, while researching an article she was planning to write about the dubious organizations selling dreams of colonizing new worlds to unsuspecting and desperate people, she'd been kidnapped and placed frozen in a capsule that was launched into space. Upon being unfrozen thousands of years later, she was assaulted and threatened by her abductors. While attempting to escape, her capsule had been struck by an EMP blast that sent her on an uncontrolled course toward the galactic center. She'd been rescued by Risto Jalonen, and then experienced the joy of reunion and subsequent marriage to Benjamin Mizello. But he left her while she was pregnant with Elsenia, on a mission to explore the possible existence of intelligent alien life forms on the planet Happiness. He was supposed to return to her and his daughter, but instead he remained on Happiness and lived out his life with Druix's mother, Xyla. Loss had been a recurring element of Ilsa's life.

She'd been happy on Aril, married now to Druix, raising the twins and Elsenia. Her unwavering intensity of purpose had sustained her through the turmoil and uncertainty. Her absolute confidence gave her strength, but that confidence was not a result of her strength. In fact, she was often doubtful of her own ability to deal with adversity. It was that she always knew what was best, what was right, what was the true path to follow. That was what made Ilsa steadfast and resolute. Even when she knew she'd fall short in achieving her goals, it didn't weaken her efforts. Where was that inner fortitude now, Druix wondered, as he watched her inanimate body? Where was Ilsa now?

Druix finally slept.

When the attendant returned and found Druix in the chair, she looked at him sternly. There was light in the room now. The dome had become transparent, and sea creatures swam by, oblivious to the humans several meters away. While the attendant performed a perfunctory examination of Ilsa, Druix left to find Petyuba. He looked through the entire house, calling her name into each of the domed enclosures. When he found the room where he'd arrived, he saw ports for three cylinders, arranged side by side. One was empty. Petyuba must have departed in it. The two remaining cylinders stood with their doors open. Druix considered taking one to see where he could go, but there was no indication of how the vehicle operated—no dials to turn or buttons to press, no steering wheel or joystick, no computer to enter instructions. Even if he were to get the cylinder to move, he'd have no way of knowing where he might go or how to get back.

He returned to the larger dome and sat in the chair Petyuba had occupied at its center. He remained there for several hours, watching the improbable creatures of the underwater world. They were very different from those Druix knew growing up on Aurora. The only marine life he'd seen on his frozen planet were food-fish, pulled from the icy waters and eaten. The tropical sea life of the warm waters of Earth couldn't have existed there. Druix had studied the plant and animal life of saltwater seas in books, and he'd seen pictures of the myriad species, but those had failed to give him even the slightest notion of the variety of underwater organisms. The ocean seemed to be one huge petri dish, within which fantastic experiments in life were carried out.

In those hours sitting in Petyuba's chair, Druix saw every manner of sea life swim by. There were the schools of little fish, some gold, some silver, some iridescent, all swimming together in unbelievable and inexplicable syncopation, their wiggling forms making the water shimmer as if it carried rivers of gems. There were the phantom-like, gelatinous masses that moved vertically up and down, disappearing into the murky glow above the dome, and then reappearing, some distance off, as if magically born in the life-giving liquid. Then there were the large, lumbering beasts swimming alone, carrying the signs of incredible age, their bulbous eyes unreadable, concealing the secrets of all they'd learned during their long lives and journeys under the sea.

When he tired of looking at the sea life, Druix returned to check on Ilsa. The attendant sat beside the bed staring blankly at nothing. It was then that Druix realized there were no books anywhere in Petyuba's house—no written materials of any kind. How could a doctor not have any books? It was possible all written information was stored electronically and accessed via some virtual device, but he'd seen nothing even faintly resembling a computer. Perhaps one of the objects scattered about the floor of the dome was a cleverly camouflaged computer. He would have to ask Petyuba when she returned.

CHAPTER 13
— Century 1646 —

WEEKS PASSED and nothing changed. Ilsa remained in the same comatose state, wrapped in plastic, immobile and unconscious. Druix wandered about the house trying to keep himself occupied with his thoughts. The creatures of the sea swimming past the dome became familiar to him—in their own dull, monotonous routine. Druix became one of them, a fish in a bowl surrounded by other fish.

Every night he confronted Petyuba with questions, that soon became requests. The requests became demands. Frustration turned to indignation, indignation to anger. Petyuba deflected these advances with the assuredness of someone in absolute control. Druix cursed himself for having let Petyuba draw them into a circumstance from which there was no escape. He had no way to go anywhere, nor even to contact another human for help. They were at Petyuba's mercy because she alone held the secret to Ilsa's recovery. Petyuba could make Druix do anything. What would these demands include? Druix wondered and imagined, and in those long days with nothing to do, at the mercy of his own imaginings, the boundaries between reality and fantasy became blurred.

The days dragged on interminably. The only event he looked forward to each day was Petyuba's return. How could that be? Each day, when Petyuba emerged from her transport cylinder and entered the large dome enclosure, she seemed to have grown younger. The wrinkled skin became smoother, her hunched posture became more erect, her white hair regained its color, and her youthful shape was restored.

Were these changes just imaginings conjured up by Druix in his stimulus-free situation? Was Petyuba changing or was he? And in those dark nights in bed, when he dreamed of Ilsa's touch, could feel her body next to his, her warm, smooth skin against his, naked flesh to naked flesh, were these really dreams? Were those

Ilsa's lips he felt on him, as if his longing for her had solidified his vaporous imaginings? Was it reality or dreams that left him feeling the next day both fulfilled and unfulfilled, satisfied but wanting, faithful and unfaithful? Druix was losing the capacity to distinguish between these discordant emotions. The weapons by which one defends oneself from insanity were failing him.

The floor of Petyuba's home was organic, a thin layer of moist, spongy grass, genetically engineered aquatic plants that thrived in the heterogeneous boundary between land and sea.

"The plant also replenishes and purifies the oxygen within the dome," Petyuba explained in response to Druix's questions. She was always terse with Druix when he probed with questions about her home. She knew, or pretended to know, little about how the undersea habitat was maintained. The dim lighting that seemed to emanate from the surrounding water during nighttime hours was filled with phosphorescent plankton illuminating the dome. But the plankton couldn't have provided power for other appliances and gadgets in Petyuba's home—the furniture that unfolded from the objects about the floor, the food that was cooked throughout and served hot. Druix wondered what hidden technology sustained the undersea home of Ilsa's doctor.

In the late hours of the evening, after his recurring dreams, Druix lay awake until he was sure the apparition who shared his bed had departed. Then he rose and wandered about in the dark. He did this partly because he couldn't sleep, and partly because he hoped to discover something in the darkness, in his heightened sensitivity, that he missed in the long hours when he was alone.

On one of these walks, he found his way to the room that held the three transport cylinders. Barefoot, he had the unmistakable sensation that the floor was warmer than in the other parts of the house. He lay down and pressed his ear against the spongy floor. Was he imagining it or did he hear a low-pitched humming coming from beneath? With his fist, he thumped the floor. Did it yield more than it should? Was there a hollowness to the sound? He crawled across the floor, scraping his fingers through the thick, biotic turf covering it, looking for something.

He found it. One hundred and fifty thousand years of advanced technology had not produced a more clever way to conceal a hidden door. His fingers clenched a metal latch. He pulled on it, and a section of floor sprung open with a hydraulic hiss, revealing a space below, bathed in the eerie glow of ultra-violet light, that mysterious radiance, which could only be seen when it impinged on white objects, and did so with spectacular effect.

A metallic staircase descended into the space. Druix stepped down carefully and quietly until he reached the bottom some three meters below. Looking about, he saw what he knew had to be there: a vast array of machinery—motors, pumps, tubes, gears, pistons, cams, rotors, axles, pipes, wires, and cables—all intricately and methodically integrated into a complex engine, every component contrived to maintain the habitability of the dome tens of meters below sea level. It was an ingenious power plant so smoothly and quietly functional that those living above could scarcely sense its existence. Here was the secret to the breathable air, tolerable pressure and temperature, and inexhaustible light and power that made the undersea home habitable.

Druix walked among the machinery and equipment trying to understand their operation, but it was unfathomable to him. All the parts were heavy and solid, and connected tightly together. He doubted it ever needed repair, yet access from above and the stairway indicated that people needed to go there occasionally.

As he returned to the stairs, Druix noticed a transparent plastic tube running along the walls, as big around as his thumb. He reached out and closed his hand around it. The vibration within the tube suggested there was moving liquid within. It could be the source of the home's fresh water.

Druix climbed out of the basement and closed the door concealing it. He returned to his bed and spent the rest of the evening pondering his discovery.

After Petyuba departed the next day, Druix pretended to have a sneezing fit during breakfast and used his cloth napkin to wipe his nose. In front of Petyuba's quiet server, he left the table still holding the napkin, bringing it to his bedroom, where he hid it beneath articles of clothing. He spent the rest of the day casually strolling about the house looking for something sharp and metallic and found a syringe in the equipment arrayed about Ilsa.

He needed one more thing, a writing implement, but there was nothing anywhere that he could use. He decided to use his own blood.

Pricking his finger with the syringe, Druix wrote on the cloth napkin: "*Petyuba is holding us against our will. If you help us, you can have our DNA.*"

The message was in Union English, gibberish unless read by someone who understood the language. Petyuba did, and Druix had to assume others did as well.

That night, after the recurring dream that was not a dream but a nightmarish reality, Druix returned to the basement area. With the syringe, he punctured the transparent hose that ran around the walls of the room. A thin stream of water spurted from the opening. It hardly seemed enough, so he inserted the syringe again and twisted it to enlarge the opening. Now a stronger stream of water emerged from the hole. Satisfied with his work, he climbed up the stairs and closed the door again.

Druix hoped that the leak he'd created would set off an alarm, but he had no way of knowing what to expect. As far as he could tell, nothing changed in the house, and he fell asleep with that thought.

He awoke to the sound of voices. He rose quickly from the bed and walked to the doorway to listen. He heard Petyuba speaking loudly, with urgency, but couldn't understand the words. He left the room and found her talking to one of the attendants.

"What's wrong?" Druix asked.

"Nothing," Petyuba answered sharply. "Go back to bed."

"Is Ilsa okay?" Druix persisted, knowing she was, but using the pretext to disregard Petyuba's dismissal.

"Your wife is okay. There's just a minor malfunction in the dome. It will be fixed today. It's of no concern to you."

Hearing what he wanted to hear, Druix went back to his

room. He hoped the repair of the plastic tube required someone to enter the house—to whom he could give the cloth napkin with his message in blood. He'd considered leaving the note on the pipe itself but feared Petyuba or her attendants would find it first. Also, a repair person seeing the unintelligible markings on the cloth might throw it away. Only by handing it to the person directly would sufficient significance be attached to the cloth for Druix's plan to succeed.

What Druix failed to anticipate, however, was that he'd be locked out of the main part of the house. After Petyuba departed, he walked down the corridor to the living room, only to find the entrance blocked by a black, impenetrable, metallic door. He knocked repeatedly, but there was no response. Druix hurried to Ilsa's room where an attendant sat, as always, beside the bed. With gestures and words she couldn't understand, Druix tried to question her about the closed door, but the attendant just shook her head and looked at him without expression.

Druix returned to his room, glumly fingering the cloth message, wishing he'd taken the chance of leaving it in the basement. Now, the tube would be fixed and his one opportunity would be lost. He lay in his bed, angry and frustrated, watching the murky water outside the dome.

He was about to doze off when his eye caught a faint flash of light in the water some distance away. Sure it hadn't been there before, he stood to get a better view. Straining his eyes, he thought he could see the faint outline of a vehicle in the water. It made sense that whoever came to repair the tube might arrive in a submersible capsule.

With a small flashlight Petyuba had given him for night use, Druix pointed at the vehicle, turning the light on and off in the ancient code developed by Samuel Morse that spelled out SOS. Was it possible that 165,000 years later, the universal code was still understood? It didn't matter. Anything to attract the attention of the vehicle's occupant might work. He repeated the signal over and over, switching hands, as the repeated motion caused his fingers to cramp. The light in the capsule didn't change.

Finally, perhaps an hour later, it started to move, rising in the water. Druix directed the flashlight to follow its upward motion, as it grew fainter in the translucent fluid. Druix had almost given up when the light on the vehicle ceased its ascent and grew larger, coming toward him. Moments later, it was right outside Druix's dome with its light pointed straight at him. Druix couldn't see anyone inside the capsule, but whoever was in it could easily see him.

Druix withdrew the cloth from his pocket and pressed it against the dome with the writing displayed toward the vehicle. He held it there. If the occupant of the capsule didn't understand the writing, perhaps he could take a picture of it to show to someone else. Druix continued to hold the cloth up. The light in the capsule blinked twice, then the capsule drifted away and resumed its ascent. Druix was exhausted, drained of emotional and physical strength by a strategy with an extremely uncertain outcome. It could well be that he and Ilsa wouldn't be rescued at all—that the occupant of the capsule would report back to Petyuba and the old woman would exact a terrible vengeance on Druix and Ilsa. He had only to wait now, without knowing for what or how long.

Nothing happened until the second evening after the repair. That night, Petyuba returned to the dome in a foul mood. Druix sat down to dinner as usual, but she neither looked at Druix nor engaged him in conversation. Druix was struck by the extent to which the old woman controlled not only what happened within her home, but the overall mood of the place. During his time there, his emotions had run to extremes, driven in one direction or the other by his own thoughts and imaginings, but upon Petyuba's arrival at the end of the day, she always managed to restore normalcy by refusing to engage Druix or entertain his indignation and anger. But now that Petyuba was disturbed and upset, she set the mood for the entire house. Even the attendants, who normally excelled at remaining impassive to all of Druix's tantrums, reacted with fear to Petyuba's anger.

In the middle of their meal, with edgy tension hanging in

the air, Ilsa's attendant entered the room and spoke briefly to Petyuba.

"Your wife has regained consciousness," said Petyuba, abruptly rising from her chair. "Come."

Druix stumbled dazedly after the two women, only half comprehending what was happening. When they reached Ilsa's bed, he could see her eyes were open, a puzzled, frightened expression on her face.

"I'm cold," she muttered.

"That's normal," said Petyuba, moving closer to the bed. "We'll remove the plastic now. Once your circulation is normal, you'll feel warmer."

Ilsa gazed at her with suspicious annoyance. "I don't know you."

"I'm your doctor. You were injured. Your space capsule crashed. You'll be better soon. Your husband is here."

Petyuba stood aside and Druix stepped forward. "Ilsa, it's me. I've been so worried about you."

He took Ilsa's hand, but her expression didn't soften. "I need water."

The attendant poured Ilsa water from a pitcher that stood by the bed. Ilsa drank it, then handed the glass back silently.

"Are you okay?" asked Druix.

Ilsa turned to look at him. Her eyes seemed to have retained the pall that had fallen on them during her comatose state. Druix had always been able to lose himself in the depths of Ilsa's eyes, but now there was no depth, only a shallow grayness.

"I'm tired," Ilsa said.

"We'll leave," responded Druix. "You'll feel better after you get some sleep."

He bent over and kissed her forehead.

When Petyuba and Druix returned to the living area, the old woman grabbed Druix by the arm and turned him around to face her.

"You and your wife will leave here tomorrow. Her treatment is complete."

With that, she turned and strode away. Druix watched her disappear into her room. Whatever happened as a result of his message had produced a profound effect.

Druix remained awake that whole night, listening for any unusual sounds in the corridor outside his room. He tried to imagine what had transpired. Within the space of 48 hours, Ilsa had recovered and the two of them would finally be released from the prison they'd been confined in for three months. It was no coincidence. Had Petyuba kept Ilsa in an induced coma to satisfy her own sick need for companionship? If so, was she now resigned to give up the hold she had on Druix and Ilsa with no objection? What force or threats had been used to compel her to release them? Or was there a sinister intent to Petyuba's acquiescence?

That night, Druix didn't have the nightmarish dream he'd come to dread over the past months, but had been helpless to prevent. The next morning, he and Ilsa departed Petyuba's home. This time, they exited through an airlock at the back of the house into a waiting submersible.

Ilsa was transported in her bed, silent and moody, whether in shock or still suffering the aftereffects of the induced coma. Petyuba was nowhere to be seen.

They reached the surface in a half hour and transferred to another vehicle that whisked them smoothly through subterranean tunnels. Druix still had not seen the surface of Earth, other than the brief glimpse when the capsules landed.

Now they were brought to a hospital, much like the one Ilsa had been treated in before. She was taken to an examination room, while Druix waited in an area that was as sterile and featureless as any hospital he'd ever been to.

Over the next several days, there were endless interviews and inquiries. Amazingly enough, in his responses to questions, Druix found himself unable to capture the indignation, frustration, and helplessness he'd experienced during those months in Petyuba's home. His examiners nodded and exchanged glances with each other, but gave no indication that they were bothered by what had happened. They concealed their reactions carefully.

Finally, the topic of DNA entered the discussion. They asked Druix to repeat his promise that both his and Ilsa's DNA would be made available. Druix repeated the promise, but added the condition that their space capsules be repaired and made ready for departure as soon as possible. He had no idea whether these Earthlings had the knowledge and technology to undertake the repairs. He was surprised when they agreed to this condition without hesitation.

Druix and Ilsa remained on Earth for three more days, till Ilsa was strong enough to get out of bed. They took walks together through the muted hallways of the hospital. The other patients and staff looked at them oddly, but no one spoke to them. Occasionally, one smiled or waved, but other than that there was no attempt to communicate.

Ilsa remained introverted and moody. Druix tried to engage her in conversation about the twins, but she seemed detached and unresponsive. He reminded her that their next destination would be the planet Happiness and a reunion with the rest of the family. Ilsa took all this in thoughtfully, but without emotion or expression. The doctors reassured Druix that it would take some time before she was normal again. The healing process was complex, involving every physiological system in her body and the intricate connections that made them work together. Until that happened, it was natural for her to feel disoriented. They also asserted that Ilsa was strong enough to withstand the launch and subsequent freezing in the magnetocryogenic chamber. Remarkably, now that they had permission to take their DNA the doctors had little interest in keeping Druix and Ilsa on Earth.

On the day before their departure, Druix made one more request. He asked to see more of the surface of Earth. His hosts obliged. He and Ilsa boarded a craft that rose through a vertical chute into the daylight. The craft moved smoothly and silently, maintaining an altitude that afforded them a panoramic view of the scenery below. It was spectacularly beautiful. 1646th Century earthlings had apparently moved everything related to human presence underground, allowing Earth's surface to evolve without artificial influence. The landscape was one contiguous parkland, encompassing tree-covered hills, grasslands and meadows, valleys and canyons, craggy mountain chains, plains and deserts, rivers and lakes, marshes and swamps, stretching to the ocean's edge, unblemished by any building, road, bridge, dam, power line, factory, mine, quarry, or even a farm. This was Earth's natural ecosystem completely restored to its natural state. Whatever animals inhabited that untouched domain did so without human influence of any kind.

Druix asked if humans were allowed to visit the surface. The Earthlings looked puzzled and confused, not understanding why anyone would want to venture into that inhuman habitat. A tremendous gulf between the minds and senses of these modern Earthlings and his existed. Through thousands of years of evolution, humans on Earth had become obsessed with their own genetic makeup. It had become so important for them to know and understand their genome that their senses and brains had become specialized for that one purpose, to the exclusion of the perceptive ability to appreciate the natural landscape. Beauty for Earth's civilization was now tied up in the nuances of the nucleotides that arranged themselves on DNA strands. Human senses had altered through the millennia so that they could only detect the genetic variations that distinguished one individual from another. The beauty of the natural world held no attraction for them any longer. That affinity had been linked to survival of the species once, but thousands of years of environmental and social pressures had altered the criteria for genetic success. On Earth's surface, bees and birds were still attracted to colorful flowers to spread the seeds of future   generations, but for humans, that beauty did nothing to facilitate procreation.

Druix tried in vain to understand—to see beauty through the eyes of these modern humans, but it was impossible. He was from a race that valued natural beauty, and it was impossible to comprehend how that could be replaced by esthetic appreciation for chemicals on a twisted molecular strand, and how that manifested itself in the physiological features of people.

The next day, officials escorted Druix and Ilsa to their capsules, after a short ceremony to thank the visitors for sharing their DNA. The officials vowed to use it responsibly, and if at some future time the visitors returned, they'd be able to see and enjoy their legacy, perhaps a familiar color in the hair or eyes of a descendant, a posture, profile, gait, or mannerism that would commemorate their time on Earth.

Petyuba attended the ceremony, but said nothing. She stood behind the others. Druix was struck by how old she looked again, even older than when he'd first met her. During their time together, he'd witnessed her become younger, but it must have been his imagination, distorted by the stress of his situation, the worry, the long days, and the trauma of those terrible nights being visited by a haunting and demanding apparition.

Feeling the familiar g-forces of the capsule lifting off, Druix wondered if he or Ilsa would ever be the same.

CHAPTER 14

— Century 1655 —

Elsenia was genuinely happy to see Hespera and Johanis again. She told them about her visit to Magnetonia. They told her about newly discovered planets with Tattoo people. Elsenia was amazed at how many planets now possessed alien civilizations and asked to remain on the supply ship to examine the data more carefully. Her stay lasted six months, during which time she conducted a systematic study of all planets explored in the Galactic Garden. The survey eventually led to Elsenia's landmark work, in which she introduced a system of classification for planets based on a variety of properties. One index, called the Common Era, or CE, index, contained the Earth-year origin of the humans who inhabited a planet. Aril, which had been established by travelers who left Earth early in the third millennium, was a CE-3 planet. Prosperity and Happiness were both CE-74 planets because they were established by humans who left Earth in the 74th millennium.

The planets settled by Tattoo People had similar classifications, except that they were indexed according to the Earth-referenced millennium when the Tattoo People sprouted from the vine. This wasn't known exactly, but it could be estimated fairly accurately using a formula based on the maturity of the vine, a method analogous to counting rings to determine the age of trees on planets with well-defined seasons. Elsenia gave planets with vines and a population of Tattoo People the designation XV. Galactic explorers had visited 28 planets with Tattoo People and their indices ranged from XV-15 to XV-155.

Not all the planets upon which the alien vine landed produced civilizations of Tattoo People. On a few planets, the vine didn't take hold, and its transformative properties on the planet's atmosphere failed to produce a life-supporting environment. In some cases, the vine eventually died, shriveling up into a mass of dry, tangled branches, lifeless and barren, a stark skeleton and a grotesque monument to the failed attempt. In other cases, the vine thrived and spread, but for one reason or another never brought forth a population of Tattoo People from which future generations would spring. It was a lingering mystery. What triggered the budding of Tattoo People? What told the vine it was time to form the pods containing the first group of fully-formed Tattoo People, like butterflies in a cocoon? Elsenia gave these planets the designation UV—U for unsuccessful. She added a number, which indicated the estimated time in Earth-referenced years that the vine was introduced to the planet. Thus, a UV-84 planet had been struck by the vine-carrying asteroid in the 84th millennium CE, but no Tattoo People had yet been produced.

It seemed like a dreary, uncreative enterprise—developing a classification system for categorizing planets in the Galactic Garden—but the scheme caught on. Everyone used it. The galactic explorers found it a quick and easy way to put a newly discovered planet in proper context. Galactic news reporters found it convenient when communicating the latest events from other worlds. Most importantly, from a planetary psychology point of view, it was an excellent way to compare planets. With newly inhabited planets being discovered and named every hundred years, Elsenia's classification scheme allowed a quick sorting to determine where they all stood on the scale of intelligent civilization. On the downside though, Elsenia feared eventually the index would be used by planets to judge one another with very little knowledge or information. She worried that it would be the basis by which one planet would assume superiority over another and attempt to dominate or conquer it.

After completing her study, Elsenia considered where to go next. Although she was anxious to visit another Tattoo People colony, she was intrigued by a new planet called Nuterra, which was colonized by humans from Prosperity. Within a few thousand years of its founding, the planet earned a reputation of being extremely well connected to other human-inhabited planets, such that it represented a new center of advanced civilization. What made Nuterra a popular destination for explorers, Johanis and Hespera explained, was that it had become a repository for all communication among the human populations of the Galactic Garden. Its societies passed on knowledge and information diligently through the generations, and were as up to date as possible. Elsenia felt she could learn much from the communication information on Nuterra.

CHAPTER 15

— Century 1702 —

AFTER HIS EXPLORATION of the asteroid, Risto stopped at Supply Ship 5, just missing Elsenia by 5000 years. He told Hespera and Johanis about the mysterious device. They immediately transmitted Risto's information to other supply ships and Admiral Chase, wanting to learn if similar objects had been observed by other galactic explorers. They suggested that Risto travel to Supply Ship 6 and time his arrival to meet Admiral Chase, who was on route there after a visit to SS4. The Admiral made sure that supply ship custodians had his itinerary and that he adhered to it, so that any galactic explorer needing aid or with news to report could meet him personally.

When Risto arrived at SS6, he saw the Admiral's command ship shadowing the supply ship. The advanced composite material of Admiral Chase's ship was a duller, darker color than the bright metallic hull of the ancient Union supply ship, which, designed to last for hundreds of thousands of years, didn't show its age—except on close inspection of the many pock marks from impacts with the rare, microscopic particles of interstellar space. The command ship looked much older, as the composite material of its construction was nonmetallic and had radiation and thermal resistant properties. The crew was able to remain onboard in magnetocryogenic chambers with excellent isolation from the ship's engines and power systems. In contrast, the custodians of the supply ship had to separate, in their own capsules to avoid the heating effects that would compromise their zero temperature states.

Admiral Chase was waiting for him on the supply ship. Risto found him in the galley with the custodians. When Risto was introduced to the couple, Nebero and Rashera, he was surprised to hear that Rashera was the daughter of Arthur Mizello, Benjamin Mizello's father. Arthur and his partner Krystal had given up command of the supply ship in the 1300th Century and returned to Earth. There, Krystal gave birth to a baby girl, who grew up in the bizarre circumstance of being a 22nd Century humanoid on a 1300th Century Earth. Understandably, when her parents died, Rashera lost no time taking to space in her mother's ancient vehicle. She'd developed a fascination for space travel, doubtlessly inherited from her parents. Like her mother, she'd quickly grown tired of the life of a galactic explorer, and after meeting Nebero during a stop at Supply Ship 6, decided to be his partner and co-custodian of the vessel. Rashera had also inherited her mother's skill analyzing data using intuition and technology.

She listened with interest as Risto related the story of his second encounter with the mysterious asteroid. She'd already received the report from Johanis and Hespera, but hearing it again directly from Risto added a new dimension to her analysis.

Rashera seemed to be in a continuous state of distraction. Often, her eyes wandered to a computer display set into the wall. Columns of numbers scrolled down the screen at speeds impossible for anyone to read, but it didn't seem to discourage Rashera. She'd notice if any of the numbers weren't what they should be.

"I believe it's some type of weapon," Risto was saying.

"And the antennas?" Admiral Chase asked.

"Part of the targeting system, no doubt," answered Risto.

"Is it possible the cylinders contained explosives?"

"It's possible. I couldn't see what was inside. I considered bringing one back. In the weightlessness of space, it wouldn't have been hard, but they were attached magnetically to their tracks."

"You said it was a spiral track," said Rashera.

"Yes."

"Were there cylinders along its entire length?"

Risto thought momentarily. "No, the inner parts of the spiral track contained no cylinders."

"How many cylinders would you estimate could sit on the empty track?"

Risto paused. Rashera had just made him realize that if the asteroid was a weapon, it had been used. The track must have been filled with cylinders when the weapon was loaded.

"I don't know," he answered.

"Of course, you don't know," said Rashera. "You couldn't possibly know. I'm asking you to estimate."

Risto became nervous.

"Sorry," said Rashera. "I think it's important how many cylinders were missing. Do you think it was more like ten or a hundred?"

"Something in between," said Risto.

"Okay, let's say forty. Each cylinder, if it was the size of a fifty-gallon drum, might weigh 200 kg. more or less. They could be hollow, but that's doubtful. All these parameters, including the length of the barrel of the device, make it comparable to the magnetic cannons once constructed on Earth for putting small payloads into orbit."

"Are you suggesting this is a booster for launching objects into space?" asked Admiral Chase.

"No. They're already in space. I'm just trying to use the comparison to estimate the muzzle velocity of the cylinders. Given the length of the barrel, we can tell how fast the cylinders are moving when they emerge. That, coupled with their mass, tells me the momentum and energy of the cylinders."

"Enough to do a lot of damage if it struck another object," said Admiral Chase.

"True, but somehow I don't think that's the point—at least not the way you're imagining it."

"Are you saying it's not a weapon?" asked Risto.

"Oh, it's a weapon all right," Rashera answered quickly. "Only you're thinking of it as a weapon to destroy another space vehicle. If that was the point, just one cylinder is overkill by a large margin. To accomplish that objective, it would be deadlier to have smaller missiles sprayed out—like an old-fashioned shotgun."

"So what type of weapon is it?" There was an impatience to Admiral Chase's question, but moderated by a hint of respect.

"It could be a weapon against an entire planet."

Risto and Admiral Chase exchanged glances. "How so?" Risto asked.

"We've already established that Risto's asteroid is too large to be carrying the alien vine. If an asteroid that large struck a planet, it would be catastrophic."

"Yes, agreed Admiral Chase. "But that doesn't explain the cylinders."

"Yes, it does." Rashera rose and began to circle the table where the two men sat. "An object in interstellar space, far from any stars, is free from gravitational bonds. It's not orbiting another object under the influence of gravitational attraction, except perhaps the combined mass of the galactic center."

Rashera held her fist aloft to illustrate the asteroid. "Now pretend you're on the asteroid. Look about you. You see millions of stars, all far away. Each one is a potential target, and it wouldn't take much impulse to set the asteroid on a course toward any of those stars."

"The cylinders." Admiral Chase said softly.

"Yes. Every action has an equal and opposite reaction. To propel the asteroid toward its target only requires the launch of cylinders in the opposite direction. It's a slow process, as each cylinder launched only accelerates the asteroid an infinitesimal amount, but after enough have been ejected and given a sufficient amount of time, the asteroid will home in on its target. Once close enough, the target's own gravitational field will take over and pull it in. No more propulsion is necessary."

"It's rather devious, when you think about it," interrupted Admiral Chase. "The target aids its own destruction. Its gravity becomes an accomplice in its own annihilation."

"Right."

"Wait," said Risto. "If your theory is right, and there are missing cylinders on this asteroid, then it has already started to move."

"Yes, it has. We know its motion, too. You've visited the asteroid twice. The direction that the asteroid is heading is quite clear."

"You already know," said Admiral Chase.

Rashera, holding her fist aloft again, now raised the other one. "It's closing in on Aril," she said, bringing her two fists together dramatically.

"We need to contact Aril right away."

"No hurry," said Rashera. "It's still thousands of years away."

"But what can be done?" asked Risto. "Once it's in the clutches of Aril's gravitational field, there's little that can stop it."

"That's not quite true. In any case though, what's more intriguing is how many of these asteroids might be out there and what other targets they have. Who is creating these devices and why? Have you heard of Fermi's Paradox?"

"No."

"I'll try to explain. For more than a hundred millennia, humanity has extended its domain to galactic destinations once deemed too far away. In doing so, we've encountered an alien race, the Tattoo People, also in the midst of spreading its influence, intent on establishing a foothold in a realm with virtually no bounds. Yet, a hundred thousand years represents only a small fraction of the age of the galaxy. If humanity has achieved the technological mastery to spread itself to great distances in such an astronomically short amount of time, why isn't the galaxy teeming with similar civilizations endeavoring to occupy every habitable planet? What's making their presence so rare? Back on 20th Century Earth, the question was raised by Enrico Fermi, and came to be known as Fermi's Paradox.

"Several possible explanations were proposed to account for the paradox. Some believed that civilized races populating the galaxy are indeed an extremely rare occurrence, a unique gift from a singular god, or maybe the culmination of a series of events so unlikely that the odds of it happening are one in a billion—one in a galaxy. Humans might have to travel to the next galaxy over to encounter another civilization similarly advanced. Of course, we've already come across another civilization within the Milky Way, and we've really only explored ten percent of its volume. Advanced civilization couldn't be too rare.

"Still another possibility for the absence of evidence of other civilizations is that technically advanced societies destroy themselves, victims of the very same intelligence that enabled them to escape the gravitational confines of their planet. If advanced civilizations rise and fall over spans of tens or hundreds of thousands of years, then the odds that two might coexist and find each other during the 15 billion-year lifetime of the galaxy would be extremely small.

"This is a gloomy scenario, but not necessarily the only one. Civilizations don't have to annihilate themselves. Advanced civilizations might just grow bored with exploring space or trying to communicate with races in other parts of the galaxy. Perhaps civilizations evolve in the same way humans do. When young, they're very exploratory, with a child-like fascination in the universe. Eventually, such fascination wanes, and discovering new worlds becomes old and tiresome, yielding rewards that aren't commensurate with the energy required. Then, civilizations, like humans, may turn inward, shutting themselves off, becoming private and reclusive. The joy of life has left them. They lapse into a prolonged geriatric phase during which they neither attempt to contact others nor open up to be contacted by others. Thus, the ultimate fate of ancient civilizations may be isolation and introversion. Perhaps the galaxy is populated not by thriving, modernistic civilizations striving to expand their frontiers and spread to new planetary homes, but by dull, decrepit societies that have lost the will and drive to grow or expand. Maybe civilization is like a star—burning brightly for millions of years, then exploding in a spectacular blast of light and energy, and finally, with all fuel and energy consumed, falling into itself, becoming a black hole from which nothing can escape, even the light that would reveal its existence to the rest of the universe.

"But the scariest explanation for Fermi's paradox is that there is a civilization, a race of aliens in our galaxy, which in the name of some cosmic version of manifest destiny, is wiping out new civilizations as they emerge. Could it be that an extremely powerful alien species has made the unilateral decision that no other civilization deserves to exist? As soon as these aliens learn of the existence of a competing species, they set out to destroy it.

Human presence has gone on long enough for it to be detected and known by other civilizations in the galaxy. If they wanted to destroy us, they certainly would've tried already. Perhaps they just haven't reached us yet. The galaxy is, after all, tens of thousands of light-years across. They could be on their way to our sector right now, with whatever destructive weapons they've successfully used thus far in suppressing the rise of advanced races. They enforce Fermi's Paradox.

"If you eliminate one by one these explanations so that only one possibility remains unproven, that must be the right one. Galactic exploration removed one of the most puzzling ones that Fermi could only guess at. The biggest uncertainty was how long it takes for an advanced civilization to populate the galaxy. Humans expanded their presence during the last 200,000 years, as have the Tattoo People, in a remarkably coincident way. So, if it only takes 200,000 years to colonize a good part of the galaxy, why isn't the Milky Way crawling with alien life forms? It's been in existence for 15 billion years."

Admiral Chase shook his head in confusion. "Then what's the answer?"

"Who knows? If we assume the worst case scenario it's just a matter of time before we're discovered and annihilated. Death by paradox, you might call it. We cannot exist, therefore we will not. There's a principle in quantum mechanics—the exclusion principle, which limits two identical states of matter existing within a certain system."

"Could this be connected to the Tattoo People?"

"Possibly. The launch of objects carrying the alien vine may be a last ditch effort to establish a permanent presence in the galaxy. Perhaps the creators of the Tattoo People believe that if they scatter enough of their race throughout the galaxy, they can escape the destructive force."

"Interesting idea," Admiral Chase mused. "But maybe the creators of the Tattoo People are the destroyers themselves."

"It's hard to imagine the Tattoo People being destructive in any way," said Rashera.

"I'm not talking about them per se. I'm thinking of the beings that created them."

"It seems to me that whoever created the Tattoo People can't be malevolent. A benign God may inexplicably create malevolent beings, but a malevolent God wouldn't create benign beings."

"Then how do they do it? How do they manage to destroy every advanced civilization that dares to evolve and launch space vehicles to colonize distant planets?" asked Admiral Chase.

"I don't know, but it'd help to see a cylinder launching," Rashera said. "That'd tell us the asteroid's intended course. Hundreds of years may go by between shots. There's probably no way to know when one is ejected. Perhaps when the target trajectory is well defined, it shoots out cylinders in quick succession."

"Are the antennas used to aid in the targeting?" asked the Admiral.

"Probably, but I'm not sure how it's done. The antennas may be receiving signals, getting directions, from somewhere else. Something or someone is telling the asteroid which way it has to go. It's a very large, very smart rock, but getting its orders from somewhere else. We need to know where and why."

"What about eliminating the threat to Aril?"

"That'll take some thought. The best way is to divert the asteroid, or interfere with its targeting system," said Rashera.

"Couldn't we just blow it apart with a nuclear weapon?" asked Admiral Chase.

"We can while the asteroid is still outside the gravitational attraction of its target. If we're too late, some debris from the blast will continue along the original trajectory and strike the planet. Instead of one large object, there'll be a barrage of smaller fragments, possibly just as devastating."

"We need to intercept the asteroid as soon as possible then and hope that it's still far enough from Aril when we do."

"Right," said Rashera. "But remember that our calculation of the asteroid's course depends on its position and speed when Risto was last there. If the cylinders have been fired, everything may've changed. You may have to search for the object."

"I can have the command ship and ten of my troops besides Risto fan out in a search pattern."

Rashera looked down at her hands, the fist of one enclosed in the palm of the other. "If you can't find it, you must advise Aril to evacuate the planet."

"Right," agreed Admiral Chase grimly.

CHAPTER 16

— Century 1711 —

UNLIKE THE HUMAN inhabited planets whose atmospheres had been conditioned by the alien vine of the Tattoo People, Nuterra had a naturally benign biosphere. A galactic explorer discovered the planet in the 1432nd Century, and within ten thousand years an expedition from Prosperity had established a permanent colony. The population blossomed, and it wasn't long on galactic timescales before its civilization rivaled that of Earth, Aril, and Prosperity—those three original bastions of human habitation.

Elsenia had mixed feelings as she approached the planet. On the one hand, she looked forward to reconnecting with fellow humans, but on the other hand, they represented a race of Homo sapiens 170,000 years further along on the evolutionary ladder. She'd be more of an outcast than she'd been on Aril. Also, she suspected her visit would do little to help her better understand the origin of the Tattoo People.

A delegation of planetary officials met and escorted her to comfortable lodgings adjacent to the modern spaceport, where her capsule was checked out, refueled, and sheltered with hundreds of others. Elsenia was surprised to learn that she was well known to the scholars because of her classification scheme for the inhabited planets of the Galactic Garden. They invited her to lecture at several of the universities—an honor she politely tried to refuse. Her knowledge was thousands of years older than that of the students. How could she possibly enlighten them on a subject that was for all intents and purposes ancient history? But her hosts graciously offered to provide her with an assistant who would help her prepare the talks, ensuring that its content would both inform the audience and honor the presenter.

In appearance, the assistant, Gabriona, typified the race of humans occupying the planet, but in an understated manner less intimidating to Elsenia. Much taller than Elsenia, Gabriona carried herself with a cautious grace and humility that underplayed her stature. Her ears were large, typical of her race, but they nestled compactly against her face, hidden beneath wisps of silky, auburn hair. The most noticeable difference between Elsenia and Gabriona was the trait that gave the humans of Nuterra their exceptional health, longevity, and beauty: their skin. Gabriona's skin was as clear, moist, and supple as a newborn baby. Its color was burnt orange, packed with melanin and naturally beneficial oils to provide the protection and insulation necessary to ensure many decades of vitality. Thousands of years of environmental stress and natural selection helped endow these humans with a layering resilient to the damages inflicted by radiation, bacteria, chemicals, dirt, soot, ash, pollution, parasites, dust, dander, and pollen—while at the same time allowing the penetration of beneficial substances.

Gabriona, it turned out, was no mere assistant at all. She led a group of a dozen Nuterrans monitoring the transmissions received from space, and responding to them, as necessary.

"We've found your classification scheme extremely helpful in understanding transmissions we receive," Gabriona said.

"In what way?" Elsenia asked. They stood before a bank of monitors, which displayed colorful graphics, not one of which Elsenia could comprehend.

"The planetary traits we observe are amazingly well correlated with your classification scheme. The length of time the vine has been on the planet, the time of the first appearance of Tattoo People, and the amount of time humans and Tattoo People have coexisted—all figure into the inherent personality of the planet."

"The personality of the planet," Elsenia repeated. "My favorite subject."

"Then you'll enjoy reviewing excerpts from the messages we receive. Keep in mind, we don't get these types of messages very often—every few hundred years or so—but the frequency is increasing as more planets become inhabited."

Gabriona read slowly, in impeccable, if slightly accented, Union English.

"I am lonely. But who am I? Who is it that feels the loneliness? I was fine once, living in oblivious contentment, not daring to imagine there were others like me in the universe. Then the visitor arrived and told me I was not alone. Now the knowledge that I am not alone has made me feel lonely."

"I feel fulfilled. Our alliance with the humans has given me a new window on the universe that our creator probably did not know existed. Happiness is a new dimension, which allows us to transcend the limits of our consciousness. It is difficult to possess this emotion without projecting it, but I fear that will jeopardize the reality of it."

"They will be here soon. Their arrival will change everything. Why does it fill me with such dread? Is it because I reject change or fear the unknown? These emotions are new to me. They presuppose an order to the universe of which I am ignorant. If I am ignorant, am I not free to define what that order should be?"

When Gabriona was done, Elsenia, looking puzzled, asked, "Who's sending these messages? Are they coming from the Tattoo People?"

"We think so."

"But how can they send messages without the technology to transmit radio waves?"

"We don't believe they're using artificial transmission. We're receiving the collective signals that the Tattoo People use to communicate among themselves."

"How can you do that? Those signals are extremely weak. You couldn't possible detect them at interstellar distances."

"You're right, except when many have collective thoughts. Then the signal is much stronger. In some sense, it's easier because we don't hear the minor, mundane communication between individuals—the babble of the crowd, so to speak. We only hear widespread expressions common to all. The distance is a natural filter, allowing us to focus on just those thoughts, emotions, and attitudes."

"And you've been able to translate these messages?"

"Yes, sometimes with great difficulty, but eventually we decipher them. Remember, the languages of Tattoo People on different planets are not that dissimilar. Their language is genetically encoded in them. They only differ to the extent that they've evolved into distinct dialects, often influenced by contact with humans. Some of the variations are quite predictable."

"This is incredible," said Elsenia. "There must be so much to be learned. I've spent most of my life studying Tattoo People, but haven't even scratched the surface. This would tell us so much more about them—perhaps give us clues to their origin."

"That's true," said Gabriona. "But the tale these messages tell us is not so simple. Let me read to you other messages.

"I am losing my memory. They are destroying it. I can no longer remember who I am or why I exist. When my memory is gone, I will be cut off from my past. One who has no past has no future."

"I feel I am being used, a pawn in a wicked game of destruction. Is it possible I've become an instrument of those whose purpose is evil? When and how did that happen?"

"I am a lie. I am not what I appear to be. I put on a face for others to fool them into thinking I am something else, but I fool my-self as well, for I am not who I want to be. I lie to myself so I can be a better liar to others. I fear I will lie myself out of existence because when there is no longer truth, there is no longer life."

"My God," said Elsenia. "These are cries for help."

"For some reason, the Tattoo People on these planets have developed collective personality disorders, suggestive of psychotic episodes, perhaps brought on by traumatic events in their history."

"You said that you answer some of these messages. Do you respond to these?"

"We do. We try to reassure them that they're not alone. We tell them they're part of an extended family in the galaxy, with common problems and challenges. We endeavor to make these planets understand that there are others who care about them, though they may be impossibly far way."

Elsenia had a thought. "I visited Lumina with my family. It was 30 thousand years ago. Have you received messages from that planet?"

"Of course. In fact, messages tell of your visit. The Tattoo People on Lumina were fascinated by your siblings. The twins."

"Vega and Deneb," Elsenia whispered, suddenly missing them dearly.

"Here's one."

"I miss them. I understand that they had to leave. It is in the nature of life that they move on. Yet, I feel that they have taken a part of me with them. And I know which part they have taken. It is the part that I would not have had if it weren't for them."

"Are you sure these messages are coming from the Tattoo People?"

"What else? We know which planets they come from. All are populated by Tattoo People."

"But why are all the messages written in the first person."

"Remember that these are translations, not exact quotes. They're transcriptions made from very weak signals. We believe that the Tattoo People think collectively as one person. Therefore, the most accurate rendition in Union English makes it sound as if a single person is speaking."

"The one that refers to memory loss—where is it coming from?"

"That's an interesting one, coming from the planet Carbonia. It has one of the oldest populations of Tattoo People."

"Can you give me its coordinates? I'd like to visit there next."

"Yes, certainly, but you should stop at the nearest supply ship before landing on the planet—just to confirm that nothing has changed."

"Of course. I have to stop at a ship anyway to refuel."

CHAPTER 17

— Century 1757 —

While Admiral Chase and Risto were speeding to intercept the asteroid, Arilians crunched away at calculations attempting to predict the asteroid's destination. Aril and its companion planet Sparil were not the only ones orbiting their star. The asteroid might just as easily be sucked into the gravitational pit of some uninhabited planet, but Arilians were not so complacent to be comforted by that possibility. It was easier for them to believe their planet had become the target of an alien civilization. It wouldn't be the first time Aril was threatened by a peril from space.

In spite of efforts at prediction, the Arilians knew that only by directly observing the missile could they be sure of its heading. The problem was that once the asteroid was close enough to be seen, it would be too late to do anything to save their planet. For that reason, they launched a fleet of autonomous space capsules equipped with telescopes that scoured the vast space within a conically-shaped volume where they estimated the object would be. Because the asteroid had no intrinsic luminosity and its blackness suppressed any reflected light from its surface, the only way to observe it was by transient occultation of starlight. The capsules carried computers programmed to detect those fleeting eclipses when they occurred.

But space is nothing if not big, and searching for a single object a hundred kilometers in diameter in a volume so large was unlikely to be successul. Decades passed with Arilian scientists fruitlessly poring over the data returned from the fleet vehicles, and the more time that passed, the gloomier Arilian people became. Other than the invasion by Carl Stormer and Andrew Harding, no acts of violence or aggression had imperiled them. Now, for some unknown reason, Aril was the target of a malicious cosmic weapon, and all the people could do was wait and hope.

With Admiral Chase's arrival, the asteroid was finally

located. The long-range radar of his command ship picked up its presence just 3.4 light-years from Aril's star. At that distance, it was still impossible to tell where the asteroid was heading, other than in the general direction of Aril's planetary system. Though alarmingly close to Aril on galactic scales, the asteroid was still far enough away that Admiral Chase could use one of his nuclear weapons to destroy it without fear that a piece of it would strike Aril anyway. Seeing how large the asteroid really was, the Admiral became uncertain how much destruction his nuclear weapon might cause. If nothing else, he could destroy the magnetic rail gun, which would eliminate the asteroid's capability to steer toward a target. Whatever adjustments were necessary in its approach to Aril would not be possible. Hopefully, even if parts of the asteroid survived, they would not be drawn into Aril's force field.

The nuclear weapons on Admiral Chase's command ship were constructed in the 550th Century, long after the time in Earth's history when the devices were used to kill other humans. Sometime between the 22nd and 50th Century, Earthlings had learned a hard lesson on their true destructiveness, as well as their uselessness. The bombs on the command ship were designed as the last line of defense against an alien force strong enough to resist all the other weaponry on board, including ballistic devices, laser beams, and EMP cannons. Consequently, the nuclear explosives were only powerful enough to annihilate anything the size of an enemy spacecraft.

The weapons experts in Admiral Chase's crew could offer no assurance how effective the weapon would be. The ship carried a half dozen devices. If the first didn't succeed in destroying the asteroid, the crew could chase down any remaining large pieces and use up another one of the arsenal. This was risky, however, because in chasing the remaining piece, the ship might be struck by the debris from the first blast.

The command ship was 100,000 km from the asteroid when the weapon was released, about a quarter of the distance of the Moon from the Earth, far enough that the ship would have a sufficiently large head start to escape flying fragments.

The weapon was self-targeting. Once released, it used optical sensors and rocket thrusters to home in on the asteroid. There was virtually no way to miss it, as the command ship was moving at the same speed as the target. From the ship's reference frame, the asteroid was standing still.

It took 20 hours for the nuclear weapon to reach the asteroid. The entire crew watched the explosion on video monitors scattered throughout the ship. Among the observers was Risto Jalonen, who had volunteered, only half-jokingly, to ride the bomb to guide it down the barrel of the magnetic cannon to make sure it exploded in the subterranean chamber where the alien nuclear reactor was located. The combined explosions of the two devices would certainly pulverize the asteroid. However, Admiral Chase's weapons experts had nixed the idea because they didn't know what kind of nuclear reactor powered the asteroid. They feared that the combination of explosions might create a singularity in space, a miniature black hole that would implode the asteroid and everything else in its vicinity. Instead, they programmed the device to explode several meters above the surface.

When it came, the blast produced a flash of light intense enough to saturate the optical sensors that fed the video monitors. All screens went momentarily white, their liquid crystal pixels unable to accommodate the impinging surge of photonic energy. Several seconds later, the flash dissipated, and the screen became streaked with white slashes caused by the penetration of energetic particles through the optical detectors. After that, the sensors recovered and the crew saw the bright toroid of flaming luminosity expanding outward from the impact point. The rate at which the shell of destructive energy expanded frightened the crew. The ship raced away at full speed, but the radiation pulse was faster. The crew could only hope it would dissipate before it overtook them. It did. When it passed by the ship, all they felt was a slight shudder of the hull. Now, they only had to worry about the blast debris. They were sufficiently far away at the time of the explosion that the remnants diffused by the time they reached the ship. The command ship's collision avoidance system easily handled these last remaining particles.

Admiral Chase knew that the pieces of the asteroid would spray out in all directions and that inevitably some might continue on the same course the asteroid had been on. These would enter Aril's planetary system, and a fraction of them would pass close enough to Aril to be drawn in by the planet's gravitational field. Admiral Chase could do little about these, other than to warn Aril and hope for the best. He considered continuing on to the planet to be there when the pieces struck, but other business called him away. Also, he wanted to arrive on Happiness in time for a special event in the year 186,000.

CHAPTER 18

— Century 1763 —

AMALIA ANATALIA KNEW she would die. It didn't matter how much she'd practiced the drill, when the time came to evacuate the children to the underground bunkers, she knew she wouldn't make it. As a teacher and safety warden, she'd be among the last to enter the bunker and at the greatest risk of being struck by the incoming barrage. But it didn't matter anyway. The cataclysmic event would no doubt destroy the bunker, the town, the continent, and the whole unlucky planet.

Amalia resented the bitter irony that the population of Aril had thrived in peace, security, and abundance for tens of thousands of years. Generations had come and gone, women and men had lived and died, over and over again, blissfully free from the threat of sudden catastrophe and violent death. Yet now, her generation, the thirty-year chunk of time during which she lived her life—this one would witness the end of Arilian civilization. Amalia did the math. The odds of a person being alive at the time of the end of the world were one in 1300. She had won the grand prize. It wasn't fair, she thought. The trite, but oh-so-human expression that she heard on the playground every day crossed her mind as if mocking her. No, it wasn't fair.

She watched the Arilian children disappear into a bunker, their red, blond, and yellow hair bobbing in time to their rushed and practiced retreat. She couldn't help but wonder what was going through their youthful minds. Were they also lamenting the tragic injustice of having their lives cut short so young? Or did their youthful spirit prevent them from foreseeing the disaster about to take place? Was this just another day's adventure for them—a field trip, a walk to a beautiful Arilian garden, a ride in a brightly colored hot air balloon? Were they thinking only of the fun they'd have when they emerged from the bunker, ambled home, and set out to play with their friends, as they'd do any other day?

With the imminent arrival of the debris from the asteroid, forecasters had made their best guess on the time. The presence of meteors in the skies above Aril had been increasing steadily over the past several days. This heralded the leading edge of the swarm of objects produced by the nuclear explosion 150 years ago, 3 light-years away. Now, at last, the products of that explosion were beginning to rain down on the planet. The smaller particles were first to arrive because they were propelled at the fastest speed from the detonation point. But no one really knew when the largest ones would come, or even if there were large ones. The explosive debris had been dispersed over such a large area it was impossible to track all the material.

The Arilians had been diligent in their surveillance and preparedness. As soon as any large object was observed in Aril's vicinity, sirens sounded across the planet and the entire population rushed to designated shelters.

Some parents, not wanting to take a chance of being separated from their children during the emergency, had played it safe and kept them home. Attendance was down thirty percent that day at school. And what of the others, Amalia thought? What were the parents thinking when they sent their children off to school knowing that a world-ending catastrophe might take place? Were they so sure that the odds would favor them and spare their children? Was it that easy to deny the reality of events, even after witnessing the spectacular displays of shooting stars over the past several nights? Had life been so good that it was impossible for them to imagine such a disaster? Or were they so confident of the imminent destruction that it didn't matter one way or the other if their children were home at the last moment of their existence? Perhaps it was more important to go through the motions of routine normalcy. Or maybe they felt that by maintaining normalcy, they could force the universe to comply with the world as they defined it—the tail wagging the dog, as it were.

The last child entered the bunker. They still had a long way to go, negotiating a series of ramps that would take them deeper underground, eventually emptying into a larger, reinforced chamber, where they'd hunker down with other children from nearby schools. There they'd wait, the children of Aril, the future of the planet, huddled together in a last resort attempt to survive the physics of a cosmic collision.

Amalia was supposed to follow them, but she held back, transfixed by the display of lights in the sky above her. Even in daylight, the streaks of burning gases sliced white, incandescent lines across the background of blue. Those were not the ones to fear, Amalia knew, at least not immediately. They were headed elsewhere, striking the atmosphere obliquely and therefore more likely to burn completely in their long transit through the resisting air. It was the point of light that grew in size that was most to be feared. Its path was directly along her line of sight, and therefore on a track toward her.

As if by thinking about it she'd willed it into existence, a bright spot appeared in the sky. It grew in size, starting out as a pinprick of light and then expanding. Amalia watched it with the sickening awareness that death was only moments away. Though there was no way of telling its distance, she'd been taught the celestial mechanics of atmospheric entry. Once an object began to burn, it was at most a couple of hundred kilometers from the surface, with speeds of several kilometers per second—only a minute or two away. It would get bigger and bigger until in the last few seconds the mass filled the sky, and then there'd be nothing. She'd be crushed as if struck beneath a falling anvil.

Amalia waited and watched. The object grew to half the diameter of the moon and exploded—nothing she could hear, but visible as a brilliant spray of burning objects radiating out from a central nucleus. A second explosion followed. Seconds passed. Amalia stared at the streaks of light and vapor emanating from the burning object. Then she heard the explosions, first one then another, and knew devastation and death were near. She squinted her eyes, waiting for the impact.

It came a half mile from where she stood. A tremendous explosion of dirt and debris erupted into the sky. The ground shook, and Amalia lifted her arms in a futile attempt to protect herself from the propelled products of the impact. Dirt rained down upon her and she shrunk to the ground, now covering her head with her arms.

Then it was over. She stood and looked about. Buildings in her immediate vicinity were untouched, wearing the same coating of dirt and dust that covered her. The explosion of light and vapor above her had dissipated. Only the blue sky remained.

Amalia shrugged, almost in disappointment. She looked about. She was alone. No one else had witnessed the impact. She turned and entered the bunker, leaving daylight behind her. A piece of asteroid debris had made it to the surface, exploding twice in the atmosphere along the way. Had she not been in its direct path, it would've looked like a bolide or fireball, a glowing streak across the sky caused by an incoming meteor. This one had not destroyed the planet, but the shower wasn't over. The all-clear sirens hadn't sounded yet.

Amalia hurried down the ramp in the dim lighting built into the walls. She came to the first turn in the series of switchbacks that descended deeper. Starting down the next ramp, she heard behind her a muffled whimper. She stopped and looked about. Against the wall, in the corner where the corridor turned, a child sat with knees drawn up and arms wrapped tightly around them. Amalia went to her. She knew the girl. Her name was Melina and she'd just turned five.

Amalia touched her arm. "Melina, honey, what's wrong?"

"Nothing," was the trembling reply.

"We have to go, Melina. We can't stay here."

"I don't want to go."

"But we have to. They'll be looking for us."

"I'm scared."

"Yes, dear. I am too. But it's safer down farther."

"I don't want to be safer."

"What do you mean, Melina? Of course, you do."

"I want my mommy and daddy."

Amalia stroked the girl's hair. She wasn't sure what to say. "You'll see them again soon," she said. "They'll be okay."

"Where are they?"

"Probably safe underground in a different shelter."

The girl looked about, as if she might see her parents on the ramp. She wiped away tears with the back of her hand. Then she raised her arms toward Amalia and wrapped them around the teacher's neck. Amalia lifted the girl. Melina's face, damp with tears, nestled into her shoulder.

"It will be okay, Melina. Don't cry."

Amalia carried her the rest of the way. The ramp turned several times more before descending into a large, dimly lit room. There, crowded into the confines of the subterranean chamber were hundreds of school children and their teachers. The room was divided with stanchions into different areas, one for sleeping, equipped with air mattresses arranged neatly in rows. Some of the children were already napping, with teachers walking among them, calming and consoling those who resisted sleep. Another area was set aside for eating. Rows of tables and benches stood beside a cafeteria counter, where children stood patiently in line.

In an area for recreational activities, children sat in circles, listening to a teacher read. Others played games, or occupied themselves with art projects. To one side was a group singing softly so as not to wake those resting, but the echoes in the room seemed to magnify their voices, carrying them into every corner. It made the children sad. Some were crying. The song was supposed to be uplifting, but echoing in the dreary volume of the chamber the song had an eerie, melancholy tone.

A group of older children stood in a circle around an object concealed from view. Amalia took Melina's hand and approached the crowd. Coming closer, they heard a curious undulating tone, modulated in frequency and amplitude to produce an otherworldly sound that kept the children spellbound. Its source was a large sphere, three meters in diameter, constructed of a metallic substance, but covered by a thin layer of gelatinous plastic.

"What is it?" asked Melina.

"It's our world. It's a model of our planet."

"But why is it making noise?"

"It's not really noise," said Amalia. "It's sound."

"What's the difference?"

"Noise is random," explained Amalia, but as soon as she said it she knew Melina wouldn't understand. "Do you like to draw, Melina?"

"Yes."

"When you draw, do you just scribble on the page?"

"No."

"Right. You draw so that it makes sense. If you put a mark on the page, the next thing you do has to make sense with what you did before. If it didn't, you'd be drawing noise. When the marks you put on the paper, the lines and curves, are compatible with each other, then your picture looks like something. It looks nice."

Melina nodded. "But what's making the sounds?"

"Aril is. Our planet is making sounds. Our planet's singing."

Melina's face contorted in puzzlement. Then she laughed. "A planet can't sing."

"Sure it can," said Amalia. "When we sing, it's because we make sounds with our voices. We have voice boxes that vibrate, just like musical instruments."

"Aril has a voice box?"

"Sort of, but it's more like a drum than a violin. When you bang a drum, it makes a sound. When something strikes Aril, it makes a sound, too."

"What's striking Aril?"

Amalia knew that question was coming. She looked toward the ceiling of the shelter, and the dread that had crippled her earlier returned.

"The meteors are hitting. Thousands striking the atmosphere, the ocean, the land. Right now."

"If we were outside would the sound be louder?" Melina asked.

Amalia smiled. "No, you wouldn't really hear anything. The vibrations in the air, ocean, and land are at frequencies the human ear can't hear. The scientists who built the model here were very clever. They put out special instruments to detect vibrations we can't hear. The data from those instruments are used to recreate the vibrations at frequencies we can hear. Meteors that strike the atmosphere make one sound, oceans make a different tone, the land still another. All combined, it's like an orchestra, an orchestra played by meteors from the asteroid."

Melina gazed at the sphere for some time, then said, "It's pretty."

"Come," said Amalia. "You can touch it."

They made their way through the crowd, other students parting respectfully for the teacher and her companion. When they were close enough, Amalia lifted Melina's hand and held it against the soft plastic coating of the sphere.

"This plastic plays the vibrations in the atmosphere. Do you feel it?"

Melina's eyes brightened. "Yes," she said, and laughed.

"When a meteor strikes the atmosphere, it creates waves. These are the waves from all the meteors at different locations. You're feeling the vibrations of all of them combined as they travel across the surface of our planet."

"It tickles," Melina said.

"Yes, it does. Maybe Aril is ticklish. Maybe the sound it's making is laughter from all those meteors tickling it."

"What happens if a really big meteor hits?"

Amalia sighed. She paused, unsure how to answer. "Maybe if that happens, we'll hear the planet say, 'Ouch!'"

Several of the children laughed at this, and the chuckling spread through the group. Amalia led Melina away, and they continued their tour of the shelter.

The meteor shower continued for a day and a half before it began to wane. Two days later, it ended completely. When Amalia emerged from the shelter and saw everything was as it had been before, she felt an incredible burden lifted from her. She had never realized how the dread of the impending meteor bombardment had handicapped her thoughts, actions, outlook, and attitude. Amalia walked to where she'd witnessed the meteoroid impact. Several hundred meters from the school, a large portion of the earth was gouged away. Amalia walked around it, awed by the energy needed to dislocate so much rock and soil. She remembered no buildings in the area where the meteoroid had struck, so she was surprised to look down and see a twisted piece of metal in the debris. She reached for it and wiggled it free from the soil. It was flat and black, about a half meter long, with sharp, jagged edges, apparently torn from something larger. She turned it over in her hands, trying to imagine what machine or building it had come from. In one corner, barely visible through the dirt and scratches that covered the surface was a symbol, lightly etched into the metal. It was the letter "V", with a horizontal line crossing the two legs of the letter, creating a triangular shape within the three line segments. Amalia had never seen the symbol before. She decided to keep the metal fragment as a souvenir—something to remind her of the planet's near catastrophic ending. She'd show it to the Arilian authorities after things had calmed down. Someone might be interested. It might be part of the object that struck the ground.

Returning to her home that day, Amalia felt as if she'd been reborn. She'd survived life's lottery after all and befriended a child who had helped her realize that one shouldn't live at the mercy of a gloomy fortune. She'd done little in her 28 years, fearing that it would be a futile endeavor. It was time to start living.

AFTER ESCAPING THE THREAT from the meteor shower, the population of Aril declared Admiral Chase a hero, but he would not learn of this honor until many thousands of years later. Risto's role in saving the planet was recognized as well. Not all the pieces of the asteroid struck Aril during the initial bombardment. Some missed the planet, circling Aril's sun, permanently captured by its gravitational field, creating a ring of debris similar to the asteroid belt circling Earth's sun. Once a year, Aril, in its own orbit about the sun, crossed through that ring, and another meteor shower entertained the people, weaker by orders of magnitude and not a threat to the planet, but extremely beautiful. The Arilians named the annual event the Ristonian meteor shower.

CHAPTER 19

— Century 1784 —

Elsenia stopped at Supply Ship 1 before continuing on to
Carbonia. It was the first of the seven launched from Earth in
the middle of the 22nd Century to support the Union's galactic
exploration enterprise. As the original custodian of that supply
ship, Adam Corkland was probably the human who'd spent the
most number of years in space, even though he looked barely forty
years of age because he'd been so frugal with the amount of time
he spent unfrozen. He was a close acquaintance of Arthur Mizello,
whom he'd met while receiving Union training in supply ship
command. Notwithstanding his efforts to minimize the time he
spent unfrozen, Adam was a serious custodian, who kept his vessel
in excellent condition. He was also well disciplined, and never
failed to seize opportunities to keep his knowledge and skills
up to date. By the vagaries of chance, Supply Ship 1 had been at
the outskirts of the parts of the galaxy where the most interesting
discoveries took place. Nevertheless, Adam remained alert and
prepared should that situation change.

Together Elsenia and Adam reviewed the newest information about Carbonia. In her notation, it was a previously explored
XV-42 planet, with a civilization of Tattoo People who had lived
there more than 136 thousand years.

Anxious to visit these Tattoo People, Elsenia still delayed
her landing. Adam Corkland had reassured her that all was well,
but an inexplicable prescience gave her pause. She programmed
her capsule to orbit the planet, setting her telescopes to image its
surface at the highest possible resolution. Projecting these images
onto the monitor of her console, she sat in rapt silence, watching
the landscape slide past.

Like so many others, Carbonia's surface was overgrown
with the hardy alien vine. The planet's name derived from the
abundance of carbon in its atmosphere. In fact, its oceans were
filled with carbonated water. Elsenia could only imagine what the

beaches might be like with ocean waves crashing with effervescent crescendos onto the sand.

Anxious to explore, Elsenia still was wary of Carbonia. She continued to orbit the planet, familiarizing herself with its physical features, observing, looking for cataclysmic changes indicating hazardous conditions. She wasn't sure why she was being overly cautious, but something told her Carbonia was different from the other worlds inhabited by Tattoo People, yet she wanted to see what one of the advanced civilizations of the Tattoo People was like.

Strong tectonic activity was evident. From space, it wasn't difficult to believe that the planet's surface was made up of plates, like a well-crafted suit of armor. At the joints, where the plates rubbed along each other, butted up against each other, or overlapped, the forces created corrugations—large mountain ranges, long, jagged scars in the planet's surface, in some cases curving around into continuous loops. The resulting landforms could have been mistaken for craters, except they weren't sufficiently circular in shape. According to the data provided by her imaging systems, the mountains surrounding these continents were several kilometers high. Even the alien vine was unable to establish a foothold on the bleak, cold peaks of those massive mountains.

Oceans covered half the planet's surface, connected via narrow straits that cut through the vegetated land surface. Because the oceans were connected, the continents were not. Each was an island. Elsenia wondered how the Tattoo People living on different continents interacted. With their superior ability to transmit thoughts via radio waves, the inhabitants of different continents must know of each other's existence, but were they able to navigate the seas that separated them? Or did they remain apart? Was it frustrating for them to communicate with each other, but never actually meet? How physically and emotionally disconnected were they? All Elsenia's prior studies were based on the premise that the Tattoo People acted as one—their extraordinary communications enforced a shared persona. The assumption had proven useful and accurate. But in the same way persona varied from one planet to another, the different continents on Carbonia might have created distinct Tattoo People. Would their world be more like ancient Earth, with its diverse races, societies, and governments, reinforced (and even encouraged) through the millennia by the physical separation of the land masses?

Elsenia knew that some explorers visited other planets but never landed on them. The captivating views provided by the precision imaging instruments provided all the adventure and excitement they needed. Why spoil it by landing, risking one's life, and having to deal with the confines of gravity, restricting how much could be seen in a short span of time? Elsenia imagined feeling disappointed. From space, she could see alien mountains and valleys, oceans, lakes, rivers, volcanoes, geysers, and graceful alluvial fans and deltas, and impossibly beautiful and improbable scars of wind and water erosion, and all the other rich and exotic features of an extraterrestrial planet's topology. Upon landing, however, the view would become frustratingly limited. In the immediate vicinity of her landing site, it might look as if she'd never left home.

Nevertheless, she landed, and soon afterward realized she should have heeded the voices within warning her. She exited the capsule in a small clearing on the crest of a higher hill where the vine hadn't been able to grow. Like all the planets inhabited by the Tattoo People, the air was perfectly breathable for humans.

She drew in the air. It was slightly cool. Looking around, Elsenia saw Tattoo People emerge from the nearby vegetation. In all encounters with the aliens she'd read about, they approached humans slowly. No matter what collective personality they turned out to have, their confrontation with humans always took place with great caution and deliberation, understandably so, since thousands of years might pass between these visits.

Every explorer carried Arilian translating devices when landing on planets inhabited by Tattoo People. Activated, the in-struments usually detected radio transmissions from the nearest of the Tattoo People—signals rendered into audible form by the translating device, which then transmitted radio signals back to the Tattoo People, essentially, creating echoes by which the aliens could "hear" their own voices. This produced sufficient astonishment in them that they paid closer attention to the strangers. If this wasn't the first visit by an explorer, then they immediately understood who the visitors were and how they might communicate. All previous experience lived in the collective consciousness of the Tattoo People. It wasn't necessary to teach them the means of communication again, nor even the language.

Elsenia knew that other explorers had visited Carbonia. As soon as she turned on her translator, the Tattoo People should have shown signs of recognition and understanding. Instead, the alien in the lead executed a series of forward flips, with the ease that only Tattoo People were capable of, and knocked her over with his full body weight. She was stunned, but conscious enough to feel her limbs grabbed and her body dragged into the surrounding brush. Tattoo People possessed a wiry strength, unexpected and often underestimated. The speed at which she was being pulled away produced in her a terrifying paralysis.

After drawing her several meters into the tangled vegetation, they abruptly released her. In shock, fearing the injuries she had sustained from contact with the branches, Elsenia was barely conscious enough to hear her attackers running back to the capsule. Her fear turned to dread imagining what they might do to it to prevent her escaping the planet. She drew the EMP weapon Admiral Chase had given her and wondered briefly if the terror she was feeling was sufficient for the weapon to fire at full lethal power. She rose shakily to her feet, but didn't fire, seeing four Tattoo People in the clearing, not attacking her capsule, but violently kicking at something on the ground. The cloud of dirt they created prevented her from seeing what it was.

She watched, with the weapon aimed and her finger on the trigger. If Admiral Chase was correct, the device was reading her grip, taking cues from body temperature, sweat production, and neural activity to automatically adjust the power level of the pulse that would be emitted when she got around to squeezing the trigger.

As it turned out, she didn't have to. The Tattoo People abruptly ceased their attack on the object. They stood in a group, staring down at it, and when the dust had settled, Elsenia finally saw that it was the translating device. She fully suspected them now to turn back to her, as she'd been the one who brought the offending instrument. She was still prepared to fire the weapon, but never had the chance. Something grabbed her from behind and she was again at the mercy of the Tattoo People. Fortunately, she was able to maintain her grip on the EMP weapon as, once again, they dragged her mercilessly through the branches and leaves of the alien vine.

ELSENIA WAS LATER to reflect on her state of mind during the unexpected abduction. It was fortunate she'd taken the extra time to study the planet's topology before landing. The mountain crest where the capsule stood was one of two parallel chains that flanked a fault separating tectonic plates. Directly above the fault, in the deep valley formed by the adjacent mountain chains, was a spectacular river, fed by water funneled into it along its entire length, growing deeper and wider, eventually spilling into one of the planet's many carbonated oceans.

The trail her captors took snaked downward from the mountain crest, soon reaching the edge of the river, where Elsenia saw a dozen canoes tied up at the shore. Three Tattoo People rudely pushed her into one of them and jumped in after her. Two grabbed oars and one a long wooden pole. Working together in uncanny unison, they propelled the craft to the middle of the stream. Four other canoes, each with its own crew of three Tattoo People, followed them.

They moved swiftly through a narrow channel formed by steep, rocky walls. After a while, the walls receded and the river ran through a broader valley where the alien vine dominated the shoreline to the water's edge. The vegetation was impenetrable, except that at random locations were clearings, within which Elsenia witnessed a series of tableaux that were unquestionably the most horrific she'd ever seen.

She'd been conceived on a planetary amusement park, born and lived her early years on Aril, lived for thousands of years on a Union supply ship, returned to Aril to be educated, worked on Aril's spaceport Sparil, and visited the planets Lumina and Magnetonia. Yet none of these experiences prepared her for the scenes presented in those clearings along that river.

In one, two groups of Tattoo People battled viciously, pummeling one another without restraint using fists, stones, sticks, and any other object that could serve as a weapon. Their screams —of victory and defeat, of agony and pain—carried to the canoes, bringing Elsenia into the fray.

In another clearing, small groups of Tattoo People were poised in various states of sexual coupling, impossible positions markedly aggressive and savage in nature. Little was known about the sex habits of Tattoo People, but if this was an indication of the manner in which they coupled, their civilization was much sicker than humans had ever imagined.

In the next tableau, the Tattoo People danced about with exaggerated flips and cartwheels, as in a show at the Happiness amusement park, except that above the dancers a trio of Tattoo People hung by their legs from thick branches of the vine. With sticks, rocks, and fists, the dancing aliens inflicted all manner of torturous and humiliating physical attacks on their helpless kin.

Farther along the river, Tattoo People were tossed from a high cliff into the river, not to land in the water, but to be maimed and mangled on the rocks in the shallow water at the cliff base. The cliff wasn't high enough to kill people instantly on impact. The victims lay on the stones in agony, trying to rise in semi-conscious states on broken limbs.

In another clearing, the Tattoo People on the shore were directing their aggression not on each other, but on the canoes drifting by. They threw rocks across the water in vain attempts to strike the swiftly moving craft. With angry shouts and threatening gestures, they expressed their uninhibited desire to destroy their fellow aliens on the water.

Elsenia stared with revulsion and disbelief at these scenes

as they slid by. Were these just glimpses of equally horrific acts being carried out over the whole planet? Regardless of how varied the personalities of other Tattoo People, she'd heard no reports of any being aggressive toward each other. That they communicated so efficiently meant that they typically acted with one mind. An attack against any one was felt by all, so it just didn't happen. What went wrong on this planet? Elsenia's immediate thought was that their ability to communicate among themselves had broken down. Perhaps this breed of Tattoo People weren't able to communicate via radio waves, or had lost the ability, so that now they were as disconnected as humans, fully capable of committing the same acts of aggression against their own kind that marked the expansion of Homo sapiens on Earth.

Elsenia vaguely recalled that in the brief interval after emerging from the capsule and before being dragged into the brush, the Arilian translating device had detected a signal not unlike any others she'd heard when encountering Tattoo People. Obviously they must be transmitting radio waves in the usual fashion. Maybe their reception had been compromised. What would humans do if everyone spoke, but no one could hear? Would this eventually lead the entire civilization to go mad?

The Tattoo People on the canoes ignored the bizarre displays appearing along the shores of the river. They seemed intent on conveying Elsenia to a destination terrifying to imagine. She still had the EMP weapon, which was the only thing preventing her from sinking into a debilitating hysteria. She knew there was sufficient power in the weapon to immobilize or kill all of her captors with plenty to spare. But after that, how many more would she have to kill before she could find her way back to the capsule? The navigation system built into her jumpsuit would show her the way, but how difficult would it be to return upriver to the place where the canoes had departed? She'd have to deal with that problem when the time came. For now, she just watched the horrible scenes being played out in the clearings along the river, trying to understand what had gone wrong with the Tattoo People on Carbonia.

It was after the river broadened into a wide delta before emptying into the sea that Elsenia began to smell the stench of rotting flesh. Soon, bodies floated toward the canoes. The Tattoo People with the long poles, one in each canoe, used their staffs to push the bodies away as they moved through the water. The delta was the resting place for thousands of dead. Their bloated bodies were dense enough that one could walk across the water by leaping among the floating corpses.

Elsenia covered her face, unable to endure the smell of decaying flesh. She forced herself to look at the corpses to see if there was evidence of a common cause of death, but there was no consistency in the appearance of the bodies. Some had gashes and bruises, victims of blunt force. Some had limbs distorted into impossible positions from falls or violent physical attacks. Many had missing limbs, and Elsenia saw with horror a sea of disconnected body parts. The entire delta was a graveyard for fallen Tattoo People. How many more reservoirs of the dead were on this planet? Were all the oceans filled with dead aliens, washed from the continents like rocks, silt, branches and other organic detritus? How many more festering wounds of a civilization gone tragically insane scarred the face of this world? Was it the emissions from these decaying carcasses that gave the planet its carbonated oceans?

Elsenia's captors steered the four canoes toward a distant shore that was nothing more than a spit of sand extending into the water, but it was the only conceivable landing site in view. She was relieved that it was on the same side of the river as her space capsule. Were she to have to find her way back from the opposite shore, she'd have to cross that horrible, corpse-filled delta, or battle the river's powerful current farther upstream.

As the canoes approached the sandbar, the density of the bodies in the water increased. The Tattoo People with the poles worked their implements rudely to part the lifeless obstacles. It sickened Elsenia, and she fought back the growing urge to vomit. When the boats struck the shore, there was no need for the Tattoo People to drag her out. She jumped off and ran inland as fast as she could, not so much to escape her captors, who could easily overtake her, but to put as much distance as possible between her and the death-filled waters of the delta.

She would have continued her flight, but looking inland, Elsenia saw another group of Tattoo People, charging toward her with great leaps, tumbles, and flips. She stopped short and looked back to see the Tattoo People who'd captured her attacking from the opposite direction. They ran past her and met the attackers, each side with equal vigor. Elsenia watched in stunned and surreal silence, eerily conscious that the object over which they fought with such violence was her.

She'd had enough. Peering along the sandbar to where it connected to the mainland, Elsenia saw the edge of the forest, a thin green line marking where the alien vine terminated. She resolved to reach the forest and lose herself in the tangled mass. She knew how impenetrable the thicket was, but now she hoped to use it to her advantage.

She ran, but found it too difficult in the soft sand. She pulled up and began a long stride with purposeful steps, saving her strength as much as possible. In the midst of their vicious battle, the Tattoo People realized she was trying to escape. She looked back to see a half dozen had broken off from their fight and with great leaps were closing the distance to her. There was no telling which side they represented. It didn't matter. Elsenia drew the EMP weapon and with six quick blasts felled them all.

It was the first time she'd ever fired the weapon. Its ease of use was both scary and satisfying. There was no recoil. The blue streak from the muzzle allowed her to see exactly where the shot went. Even if she'd missed the target on the first shot, the second attempt would have been true.

Elsenia hoped that seeing their comrades fall with such ease would discourage the rest from pursuing her, but the Tattoo People's insanity extended into imperturbable courage, or a death wish. They rushed at her. Elsenia proceeded to shoot every one. In no more than five seconds, the spit of sand was littered with dozens more bodies —her contribution to the thousands in that hideous delta of death.

She wondered only briefly whether the EMP weapon had killed them or just stunned them. What had the chip built into the weapon concluded about her state of mind as she numbly and coolly fired at her pursuers?

Elsenia walked the remaining distance to the edge of the thicket, no longer being followed by the Tattoo People, whose intentions she'd never know. Once in the forest, she climbed over and through the tangled branches of the vine until she could no longer see the water behind her, nor smell the stench of the rotting corpses. Only then did she rest.

She'd never had the need to use the full capabilities of the Union jumpsuit, but now Elsenia knew she'd have to take total advantage of it. The navigation system told her exactly how far she was from the capsule, both in distance and elevation. The food and water built into the backpack was sufficient to keep her alive for seven days. The cutting tools were mechanical, electronic, and laser-based. She'd no doubt need them all to get through the dense jungle. A thermal blanket and inflatable mattress would provide her with a comfortable sleep. The Union system also had a perimeter alarm to warn her of any approaching aliens while she slept. Elsenia didn't know it at the time, but she'd make use of another piece of survival equipment built into the jumpsuit that would not help her, but put her in grave danger during her return to the capsule.

As she made her way through the forest, Elsenia gained an unanticipated appreciation for the alien vine. She'd studied its biological and genetic properties extensively, and spent many hours on paths sculpted from it. Yet she'd never before experienced the essence of the vine as she did during her trek back to the capsule. She was armed with the tools necessary to physically hack her way through, but something told her to refrain from using that approach unless absolutely necessary. The Tattoo People trained the vine into the desired shape. They rarely cut it. Knowing that made her reluctant to harm the plant, and her progress was at first agonizingly slow. Unlike trees, where the branches tend to grow in a vertical direction, the main branches of the vine grew horizontally, twisting and turning about one another to form an impossible barrier to a vertical being like Elsenia. She could crawl on her stomach except that the vine also featured a system of roots extending downward into the ground from the branches. These roots probably tapped underground sources of moisture and nourishment for the vine, but the Tattoo People believed they were connected to the soul of the plant, residing beneath the surface of the planet. The aliens might occasionally cut the horizontal branches, but they never harmed the roots. The tough fibers provided still another obstacle to Elsenia's progress, though it would've been easy to sever them with the tools she carried.

The route the navigation system took her on was a straight line path. It rose sharply, as Elsenia knew it must. If she were to stay on level ground, she'd soon find herself facing the steep, rocky cliffs that formed the valley where the canoes had been waiting. As the slope steepened, Elsenia felt grateful to the vine, as its tangled branches prevented her from falling backward. Climbing, she gained the eerie sensation that the plant might actually be helping her. Whenever she needed something to grab or a place to put her foot, a branch seemed to be situated exactly where she needed it. Her progress was slow due to the contortions necessary for her to move through the vine, but other than that, it was not an unpleasant journey.

She stopped to rest on a saddle point along the ridge she'd been following. When her breathing slowed, she remained still, listening, enjoying the silence, alert for any sounds that might indicate others moving about. Sitting on the ground with her back against the vine, Elsenia experienced an uncanny connection with the plant. She felt that it was reaching out to her—crying out for help. It could have been merely a projection of her own emotions. Or perhaps it was the realization that the plant had established itself on this planet for the sole purpose of building a new civilization but that had inexplicably gone wild. What does a creator do when the creation turns bad? There must be helplessness and frustration when something meant to be beautiful becomes evil and destructive. Elsenia had the inescapable sensation that the vine was inconsolably and irrevocably sad.

Or perhaps it wasn't the vine she was connecting with at all, but the trauma of the situation allowing her to do what her father's second wife Xyla had done: reach back and activate some long-suppressed genetic ability to detect the collective radio waves transmitted by the aliens, and sense the regret of succumbing to evil forces they couldn't resist or reverse. In spite of the horrible acts of violence and aggression she'd witnessed, perhaps there was still collective sadness and regret—a recognition that they'd all fallen victim to evil forces. What if good still existed in the collective soul of the Tattoo People of this planet? Was that what she felt—not a cry for help from the vine, but a lament multiplied thousands of times? Or perhaps they were one and the same. What if the vine itself was the collective soul of the Tattoo People?

Even though she suspected these thoughts were random imaginings born by exhaustion and fear, Elsenia felt the need to ensure they be communicated to the explorer fleet. Admiral Chase and others should know about the strange path the aliens on this planet had followed. Should she not make it back to the capsule, that knowledge would die with her.

She brought out the emergency radio transmitter included in the Union jumpsuit. Elsenia was close enough to the capsule to transmit a message to it. The message would be stored in the vehicle's computer and could be accessed remotely anytime in the future by other members of an explorer fleet—perhaps one sent out to search for her. As long as the vehicle was intact, someone would find it eventually. The capsule's radio beacons activated and broadcast periodically in any case

Elsenia turned on the transmitter and spoke a message quickly, describing concisely and accurately what she'd seen. She tried to imagine her mother, or Druix, or Admiral Chase listening, perhaps thousands of light-years away, sadness and despair written upon their faces, to what could be her last words.

Elsenia was surprised though at the detached, emotionless quality of the words she used to describe the dangers that still faced her before she reached the capsule, and what she might find upon returning. She signed off and stored the device in her backpack, ready to resume the trip to the capsule.

She hadn't gone far before she heard a rustling sound nearby. Looking about, she caught a fleeting glimpse of one of the Tattoo People, not more than ten meters away, barely visible through the thick vegetation. Then she spotted another one. And another. Before she knew it, she was surrounded. She drew the EMP weapon from her side.

These Tattoo People were more cautious than those she'd shot earlier on the sandbar. That attack had been reckless and sloppy. These were circling her, searching for an opening through the tangled brush. She briefly entertained the vague hope that they were friendly, exhibiting more of the shy curiosity she was more accustomed to from Tattoo People, but her hope shattered when the first broke through the branches and rushed at her.

Tattoo People make no sounds. They have no vocal chords. However, the expression on this one's face told Elsenia all she needed to know about the intent of the attack. Eyes wide, mouth open, and hands outstretched in a gesture that suggested the creature meant to tear her apart, he negotiated the final obstacle that separated them with astonishing ease and was about to grab her throat when she fired the EMP weapon. There was no doubt that the shot fired by the weapon now was deadly. The blast immobilized the creature instantly. A moment later she saw the life depart from its body like air escaping from a burst bubble.

The battle that ensued was a strange one. Elsenia refrained from firing at the fleeting people in the brush surrounding her, because she was afraid to miss and waste valuable energy, but also partly concerned about hurting the plant. She was still conscious of the bond she imagined she'd established with it. Thus, she waited, trying to anticipate from which direction the next attack would come. She wondered how many were out there. The power in the EMP weapon wouldn't last forever. She considered switching it from automatic mode to reduce the output level to only stun the attackers. But would the weapon adjust the output power automatically when it began to wane? How smart was the weapon? Smarter than she was, she concluded, and left it on automatic.

Elsenia had shot no more than three of the Tattoo People when she noticed they began to disappear—not disappear as in going away, but disappear as in becoming more difficult to see. They were out there. She could hear them moving about in the brush, but she could no longer get transient glimpses as she had before. The space she was trapped within darkened, almost as if the sun were setting. But it wasn't. It was still high in the sky above her, its light barely visible through the branches of the vine.

When she realized what was happening, she couldn't believe her own senses. The vine was reconfiguring its branches, closing up the gaps and spaces about her, like a braid that's pulled tightly. Before long, the vine had surrounded her with a tightly knit shield of branches and leaves that even the Tattoo People couldn't penetrate. She holstered the EMP weapon and watched in amazement as she was completely shrouded in a protective shell, thanks to the alien vine. What now?

As the last of the daylight disappeared, she stood in the dark of the shell. In a strange paradoxical way, she felt safer than she'd ever felt in her life—not only because of the protective cocoon, but from the awareness and confidence that she had a very powerful ally.

Exhausted and confused, Elsenia inflated the mattress from her backpack, covered herself with the thermal blanket, and slept. Just before dozing off, she had a fleeting thought that her radio transmission back to the capsule had brought the Tattoo People upon her. Until then, she'd seen none during her journey. When she'd first arrived on the planet and tried to use the Arilian translating device, the Tattoo People had viciously attacked not her, but the instrument, only returning their attention to her after they'd pummeled the device into lifelessness. For some reason, the civilization of Tattoo People on this planet reacted violently to any artificially produced radio waves. Perhaps it wasn't just artificially produced radio waves that they reacted to. Maybe it was all radio waves, regardless of their origin. Was this why they were so intent on destroying each other? Elsenia wanted to understand, but above all she needed to get back to the capsule.

She'd forgotten to look at her watch, so she had no idea how long she slept. It could've been forever, except it began to grow light again. The vine was retracting its branches, loosening the braid to admit daylight. Her hand reached for the EMP weapon, but it wasn't necessary. The Tattoo People were gone. Had they gotten a message from the vine and called off their attack? It was all the reassurance she needed to resume her trek. She resolved not to use the radio transmitter again, sure that her message to the capsule had allowed them to find her.

The remainder of her trip was uneventful. For whatever reason, she encountered no more Tattoo People. She suspected they weren't far away. They'd found her very quickly after her transmission.

When she reached the capsule and saw it undamaged, she was relieved and elated. Before entering it to prepare her departure, she peered at the vine surrounding the landing site. She felt an enormous remorse that bordered on guilt. She would lift off and be free from the terror and savagery, but the poor plant was doomed to remain, a helpless witness to the barbarism being committed. She suspected the plant would soon die, one more victim of the brutality, and with its death, the soul of the planet would cease to exist. The vine and the civilization it had spawned would become extinct. The thought of it filled her eyes with tears, and Elsenia wondered what gesture of sympathy she could leave—a message of communion with the vine. She thought of the braided necklace that Ilsa had given to her. It still hung about her neck. Now it would be a gift to the vine. She removed the rendezvous plan from the necklace and strode to the edge of the thicket. She draped it over one of the protruding branches, hoping the plant would understand.

Before entering her capsule, she glanced back at the vine where she'd left the necklace. Was it her imagination or had the vine acknowledged her gift by reconfiguring its branches about the necklace? Two branches stretched upward, creating a "V" shape, and across the top of the letter was a horizontal branch, where the lanyard now hung. Elsenia studied the arrangement for some time, wondering whether it'd been there before, or whether it could have formed by chance.

Finally, she boarded her capsule and barely fifteen minutes later, blasted off, leaving the planet and all its madness behind.

Chapter 20

— Century 1810 —

Max had been unfrozen often over the last forty thousand years, each time because the aliens needed help in their efforts to reverse engineer the systems of the space capsules. They'd been able to access all the internal documentation, circuit diagrams, maintenance instructions, repair manuals, and user guides, along with the unlimited archive of data about Earth. They'd quickly mastered the written form of Union English, and even though they couldn't speak the language, they were able to write out for Max specific details on what they wanted from him. They never unfroze Sadie. They'd made it very clear that it was important Max comply with their demands or he would never see his wife alive again.

Max was impressed by the determination of the aliens to develop the technology that humans had mastered. The sustained effort over thousands of years demonstrated their resolve to explore the galaxy as humans had done. The four most important technologies were the magnetocryogenic systems for deep freezing, the shielding from lethal cosmic ray fluxes, the propulsion systems providing sustained acceleration reliably and consistently through the millennia, and the weapons systems, used to neutralize objects that might damage or destroy vehicles during their voyage. Max was surprised to learn that the aliens were unfamiliar with the concept of weapons. They had little need to use them against each other, and against other beings they might encounter in space, they could rely on the strength of their arms and hands, combined with speed and agility surpassing that of any animal.

Max helped the aliens, time and again. Before each of his exits, he made a point of looking at the location and time display on his control console. Although thousands of years passed between each unfreezing, the location remained the same, near the center of the galaxy. But not this time. Now, the coordinates shown by the capsule's navigation system indicated that the aliens had moved to a new location, about eight thousand light-years from Earth and about fourteen thousand light-years from Aril. This was still far away on galactic scales, but the fact that they were closer to the section of the galaxy occupied by humans now bothered Max. What had he done? Helped these aliens develop the technology to travel across interstellar space? What if their ultimate goal was to conquer humanity? At the time Max and Sadie's supply ship was hijacked, there were only two planets with well-established human civilizations: Earth and Aril. How many more might there be now? Was this what drove the aliens in their relentless effort to understand and use human technology? Max wanted answers, but was forced to cooperate with the aliens. Sadie was at their mercy.

This time, after leaving the space capsule, he was escorted to the same room where he and Sadie had first met the large alien leader, who still occupied his position on the platform overlooking the controls and computers. Either these aliens lived a very long time, or they'd taken advantage of the magnetocryogenic technology to preserve themselves through the millennia. Next to the alien was a video monitor with words in Union English, scrolling slowly from bottom to top on the screen.

"You have done well. With your aid, my people have begun our long awaited expansion to new planets throughout the galaxy. We have reached the first destination."

The scrolling text stopped. The alien stared at Max, as if waiting for a response. In the past the aliens hadn't shown any indication they were able to hear or understand what Max said. He returned the alien's stare.

"You may speak. The acoustic vibrations you create will be interpreted and shown on the screen."

A million responses occurred to Max in that moment, most of them wouldn't have pleased his alien hosts. Instead, he said, "Who are you?" and watched his words appear immediately on the screen above the alien's head.

"In your language, my name would be pronounced Abnaxes. We have mastered your language and your technology for space

157

travel. We will soon depart on the next phase of our journey, but we require further help from you."

"What more do you want?"

Abnaxes pointed at another video screen with one of his long knobby fingers. Max was amazed at the intricate reticulations of the enormous digit. It allowed for minute and precise movements, even in a rotational direction, as if each finger of the alien was a viper, able to deliver instant death with chilling certainty.

The second monitor came to life. It showed a map of the galaxy, the Milky Way's spiral arms all too familiar to Max. Like maps produced by humans, it was impossible to show every star individually. A filter had been used to ensure the image appeared realistic without rendering billions of points of light. Max recognized where Earth was on the alien map, and the approximate location of Aril and the Galactic Garden. At the time his supply ship was hijacked, Aril had only recently been established.

Bright yellow dots appeared on the background of galactic stars, and a new message appeared on the adjacent video screen.

"Each of these dots represents a planet that will be a future home for our civilization. They are already being prepared for our arrival. By the time we get to those planets, their atmospheres will be perfect, and the surface will be covered by a plant that will provide all the food, clothing, and building materials we need."

Max was stunned. Hundreds of yellow dots appeared, concentrated in the sector of the galaxy that included Earth and Aril. Could it be possible that these aliens would completely populate the Galactic Garden? Had Max and Sadie really delivered to them the necessary technology?

After the yellow dots, a group of larger red dots appeared. Max read the accompanying text.

"These are the planets occupied by humans. Your people now inhabit many of the planets that were prepared by our plant for us. Like scavengers, humans have exploited our accomplishments. You are interlopers on planets that do not belong to you. Not only have humans taken over our planets, but they've polluted the galaxy with their filthy radio waves, which interfere with the primary means by

which we communicate among ourselves. This cannot be allowed. The human species must be destroyed."

Max stared at the map incredulously. In the time he and Sadie had been forcibly ejected from their ship, humans had settled more than a half dozen planets. He and Sadie, frozen, had been completely oblivious to this unprecedented expansion of humanity. And now, they'd been unwitting accomplices to a race of aliens that sought to destroy human civilization.

"Let me and my wife go," he said to Abnaxes.

The reply came immediately to the video screen.

"No. You both will accompany us on our journey to conquer your people. We are still in need of your knowledge."

"I won't help you destroy our own race."

"Then we will have to kill you and your wife."

Seeing the words printed on the screen gave them a coldness that was even more threatening than if they'd been spoken.

"What would you have me do?"

"Explain these things you call weapons."

Max obliged. Over the next several hours, he told Abnaxes about the full arsenal of the supply ships, embellishing their destructive power and lethality. This was his chance to undo the damage he'd done by unknowingly helping the aliens. He told them of the laser weapons that could slice through the metal hulls of ships, melting impossibly thin fissures with sizzling instantaneity. He told of the EMP weapons, whose blast neutralized all the electronic circuitry of a spacecraft, even if it was deep within the interior of the vessel. The electromagnetic fields of the EMP pulse would strike the exterior surface and set up electrical currents in all parts of the hull, finding its way along metallic pathways to the ship's circuitry. Then there were the ballistic weapons, simple but highly destructive to vehicles in the merciless environment of space. Ballistic missiles would tear through the protective shells, exposing critical systems to the lethal vacuum of space, causing the loss of whatever oxygen the ship carried. Then there were the nuclear weapons. Max didn't need to embellish their destructiveness. If the alien was curious, all he had to do was bring up images stored in the computer on his space capsule showing the power of a nuclear blast.

"Humans would use these weapons against our people?"

Max hesitated. The alien, either intentionally or for lack of knowledge about the nuances of Union English, had phrased the question in such a way that Max was unsure how to answer.

As if to clarify the inquiry, an image on another monitor appeared. It showed one of the enormous alien spacecraft, executing a slow rotation in its orbit about Aurora. Abnaxes pointed to the image.

"Our spacecraft carry no weapons. They only carry people. They are all frozen now, but when they arrive at their destination, they will establish new populations on the planets that have been pre-conditioned by the vine. Your human cousins would destroy these ships with their weapons?"

What was the right answer? If he said yes, he'd be admitting to the aliens that humans were a flawed species—that they were capable of committing mass genocide against an alien race. They'd been known to kill each other en masse in historic times. Why would they hesitate, if faced with imminent invasion by aliens—even unarmed aliens?

If he said no, he'd be giving the aliens a green light to continue their invasion. Or perhaps worse, he'd be lying, and humans on those target worlds would unleash weapons against defenseless alien spacecraft. The humans were many thousands of years evolved from Max and Sadie. In fact, the last humans Max and Sadie had seen were ruthless, indiscriminate pirates, who'd terrorized them and stolen their supply ship. Had human civilization been taken over by such criminals? Max couldn't know how present humans might respond to spacecraft carrying an alien population.

"I'm not sure. I don't know," Max answered, finally.

The words appeared on the screen, a glowing testimonial of his doubt and ignorance.

Abnaxes looked at him with bottomless eyes. Had he learned enough about humans to assess Max's sincerity from the expression on his face?

"But it doesn't matter," Max added, thinking of Abnaxes' earlier words. "Humans possess a technology that is far more dangerous than any of these weapons." He let the words hang, watching them appear on the screen.

"What is that?"

"You said it yourself. Radio waves. The human world is bathed in such waves. They are ubiquitous and pervasive. If it is true that your civilization can't tolerate these waves, then the world of humans will be poison to you. Find another part of the galaxy to go with your people. The domain of humans will never be your home."

Max waited for the inevitable rage to appear on Abnaxes' face as these words appeared on the screen, but the alien showed no reaction. Max's words remained on the screen, inscribed in brilliant light, a challenge to the power of Abnaxes. Finally, the response scrolled onto the monitor.

"We will overcome the humans and their radio waves because you will help us. You will tell us how to protect ourselves from this radiation. If you do not..."

Abnaxes didn't complete the threat. He'd already learned the human art of intimidation through words unsaid.

Max hesitated before answering although he already knew what he'd say. He was negotiating with an alien using words on a video monitor as a means of communication, but the principles were no different. If Abnaxes was to believe Max's words, he had to make it seem as though they didn't come easily.

"I will help if you will release me and my wife."

A single word appeared on the screen.

"Agreed."

CHAPTER 21

— Century 1836 —

AFTER ESCAPING CARBONIA, Elsenia returned to Supply Ship 1. Adam Corkland was contrite for not having anticipated dangers on Carbonia. He took pride in being alert and prepared, to safeguard the explorer fleet from anything unforeseen on newly discovered planets. Elsenia reassured him that he couldn't have known of the damage and chaos on Carbonia. She'd made her own decision to travel there based on the frenetic signals from that ill-fated world received by the radio telescopes on Nuterra.

One of Adam's exceptional skills was first aid, which he immediately and expertly administered to treat Elsenia for the bruises and abrasions she'd suffered at the hands of Carbonia's Tattoo People. After she'd rested, Elsenia joined Adam in the galley of the supply ship. Over a bowl of hot soup, she told him what had happened, leaving nothing out. Adam listened intently. Elsenia knew she was being recorded and that Adam would transmit the report to other supply ships. Eventually, everyone in the Union fleet would know to avoid landing on Carbonia.

Adam was intrigued when Elsenia related her impression that the vine had protected her. But his strongest reaction came in response to Elsenia's description of the V-shaped configuration the vine had formed over the spot where she'd left the iridescent necklace that Ilsa had given her.

"I've seen that symbol before," pronounced Adam immediately.

"Where?" asked Elsenia.

"Come with me."

Elsenia followed him into the control room. He activated the computer's monitor and called up a message received from Aril just two hundred years earlier. Admiral Chase had destroyed an approaching asteroid with a nuclear weapon. Years later, Aril was bombarded by the debris from that explosion. The entire population of the planet had taken cover during the shower.

All had survived, even though several large fragments struck the surface. One fragment produced a crater about a half kilometer in diameter. Within the crater, a woman named Amalia Anatalia found a metal plate with a strange symbol etched into it. Adam showed Elsenia an image of the plate. It was exactly the same as the shape formed by the branches of the alien vine on Carbonia.

"What does it mean?" asked Elsenia.

"That's impossible to know, but there's one thing it tells us: there's a connection between that asteroid and the vine on Carbonia."

"Could that asteroid be one of the ones that carry the alien vine? According to Alphons, it was too big for that."

"It doesn't have to be one of the asteroids carrying the vine to be connected with the vine. Whether the purpose is to plant a vine or destroy a planet, it's the same transportation system being used. The race of intelligent beings that deployed them is out there in the galaxy somewhere."

"And whoever they are, they've adopted this symbol. It could be their calling card."

"Possibly. It certainly meant something to your friendly vine on Carbonia."

Elsenia nodded, remembering her narrow escape from the perilous planet.

"You're not thinking of going back there. Are you?"

"No. Not yet, anyway. I have to go to Happiness first. Our family agreed to meet there in 3000 years—a sort of family reunion."

Adam smiled. "Sounds like fun."

"Sorry," said Elsenia. She had to keep reminding herself of the lonely lives the custodians led.

"No need to feel sorry. We all knew the choices we were making. I like to think of all the galactic explorers as my family. In that sense, I've many family reunions—every time an explorer shows up."

"I hope you have many more," said Elsenia, finishing her soup.

"I'll make sure Admiral Chase gets your report He may wish to look into it further."

"Yes, of course," said Elsenia, wondering why hearing the Admiral's name gave her such comfort.

CHAPTER 22

— Century 1860 —

THEY'D SELECTED the planet Happiness for the reunion because it was centrally located in the Galactic Garden and had much significance for the Mizello family. Ilsa had been there twice before—once with Benjamin on their honeymoon and then again to visit the place he lived with Xyla, the woman he'd met on Aurora. Druix had also been there twice—once with Benjamin and Xyla, when they'd first explored the planet and forged an alliance between the humans and the neighboring Tattoo People, and again when he went to meet Ilsa and Elsenia during their return visit. Elsenia had been to Happiness only once, but it was the experience that had sparked her lifelong interest in the Tattoo People.

Happiness had grown and prospered in magnificent ways. The partnership between the Tattoo People and the humans benefited both. The two populations still lived separately, the Tattoo People within the confines of the vine and the humans in the reconstructed amusement park. But now it wasn't unusual to see humans visiting the alien domain in the forest, enjoying the tranquility of the lakes, rivers, and waterfalls, as well as the majesty and mystery of the three pyramids on the island replica of Nucleanis. Similarly, many Tattoo People emerged from the forest on a daily basis and worked side by side with their human friends, caring for crops, learning the skills of metal work, and most of all entertaining visitors to the amusement park. Consistent with the model upon which Happiness had been established, the amusement park and the places where the humans lived were completely integrated. The humans on Happiness worked where they played and played where they worked.

Druix and Ilsa arrived first for the reunion. Ilsa's temperament had not changed from when she and Druix left Earth. She remained in a dark and somber mood, even though she seemed to understand that their journey to Happiness would reunite them with their children. When she and Druix disembarked at the Happiness spaceport, they were greeted warmly by a delegation that included both humans and Tattoo People who knew that the two visitors were related to Benjamin and Xyla, honored and respected for the role they'd played in bringing the populations of Happiness together. Yet the warmth of the greeting they received did little to break the shell of bitterness that seemed to envelop Ilsa. She followed Druix and the delegation from Happiness through the spaceport in silent resignation.

For the reunion, they had arranged in advance to stay in the recreated Caribbean seaport. It had been Ilsa's choice, which she'd expressed to Druix prior to her ill-fated crash landing on Earth. Druix now worried how Ilsa would react to the inevitable memories of her time there with Benjamin, when they strolled as newlyweds through the cobblestone streets and enjoyed the music, excitement, and romance of that tropical resort. Although it was also somewhat strange for Druix to be in the same place where his father honeymooned with the woman who was now his wife, concerns for Ilsa's health overshadowed those worries.

Druix and Ilsa drove in an electric cart to a picturesque hotel with a spectacular view of the ocean and the replica of an old Spanish fort, the kind that had been built long ago on Earth to protect seaports from marauding pirates and hostile invaders. It wasn't really situated on an ocean, but the adjacent lake was large enough that one couldn't see the opposite shore. A variety of watercraft speckled the lake's surface. Some took visitors to one of the few access points for humans wishing to visit the empire of the Tattoo People. Druix gazed out at the water, remembering his previous visit with his mother and Benjamin. He felt an irrepressible desire to explore the planet again, to recapture the mystery, excitement, and uncertainty of those months that had been the turning point in all their lives.

Once in their hotel room, Ilsa washed up perfunctorily and went to bed. Druix offered to call one of the local physicians to examine her, but Ilsa angrily resisted any such intrusion on her privacy. Druix slipped quietly out of the room to explore the resort on his own. He was anxious for the rest of the family to arrive, hoping they'd be able to help Ilsa regain her former warmth and friendliness.

FOR ELSENIA, the excitement of seeing her family was mixed with an inexplicable desire to see Admiral Chase again. She still had the rendezvous plan he'd given her and was tempted to display its contents on her capsule's computer to see where and when she might meet him, but she didn't. Although anxious to tell him about her nearly catastrophic visit to Carbonia, she'd committed herself to the family reunion. Admittedly, she missed Ilsa, Druix, and the twins, and looked forward to seeing them. Even though galactic space travel and magnetocryogenic technology was such that most of the life-threatening risks had been eliminated, there were always lingering doubts and fears that crept into one's consciousness. When two people separated to follow different courses in space and time, many events could take place along the way, and the travelers never knew for sure whether they'd ever see each other again, even with the best rendezvous plans in hand. It wasn't unlike air travel in the 20th Century. No departure was ever completely free of the worry that it would be a final one.

Elsenia looked for her parents immediately upon arriving at the hotel. She found Druix alone, waiting anxiously in the hotel lobby. Druix had aged visibly, and Elsenia wondered how long he and Ilsa had remained on Earth. During the same time, Elsenia had visited three planets, they'd visited just one. It was to have been a homecoming for Ilsa and an opportunity for Druix, who was still the curious student of history; for him, Earth was where all human history began. Elsenia could believe that her parents had decided to stay several years on the planet, but Druix's appearance told her there was more to it than just the passage of time.

That night, Elsenia and Druix dined alone. He told her of their crash landing on Earth and Ilsa's bizarre medical treatment under the care of Petyuba. Ultimately, Ilsa had been healed of life-threatening injuries, but the experience had left her emotionally scarred. Druix was preparing Elsenia for the impending reunion with her mother, adjusting her expectations so that it would be less of a shock for the young woman.

That reunion took place the next morning. Ilsa still refused to leave the hotel room, though she was dressed and sat in a chair facing the window, looking out at the variety of watercraft that skittered across the lake in the slanting light of the recently risen sun. Elsenia bent to hug her mother, who returned the embrace stiffly. Elsenia was grateful that Druix had warned her. Otherwise, she'd have questioned whether the pale woman in the chair was the same person. Ilsa's beauty had always been accentuated by the stunning contrast between her smooth, pale skin and her dark eyes, but now those same features gave her an appearance of morbidity that was almost frightening. Elsenia had inherited a subdued version of her mother's distinctive beauty.

"Mom, what's wrong?" Elsenia said, deciding not to waste time on false pleasantries.

Ilsa turned her head only slightly to look at her daughter. "I don't want to be here. I don't know why he brought me here."

"We're here for a family reunion. Don't you remember? It was your idea. The twins will be here soon."

Ilsa's face twisted. "The twins?" she said absently.

"Yes, Vega and Deneb. You remember them, don't you?"

"Where are they?"

"They're not here yet, but they're on their way."

This seemed to revive Ilsa. They all took a walk on the hotel grounds. Druix remained worried, but every time he suggested Ilsa see a doctor an argument ensued. Elsenia couldn't remember ever seeing her parents quarrel as they did now. It was contentious and uncomfortable, and Elsenia found herself looking forward to the twins' arrival, when the attention of her parents would be shifted away from each other. Elsenia resolved to explore the Happiness amusement park on her own. Occasionally, Druix joined her, but even away from Ilsa, he was pre-occupied worrying about her.

CHAPTER 23

— Century 1860 —

TWO WEEKS INTO THEIR STAY ON HAPPINESS, the feuding and animosity between Ilsa and Druix became of secondary importance when Admiral Chase and Risto Jalonen showed up at their hotel. Elsenia couldn't conceal her emotions, complex as they were, on seeing the Earth Fleet Commander enter the dining area of the hotel while she was seated for dinner with Druix and Ilsa. Risto strolled in awkwardly behind the Admiral, looking equally out of place among the vacationers. The last time Elsenia had seen him he was undergoing a process of semi-frozen rehabilitation from lethal dosages of radiation he'd received during many millennia in space. Remarkably, he seemed to have recovered his vitality, but he'd aged considerably. Whatever treatments the Arilians had given him must have taken many years. With eyes downcast, he followed closely behind Admiral Chase.

Elsenia and Druix rose in unison to meet the two, but Ilsa remained seated. There was no denying the attention this meeting was drawing from others in the dining room. Admiral Chase embraced Druix in greeting, but held back from Elsenia, unsure of what to do. So it was Elsenia who moved forward to hug him. It was a different kind of hug than one would give a friend. Elsenia wondered where she'd learned it. Admiral Chase must've felt it too, because he blushed visibly—or at least it was the equivalent of a blush for someone with the leathery skin of a 550th Century human.

Risto Jalonen clearly wanted nothing to do with all the hugging, but he couldn't escape. Elsenia embraced him warmly, unable to conceal her surprise at seeing him, especially given his condition the last time they spoke. She'd fully expected never to see him again.

Chairs were moved and tables rearranged to make room for the two new diners. When they were seated, Admiral Chase spoke first. The air of familiarity and friendship disappeared from his voice. He was once again the Commander of the Earth fleet.

"I have some worrisome news. Please don't overreact because we're still analyzing the data to determine what happened."

"What's wrong?" said Druix, his voice filled with dread.

Admiral Chase leaned forward. "The twins were supposed to join you here on Happiness. Correct?"

"Yes, but they haven't arrived yet." said Druix, cautiously.

"Right. We don't know where they are."

"What?"

"We're still sorting it out. We know they both went together to Supply Ship 2 after leaving Lumina. According to the custodian of that supply ship, they left sixteen thousand years ago, and were both supposed to be on their way here."

"That's odd," said Elsenia. "Why would they leave Lumina, stop at a supply ship and then come to Happiness without visiting any other planet along the way?"

"We don't know. All we have is a report from Alphons Demetriano, the custodian of the supply ship. They certainly had enough time to visit other planets before coming here, but apparently decided not to."

"Then why aren't they here?" asked Druix.

Admiral Chase shook his head. "We've sent inquiries out to other supply ships and requested they forward the messages to any galactic explorers in the vicinity. It's too soon to hear back from any of them though. The good news, I suppose, is that they're both missing. It means that whatever happened, they're probably still together. It argues against an accident. The odds that both capsules suffered failures or collisions are impossibly small."

"So what does it mean?" asked Druix.

"We've considered the possibilities and narrowed them to two, both equally puzzling. The first is that they were attacked by a hostile force in space. The problem with that explanation is that we haven't met any hostile forces in space. The second explanation is that the twins decided to go somewhere without telling anyone."

"Why would they do that?" asked Elsenia.

"We were hoping you might be able to tell us. Do you know of any reason Vega and Deneb wouldn't want to reveal their destination?"

"No, of course not," answered Druix.

"Except…" put in Elsenia.

"Except what?"

Elsenia reminded Admiral Chase of how the twins had been whisked away by the Tattoo People of Lumina for some unknown reason.

"And you never found out what happened that day?" the Admiral asked.

"No," Druix admitted. "There were too many other things going on at the time. We never had the chance."

Admiral Chase nodded. "I'll send an inquiry to my command ship. They'll do a complete scan of all information we have on Lumina and its Tattoo People. There've been recent visits by explorers that might give us a clue to where the twins went."

Risto had been listening to the conversation quietly, all the while watching Ilsa. During the ensuing lull, he leaned toward her and said, "Miss Montgomery, are you okay?"

He addressed her by her maiden name, apparently forgetting that she'd been married to Benjamin and still carried his surname. Risto had rescued Ilsa from her space capsule after it was struck by an EMP blast from Andrew Harding's supply ship. He'd pursued the capsule for fourteen thousand years before overtaking it. The rescue had established an unbreakable connection between the two, but now Ilsa gazed at Risto with the same vacant look she directed to everyone else at the table. Failing to elicit a response, Risto sat back in his chair uncomfortably, all too anxious to resume his silent participation at the table.

After the meal, Druix led Ilsa back to their room. Risto disappeared, probably to sample some of the local beer in the hotel's lounge. Admiral Chase and Elsenia found themselves alone in the lobby.

"Walk?" the Admiral asked.

"Sure," replied Elsenia without hesitation.

They strolled outside to the recreated cobblestone streets flanked by pastel-colored stucco structures housing shops, cafes, and bars, where loud, rhythmic songs from ancient Earth echoed resonantly about them. The couple walked silently until they reached the end of a street where a low wall allowed a view of the lake, dark now, with just a few lights from distant tour boats speckling the liquid blackness. Here, only the deep, periodic beats of the music could be heard, like the waning thunder of a passing storm.

"I read your report on Carbonia. I'm sorry you ended up there. We've initiated a thorough investigation into what may have happened to the planet and why we were unable to anticipate the breakdown in their civilization. We like to think we know what's happening and are well prepared whenever an explorer lands somewhere."

"You can never be sure what conditions are," said Elsenia, "Thousands of years might pass between consecutive visits to a planet. Anything could happen. Cataclysmic events, either natural, or societal, or political could completely alter its usual state."

"That's true, but we take that into consideration. The state of a world at any given time is used to make forecasts. When we're not correct, it's because something unexpected has taken place. We need to know what that is."

"So the next time it's expected? The catastrophe might still happen, but at least now it's an expected catastrophe?"

Admiral Chase smiled. "Right." Then he told her about the asteroid that had been moving toward Aril, and how they'd used a nuclear weapon to render it harmless. He explained how the debris produced a fantastic meteor shower on Aril that repeated annually, which reminded Elsenia of the V-shaped configuration of the vine on Carbonia, and how it was identical to the symbol found on a piece of metal debris from one of the meteor strikes on Aril.

Admiral Chase was intrigued. "I should visit Carbonia."

As if to punctuate his words, a bright meteor streaked across the sky, so bright the surface of the water reflected it. The two streaks, one real and one a phantom, converged, but dissipated, failing to survive across the last gap that separated them.

Admiral Chase and Elsenia returned to the hotel, taking the longer route along the lakeshore which avoided the rousing nightlife of the cobblestone streets. When they said good night in the hotel lobby, they hugged awkwardly and parted.

CHAPTER 24

— Century 1860 —

DISTRAUGHT WITH WORRY ABOUT THE TWINS AND ILSA, Druix announced that he was going to Nucleanis to escape for a while and think. He hadn't been there since his previous visit to Happiness, when he'd found Ilsa and Elsenia touring the island, which was actually a smaller replica of the continent of Nucleanis on the planet Prosperity. The artificially constructed island held the triad of pyramids that commemorated three different civilizations of ancient Earth. One of these was where the interstellar pirate Stella had hidden the earthly treasures she and her pirate band had stolen.

A Tattoo woman met Druix upon his arrival at the lakeshore, where he'd be escorted by boat to Nucleanis. She introduced herself with a name her translating medallion rendered as something like "Vendema". Druix shook her hand. It was thin and delicate. She was such a slight being, he thought she might fly away or turn to vapor before his eyes.

"Welcome back, Druix. It's been a long time. Your mother has been waiting for your return."

Druix registered obvious shock. "My mother is dead," he proclaimed. Druix had a powerful voice, but these words emerged broken and hesitant.

Vendema flashed a sympathetic smile. "Yes, of course. I'm sorry. I forgot how humans see death."

Druix was too upset to pursue her comment. He allowed himself to be led away, trying to concentrate on the sights and sounds of the present. Being back on Nucleanis was drawing him into the past—a past he wasn't sure he was prepared to revisit.

Vendema led Druix along the shore of the lake, stopping at a spot with a narrow, sandy beach, surrounded by vegetation formed by the alien vine. They approached a house, also formed by the vine, with a porch and sloped roof. It was the home where

Benjamin and Xyla had lived.

Druix and Vendema sat on the porch, looking out over the lake.

"What'd you mean about how humans see death?" Druix asked.

Vendema drew her knees up, then wrapped her arms around them, a child-like posture that made it difficult to believe she'd have anything profound to say about death, or life.

"Your mother is very much still with us, Druix. Just because you can't see her doesn't mean she isn't present."

"Ah, yes," said Druix. "You're right. She'll always be present in my heart. I see what you mean."

Vendema looked at him as if measuring his sincerity. She waited, deep in thought. Finally, she said, "It's more than that."

Something in the electronic precision of the translating device gave Vendema's words a mystical quality.

"What do you mean?"

Vendema looked out at the lake. Through the haze, the peaks of the three pyramids were visible. "I mean that Xyla is here. Her mind and her thoughts are still with us."

"I don't understand," said Druix.

"It's getting late," said Vendema suddenly. "You've had a long day traveling here. It's better if we discuss this another time." She rose to leave.

"No," said Druix, more sharply than he'd intended. "I want to understand. Now."

Vendema sighed and sat again. "I thought you understood already. Your time on Happiness in the past didn't teach you more about us, about..." She stopped, unable to find the right word.

"Go on," encouraged Druix, more gently now.

"When someone you love or care about is injured, or is in pain, or dies, you feel bad. Don't you?"

"Of course," answered Druix, thinking of Ilsa.

"Loved ones become an extension of yourself. It's no longer possible to separate the things that happen to them from your own thoughts and emotions, whether they're good or bad."

"That's true."

"So by loving someone, you extend your sentience to that other person. You become a bigger self."

"Yes," affirmed Druix, beginning to see where Vendema was taking him.

"Your mother spent her entire life working with the Tattoo children of Happiness. She loved every one of them, and they loved her. She willingly extended her psyche to them, feeling whatever they felt, sharing their triumphs, suffering through their anguish. The Tattoo children were very receptive to this extension of her consciousness because that's what we do—naturally—with one another. When Xyla's body stopped working, that part of her mind that was contained within her body did as well."

Druix interrupted her. "What do you mean?" His voice expressed alarm.

Vendema chuckled. "Please don't think we removed part of her brain. That's not what I'm saying. I'm trying to say that by the time her body stopped functioning, your mother had already spread her psyche to thousands of Tattoo children, and if there's one thing we're good at it's sharing thoughts among us. Thus, part of Xyla's consciousness survived, even after she died."

Druix shook his head. "Even if I accepted the idea that my mother could perpetuate her thoughts in sharing them, that was thousands of years ago. Those children are gone—dead long ago."

Vendema looked disappointed. "Can you stop being human long enough to understand? Thoughts don't die when people die. Ideas don't die when people die. Emotions don't die when people die. They live on within the minds of others, and they're passed on from one generation to another. They survive for a very long time."

"I don't buy it. By that logic, Albert Einstein is still alive because his thoughts and ideas are still remembered—even now."

"Exactly," said Vendema.

"But that's absurd," returned Druix. "We may be thinking Einstein's thoughts, but I'm sure Einstein doesn't feel alive."

"How do you know?"

Druix opened his mouth to answer, but stopped.

"You don't know. Do you?"

Druix sighed in exasperation. "Right. Einstein could be with us still, pondering the mysteries of the universe, trying to learn the unified theory of physics. There's no way we'd know."

"You'd know if you could speak to him," Vendema said.

Druix looked at her sharply. "Now you're just playing with me."

Vendema lay her hand on his. It was cool—like a damp leaf, as the body temperature of Tattoo People was lower than humans.

"I'm not playing with you Druix. Your mother is here with us. With you. I know this is hard for you to understand, but if you were one of us you'd realize how it is to be so strongly connected with others that your consciousness is not localized to just your own mind. You have an extended soul that transcends an individual. Your mother came to understand that. She became one of us. She's still one of us. She lives as long as Tattoo People exist on Happiness."

Druix rose slowly and took several faltering steps toward the edge of the lake. The mist was clearing. The outline of the island with its three pyramids was more distinct. He gazed at the shimmering water for some time, then turned to face Vendema.

"I want to speak to my mother," he said.

Vendema nodded. "Very well. I'll arrange it."

THE MEETING between Druix and his mother was to take place on the island of Nucleanis. Hundreds of Tattoo People gathered about the smallest of the three pyramids. Vendema led Druix up a set of stairs that led to a terrace-like platform half way up the structure. It was almost noon. Druix was warm, sweating profusely after the ascent. His ears throbbed, echoing the beat of his heart. He felt dizzy and disoriented. Vendema sensed it and held his hand. He looked out at the crowd below.

"Why are they all here?" Druix asked.

"It's been many years since your mother was alive. Her presence is no longer as strong as it once was. We must work together to resurrect her thoughts." Vendema motioned to a heavy wooden bench on the terrace. "Sit."

Breathing heavily, Druix was glad to be seated. He wasn't out of shape, but the heat and climb up the stairs had exhausted him. He shielded his eyes from the sunlight and scanned the crowd. Then he looked upward past the lake surface to the line of vegetation beyond and closed his eyes. In the silence, he heard the electronic voice from Vendema's translating medallion.

"Your mother is overjoyed that you've returned. She was desperately worried about you when you departed. She thought of you every day. She has much to tell you, but first she asks if you remember what you told her on the day you both left your birth planet, Aurora."

"Yes," said Druix, weakly.

"You said you understood that there are times when choices have to be made that will determine the course of your life forever after."

"I remember."

"You may soon have to make another of those choices, she says."

Druix nodded, numbly. Some combination of the heat, his exhaustion, and the bizarre surroundings in which he found himself transported him to another place and time. The voice emanating from Vendema's device was his mother's. With his eyes closed, he could easily imagine she was sitting next to him, talking as they had done so often during their travels across the galaxy.

"The twins are okay, but they're far apart," his mother said. "They've been summoned to serve a higher purpose. You can help."

"What?" Druix said.

"You can help," Xyla repeated.

"How?"

"You must return to Aurora."

"Why?"

"To help your children. To help the twins."

"But why?"

"I can't tell you why. I don't know. I feel it. It's good to be with you again, Druix."

"I…" stammered Druix, unable to respond.

"Go to Aurora, Druix."

"I will," he answered but the pounding in his ears and the heat made him feel faint. He could barely sense Vendema's hand, clutching his tightly, reassuring him.

"And Druix, I feel something else."

"What?"

"I'm not sure. It's a strange feeling."

Druix shook his head, and Vendema had to steady him so he wouldn't slump off the bench.

"Beware the ship of Theseus. Take care," Xyla's voice pronounced.

With that, Druix lost consciousness, caught like a child in Vendema's frail but certain arms.

AT DINNER THAT NIGHT, with Ilsa, Elsenia, Admiral Chase, and Risto, Druix announced he was going to Aurora.

"Why?" Elsenia asked.

"Call it a hunch. I believe the twins are there."

"You can't travel all the way to Aurora on a hunch," said Admiral Chase.

"It's more than a hunch. It's a premonition."

"We have no information about Aurora," said the Admiral. As far as we know, it hasn't been visited since you and your mother left. Its sun was fading. It's probably frozen solid by now. Certainly there's no life left on the planet."

"I have to go there," said Druix. "It's hard to explain, but I have to do it."

"I'm not going with you." Ilsa said, breaking her silence.

"You don't have to," said Druix.

"Then you're leaving me," she answered, bitterness in her voice.

"No. I'll be back."

"And what am I supposed to do until you return? Wait here for you? You just want to leave me on this phony, ridiculous planet to die so you can be rid of me. Is that why you brought me here from Earth?"

"If you don't want to go with me, you don't have to, but you don't have to stay here. Perhaps you should go to Aril. They have excellent doctors there." Druix regretted his last sentence as soon as it left his mouth. Ilsa stood angrily.

"I will not go to any doctors on Aril. And I will not go with you to Aurora. Just do whatever you want to do and forget about me. I don't need any of you!"

Ilsa turned and stormed from the dining room, leaving Druix and everyone else in stunned silence.

LATER, alone with Elsenia, Druix told her about his contact with Xyla. Elsenia, who felt more and more that the Tattoo People and the vine were magical, was not the least bit skeptical of Druix's story. She agreed with his decision to go to Aurora.

"What do you think she meant by 'Beware the ship of Theseus'?" she asked.

"I think I understand that, although I'm not sure what to do about it."

They strolled along Broadway in the recreated city of New York. It was late, and the bright lights of the shops and restaurants began winking out. The giant billboards were black now, no longer assaulting the senses with gaudy displays of lights advertising products and services obsolete.

"During our visit to Earth," Druix said, "the planet was undergoing a global identity crisis. Over the past 150 thousand years, humans had launched one expedition after another into space. If you remember, the mass migration from Earth to Prosperity created a highway in the galaxy over which humans emigrated from their home planet. Later, after other worlds were colonized, the emigration continued. Of course, some remained on Earth. The population stabilized, but that raised the question of what place in the galaxy should be thought of as humanity's home. It's largely a philosophical question, akin to the ancient paradox about the ship of Theseus. As Theseus' ship grew old, pieces of it were removed and replaced with new parts. After every piece had been replaced, was it still Theseus' ship? What if the pieces that were removed were used to build another ship? Then which one would be the ship of Theseus?"

"So with all the people removed from Earth, where then is humanity's ship?" Elsenia mused.

"Exactly."

"I still don't see why Xyla would warn you about the ship of Theseus, or Earth."

"I asked Vendema about it later. She reminded me that my mother always enjoyed the classics, Greek mythology, and ancient history. She read many of those works to the Tattoo children. It wouldn't be unusual for her to draw on an ancient paradox, the ship of Theseus, to express a vague premonition."

"Beware of Earth," Elsenia repeated. "We should probably tell Admiral Chase."

"Yes, but I hope he doesn't ask too many questions. I don't think it will be as easy for him to believe the tale I've just told you."

"No, but he's from Earth. He may know something about possible threats from there."

By now, the only illumination remaining was from the dim streetlamps, but the darkness afforded them a view of the night sky. The stars appeared brilliantly above them, and Elsenia found among the random patterns the constellation within which Earth's sun shone, so very far away.

CHAPTER 25

— Century 1860 —

ADMIRAL CHASE REPORTED that they'd learned nothing from examining the archived messages received by the command ship. None had given any clue that there were unusual events connected with either Lumina or Aurora. He'd decided to initiate a galaxy-wide search for the twins. Elsenia's heart sunk when she heard this. How does one go about finding two missing children (for to Elsenia they were no more than teenagers) in a portion of the galaxy tens of thousands of light-years across, and populated with potentially habitable planets too numerous to count? Add to that scale the dimension of time, which could make it impossibly difficult to find missing persons even if their exact location were known. Imagine arriving somewhere days too soon or too late. At the speed space capsules travel, the objects of the search could be as far away as the distance of Earth from the Sun. A search might be successful if those being sought wanted to be found, but what if they didn't? They might be deliberately avoiding the family. It seemed far-fetched, but how else to explain the disappearance of both of the twins.

After discussing it for some time, Elsenia, Druix, and Admiral Chase agreed that the twins had intentionally gone somewhere without telling anyone, and somehow the Tattoo People were implicated.

They decided to search separately. Risto volunteered to go back to Earth, one of the places the twins had expressed interest in, based on the stories Ilsa had told them about her home planet—their ancestral world. Elsenia had an uneasy feeling that Risto wanted to return to Earth for another reason. Though he'd survived radiation exposure, he probably didn't have much longer to live, and he certainly didn't have the youth and vigor to carry on with galactic exploration. Elsenia suspected he would remain on Earth after he returned and live out his life there.

Admiral Chase said, he'd have to remain in the Galactic

Garden to continue his command of the Earth fleet. He would stop at Prosperity first, then Lumina, and then head back to Aril. Along the way, he'd visit Carbonia to see if the conditions described by Elsenia had deteriorated further. If the twins were in any of those locations, there'd be historical records of their visit. In the meantime, he'd continue to monitor messages received by the command ship. If any transmission offered a clue as to the whereabouts of the twins, he'd broadcast it to all the others. After describing his plans, Admiral Chase paused and looked at Elsenia expectantly.

"I'll go to Supply Ship 2 to talk to Alphons Demetriano," Elsenia said.

"What?" Admiral Chase asked. He almost appeared disappointed.

"That's the last place we know the twins were before they disappeared. They may have told him something about where they were going."

"We've received a report from Alphons already. It says only that they were coming here."

"I know, but perhaps I can learn more by talking to him directly."

"Very well," said the Admiral, weakly.

Was Elsenia imagining it, or had Admiral Chase been about to invite her to join him? Later, she wondered whether she should have hesitated before offering to go to Supply Ship 2. It was the kind of moment that would plague her thoughts for a long time. How different might Elsenia's life had been if she had just given Admiral Chase a chance to finish his thought? He was shy and uncertain. Words didn't come easily to him, especially in these types of situations.

But that was that. The moment had passed. Several more of silence ensued before Elsenia excused herself. As they parted, it came to Elsenia that in all her encounters with Admiral Chase, he never left her. It was always she walking away from him. What did that say about him, and her? How different the world looks to two people, when one is walking away from the other? One sees only the future, the other sees that person from behind, moving into an unspecified future. How many fewer such partings would take place if the person walking away saw the same way as the person left behind?

That was the last Elsenia saw of Admiral Chase on Happiness. He and Risto took off the next morning. Several days later Druix departed. Ilsa wasn't there to say goodbye. There were tears in Druix's eyes when he left her in the hotel on his way to the spaceport. He said nothing to Elsenia about his last conversation with his wife, but it couldn't have been easy. Elsenia had never felt so close to Druix. It seemed now that they were the only two remaining members of the Mizello family. Before he left, Druix removed the iridescent necklace that carried the Mizello family rendezvous plan, and once belonged to Benjamin.

"You left yours on Carbonia. Take mine."

Elsenia took the necklace and embraced Druix. He turned and strode resolutely to the waiting space capsule.

With the departure of the others, Elsenia found herself for the first time alone on Happiness with her mother. While preparing for her own departure, she visited Ilsa in her hotel room one last time. Rather than try to engage her mother in conversation, Elsenia described everything that had happened to her. She told her of Magnetonia, where humans lived disease- and illness-free for hundreds of years. She spoke of the enigmatic messages being received on Nuterra, the pleas and exhortations of Tattoo People, inadvertently baring their collective souls into the galactic void. And she described the horrors she'd seen on Carbonia, and how she had just barely escaped with assistance from the alien vine and the aid of the EMP weapon Admiral Chase had given her.

Ilsa listened to these stories without response or emotion. She sat in her usual place, staring out at the lake, her face registering no reaction. Elsenia concluded and told her mother she had to leave Happiness the next day.

"Do what you have to do," was the impassive reply.

"What will you do?"

Ilsa turned slowly toward Elsenia, an eerie motion that

chilled her. "That's of no concern to you."

With a trembling hand, Elsenia showed Ilsa the rendez-vous plan her mother had given her on Lumina, now attached to Druix's lanyard.

"Do you remember you gave me your rendezvous plan?"

"Yes."

"You still have yours, don't you?"

"I suppose so."

"Don't forget it."

Ilsa didn't respond. Her head executed a slow rotation back to stare out the window at the water.

"Good bye, Mom," Elsenia said. She gave her one final hug and left.

CHAPTER 26

— Century 1964 —

ELSENIA HAD HEARD many stories of the mad physicist, Alphons Demetriano, who'd been the replacement custodian for Supply Ship 2. He had guided Xyla on a course that eventually led to her finding Benjamin, the father of her child. How different Elsenia's life would have been if the meddling, old scientist had not seen fit to help Xyla in her search.

Elsenia also remembered her conversation with Admiral Chase relating his visit to Alphons' ship. The old man had rambled on about his theories of the origin of the Tattoo People. She knew that Alphons was a data gatherer, hoarding it as if it were gold. Maybe that's how Alphons maintained his sanity, although after talking with him, Elsenia had her doubts about how much sanity remained in his withering mind.

Alphons didn't look much older than what Elsenia had imagined based on Admiral Chase's description. Either she exaggerated his age, or perhaps he'd reached that point where aging no longer produces substantive changes. The difference in a person's appearance between the ages of twenty and forty are dramatic because the age has doubled. But between 100 and 120, a person's age has only increased by 20 percent. A white beard can't get any whiter, and one's skeletal structure can only relax to a certain level of curvature before the frame can contract no more. The skin becomes thinner until it has a translucent sheen that no longer changes color. There can be no more loss of elasticity after all elasticity has been lost. Alphons had reached a steady state. He might indeed live forever, with bits of data flowing through his veins instead of blood.

"I'm honored to meet you," he greeted Elsenia. "I've read your works. Who would have thought one could make a career out of classifying planets?"

Elsenia wasn't sure whether there was a degree of sarcasm in his remark. She ignored it.

"I'm here in search of my brother and sister."

"Yes, I know. Vega and Deneb. They were here. I received an inquiry from Admiral Chase and transmitted a full report of their visit."

"I know. I've read it. But perhaps you can tell me more. We were very close. Perhaps I can learn something from your recollections to shed light on their disappearance."

Alphons seemed to take offense at this. Elsenia sensed a mild hostility that she hadn't anticipated. In the accounts of their visits to Supply Ship 2, neither Admiral Chase nor Xyla had described Alphons as being the least bit defensive or standoffish. Why was he treating her differently? She changed the subject.

"I didn't start out to classify planets," Elsenia told him. "My interests evolved from my curiosity about the Tattoo People and their origin."

He laughed. It was a derisive laughter, and Elsenia found herself disliking the ancient physicist even more.

"The Tattoo People are nothing," he said. "They're a race of alien beings spread across the galaxy by seed-carrying asteroids. You're wasting your time. You're studying the fruit. You should be studying the tree."

"The vine?" she asked.

"Of course, the vine," he said rising from his chair. "You're a biologist. That's what you should study. Come with me."

Elsenia followed him to a room, which she knew to be the one he'd constructed for three-dimensional images. He'd used it at first to create realistic likenesses of galactic explorers. Now, with the light extinguished, the space filled with an incredibly precise rendition of the alien vine. Elsenia felt as if she were back on Carbonia again, desperately trying to return to the space capsule. She wondered how Alphons was able to simulate the appearance of the plant with such detailed accuracy. He certainly would have access to images, but the 3-D display held far more information than could be derived from one image. He must have used thousands in combination to reproduce the dimensions, color, and texture of the plant.

"It's beautiful," she said in awe.

"Thank you. I knew you'd like it. I spend much time in this room, observing the plant. It fascinates me, as it should you."

"Of course," Elsenia said. "Everyone appreciates the multifunctional design of the vine—that it was genetically engineered to be both the source of the Tattoo People and their sustenance."

"Is that all?" Alphons challenged.

"Well, ultimately I want to learn about the beings who created the vine—the race of aliens who produced the asteroids carrying the seeds from which the vine grew. But we've drawn a blank. Until we actually find one of those asteroids before it crashes into a planet, we'll remain ignorant of the vine's origin."

"True, but have you really learned everything there is to know about the vine?"

"The studies have been exhaustive—at least to the extent the Tattoo People will allow."

"Yes," mused Alphons. "And what is it that the Tattoo People will not allow?"

Elsenia thought about this. "They don't permit any disturbance of the root system." She pointed to the tendrils that hung from the vine's branches and disappeared into the ground. "They claim that when those tendrils are disturbed, the plant is injured."

"Injured how?" persisted Alphons.

"I'm not sure. I supposed it's because those roots are how the plant draws water and nutrients from the ground."

"In science, one should never suppose. And whenever the answer to a question is, 'I'm not sure', then that should be the impetus to pursue the answer even more vigorously."

"To really study the functionality of the tendrils, we'd have to dig them up."

"And that's never been done?"

"I don't believe so. It's not allowed."

Alphons laughed again, but this time it was not derisive or condescending. "I admire your naivety—that you believe because something is not allowed it has never been done. I can tell you, it has been tried."

"It has? By whom?" This surprised Elsenia.

Alphons hesitated, seeming to consider whether or not to answer her. Finally he said, "There have been hundreds of visits to planets infested by the vine. Explorers report the results in great detail. Usually, only the most exciting events and discoveries are noticed due to the tremendous volume of data examined. But I have more time on my hands than others, and I make a point of reviewing the reports of all planetary explorations—exciting or not. All of them."

Alphons rose and walked into the display. His body obstructed some of the laser beams producing the image and it began to dissolve. He bent to examine the quivering, pixilated remnant of one of the tendrils, pointing to where it disappeared into the floor.

"Every time one of the explorers attempted to dig up the root system of the plant, Tattoo People showed up immediately and stopped them."

"It's not allowed," Elsenia repeated.

"Right, but how is it that the Tattoo People show up so quickly to stop them?"

Elsenia started to answer. She was going to explain to him how the Tattoo People communicate so easily by radio waves, but Alphons knew this. That wasn't his question. When she realized what he was getting at, she knew the answer. "The plant called them."

"Right," said Alphons. He returned to his seat against the wall and the full image of the plant reappeared. "Once you accept that the plant is not just the vehicle carrying the seeds to start a new race of Tattoo People—once you begin to see the vine from a different perspective—it's very clear that the vine itself is a being."

Elsenia was stunned. It was the classic case of not being able to see the forest for the trees. Everyone concentrated on the Tattoo People because those were the beings that moved about and communicated with humans. No one had thought that the plant itself might be a fully conscious alien being. Alphons noticed the awareness settle upon Elsenia. "When you look at it this way," he said, "Your Tattoo People may be no more than caretakers of the vine."

Elsenia couldn't conceal her amazement. "All this time we've thought of the vine providing protection and bounty for the Tattoo People, but it's actually the other way around."

"Admittedly, it's a symbiotic relationship, but which one came first: the chicken or the egg?"

Elsenia remembered her experience on Carbonia. The vine had protected her. She was sure of it. She recalled the inescapable feeling that the vine felt sad—that it needed help. Imagine creating a race of beings whose job it was to protect you, but then watching them relentlessly and systematically destroy each other.

Alphons was smiling, a mischievous smile. "Don't beat yourself up over it. Think about it. It offers a rationale for classifying planets. You want to be a planetary psychologist, except it's not the planet you should be psychoanalyzing. It's the vine. Each one has, or develops, a unique personality, with both nature and nurture entering into the final outcome."

It made sense. Enlightenment fell on Elsenia like the first rays of the rising sun, but her next thought was more startling. Had Alphons told Vega and Deneb his theory? Did their visit to Supply Ship 2 have anything to do with their secret meeting with the Tattoo People on Lumina?

"Where are the twins?" Elsenia asked suddenly.

Alphons' face darkened. He spoke a command and the image of the vine disappeared. They were plunged into darkness momentarily until the lights in the room came on.

"I don't know."

"But you do know something."

Alphons walked from the room. He seemed now to show his full age, whatever that might be. He shuffled with a weary gait back to the galley, where he slumped into a chair.

"Could you please bring me a juice pack? In that cupboard."

He pointed with a trembling finger. Elsenia set the packet before him and watched as he fumbled to open it.

"Why hasn't the Union replaced you yet? You're too old to be a supply ship custodian. You should go to Aril and live out your life there. They have doctors."

Alphons sighed. "A replacement is on the way. Admiral Chase made the decision after his visit. But I won't leave except as a corpse. I have no planet to return to. And besides, I'd never be able to tolerate full gravity again. My body is too frail."

Elsenia watched him drink the juice, feeling profound pity for him. Here was a man not in the least ready to die. There were still too many questions in his mind, whose answers were "I'm not sure." Elsenia waited.

"Your siblings are performing an experiment for me," he admitted.

"An experiment?" she repeated, her pity disappearing—turning rapidly to rage. "What kind of experiment?"

"Actually two experiments," he said weakly. "Maybe three."

"What kind of experiments?" Elsenia demanded, unable to conceal her growing anger.

Alphons perked up. Whatever was in the juice pack had remarkable restorative properties.

"One you will appreciate; the other you may not."

"Where are they?" Elsenia asked.

"They arrived at my supply ship when I was formulating my theory about the vine. We discussed the idea. They were both intrigued by it, although not unusually surprised. It was actually Deneb who concluded that the only time we can study the root system of the vine is before the Tattoo People are created. Deneb's idea was to visit one of the planets—a UV type according to your naming system. At that stage in the plant's growth, the vine is unprotected, as we might surmise from the devastation brought upon planet Alpha by Carl Stormer and his men."

"So the twins are on their way to a UV planet?"

Alphons was quiet for a moment. "Not quite."

"What do you mean?"

"I mean one of them is."

"One of them?" Elsenia cried. "Just one of them! They're not together?"

"I didn't separate them. You make it sound as if I used force. They agreed to it. They are, after all, trained and Union-certified galactic explorers."

"Yes, but they've never been apart. How could you let them go different ways?"

This question produced another sigh from Alphons, long and drawn out. "They didn't go to different planets."

"Then..."

"Vega is here."

Elsenia stood, planting her hands on the table separating them. "Vega is here? What do you mean? Alphons, stop teasing me with bits of information and tell me what the hell's going on!"

He looked at her steadily, unflinching.

"If you sit, I will tell you."

She sat.

"As you pointed out, I'm an old man. The distance to the planet, a UV-60 planet, is such that it would take the twins three thousand years to reach it and then another three thousand years to return here to report their findings. They could, of course, send back the results via radio wave messages, but that also would take considerable time before the transmissions worked their way across the network. In either case, I feared I wouldn't be alive to hear about the results of Deneb's investigation."

Elsenia noticed that Alphons was choosing his words carefully. Much as she tried to anticipate him and draw him out more quickly, she held back, allowing him his own pace.

"This is where the other experiment comes in." He sipped more juice, a signal that this part needed additional strength. "I believe the twins can communicate by a mechanism that is not at all understood. Am I right?"

Elsenia nodded. The twins' ability had been inexplicable, even to the wise Arilians.

"I suggested to the twins that it might work even across

192

vast distances—instantaneously."

"That's ridiculous," she declared. "There's no evidence to suggest that the twins can read each other's thoughts at very large distances."

"As I understand it, there's no evidence to suggest they can't. There is no evidence because your mother would never allow the twins to be separated by a sufficient distance to test the hypothesis. They told me that."

"Yes, but it's also impossible because it's a fundamental law that information can't travel faster than light-speed."

"That's true in the classical world, but not in the quantum world. There's experimental evidence that quantum states can interact over large distances instantaneously. It's called the EPR paradox. EPR stands for Einstein, Podolsky, and Rosen, the three physicists who first posed the paradox."

"But the twins don't represent a quantum system. They're just brother and sister—not two spin states." Though Elsenia was a biologist, she had learned quantum mechanics at a young age.

"Are you sure? Do we know that macroscopic systems can't exhibit quantum mechanical behavior? Especially when..." Alphons stopped.

"Especially what?"

The old man was thinking. "In discussing spin states in quantum mechanics, a pair of photons is believed to exhibit quantum behavior if the two are entangled."

"Entangled?" Elsenia vaguely remembered the term.

"Yes. The simplest form of entanglement is when the two photons are created at the same time. They represent an entangled system."

"Do you mean to say Vega and Deneb are entangled because they're twins, created at the same time?"

"It's a hypothesis that has to be tested."

"But that's absurd. Why just them? There've been twins all through human history with no evidence to suggest they're quantum systems."

"No. Nothing obvious, but you have to admit that Vega

and Deneb are special. They exhibit a connection that's hard to explain. They often act as a single person."

Elsenia found herself wondering how Alphons could have known the twins so well after one visit, but she postponed that question for later. "Are you telling me that Vega stayed here to receive the results of Deneb's exploration of the UV-60 planet? Vega is here?"

"Not right here. She's frozen in her space capsule, executing a halo orbit about the supply ship."

Elsenia shook her head. "Then I can see her. Bring her here. I need to talk to her."

"Yes, we can do that, but there's more to tell you first."

The dark tone of his voice chilled her. "Go ahead."

"The twins expressed concern about not showing up for their rendezvous with the rest of your family. We selected a UV planet close enough so that if the experiment was successful, we'd send a message to Happiness to report the results and explain the twins' absence."

"And if the experiment wasn't successful?"

"Then Deneb was instructed to send a message to you explaining everything. It would get to Happiness before our message."

"But we never received any message."

"No," Alphons pronounced slowly. "Because there was a delay."

"What kind of delay?"

"We're not sure. We think Deneb had to reroute to a new destination. We believe by the time Deneb reached the UV-60 planet, it already had a population of Tattoo People."

"You're telling me Deneb didn't reach a test planet yet?"

"Right. I anticipated that might happen, so I gave Deneb an alternate destination. We believe he's on his way there now."

"How do you know that?"

Alphons' hands returned to the table, fingers set upon the surface, as if he were a professor instructing a student.

"We knew exactly when Deneb would arrive at the UV-

60 planet. I unfroze Vega at the prearranged time. They were supposed to make contact then."

"How did that go?" Elsenia asked, unable to conceal her contempt.

"Vega sat just where you're sitting now and told me Deneb had to divert."

"How can she know that?" said Elsenia with exasperation.

"She knows."

Elsenia's fist slammed down upon the table. "She knows nothing! Her brother is thousands of light years away. He may be dead for all she knows. How can she tell the difference?"

"I asked her the same question. She asserted with absolute confidence that Deneb is alive and frozen in his space capsule. There is a difference."

"There is no difference. There can be no difference. She's fooling herself. Get her back here. I need to talk to my sister."

Chapter 27

— Century 1964 —

Elsenia embraced Vega, never happier to see anyone in her entire life. Vega hadn't changed. Apparently, she hadn't spent much time unfrozen. She was still the petite beauty she'd grown up to be, thin-boned, but with impeccably carved features, and skin as lustrous as her mother's and eyes as dark and penetrating as her father's.

Her smile was weak. Elsenia could tell she was worried.

"Deneb?" was the first word she said, addressing this to Alphons, who just shook his head in response.

Vega seemed to drift off, turning inward, which irritated Elsenia because there was so much she wanted to ask her. She turned away, fixing her eyes on a computer monitor showing status data.

"He's still frozen," Vega pronounced. "He hasn't gotten there yet."

Elsenia grabbed her shoulder and spun her around, more strongly than she intended.

"How do you know? How can you know your brother's not dead?"

Vega looked at Alphons for help, but the old man sat with his elbows on the table, head resting on his hands. She turned to fix Elsenia with a defiant stare. "How do you know your hand is still attached to your arm?"

Elsenia was momentarily taken aback, but then said, "Because I can move my hand. How can you tell the difference between your brother being frozen and being dead?"

She responded by touching her hand to her heart. "I know."

Elsenia sighed in exasperation.

Alphons spoke. "Deneb would have sent a message if anything was wrong. The fact that we haven't heard from him means he's just following the prearranged plan."

"He's going to the second destination," added Vega. "I'm sure of it, Elsenia."

Elsenia looked sternly at her sister. "How can you be sure?"

"Don't be so skeptical, Elsenia. You know Deneb and I have had abilities that no one could explain—not you, or Mom, or Dad, or all the scientists and physicians on Aril who studied us through the years. I can't explain how I know what Deneb is doing and thinking, but I do."

Elsenia sighed. Alphons cleared his throat. "There is one other thing to worry about."

"What is that?" Elsenia asked.

He hesitated. "Until we hear something from Deneb, I think it best if Vega remains frozen until the actual time he reaches the alternate destination."

Talking to Alphons was like a puzzle. There was more content in what he didn't say than what he did say.

"Meaning…" Elsenia said.

"Meaning that I worry if Vega and Deneb's ages begin to diverge significantly, their abilities to communicate may be compromised. They may become disentangled, as it were."

Elsenia's rage had reached its limit. "You despicable old man!" she cried. "You can't keep yourself from meddling in other peoples' lives. It wasn't enough that you orchestrated the reunion of Xyla with Benjamin, leaving my mother widowed and me fatherless. Now you have the nerve to play with the lives of Ilsa's two children! It's a good thing my mother isn't here or she'd stuff you into the airlock and expel your pathetic body into space. I may, in fact, do it myself. You have no right using my siblings in your silly, sick experiments."

Vega had turned away from the computer monitor and was watching Elsenia intently.

"It wasn't all his idea."

"It doesn't matter if it was all his idea or not. It matters that it was any part his idea."

"It may yet work out," Alphons said quietly.

"How?! How can it work out if Deneb is frozen thousands

of light-years away and may be in trouble or dead—in spite of Vega's instincts?"

Alphons had no answer to this. Elsenia turned to leave the room. "Give me the coordinates of the alternate destination."

"What are you going to do?" Alphons asked.

"I'm going there to find Deneb."

"That's impossible. You'll get there way too late to find him."

"I don't care. I'm going to try. Do I need to send a message to Admiral Chase telling him what's going on, or can I trust you to do it?"

"I'll do it," Alphons answered somberly.

"Good. Be sure to send me any updates with commands to automatically unfreeze me. I want to hear any news as soon as possible."

"Right," he said, contritely. Elsenia's outburst had been effective in getting Alphons' cooperation.

"And freeze Vega again as quickly as possible. Don't unfreeze her unless you have a damned good reason."

"Okay," Elsenia heard Alphons say as she left.

A half hour later, Elsenia said goodbye to Vega, and her visit with Alphons Demetriano on Supply Ship 2 ended.

CHAPTER 28

— Century 1998 —

ALPHONS HAD PICKED POSSIBLE destinations for Deneb which, based on the best models available, were still thousands of years from being populated by Tattoo People. That should have given Deneb sufficient time to reach the planets before the vine's protectors hatched from its fruit. But these were only estimates. In any case, when Elsenia arrived at the second planet on Deneb's list of destinations, it too had a thriving population of Tattoo People. Perhaps this was better, because if Elsenia landed on the planet before it was inhabited, she wasn't sure what she'd learn. Now, she could ask the Tattoo People if they knew about a prior visit by a human from space, which was a longshot, as there was little reason they'd know about Deneb's visit if it happened before the first Tattoo People were born. She wondered whether she should have stopped at Deneb's first destination and asked the Tattoo People of that planet, but Vega seemed certain that Deneb had not landed there.

Elsenia hoped it wouldn't be difficult communicating with the Tattoo People on this planet. She was nervous and uncertain. Alphons had altered Elsenia's entire perception, now that she understood the Tattoo People to be merely protectors of the vine. Also, her experience on Carbonia gave her insight into their frailties—that they could be influenced to commit the types of atrocities she'd witnessed was enlightening in the most negative way imaginable. Elsenia fully recharged her EMP weapon before exiting the capsule. She planned to use the Arilian translating device, as usual, but was prepared for any adverse reaction after turning it on.

Thankfully, the Tattoo People who approached her displayed the same curiosity and interest reported by all galactic explorers. The translating device rendered her voice into a pattern of radio waves that must have been somewhat familiar to them. All Tattoo People used approximately the same language, with some variation from one planet to another. Arilian linguistic experts concluded that this language had been encoded into their genetic makeup in the same way other cognitive abilities were. This made sense. The creators of the Tattoo People wouldn't want the newly formed beings to have to go through the long arduous effort required to develop a new language. Even with the Tattoo People's excellent communication abilities, this would take time. If their job was to protect the vine, it would be counter-productive to have them spend several generations settling on a language.

The Tattoo People on this planet greeted Elsenia warmly. She spent a while explaining to them where she came from. They were predictably intrigued when told there were other populations of Tattoo People on distant planets. Elsenia talked to them about the vine. They were extremely forthcoming, extolling its virtues. Their admiration of the plant bordered on worship. They took Elsenia on a tour, proudly showing her the wonderful roads, tunnels, and watercourses they'd created. In the evening, they escorted her back to her space capsule. As they disappeared into the thicket, Elsenia saw them start to glow—that unique sapphire luminescence they emitted to illuminate the darkness.

Before Elsenia slept that evening, she considered how she might ask them if they knew of prior visits by humans—a visit that took place before their appearance. If they'd discovered an empty space vehicle on the planet, would they trust her enough to tell her? Elsenia suspected they would.

Before sleeping beneath her thermal blanket next to the space capsule, Elsenia activated the perimeter alarm, just as she had on Carbonia. She also kept the translator turned on. If Tattoo People were nearby, it would lock on the radio frequencies used in their silent communications and produce an audible tone. She'd be able to listen in on their conversation. Essentially, she'd be eavesdropping. Even though she understood this might prevent her from sleeping, she didn't want to miss out on any information she'd gain from their conversations.

As it turned out, the device was silent through much of the night, suggesting the Tattoo People were too far away for the translator to detect any signals. Elsenia slept soundly until early morning, when the sky first started to brighten with the rising sun. Then the translating device began to emit a faint, high-pitched wailing tone. It grew stronger, an eerie sound not unlike the mournful cries Elsenia remembered in recordings of ancient Earth societies after someone had died.

She rose from the ground, fully awake, trying to understand the source of the sound. She'd never heard anything so painfully sad. Elsenia spoke into the translator, moving about the clearing where the capsule sat.

"Hello!" She called. "Is anyone there? Is anyone out there?"

She heard no response and tried again, speaking loudly. The translating device emitted more powerful radio transmissions the louder one spoke into it.

"Can anyone hear me? Is everything okay?" She shouted into the instrument.

The thicket moved near her and she turned to see three Tattoo People emerge. Elsenia would've been frightened, but their expressions showed they were just as worried as she was.

"Everything is okay." The voice came from the translator, momentarily replacing the wailing sound. "It is okay. It is just the children."

Elsenia was confused. Tattoo children learn to speak via radio waves when very young. She'd never heard them cry.

"Are they sick?" she asked. "Why are they crying?"

"They are not sick. They are just too young. They are not used to the pain. The very young will cry until they grow accustomed to it."

"Accustomed to what? Why are they in pain?"

The one who'd been speaking paused as if thinking how to answer the question. Then he said, "Their heads hurt inside."

"But why?"

"It is the noise. The noise makes their heads hurt. We all hear it, but we are used to it. They are not."

Elsenia knew the Tattoo People couldn't hear sounds. The translating device was using the word "noise" in the technical sense of the word—random, incoherent signals that lack information and often obscure the intended signal.

"What noise?" she asked. "Where is the noise from?"

The Tattoo man raised his arm and pointed a thin finger toward the horizon. "The noise will continue all day as the star moves across the sky. Sometimes the noise is worse than other times."

Elsenia caught her breath. She knew exactly which star the man pointed to. It was the star around which the two planets Prosperity and Happiness orbited. She knew it well.

"Do any other stars produce noises when they're in the sky?" she asked.

"Yes. There is another—not so strong, but still painful to our young. They will get used to it eventually."

"When does the other one rise?" Elsenia asked.

It was a bad question. There was no commonality in the units of time used by the Tattoo People on different planets. The translating device wouldn't know how to interpret the answer.

The Tattoo man must have understood this because instead of answering, he stretched out his two arms, one pointing toward the star that had just risen and the other pointing downward toward the ground at almost a ninety degree angle. It meant the other star would rise a quarter of a day later, when the first star was overhead.

"It is worse when both stars are in the sky," he said.

Elsenia nodded. That was exactly where Aril and Sparil would be relative to the other two planets.

"There is a third star that produces pain, but not as strong. It is in that direction. He pointed downward, but at a smaller angular separation from the star on the horizon.

"Earth," Elsenia said softly.

"You know these stars?" the Tattoo man asked in a tone that was both accusatory and hopeful.

"Yes," she admitted.

The man's expression changed. Elsenia's hand instinctively reached for the EMP weapon.

"Can you make them stop the noise?" he said.

It was at that moment that many disconnected facts congealed in Elsenia's thoughts: the attack of the Tattoo People on her translator and their attack when she attempted to transmit back to her capsule. The Tattoo People, with their extraordinary sensitivity to radio waves, couldn't tolerate the noisy artificial signals generated by human transmitters. Apparently, they could tolerate them at low doses and at weak levels, but continuous exposure over many years produced irreparable damage to their minds. With the spread of human civilization, the use of radio waves to establish communication had increased a hundred-fold. Each of the communication hubs constructed powerful transmitters with huge antennas, almost competing with one another in their efforts to dominate the airways.

Carbonia was an XV-42—a very old planet. Its population had been exposed to radio waves from human transmitters for many thousands of years, which had driven them crazy. Was this their common fate?

"I can make them stop," Elsenia said without thinking. "But it will take a long time. I have to go there and tell them."

"It does not matter how long it takes. If you can make the noise stop, we will be very grateful."

"I'll do my best, but you must understand that the people producing this noise don't know they're doing anything harmful. They're just trying to communicate with each other in the same way that your people do. Except these people are separated by great distances and they must transmit very powerful signals to hear each other.

"We understand. Please let them know that their signals are painful to us."

"I will. I promise."

The wailing of the children coming from her translator had ceased, replaced now by a haunting melody, eerily tranquil.

"What is that?" she asked.

"It is what you call a song. We sing it to the children to calm them down. It makes the noise from the sky less painful, and then puts them to sleep."

Elsenia listened. The Arilian translator converted the radio wave song into something that sounded very much like a lullaby for human ears. In fact, she found herself growing relaxed and sleepy under the spell of its slow, lilting melody. She hoped she'd remember the song later. It was really quite beautiful.

The Tattoo People departed and Elsenia was left alone in the clearing, listening to the song and pondering the implications of what she'd just learned. In humanity's efforts to maintain communication among the planets and space vehicles scattered over this sector of the galaxy, it had bathed the cosmos in radio wave energy, seemingly benign and almost negligibly feeble. Yet to the sensitive Tattoo People, it was like a bright light flashing in one's eyes, or the irritating scrape of a fingernail across a chalkboard. One could easily imagine going insane after continuous exposure to such irritations.

When galactic exploration first began, the levels of radio wave signals were relatively low, and no doubt tolerable to early civilizations of Tattoo People. But gradually, as humans established civilizations on more planets in the Galactic Garden, signals not only grew stronger, but more pervasive. Humans unintentionally tortured the Tattoo People, who'd been unlucky enough to sprout from vines in this part of the galaxy.

Elsenia was anxious to leave and report back to Aril what she'd learned. Once in space, she'd transmit her report and hope that it'd find its way to Admiral Chase and Arilian authorities, but it would still be thousands of years before anything could be done to eliminate the transmissions.

Distracted by the plight of the Tattoo People, Elsenia still had learned nothing to help in her search for Deneb. The pitiful wailing of the suffering children stayed with her throughout the day. The Tattoo People did not reappear. She supposed they were waiting for her to take off on the voyage to fulfill the promise she'd made. Yet she couldn't leave until she'd made some effort to find out if they knew anything of Deneb.

In the waning light of day, Elsenia once again circled the

clearing, calling to the Tattoo People through the translating device. After a while, the three aliens returned.

"You are still here." It was both a question and a statement.

"I can't leave yet. I need to ask something."

From her previous studies, Elsenia knew that the question and answer concept didn't come easily to the Tattoo People. Their incredible communication skills made asking questions unnecessary. In their conversations, questions were answered without being asked. The Tattoo People now processed her questions before replying.

"You wish to know something?"

"Yes. I'm trying to find my brother. He may have visited your planet very long ago."

"Your brother is human?"

"Yes. Of course."

"You're the first and only human visitor we know of."

"And my spacecraft. Have you come upon similar vehicles anywhere on your planet?"

The translator was silent. Elsenia suspected and hoped that in the few seconds before they answered, a query went out to other Tattoo People all across the planet. They were readily capable of such feats of communication.

"No. We've found no such vehicle as yours."

Knowing how important her next question was, Elsenia chose her words carefully. "Do you know if my brother may have visited the planet before your people existed?"

This clearly confused the leader of the group and he looked at his two companions for help. Finally, he said, "We know nothing about what happened before we existed on this planet."

Then Elsenia took a huge gamble, and formed her fingers into the V sign she'd seen the vine make.

"Perhaps you can ask the vine if it knows anything about my brother."

This paralyzed the three. She watched them carefully to gage their reaction, but Tattoo People are as unreadable as the primitive robots manufactured by humans eons ago. In the next instant, they turned and disappeared into the forest.

Elsenia spent the evening trying to recreate her brief conversation with the Tattoo People, recalling their responses. What could she infer from their words and sudden departure when asked about the vine? She knew they depended on her to help them, but how much would they do for her in return?

The next day, Elsenia decided to delay her departure. Perhaps if they thought she wouldn't leave until they'd answered her question, they'd be more forthcoming.

It was midday before they showed up.

"We have little knowledge of events that took place here before our kind was created. It is knowledge hidden deep within our collective consciousness."

"I understand." Elsenia did understand. She understood that they wouldn't admit to their ability to communicate directly with the vine. They wanted her to believe the knowledge was coming from within their own minds. She was okay with that. She didn't care where the information came from, or how they pretended to get it.

"There was another of your kind who visited the planet before our civilization was created."

Elsenia's heart was pounding. It must have been Deneb.

"Did he leave the planet safely?"

This seemed to confuse the Tattoo man. "Yes," he said. The word emerged weakly from the translating device. The translator detected hesitation in the alien's response.

"Are you sure? Did the visitor leave safely?"

"Yes, I am sure, but the visitor was not your brother."

"Not my brother? How can you be sure?"

"Because the visitor was a female human."

Elsenia gasped. "A female?"

"Yes. If it will help you, I can tell you her name as it was remembered and passed down to us."

"Please tell me her name."

"The female visitor's name was Vega."

A thousand thoughts raced through Elsenia's mind at that

moment, none of them making any sense. The Tattoo man must have noticed her confusion and shock.

"Are you well? Do you know this person?"

"Vega is my sister, but she can not have been here."

"That is what our collective memory tells us."

"When was this visit? Can you tell me?"

"No," the alien said definitively. "We measure time by generations. There is no way to measure time before our creation."

"And are you sure this was the only visitor to your planet before me?"

"She was the only visitor we have any record of. We can not say for sure, but our memory is very complete."

Elsenia tried to think of some explanation that would account for Vega's presence on this planet thousands of years earlier, but nothing made sense at all. She needed to concentrate, but couldn't do it with the Tattoo People standing before her. They'd given her what she asked for.

"Thank you," She said. "I'll go now."

But where would she go? Her first inclination was to return to Supply Ship 2 and confront Alphons and Vega—tell them what the Tattoo People had said and ask for an explanation. Somehow, Elsenia didn't really believe she'd learn anything from them that would account for the inexplicable visit of a woman named Vega thousands of years ago. Elsensia could do the math in her head. There was no way Vega was there and on Supply Ship 2 at the time she saw her there. Something was very odd. And where was Deneb? She still knew nothing that would help in that search.

She was about to reenter her capsule with these contradictory facts in her head when she glanced back and saw the three Tattoo People, still standing at the edge of the thicket, watching her with expressions of curiosity and concern. The leader of the group walked toward her and Elsenia turned to him, making sure the translating device was still on.

When he was a meter away, he held out his hand and touched her arm. Then he extended the other arm skyward. It was a purposeful gesture, with his index finger fixed at a point in the sky somewhat lower than the afternoon sun.

"She said she was going there."

Elsenia looked in the direction he pointed. What did he mean? If he was just telling her she had blasted off into space, why point in that direction? Why not point straight up, which was the way the capsule would ascend?

"What do you mean? She returned to space. Right?"

"Yes. There," he repeated, his finger still directed to the same spot in the sky.

Elsenia raised her arm and pointed in the same direction. "There?"

"Yes."

She peered into the blue sky as if it might suddenly reveal the destination of the mysterious space traveler who had the same name as her sister.

"How could you know where she was going?" I asked.

He lowered his arm. "I cannot say."

With that, he turned and disappeared with his two friends into the vine.

AFTER she lifted off from the planet and was enjoying the familiar weightlessness of space, Elsenia activated the computer system to display the stars of the Galactic Garden. She circled the star system she'd just visited. Then she located the stars around which Aril and Happiness orbited, highlighting them in different colors. She used other symbols to display the Union supply ships. Finally, she found Earth and its sun. She centered her current location on the screen, then rotated the display so that Happiness was to the right. This was the first point the Tattoo man had indicated when he directed his arm toward the horizon. The second source of radio waves he'd identified was downward and to the right of center in her display. As she expected, this was the direction of Aril and Sparil. The third direction he'd pointed was toward Earth. She marked the final destination the alien had pointed to, the one where he said Vega had gone. It was also to the right and downward, on a line that passed in between Happiness and Aril. Elsenia followed this line from her current location to distances well outside the Galactic Garden. There was no destination of note along that line. She commanded the computer to display every planet with Tattoo People, wondering whether Vega had decided to visit another of those. There were two, approximately along the line. Had Vega gone to one of those planets?

While she considered this, Elsenia recalled the message that Druix had gotten from Xyla. She'd told him to go to Aurora. Elsenia felt a shiver pass through her as she zoomed out to show a larger portion of the galaxy. Extending the superposed line, she saw that it passed directly through Aurora's star. Vega, or she who called herself Vega, may very well be going to the same planet as Druix. The questions tumbling about in her head confused and troubled her. She suddenly felt extremely tired, almost anxious to enter the magnetocryogenic chamber and enjoy the oblivion of being frozen, even though she knew it would in no way provide the rest she craved.

How was it possible, that she'd seen Vega on SS2—embraced her and talked to her—but then been told she'd visited the UV-60 planet long before Elsenia got there? Had Vega left after her and traveled faster, arriving several thousand years before her? Had she been there even before she showed up on SS2? It was possible, but according to the observations and models, that visit would have predated the impact of the asteroid carrying the alien vine. Was it possible another explorer named Vega had showed up coincidentally? Or had the visitor been Deneb? Could he have been mistaken for female? Then why did he use Vega's name? The name would've been translated through the Arilian translating device. Maybe something was lost in the translation from radio waves to audible signals.

In spite of her confusion, one thing was very clear, and the clarity of that fact both comforted her and added to her confusion. She wanted to see Admiral Chase—that of all the people in her life, he was the one she most wanted to sit with and puzzle over what she'd learned on this UV-60 planet.

Elsenia dug in the pocket of her jumpsuit and retrieved

the medallion the Admiral had given her, wondering whether she should take advantage of his invitation and meet him at the next possible rendezvous point programmed into its memory. She put the decision off and set a course to visit her old friends Hespera and Johanis on Supply Ship 5. She needed to resupply her capsule in any case. Without further thought, Elsenia departed the planet.

CHAPTER 29
— Century 2025 —

NIGHTMARISH AS ELSENIA'S visit to Carbonia had been, it turned out to be extremely fortunate that she'd gone. When Admiral Chase landed there, he found conditions hadn't changed from what Elsenia described. The Earth Fleet Commander felt the circumstances were such that drastic measures were called for. Thus, although strictly forbidden by the Union, the Arilians, and the universal code of exploration ethics, he and his men used an EMP weapon to stun one of the wild Tattoo People and capture him. They transported him to Sparil, where Arilian scientists could examine the complex wiring of his mind to determine what had gone wrong.

After they performed many weeks of tests, the Arilians diagnosed the problem by probing the alien with a variety of sensitive electromagnetic detectors to determine the abnormalities in his brain activity causing the madness. Once they did, they were able to find a remedy, but not a cure. The Arilian scientists confirmed what Elsenia had suspected. The Tattoo man was reacting to low levels of radio wave energy in the ambient medium. His expected ability to focus on a specific radio transmission from a nearby source and filter out all other background signals was completely absent. He attempted to listen to all transmissions without discrimination, a form of attention deficit, which in its extreme form produced psychotic behavior, as he was also unable to block out violent and destructive thoughts. He heard voices, and the voices told him to commit vicious, indiscriminate acts of violence.

The captured Tattoo Person was completely irrational and uncontrollable until placed in an anechoic chamber. The room, whose walls, ceilings, and floors were covered with conically shaped radio wave absorbers, created an electromagnetic environment completely free of interference or noise. The tranquility and calm exhibited by the alien was striking. The discomfort and pain returned dramatically whenever the door to the room opened.

The alien immediately resumed his extreme behavior. The Arilian scientists concluded that the aliens were being simply driven mad by exposure to radio waves from space.

The captured Tattoo man was given a prolonged period of rehabilitation. Under careful treatment by Arilian physicians, he fully recovered his capacity to reason and communicate. He was fitted with a metallic helmet, that protected him from a large fraction of the ambient radio wave energy. After a while, he was able to remember his name. It was Nolondi. Like other Tattoo People, he was inherently bright, and his capacity to assimilate information quickly facilitated his education and training. Eventually, he fully understood what had happened, and he expressed a willingness to help his human friends mitigate the destructive effects of radio wave transmissions on his people. Admiral Chase asked if he'd be willing to become a member of his crew. Having one of the Tattoo People on board would be a tremendous benefit when they visited planets with alien populations. Nolondi accepted the offer without hesitation. He underwent an accelerated course in the skills and knowledge needed for space travel. Six months later, he joined Admiral Chase's command ship as it departed from Aril, continuing its patrol of the Galactic Garden.

CHAPTER 30

— Century 2031 —

HESPERA AND JOHANIS were as bubbly and effusive as ever when Elsenia boarded their supply ship. They seemed unable to perceive that Elsenia was preoccupied with matters far beyond the limited world of a supply ship. She related to them the outcome of her visit with Alphons and her success in finding Vega. She recounted her visit to the UV-60 planet, where the children of the Tattoo People wailed in pain from the radio transmissions of other planets. Then she told of her astonishment when finding that Vega had visited the planet earlier, even though she couldn't explain her sister's simultaneous presence there and on Supply Ship 2. Hespera and Johanis listened with polite interest but failed to understand the full import or seriousness of Elsenia's experiences. The couple's world on Supply Ship 5 wasn't easily shaken by external influences.

While Elsenia puzzled through events, she considered where to go next. She could return to Supply Ship 2 and confront Alphons and Vega with what she'd learned. Or go to Aurora where Druix, and possibly Vega were. Or perhaps she should make use of Admiral Chase's rendezvous plan and find the intrepid Earth Fleet Commander. Certainly he'd be intrigued by what had happened to her. Hespera, who clapped her hands together in matronly concern, interrupted her thinking.

"Why Elsenia, we thought you'd go back to Magnetonia."

"Why would I go there?"

"Because that's where your mother is going."

"What!?" said Elsenia in surprise.

"You didn't know?"

"No, I didn't," answered Elsenia thoughtfully.

"She stopped at Supply Ship 6 five thousand years ago. She told Rashera she'd visit Magnetonia. She seemed excited by the longevity of the people there."

"Longevity!" Elsenia cried. "What longevity? They live for

a few hundred years. That's not longevity. She was injured. She's not thinking straight. When's she getting there?"

Hespera looked at Johanis, who mumbled some calculations and produced an answer. "In about two thousand years. You may not be able to get there in time to meet her."

"I have to get to her. She doesn't know what she's doing. She'll die on Magnetonia."

Johanis seemed to finally understand the urgency of the situation. "Stay here. I'll perform more accurate calculations."

With some effort, Elsenia remained in the galley with Hespera till Johanis returned, scratching his head in thought.

"We can remove all excessive weight from your capsule. I've analyzed the possible routes between here and Magnetonia, making use of gravity assists from stars in the vicinity. With a stripped down space vehicle and using the maximum amount of fuel while still leaving enough for a landing and lift-off, you'll arrive on the planet within a few years after your mother."

"That's good enough," said Elsenia. "Please, tell me what I need to do."

CHAPTER 31
— Century 2064 —

ELSENIA arrived on Magnetonia five years after Ilsa. She wondered what had happened to her mother in the intervening time. She remembered her discussions with the robotic Lemmy during her last visit. Elsenia was concerned that Ilsa had become the type of person with negative energy that would be repelled by the planet. She'd certainly have difficulty surviving there.

Upon her arrival, Elsenia was happy to see little changed since her last visit. The beauty of the alien vine guided into graceful arches and loops by the planet's strong magnetic field was still evident. With the long life spans of the population, not as many generations had passed in the interim, perhaps giving the society more inertia and permanence than other human civilizations. Still, enough time had lapsed that Elsenia wondered if they'd remember her last visit. Would they have records of Ilsa's arrival, just five years earlier and know where she was now?

At Magnetonia's spaceport, Elsenia was met by a young woman. Although Magnetonians lived hundreds of years, people didn't remain youthful any longer than they did on other planets. Developmentally, the first hundred years of life were very much like that of other humans. It was only after the first century that the miraculous restorative powers of the planet became noticeable. Thus, the young woman who met Elsenia was no more than thirty years old, and she displayed an almost child-like exuberance at the opportunity she'd been presented. Space travelers didn't arrive on Magnetonia often. Even if one lived a few hundred years, the odds that such an encounter might take place during one lifetime were very small.

She introduced herself as Jaylene. Union English was the adopted language of Magnetonia, and Jaylene's was more than just understandable; it was precise and flawless. It occurred to Elsenia that she and this young woman were only a couple of years apart in age, yet the differences between them were vast. Compared to what Elsenia had experienced in three decades, Jaylene had hardly lived at all, but she was extremely intelligent. In the course of conversation, Elsenia realized that not only did Jaylene comprehend what was said, she also understood the deeper meaning behind the words. Jaylene seemed to know the intent of Elsenia's sentences before she completed them. Given it was customary for galactic space travelers to announce their arrival on a planet weeks in advance, had this smart, young woman researched Elsenia to the extent of knowing not only the facts of Elsenia's life, but also the hidden forces that shaped them? Thus, Jaylene knew that Elsenia had returned to Magnetonia to find her mother. Within a day after she arrived, Jaylene drove Elsenia along magnetized tracks in a slim, bullet-shaped vehicle to Ilsa. Jaylene explained that Ilsa wasn't well and was being treated in a special facility several hours outside the city. In the car's back seat, Elsenia fixed on the panoramic views of the curving, twisted arcades formed by the alien vine, growing along the invisible lines of Magnetonia's magnetic field.

Elsenia wondered whether the vine was happy. She'd grown accustomed to thinking of it as a sentient life form, and regularly looked for evidence of that sentience. Just how smart was the vine? Elsenia knew of no metric by which to measure it. With Jaylene, the quickness of her wit, the depth of her understanding, and the precision of her words were all hallmarks of the young woman's intelligence. But how might one measure the intelligence of a plant? To what depths did the vine's awareness extend? Did it know it was being trained by humans to decorate their parks, shade their walkways, and support their bridges? Did the vine mind being used by another species? Was it disappointed that it'd been unable to produce a race of Tattoo People, which was perhaps the ultimate purpose of its existence? In the past, Elsenia would've spent little time worrying about the feelings of a plant, but her experience on Carbonia had indelibly altered her perceptions of the vine, and to some extent all plants.

The vegetation became denser as they traveled out of the city. Soon, the corridors were little wider than the bullet-shaped vehicle itself. The branches of the vine scraped against the windows of the car, accentuating the swiftness of its motion. Then, abruptly, the vista opened up, revealing a large concrete building surrounded by grass. Its angular lines stood out in sharp contrast to other buildings they'd passed. It might have been a prison, or some other type of institution where architectural accents were eminently superfluous.

Jaylene stopped at the front entrance and the transparent shell of the vehicle hissed open. Elsenia climbed out. The staff of the hospital seemed to be expecting them and greeted Elsenia warmly. Once inside, Jaylene left Elsenia in a waiting area. She sat on a chair padded with soft plastic that yielded to her almost as if it were living tissue. It shifted and reshaped itself in response to her weight and movements as if it were embracing her, adjusting its grip for added comfort.

Elsenia was oblivious to the strange furnishings distributed around the waiting area. There were straight lines where there should have been curves, and angles where there should have been arcs. The human mind grows accustomed to shapes and colors just as it adapts to sounds and smells. In the same way the brain ignores confusing or offensive signals, Elsenia's mind was shutting out the odd surroundings of the waiting area.

Several minutes later, Jaylene returned with one of the doctors, a middle-aged man with no hair, wearing a white smock that made him look more like a monk than a physician.

"Good afternoon, Ms. Mizello," he said. "I am Artaxo Saint Garibal. I am your mother's physician. You may call me Art."

"Thank you, Art," Elsenia replied, feeling odd.

"I hope Jaylene has warned you that your mother isn't doing well. She's shown little improvement since she was brought to this facility two years ago."

Elsenia nodded, unsure of what to say. Artaxo took her arm and escorted her through the hallways of the hospital. The lighting was greenish in color, a glow cast by a pair of parallel beams of light running the length of the hall. The luminescence was not confined by glass in any way. It was the air itself that glowed, producing the eerie illumination.

They passed many doorways. Elsenia wondered how far into the facility they'd have to go before they came to Ilsa's room. As it turned out, they passed every door in the corridor and exited the building at the back. Crossing a small patch of lawn, they entered a separate building in the shape of a half cylinder. Elsenia was reminded of old hangars that protected aircraft. Inside was an enormous coil of copper wire that was wound around the interior surface of the structure. Half of the cylindrical coil was below floor level. Within the center of the coil, oriented along its axis, was a bed on which Ilsa lay.

Elsenia approached, her boots echoing in the emptiness of the space within the building. Other than the bed, there was nothing else. When she was close enough to see her mother, her heart sank. She could barely recognize her. Ilsa's cheeks were sunken, and the dim light of the room cast cadaverous shadows across her face. Her eyes were open, but they stared upward, unblinking, seeing nothing. Elsenia moved to stand next to the bed. She reached for Ilsa's hand to hold it. It was warm, but otherwise lifeless and inert.

"Mom," she said.

"She doesn't respond," said Artaxo.

"Why is she in this place?" asked Elsenia.

"We're treating her with magnetic fields. We're attempting to correct her polarity."

"Her polarity?"

"Yes. When people get sick on Magnetonia, it usually means their magnetic equilibrium has been disturbed. We correct that by subjecting them to strong magnetic fields to help them get realigned."

"You've been subjecting my mother to magnetic fields for two years?"

"Yes, but not always in the same direction. We alternate the polarity every few weeks."

"Why?"

"We're not quite sure what polarity she's supposed to

have, so we try both."

Elsenia let Ilsa's hand fall to the bed. She turned to face Artaxo. "Let me get this straight. You don't know which polarity my mother is supposed to have, so you're subjecting her to magnetic fields of reversing polarity just to make sure."

"Yes."

"And you've been doing this for two years and she's not getting better."

"I'm afraid not."

"Given your lack of success with this treatment, shouldn't you try some other treatment?"

Artaxo looked confused. "There is no other treatment."

"No other treatment. No drugs, no surgery, no X-rays?"

Artaxo was deep in thought. "I've heard of such things, but certainly they're not necessary here on Magnetonia. People seldom get sick here, and when they do, it's usually just a matter of adjusting their polarity."

Elsenia was appalled at the primitive state of Magnetonian medicine, but she tried to keep her patience. Compared to Aril, Magnetonian medical science was in its infancy. How could they be so behind other human-inhabited planets? She turned away from Artaxo, barely concealing her disgust. Sitting on the bed next to Ilsa, she held her hand again.

"Mom, can you hear me?"

There was no response. Ilsa's eyes didn't move.

Elsenia felt something tugging at her neck. She glanced down and saw the rendezvous medallion that Ilsa had given her floating upward. The magnetic field generated by the coils about the room was lifting the medallion. It drifted slowly, suspended just to one side of Ilsa's field of view. Ilsa turned her head, and her eyes found the medallion. Then her hand reached up to grab it. Elsenia, sobbing with joy, removed the iridescent strand from around her neck and placed it in Ilsa's outstretched hand. Her mother's mouth began to move, trying to speak words that just wouldn't emerge.

"Don't try to speak, Mom. Just rest. Don't worry. I'll get

you out of here. I'm going to take you elsewhere to be treated."

JAYLENE WAS WAITING in the lobby of the hospital. "You're going to take your mother from the hospital?" she said.

"Yes. How can we do that?"

"I can help with that." Jaylene rose from where she was sitting and gave Elsenia's arm a reassuring pat. "The treatment wasn't working?"

"What treatment?" Elsenia replied, exasperated

"The magnetic field," Jaylene offered.

Elsenia lifted her arm and showed Jaylene an LED indicator built into the sleeve of her jumpsuit. "Jaylene, this is a magnetometer. It measures magnetic fields. I've been watching it since my arrival here. There are strong magnetic fields all over the planet and they change direction and strength all the time. Your whole planet is bathed in magnetism. How is putting my mother inside a coil of artificially created magnetism going to do anything for her that just moving around the planet hasn't done?"

"You know of other methods of treatment?"

Elsenia sighed. "Yes, Jaylene. I know of many other treatments."

Jaylene was quiet, almost wistful. "Okay," she said finally. "I will make the arrangements to have your mother removed."

She turned to walk away.

"Jaylene," Elsenia called. "If you help me, if you help me get my mother out of here and back onto her space capsule so we can leave Magnetonia together, I will give you something to read. I will give you many things to read. There's knowledge in the computer of my space capsule—books on medicine and the treatment of illness and disease. You'll have it all to read and study."

Jaylene's face brightened. "I'd like that very much!"

She hurried away, the youthful vigor back in her step.

By the next day, two space capsules had been readied for launch at Magnetonia's spaceport. Elsenia fulfilled her promise and downloaded all the books and documents on medicine onto a reading device, which she presented to Jaylene. It would keep the young woman occupied for many years, and perhaps motivate others on Magnetonia to study medicine as well. On the other hand, maybe the inexplicable longevity of Magnetonia's population made the study of medicine obsolete. If no one ever got sick, what was the point? Was knowledge only worth knowing, if it contributed to matters of life or death? Shouldn't the people of Magnetonia understand human physiology even if they didn't need that knowledge to stay alive? Elsenia promised herself she'd return to Magnetonia in the future to see if the seed of knowledge she'd planted with Jaylene produced any change in the fabric of the planet's civilization. For now, she was just anxious to help her mother.

Their first stop was back at Supply Ship 5 to refuel before going to Aril, where Ilsa would get medical treatment far superior to what she'd been receiving.

CHAPTER 32

— Century 2088 —

AFTER LEAVING ARIL, Admiral Chase's command ship stopped at Supply Ship 6. The Admiral was anxious to speak with Rashera again about the asteroid he'd destroyed. Her instincts had been correct about the purpose of the missile, but he felt there was more to the story. As he expected, Rashera had continued her analysis and research. Like her mother, her mind often wandered into areas not frequented by others.

"I've been thinking more about the asteroid and Fermi's Paradox," said Rashera. "If I were a civilization that wanted to destroy others in competition for control of the galaxy, I'd devise a scheme for detecting and attacking advanced civilizations as they arose."

"The first challenge would be detecting them," Admiral Chase asserted.

"Right. What features would you look for in a civilization to suggest it might be a threat? Certainly, the ability to travel into space would indicate a race that wants to expand beyond the limits of its own planet. Space travel requires communication with the home planet through transmission of coded signals via electromagnetic radiation. Based on practical limitations, we've found radio waves are the most efficient means for interstellar communication. Any civilization wanting to seek out other advanced beings, for whatever reason, would conduct that search with large radio telescopes. Earthlings did that long ago, unsuccessfully, fueling discussion of Fermi's Paradox. The Arilians were successful though. If you remember, that's how they suspected life on the planet Happiness, a suspicion proven correct with the discovery of the Tattoo People."

"Okay, so first you look for radio wave sources in the galaxy."

"Yes, and the next step, if yours is the type of civilization not wanting competition in the game of galactic colonization, is to develop a weapon to destroy all upstart civilizations."

"The planet-destroying asteroid."

"Right, but this isn't as easy as it sounds."

"It doesn't sound easy at all."

"It's not, except that I've already told you how devastating a large asteroid can be to a planet, by virtue of doing nothing more than falling on it. You don't need nuclear weapons, disintegrating rays, or black holes."

"But how do you get the asteroid to fall on the planet?"

"That's a challenge. The propulsion required to move a large asteroid out of its own orbit is tremendous. I've done calculations based on the asteroid you destroyed to see if shooting metal cylinders out of a magnetic cannon could move something that large to a distant target."

"Can it?"

"Yes, but only if the asteroid is out in interstellar space, far from the gravitational field of any star or planet. It has to be, or the propulsion needed to disengage it from its orbit would be far greater than could be supplied by a simple magnetic cannon."

"So how do they get the asteroid to escape?"

"That's the problem that baffled me for a long time, but I think I have an explanation."

"We're listening."

"Have you heard of Lagrangian points?"

"Sure. They're locations in Earth's solar system where satellites can remain in stable locations relative to the Earth and Sun."

"Close, but more precisely, if you have two large bodies, like Earth and the Sun, where one is orbiting the other, then there are points where objects, like satellites, can be placed and remain, stably locked because the gravitational forces of the two larger objects balance each other. In Earth's solar system, there exists a collection of asteroids at the Lagrangian points defined by Jupiter and the Sun. In a galaxy with billions of stars, each with its own gravitational field, there may be a great number of stable Lagrangian points, where any matter arriving with just the right speed and direction becomes locked, exactly balanced by the competing gravitational attractions from all the stars around it. Once at that point, the object will stay there forever.

"The calculation of stable Lagrangian points is complex. If there are three large objects instead of two, the calculation becomes much more difficult. But just because it's difficult, does not mean it can't be done."

"How many of those points might there be in the galaxy?"

"There could be millions."

"Is this the explanation for the missing mass in the universe?"

"Probably not. Even with millions of stable points in the galaxy, the likelihood that an object will reach it with the right velocity to become trapped is very small. But if I'm right and there are unknown objects at the galaxy's Lagrangian points, then my guess is they've been there a long time—since the earliest times. Remember, if there's enough matter at any of these points, then it will coalesce into a star, so we need locations where there isn't enough matter to form a star. I believe our xenophobic aliens took advantage of such objects to construct their planet-destroying weapons."

"How did they find them?"

"Good question. They may've developed computers sophisticated and fast enough to calculate the Lagrangian points given the masses and locations of the stars, which would be an incredibly difficult calculation, but still not impossible. Another likely possibility is that they developed a means of finding them observationally. I favor that explanation because the numerical approach would yield far too many locations. An observational technique would only give the Lagrangian points that contain large masses. Perhaps a combination of techniques was used."

"So you're saying this alien civilization found asteroids already waiting in interstellar space and decided to use them as ballistic projectiles to destroy planets?"

"Right. All they'd have to do is excavate holes, install a small nuclear reactor, construct a magnetic cannon, and then put an array of antennas on the surface as part of the weapon's guidance system. With a source of radio waves detected, the magnetic cannon can be activated and the asteroid nudged out of an orbit that's been its home for billions of years. If the aliens were really smart, they'd use a gravity assist from nearby stars in navigating the asteroid to its target more quickly."

"It seems like a very slow process."

"Extremely slow. The asteroids would never move faster than a fraction of light speed, and most of the time travel slower than that. But remember, this civilization may be ancient. Perhaps it arose in the first billion years of the galaxy's fifteen billion year lifetime. That allows plenty of time to find the objects, convert them into ballistic weapons, and set them to work scouring the galaxy of other advanced civilizations. It might take millions or hundreds of millions of years. Eventually they'd find their targets."

"It seems a lot of trouble to go to just because a civilization on another planet might become a threat. Human civilization has space technology. We've launched thousands of vehicles to explore the galaxy, but we're a long way from looking for other planets to conquer."

"You're right.It's more than just planetary paranoia."

"What else?"

At this, Rashera looked at Nolondi. He sat impassively, watching the humans, his face expressionless. He shifted nervously in his chair.

"I don't know," Nolondi said. "Other Tattoo People might. Although all knowledge is shared among the population, I believe there's information that only a few of our people possess. It's an ancient secret. I'm sorry I can't help you."

"In any case," put in Admiral Chase, "We need to alert the galactic explorer fleet of the possible presence of these asteroids in interstellar space. It would help to have computer calculations of where the Lagrangian points are. It'll increase the odds that an explorer will find one to confirm the existence of other asteroids."

"I've already started," said Rashera. "The computer is cranking away, but slowly. I'll transmit updates as I have them."

"I'll check out one of the locations with the command ship," said Admiral Chase.

"Admiral Chase, can I make a suggestion?" It was Nolondi.

"Certainly. Anytime."

"Given your questions about what my people might know about the origin of the asteroids you seek, a visit to a planet with Tattoo People might be helpful. Perhaps they will talk to me."

"Excellent suggestion," agreed Admiral Chase. "Do you recommend any planet in particular?"

"Preferably one where you've been before. If they know you, they'll be more open."

"Either Happiness or Lumina. I don't suppose Carbonia would work."

"No, Carbonia won't work. One of the others."

"Lumina is closer," said Rashera.

"Okay," said Admiral Chase. "We'll go there next."

CHAPTER 33

— Century 2167 —

ELSENIA AND ILSA never made it to Aril. While still a thousand light-years from the planet, a high priority message from Admiral Chase triggered Elsenia's unfreezing. The message contained two pieces of information, each equally surprising.

The first was a report from Risto Jalonen, relayed through the Admiral's command ship. Risto had arrived at Earth in the year 211,113. Unable to find information about the twins, he turned his attention to historical records of when Druix and Ilsa had visited Earth. He learned that Petyuba was a legendary healer of that era, a brilliant physician regarded with awe and admiration by Earthlings. She had pioneered the use of stem cells to repair damaged tissue, a procedure that had been in use for thousands of years, but Petyuba perfected the practice to such an extent that virtually any illness or injury could be cured. With Petyuba's implementation, stem cell replacement was almost a panacea for death itself.

However, Petyuba's life was surrounded by controversy because she was a difficult and eccentric person, a social outcast whose genius did not extend to her ability to communicate or collaborate with her peers. She did her work in total isolation, and her accomplishments were viewed with doubt and suspicion. Among the transgressions she was accused of was using her own stem cells to treat her patients. At that time on Earth, DNA was carefully controlled, but the use of stem cells in the treatment of illnesses confused the DNA make-up of the patients treated. Some of Petyuba's serious cases had been given so many of her stem cells that they became more and more like the insular and irritable physician. This was viewed as a breach of ethics, and Petyuba was eventually prosecuted. As a part of a plea-bargain agreement, she lived out the remainder of her long life in a self-imposed house arrest at her undersea home.

Risto concluded his report by saying that in all likelihood,

Petyuba had been using her own stem cells to treat Ilsa. Given the extent of her injuries, described by Druix, substantial quantities of the old woman's stem cells undoubtedly performed the miraculous healing during the time Druix and Ilsa lived in her house.

Risto's report contained a postscript, in which he admitted that he'd considered remaining on Earth for the rest of his natural life. Instead, he decided to resume his galactic explorations. Given his brush with death from exposure to cosmic rays, he didn't expect to last long , but somehow this seemed better than spending many years in the confines of Earth society and gravity, two equally restricting burdens to his spirit.

Before Elsenia could ponder the implications of Risto's report, she read the second part of Admiral Chase's message. The Admiral had received a transmission from Alphons Demetriano reporting that Vega departed Supply Ship 2 in the 2040th Century to return to Lumina and would arrive in the 2200th Century. As enigmatic as ever, Alphons had advised Admiral Chase to be ready to receive a report from Vega that could be vital to the survival of human civilization in the galaxy.

Elsenia looked at the galaxy clock in her space capsule and performed a quick calculation. She could make it to Lumina almost in time, but she'd have to abort her trip to Aril with her mother. She considered letting Ilsa continue the journey alone, but somehow she couldn't bring herself to abandon her mother. The fact that Ilsa might not be sick at all, but simply suffering from an excess of stem cells from an unscrupulous 1646th Century healer seemed to detract from the immediacy of her treatment by Arilian physicians.

Elsenia broadcast a brief reply to Admiral Chase that she was on her way to Lumina and would be there in time to meet Vega. Then she reprogrammed the navigation systems in her own capsule and Ilsa's to change course. She would've liked to spend several hours pondering the gist of Alphons' cryptic message to Admiral Chase, but she knew it was a waste of time without more information. Her last thought before being frozen in the chamber for the voyage to Lumina was about Alphons' warning. She puzzled over what she, Ilsa, and Vega could possibly do to save human civilization in the galaxy.

CHAPTER 34

— Century 2190 —

DRUIX PROGRAMMED his space capsule to unfreeze him as soon as its proximity sensors detected another vehicle. Other galactic explorers were unlikely to be near the planet Aurora. Thus, when he was unfrozen, he was confident that he'd found Deneb. Two vehicles moving at half the speed of light required several years to safely approach and dock with each other. So Druix returned to his magnetocryogenic chamber, relying on the two capsules to handle the rendezvous automatically. Deneb was warned, of course, that another vehicle was approaching. By the time the docking procedure was complete, he anticipated correctly the reunion with his father.

They embraced, steadying themselves in the weightlessness of the docked space capsules.

"What are you doing here?" asked Deneb.

"That's my question to you," answered Druix. "We were expecting you and your sister on Happiness. Where's Vega?"

"She's with Alphons Demetriano on SS2. It's a long story."

"Druix glanced at the oxygen gauge of his capsule. He had about 38 hours remaining. He didn't know how much Deneb had in his. It was never good to let the oxygen level fall below 24 hours. It might be needed in an emergency.

"You're going to Aurora?" he asked his son.

"Yes. How did you know? How did you find me?"

"It's hard to explain. I can tell you when we have time, but first I want to hear what you know about Aurora. What made you decide to go there?"

"That's hard to explain, too. I decided to come here after visiting a planet that had a mature vine, but no Tattoo People. While there, I had a premonition. Or, strictly speaking, Vega had a premonition."

"She was with you when you visited the planet?"

"Yes and no, it doesn't matter. She had the premonition."

"What kind of premonition?"

"That we're all in danger," Deneb answered.

"Danger from what?"

"She couldn't tell. All she could say is that it comes from Aurora. I'm going there to find out."

"You're saying that you embarked on a 25000 year voyage across the galaxy because your sister, who may or may not have been with you on a planet with an alien vine, had a premonition?"

"Something like that," said Deneb. "Dad, don't be shocked. Vega and I have had expanded perception all our lives. Most of the time we have feelings about things, they turn out to be true."

"I know," agreed Druix. "And you don't have to convince me. I found you because of a similar experience with expanded consciousness."

"There's something happening on Aurora that we need to know about. Vega was confident of that."

"Why didn't you let anyone else know where you went?"

"That would have meant others might come with me. Word would have reached Aril and Admiral Chase. Before long, there'd have been dozens of explorers heading for the planet. Vega and I felt that so many vehicles approaching Aurora at one time would alert the enemy."

"What enemy? I thought it was just a premonition. Now you're saying there are hostile forces on Aurora and you're going to face them alone."

"I'm not alone anymore," said Deneb, smiling. When his father didn't return the smile, Deneb added, "I have no intention of confronting hostile forces. I'm just going there to observe and report what I find."

"Report? You'll be way out of range for radio emissions to reach another vehicle."

"That's true, but I don't intend to use radio emissions. I'll report directly to Vega."

"That's impossible," said Druix.

"It's not, Dad. We do it all the time. You know that."

"Yes, that works when you're close to each other. How

could it work when you're thousands of light-years apart?"

"I can't explain it, but it does. We don't really understand how it works. If we don't understand the mechanism, how can we make assertions about the working distance?"

Druix shook his head. "So the plan was for you to observe the planet and communicate back to Vega?"

"Right. That is still the plan."

Druix sighed, looking with exasperation at his son. "I'm going with you."

"That would be great," said Deneb. He reached out his hand and offered his father the Union handshake, but Druix hugged the young man instead.

"I'm just glad I found you."

"It'll be okay, Dad. Believe me. How is Mom?"

At this, Druix's face darkened. "Not well, I'm afraid. She was badly injured in a crash landing on Earth. She's recovered, but the experience has left her disoriented and depressed. She's not the same."

"Where is she?" asked Deneb.

"She didn't want to come with me to look for you. To be honest, I don't know where she is. She wouldn't tell me."

"I'll see if Vega knows," said Deneb thoughtfully.

"You mean you can just talk to Vega anytime you want?"

"No, it doesn't work like that. It's difficult to explain, but basically if I concentrate on a thought or image hard enough for a long time, Vega will pick up on it. Any thought or emotion that one of us feels, the other one senses as well."

"It must be strange," said Druix.

"We're both used to it by now. It's second nature to us. We do it without trying." Deneb paused, then added, "Pain, too."

"You feel each other's pain?"

"Yes. The worse the pain is, the more easily we feel it."

"Is Vega okay?"

"Yes," Deneb answered quickly. "She's fine."

Druix sighed. "Let's get back in our magnetocryogenic chambers and preserve oxygen for when we arrive at Aurora. We have no idea what we'll find there. Do we?"

"No. I have extra-sensory abilities, but seeing the future is not one of them."

With that, father and son departed, returning to their capsules to resume their journey to Aurora.

CHAPTER 35

— Century 2200 —

ELSENIA AND ILSA LANDED on Lumina at the same site they'd camped at during their initial visit with the rest of the family. Ilsa emerged from her capsule stunned and weak. The g-forces of the landing had eroded what little strength remained in her whittled frame. Elsenia set up a camp chair and made her mother sit while she carried other gear from Ilsa's capsule. Elsenia's vehicle had been stripped of all unnecessary supplies, so the two would have to survive on what remained in Ilsa's. Elsenia wasn't sure what they'd do now that they were back on Lumina. She only hoped that either the Tattoo People or Vega would show up soon.

"Why did you bring me here?" Ilsa asked, after Elsenia had finished her work and taken a seat next to her.

"We're trying to find Vega, Mom. I was told she would be here."

"Vega…" Ilsa repeated, saying the name as if it were unfamiliar.

"Yes, Vega. She's your daughter, Mom. Do you remember Vega and Deneb? Don't you remember this place? We were all here together, with Druix, your husband."

"I don't feel good," said Ilsa. "I'm tired."

It was late in the day. The sun was low in the sky, casting long shadows of the alien vine across the camp site. Elsenia would have to light the lanterns soon.

"I'll set up your bed. We should both get some rest. In the morning, we'll make contact with the Tattoo People. They'll know if Vega has arrived."

They slept on air mattresses under the strange stars that peppered the skies above Lumina. It took a long time for Elsenia to fall asleep. In the nocturnal silence, she listened to her mother's breathing. Something about the irregularity and shallowness of Ilsa's respiration suggested she wasn't really sleeping. Elsenia stayed awake for as long as possible. If Ilsa wasn't sleeping, what was she thinking about? Was she trying as hard as Elsenia to understand the changes that had come over her since crash landing on Earth? What thoughts were going through her muddled mind? Were they Ilsa's thoughts or Petyuba's?

Elsenia finally dozed off, but it was only for a brief time, interrupted when a shadow fell across her, blocking the rays of the rising sun. Through eyes blurred by sleep, Elsenia saw Ilsa standing over her, aiming an EMP weapon directly at her. It was the one Admiral Chase had given to Elsenia. Ilsa must have taken it from her backpack during the night. Elsenia sat up quickly.

"Mom, what are you doing?"

"You shouldn't have brought me here." Ilsa's voice was cold.

"Don't you remember, Mom? We're here to meet Vega."

"I don't care about Vega. I just want to leave this place."

"You do care about Vega. She's your..." Elsenia caught herself. She stood and faced Ilsa.

"Petyuba, give me the weapon."

"Don't call me that!"

"Why not? That's who you are. Isn't it?"

"I don't know who I am," Ilsa cried. Her hand tightened around the EMP weapon.

Elsenia held her hands up. "Okay. It's okay. Let's start from the beginning. Can you put the weapon down?

Ilsa lowered her arm, the EMP weapon now pointed at the ground next to her.

"Okay," said Elsenia. "Now, do you remember your crash landing on Earth?"

"Not really."

"Do you remember being treated for injuries while you were on Earth?"

"No. I remember being under water, and fish, many fish swimming around."

"I'll tell you what happened to you. Do you want to know?"

"Yes," Ilsa answered uncertainly.

"You were injured when your capsule crashed. You were taken to the home of a physician to be treated. You were in a coma for many months. Her home was a transparent dome under the sea. That's why you remember water and fish."

Ilsa shook her head.

"Mom, do you remember Petyuba?"

Ilsa's face came up sharply. "I told you not to say that name!" She raised the EMP weapon again to aim it at Elsenia.

"Why, Mom? Why can't I say that name?"

"Because it hurts, I told you. Don't say it."

"Why does it hurt?"

"I don't know why. Just don't say it."

"I'll tell you why it hurts you."

"Don't!"

"Yes, Mom. Listen to me."

Still holding the EMP weapon, Ilsa tried to cover her ears.

"Petyuba, listen to me!"

"Don't call me that," Ilsa hissed.

"I know it's you, Petyuba. You have to listen. You both have to listen."

"I don't have to listen." The voice was not Ilsa's.

Elsenia wondered about the EMP weapon. Once it had belonged to Stella, and sensed the emotions of the person gripping the handle. It was also supposed to be smart enough to adjust the pulse to the true mental and emotional state of the person firing it. Which person was Ilsa's weapon detecting? Was it Ilsa or Petyuba? Would there be a difference in the power of the pulse? Certainly, Ilsa did not really want to harm her own daughter, but what if Petyuba's psyche determined the output power? Elsenia meant nothing to the ancient physician from Earth, and if Petyuba genuinely perceived Elsenia as a threat to her existence, then a shot from the weapon would be lethal. What if the weapon was as confused as the mixed-up person holding it?

These thoughts flashed through Elsenia's mind in the briefest of moments, but they occupied her attention long enough for her to fail to anticipate Ilsa's next action. Her mother turned the EMP weapon on herself and fired point-blank into her own tortured face.

EMP pulses carry no momentum. Ilsa did not fall backward in response to the impulse of the blast. She simply slumped to the ground as if her bones had suddenly turned to dust. The shock that struck Elsenia at witnessing her mother shoot herself rendered her as limp as if she'd also been shot. She stood frozen for several seconds before collapsing to the ground next to Ilsa. She cradled her mother's head in her lap, sobbing uncontrollably. A blast from an EMP weapon produced no localized injury that one might treat. The electrical pulse penetrating the body produced widespread, random injury, concentrated in the organs most vital for survival. There was no first-aid for the physiological damages caused by an EMP pulse. All Elsenia could do was weep and wait.

She felt her mother's head move before she noticed her eyes were open.

"Where am I," Ilsa said, weakly.

"Mom," Elsenia cried. "Are you okay?"

"What happened?" Ilsa stammered.

"You were shot with an EMP weapon. Can you move?"

Ilsa sat up. She looked about in confusion, taking in the campground, the two space capsules in the distance, and the surrounding vegetation, above which the sun now shone brightly.

"Is this Earth?" she asked.

"No, Mom. You're back on Lumina. Do you remember Lumina?"

"Yes. I think so. I feel strange. There's something…"

"Mom, listen to me. Do you know who Petyuba is?"

Ilsa didn't answer. She stared at Elsenia, as if she were a stranger.

"Mom, you have to listen to me. Your capsule crashed on Earth. You had terrible injuries and would've died. Petyuba was the physician who treated you the only way she knew—using her own stem cells. She could have used anyone's stem cells. She could have used Druix's stem cells, but she used her own. Isn't that right, Petyuba? You used your own stem cells to heal my mother because you wanted her youth. You were old and dying, and you wanted to move yourself into her body. Isn't that right? You kept her in your home for many months, transferring more and more of your cells into my mother, healing her, but also replacing her."

Ilsa was shaking her head in denial.

"It's true, isn't it? Druix alerted the authorities and the transfer process was never completed. Ilsa is still herself, but she has much of Petyuba in her as well. The Ship of Theseus is not quite complete. Petyuba died many years ago on Earth, but part of her still lives within Ilsa."

Ilsa was sobbing now. Elsenia embraced her mother, rocking her until the crying subsided. When she spoke again, Elsenia could hardly form the words. "The good news, Mom—Petyuba— is that you're well. The treatment was successful. You survived the damage to your body caused by the crash. There's nothing wrong with you. You're just not yourself. You're two people now. It's tiring for you, and confusing, but only if you continue to fight it. Stop fighting it. You're two souls in one body. You must join together and become one—a mother and a healer. It's not so difficult. Accept it, and you can start to deal with it."

Ilsa was looking at her daughter now, but it was a different look, of awareness and resolve. "Of course," she said, but it wasn't Ilsa who said it.

"Petyuba, you both must give up a little. You must allow Ilsa to recover some of herself. Otherwise, you'll both lose your lives."

Ilsa nodded. "Yes, of course. You're right. Help me up."

Elsenia lifted Ilsa by the elbows. The two women stood facing each other. Ilsa raised her hands to Elsenia's face and traced the lines of tears. "I remember you."

Now it was Elsenia's turn to cry.

"I remember you and Druix and the twins. I remember this planet. I remember everything."

"And Petyuba?" Elsenia asked.

"I am Petyuba, and I am Ilsa. I am both."

"And I am Vega." The voice came from the thicket at the edge of the clearing. Vega stood there with four Tattoo People, their bodies beginning to glow blue-green with the failing light of day. The three women converged and embraced each other, while the Tattoo People stood gazing at them in mute wonder.

When all the greetings were over, the Tattoo People approached Ilsa.

"She will come with us," came the electric voice from the translating medallions.

"What?" said Elsenia in alarm.

"It's okay," put in Vega. "They understand. They can help her."

Elsenia shook her head. She couldn't conceive of letting Ilsa go with the Tattoo People given the weakened and confused state she was in.

"Don't worry," said Vega. "They know what happened to her. They want to help. Believe me."

Elsenia still looked skeptical. She went to her mother, who was following the conversation with a puzzled look upon her face.

"Mom. Petyuba. These Tattoo People want to help you. Is it okay? Will you go with them?"

Looking uncertain, Ilsa nodded. A moment later, two of the Tattoo People came forward and reached for her hands. Ilsa allowed herself to be led away, leaving Elsenia and Vega alone in the clearing.

"They're good," said Vega. "They'll know how to treat her. You and I have to concentrate on what will happen on Aurora."

The next morning, when they awoke in the clearing, Elsenia looked about her. Vega rose from her air mattress, but Ilsa was nowhere to be seen.

"Vega, Mom isn't here."

"It's okay. Really. They told me they'd keep her overnight. It was too late when they took her away to bring her back the same evening."

Elsenia was uneasy, but she forced herself to trust Vega. A

short time later, they enjoyed artificial eggs for breakfast with a canister of juice.

"Vega, perhaps you can solve a riddle. It's been bothering me for a long time."

"I can try," she answered with a half-smile.

Elsenia told her about her visit to the UV-60 planet and how she'd asked the Tattoo People about prior visits by space explorers. When she reached the part of the story where the Tattoo People identified the previous visitor as someone named Vega, her sister's smile broadened and she nodded knowingly.

"Yes, that was another of Alphons' little tricks."

"What little trick?"

"Actually, quite amazing, and not a trick at all."

"Are you telling me that it was really you who visited the planet before me?"

"Sort of." Vega picked up a stick and scratched two figures in the ground. "Let's say this one is Deneb and this one is me. According to Alphons, Deneb and I represent a macroscale quantum system. Do you know what that is?"

"Yes, of course. That's how Alphons planned for Deneb to send information to you instantaneously. He claimed that because you were both created at the same moment, you're an entangled system. He hoped that would enable you to communicate instantly no matter how far apart the two of you are."

"Right, but it's not just a claim. It works. I do know what Deneb is feeling and thinking at all times, and he knows the same about me. For example, I know that he's frozen right now. Unfortunately, most of the time we're both frozen."

"It seems incredible, but let's just assume you and Deneb can communicate instantaneously no matter where you are, how does that explain your being on that planet?"

"Because there's more to this quantum business besides communication. This you will find more incredible."

"Go ahead," Elsenia said, looking down at the stick figures on the ground.

"Quantum mechanics is all about probability. The state of

a system is given by a probability function. The system can be in an infinite number of states, but most are highly unlikely. For Deneb and me, most of the time Deneb is Deneb and I am myself. But it is possible, for a very brief time—nanoseconds—for me to be Deneb and he me. We switch places."

Elsenia was already shaking her head. "Vega, you're not going to tell me that you and Deneb underwent one of these switches during his visit to the UV-60 planet."

"Yes, that's exactly what I'm telling you. I'm also telling you that we did it intentionally. It wasn't just a chance, random switch."

"Continue," Elsenia said.

"You know that Alphons made it a practice to examine the physiological data of all explorers while they're frozen in their magnetocryogenic chambers."

"Yes, he's obsessive about it. I consider it a bit invasive."

"In retrieving the data from my capsule and Deneb's, he saw anomalies. They were rare—every few hundred years or so—and random, sometimes occurring more frequently than other times. But what intrigued him was that they occurred at the same time in both our capsules. He looked into it more carefully and noticed something even more perplexing."

Vega stopped, as if considering how best to explain.

Finally, she said, "Deneb and I are almost identical in most physiological functions. There are physical differences between the two of us, our gender for example, but the characteristics of our bodies that are monitored by the magnetocryogenic chamber's life support system are virtually indistinguishable. Differences are very slight. Body mass is one example. My body mass index is lower than Deneb's, a common variation between male and female. Alphons noticed that during these anomalous readings in our physiological data, Deneb's BMI dropped at the same time mine increased. On further analysis, Alphons found that for these fractions of a second, my physiological data became that of Deneb's, while his became mine. It was as if momentarily, I became him and he became me."

Elsenia felt a shiver run through her spine as she realized where this discourse was heading. Had she not personally heard of Vega's appearance on the UV-60 planet, she wouldn't have had the patience or interest to listen to the rest of the story.

"That's what made Alphons speculate that he was witnessing rare and transient changes in our quantum states. Over the thousands of years during which Deneb and I are frozen in our space capsules, it may only happen half a dozen times. It's virtually impossible to calculate the quantum probability of a macroscale function, but if you could, you'd find a finite probability that the individual elements of an entangled pair can switch places every once in a while for brief instants."

"Okay," Elsenia said, holding up her hands to slow Vega's rising excitement. "Even if I accept all that, I still don't understand you taking Deneb's place on his visit to that planet, if that's where you're heading. That would take more than a transient change in state function."

"That is the next part of the story," said Vega. "This part really shows Alphons' genius—or madness—if you want to look at it that way."

"Keep going."

"Going back to quantum mechanics, remember what you learned about the dual nature of light."

"Particle or wave."

"Right. Light can behave as if it's a stream of particles—little bundles of energy that can strike a surface and actually be counted individually. Light can also be a wave. If you shine light on a plate with a row of holes in it, the waves can interfere and produce a pattern resulting from the superposition of waves."

"Yes, the nature of light changes depending on how you measure or detect it."

"This remains one of the fundamental mysteries of quantum mechanics—a paradox yet to be explained. Quantum mechanics claims that at the moment an observer interacts with a system, the system assumes the observed state. All other possible states of the system are no longer allowed."

"So if I observe you as Deneb, then you become him."

"Not quite. You're jumping ahead. This concept has been proposed as a way to achieve quantum teleportation—instantaneous travel from one place to another. It's even been demonstrated in the laboratory. Two particles that are entangled, created simultaneously, can be far apart. At the moment you measure the spin state of one of the particles, you instantaneously alter and fix the spin state of the other particle—instantaneous action at a distance."

"So the problem becomes how to observe or set the state of one of the elements of the system."

"Exactly. And the solution that Alphons came up with actually worked—the very first time he tried it."

"What did he do?"

"He assumed, that the BMI indicated when the random switch between me and Deneb took place. Then he reprogrammed the automatic system, so that when the change in BMI occurred, it initiated an immediate unfreezing sequence, beginning with the application of a sudden, intense magnetic field. This produced the desired effect of preventing the immediate transition back to the most probable state—the state where I am in my chamber and Deneb is far away. Thus, when the unfreezing process was complete, it was I, not Deneb, who was on the planet. Of course, I was totally surprised by this. I knew I'd been frozen in my space capsule. Why was I now exiting from the chamber on Deneb's capsule? It wasn't teleportation in the usual sense. I hadn't been transported. Not really. I'd changed places with my brother. The most astounding aspect of this feat, that most excited Alphons, was that Deneb carried information back with him after the change. In other words, information traveled instantaneously from one location in space to another. Einstein would be amazed. All his theories were based on the premise that information can't travel faster than the speed of light."

"What about Deneb? He must've been surprised."

"Surprised and confused. He had expected to be unfrozen during the capsule's approach to the UV-60 planet. Instead, he found himself orbiting Supply Ship 2, where I had been. Only after he met Alphons did he realize what had happened."

"He must have felt cheated," Elsenia commented.

Vega smiled and continued, "He took it well. We were all amazed that the experiment worked. He and Alphons celebrated and then froze themselves again to wait for me to return. When I did, we agreed that Deneb would get to explore the next planet while I stayed with Alphons, who promised not to try his entanglement experiment again."

"And this all happened after my visit to the supply ship?"

"Right. Remember that Deneb hadn't yet reached the planet when you arrived."

"So what did you find out from your visit to the alternate planet?"

"That one of us had to go to Aurora."

"Yes, but why?"

Vega sighed, resigning herself to the imperative of revealing what she'd been told not to. Vega, still a child in some ways, had been entrusted with a grownup secret, but the child within her wasn't strong enough to keep it.

"To answer that I have to tell you about Lumina."

"Vega, Deneb may be in danger. You'll have to tell me everything."

"I don't know where to begin," she confessed.

"What did the Tattoo People want with you?"

"They asked for our help."

"Help with what?"

"They believed their planet was in danger."

"Danger from what?"

"That's not clear."

"Vega, you and Deneb were gone for a good part of a day. When you returned, you were both different. Whatever happened in those hours changed you both."

"It's hard to explain, Elsenia. I'll tell you. You can come to whatever conclusions you want."

"I'm listening."

"First, they separated us—brought us to two different rooms. This scared me a little, but there seemed nothing sinister or threatening in their intent. They talked to us separately, asking us to perform simple manual tasks like breaking a branch or scratching a shape in the ground. They gave us food and asked whether we liked it or not. They didn't tell us why they were doing this, but Deneb and I figured it out."

"You both figured it out? You were separated."

"Yes, Elsenia, but Deneb and I are never completely apart. The Tattoo People were testing our ability to think alike, act alike, respond as one, see what we each see, experience what the other experiences. We've been subjected to those kinds of tests before. The Arilians did it all the time. Once we both figured out what they were after, we were better at it. I think they were impressed. Remember, the Tattoo People communicate among themselves as if they have one brain. Maybe it was because they'd never seen that ability in humans before and couldn't figure out how we did it. We don't send out radio waves like they do. In any case, they must have been satisfied with the outcome because afterward they did something else. They put us both together in a room, much like all the rooms they make by training the vine, except it was larger and dome-shaped. There were benches in the center of the room, at the focal point of the curved ceiling overhead. It was very dark, only a few beams of sunlight penetrated the dense foliage that formed the roof. The way these beams of light slanted through the space of the room made it look almost as if it were a church. They asked us to sit quietly on the benches without communicating. This was an odd request. For Tattoo People, communicating is the same as thinking. Asking us not to communicate was their way of telling us not to think. The way we interpreted that was they wanted us to make our minds blank. They wanted us to sense something in that room. We did as they asked."

"And did you sense something?" Elsenia asked.

Vega swallowed. "Yes. Very strongly. It was unmistakable, and Deneb and I confirmed with each other later that we both felt the same thing."

"What was it," asked Elsenia, impatiently.

"Danger."

"Danger?" Elsenia repeated. "What type of danger?"

"Who knows?" Vega shrugged, and continued before her sister could react. "Elsenia, I know you want details, but that's not how we perceive the world. It's like smell is for you. You smell something bad, but can you explain why it smells bad? What is it making the smell bad? How do you answer questions like that?"

Elsenia considered this. "Then what's the point of putting you two in the room if you can only learn what the Tattoo People knew already?"

Vega held up a hand. "Who said the Tattoo People knew there was danger?"

"You did. You said the Tattoo People asked for your help because their planet was in danger."

"Right," said Vega. "But they didn't know that before they learned it from us."

"What!" cried Elsenia. "You and Deneb told them their planet was in danger? What if you were wrong?"

"We're not wrong. Anyway, after we were in the room for a while, they came to get us and separated us again and asked us questions about what we'd sensed. Independently, we both told them the same thing. This is what they wanted from us all along, we believe. They wanted us as intermediaries to relay a message to them."

"You mean like ancient mystics who communicate with the dead?"

"Sort of, but we weren't communicating with the dead."

"Then who with?"

"The vine," Vega replied.

The words froze Elsenia. "It's what Alphons said. It's the vine that's important—not the Tattoo People," she said softly.

"Exactly. The vine was warning them of danger."

"But how could the vine know of any danger?"

"Deneb and I discussed that. We believe the vine knows

more because the vines on different planets communicate among themselves."

"How do you figure that?"

"Humans believe that a race of aliens put the seeds of the vine on asteroids to launch them into the galaxy and start new planets. That's true, but perhaps it's not all. What if the plant is the alien means to establish a network? Humans from Earth did that at the start. They launched the seven supply ships as communication hubs. Perhaps our alien friends did the same."

Elsenia was impressed. The twins were barely more than teenagers, but already their power of reasoning and deduction were phenomenal. Was this because of Alphons' influence? Had the time spent with the ancient physicist trained them to reason out problems—look for exotic and unexpected explanations? Or was it their ability to think together—pass ideas and information back and forth nonverbally—kneading unformed thoughts into well-formed ideas?

"You could be right," Elsenia admitted. "But I still don't understand where the danger is. There's no evidence that either the vine or the Tattoo People are inherently aggressive or threatening, either to us or each other."

"True," mused Vega. "But it's very possible the danger hasn't arrived yet. The deployment of the vine with the Tattoo People as their caretakers, and the launch of the planet-destroying asteroids may represent the first phases of the assault. The aliens are setting the stage for the actual attack."

"On Aurora," said Elsenia quietly.

"Right."

"We need to let Admiral Chase know," said Elsenia. "You should've told him immediately instead of sending Deneb there."

"There's too much we still don't know, Elsenia. How fast the aliens can travel across the galaxy, for example. Their asteroids travel very slowly, much slower than our galactic space vehicles. It may take them tens of thousands of years to travel anywhere. The biggest threats to humans right now are those asteroids. It's more important that Admiral Chase and his fleet deal with that threat first."

"Yes, but he still needs to know if this is the start of a larger invasion."

"There's something else that Deneb and I worried about—why it's important we don't get this wrong."

"What's that?"

"If humans believe the vine and the Tattoo People are the advance force of an alien attack, what would keep humans from attacking them? The friendly coexistence would end. If Deneb and I are wrong, then we'd have initiated a war for no reason—by mistake. Deneb didn't want that to happen, and he was perfectly willing to risk his own life finding out."

"And how will we know what he learns on Aurora?"

"We calculated exactly when Deneb will arrive there. When he does, I'll know it, whatever happens."

"When is that supposed to be?" asked Elsenia, already knowing the answer.

"About now."

Elsenia rolled her eyes and shook her head in disbelief. "Vega, are you sure your ability works? Aurora's so far away."

"It will work. There's no reason it shouldn't. And besides, we aren't the only ones with this power."

"Really. Who else has it?"

"Not who else, but what else. The vine."

"I forgot, the vines communicate among themselves."

"It's plausible," said Vega. "Imagine that all the vines come from the same, original plant. According to Alphons, as long as they all share a common origin, they have a connection."

"Do they communicate with each other instantaneously?"

"That's the reason to deploy the vine as a communication system. If it is, the aliens know everything that's going on in the galaxy at the same instant in time. There's no delay between when an event takes place and when the aliens learn of it."

"Then the aliens have almost god-like powers. That's a tremendous advantage over humans."

"Yes, but not all humans."

Elsenia stared at her younger sister. "Everyone but you and Deneb."

"Exactly," said Vega.

"This idea of entanglement intrigues me," said Elsenia. "Alphons' theory is that the alien vine, like you and Deneb, are entangled because of your simultaneous creation."

"Right," agreed Vega. "You can't be entangled with Admiral Chase, because you were created at different places and times."

She said this with a mischievous smile.

"All right," Elsenia answered, "but considering how big the universe is, and that time is for all intents and purposes infinite, then on that scale, Admiral Chase and I are entangled."

"Of course, but you can say that about every human in the galaxy."

"That's exactly what I am saying. What if all humans are to some degree entangled because, on cosmic time and space scales, we were all created at the same time?"

"You're not suggesting what I think you are. Are you?"

Now it was Elsenia's turn to smile mischievously. "I'm not saying it. Quantum mechanics is saying it. It's saying that we're all who we are because that's who we're most likely to be, but every once in a while, we could be someone else, even if only for a very brief instant."

Vega nodded. "Interesting. Sometimes I imagine being someone else, or experiencing something with amazing accuracy and clarity, and I wonder how I can do that. I attribute it to imagination inspired by subtle hints I've received and perhaps some subconscious experience passed to me genetically."

"Or it could be that sometime during your life you were someone else."

"Yes," mused Vega. "But there's another implication to what you're saying."

"What's that?"

"In quantum mechanics, a system, whether it's two or multiple particles, is described as a mathematical expression—a state function. What you're saying is that there is a single state function for all humans in the galaxy. It's a complicated function, to be sure, but its value is close to zero everywhere except where a person is. It's a function that is constantly changing, randomly and chaotically, but most of the time it looks pretty much the same." Vega was drawing the function in the air with her finger.

"I hope you're not telling me the state function follows a twisting path."

"Yes, something like that. If you saw it in three dimensions…"

"Someone else told me that. He said, all the possible paths were like a big bowl of spaghetti," Elsenia remembered, thinking of Lemmy.

"Alphons said it best," added Vega. "He believed there's a special connection linking everything created in the same moment—whether people, planets, stars, or galaxies. The essence of their shared creation binds them eternally and instantaneously, transcending all dimensions. This shared essence can be a source of great power because it enables communication, the flow of information, more effectively than by any other means. Even the sanctity of light speed can be overcome."

"You still haven't explained why you decided to return to Lumina. If all you have to do is be unfrozen during the time Deneb is on Aurora, couldn't you be anywhere? Wouldn't it be better if you were on a supply ship, maybe not Alphons', but another where you could communicate whatever happens back to the explorer fleet and Admiral Chase?"

"Alphons and I discussed that. We agreed, it would be best on Lumina. Its Tattoo People are the ones who first approached us for help. They've already demonstrated their concern about the danger, whatever it is. I believe it was the right decision. After I landed here, I spoke to the Tattoo People. They've even allowed me back to the original room where Deneb and I communicated with the vine."

"Have you learned more?"

"A lot more."

"Tell me."

"I can't."

"Why not?"

"Because I promised the Tattoo People, I will keep their secrets my secret."

Bothersome as this was to Elsenia, she accepted it. Somehow, she knew that circumstances would make it impossible for such secrets to remain so much longer.

CHAPTER 36

— Century 2200 —

OVER THE NEXT SEVERAL DAYS, the three women established a routine that was as close to normalcy as any of them had known for a very long time. They ate, slept, talked, and explored the world of the Tattoo People, who were gracious and welcoming, much more so than on the family's first visit. Ilsa was growing stronger, both physically and mentally. Her sessions with Tattoo People seemed to be helping her adjust to the two people inside her. At various times she was like the mother Vega and Elsenia knew and loved, while at other times she was the introverted, thoughtful and distant, Earth doctor. Vega and Elsenia learned to adjust their behavior in Ilsa's presence, based on their best guess on which of her two personalities happened to be prevalent at the time. When asked about her sessions with the Tattoo People, Ilsa only said, "They too are great healers."

Elsenia was also curious about Vega's relationship with the Tattoo People, and what they expected of her. She only knew that Deneb was on his way to confront some unknown threat to the Tattoo People, and perhaps human civilization as well.

But, what compelled their hosts on Lumina to seek help from two humans who were no more than children on a human scale, and infants on cosmic calendars?

Elsenia had spent many nights camping out on planets dominated by the alien vine. She'd grown accustomed to the complete absence of sound during dark hours. With no animal life, absent were the chirps of birds, the scurry of squirrels, and the buzz and whir of flying insects. Even the creaking and groaning of branches with the changing temperature or the falling of dew drops couldn't be heard, as if the vine itself slept, slipping itself into its own silent bed to await the morning's light. Thus, Elsenia woke with a start when she heard a distant roar that was as unnatural to Lumina as an alarm bell might have been. She rose from her air mattress and stood gazing at the night sky, filled with sparkling, incandescent stars, too numerous to count. One of the stars became brighter as she watched it descend from the heavens. She felt Vega walk up behind her.

"It's Admiral Chase."

"What?"

"I'm expecting him. I wasn't sure when he'd get here. I'm glad. Now maybe we can get some answers."

"Why didn't you tell me?"

"I didn't think you cared." There was a note of irony in Vega's voice.

"Vega, I'm getting very tired of your games. From now on, I expect you to tell me everything. I'm your older sister."

"Yes, Elsenia," Vega answered, amused. "Admiral Chase has arrived on Lumina. I suspect we'll see him in the morning." With that, she returned to her air mattress, leaving Elsenia alone to watch the remaining descent of the Admiral's vehicle, a star more brilliant than all others.

When Admiral Chase arrived at the campsite in the morning, he wasn't alone. Two of his troops accompanied him, along with a Tattoo man and a woman Elsenia didn't recognize. The woman's presence made Elsenia feel oddly uncomfortable, and she turned her attention to the Tattoo man who, remarkably, wore the uniform of one of the troops of the Earth fleet, except with a metal helmet set snugly upon his head.

Elsenia held back while introductions and greetings were carried out. She waited nervously till Admiral Chase approached and gave her an awkward hug. Holding her shoulders at arm's length, he asked, "Are you okay?"

"Yes. Thank you."

"I want you to meet someone."

He took Elsenia's hand and led her to where the Tattoo man stood, looking uncomfortable and shy.

"This is Nolondi. He's from Carbonia."

Elsenia took a step back. "Carbonia?"

"Yes. When I went there, the situation was still the same,

perhaps worse. I thought circumstances justified an extraction. I brought Nolondi to Aril, where he underwent a series of tests. He was uncontrollable when we captured him, but he responded well with treatment. He's become very useful to us. He's heard about your visit to Carbonia and has been anxious to meet you. He also has terrifying tales to tell of his life on that cursed planet."

Nolondi's face twisted into the closest expression Tattoo People had to a smile. He shook Elsenia's hand and bowed slightly. His touch was firm and reassuring. Elsenia smiled back at him.

"Hello, Elsenia." It was the woman, who'd accompanied Admiral Chase.

"Hello," Elsenia answered, offering her hand tentatively.

"My name is Rashera. I'm your aunt."

"I…" Elsenia was at a loss for words. She knew of Rashera, but they'd never met. "Your parents—Arthur and Krystal. I miss them…" Elsenia began to cry.

"They talked about you all the time. They loved you very much."

Elsenia embraced her aunt. The hand shake seemed no longer adequate. "I thought you were on Supply Ship 6," she said.

"I was, but I decided to come with Admiral Chase. My curiosity got the best of me."

Elsenia should've felt relief now that she was surrounded by others all willing to confront the ill-defined threat from an unknown enemy. Instead, she felt uneasy by her loss of control owing to the presence of Admiral Chase and the others. As Vega was her younger sister and Ilsa was still recovering from her medical treatments on Earth, Elsenia had assumed the role of the responsible person in their camp. True, Vega seemed to understand more about what was happening, but it had been Elsenia who'd taken charge of the diminutive outpost. Now, it seems, she had to yield to Admiral Chase and her aunt.

Elsenia forced a smile.

The introductions completed, they stood in the clearing, awkwardly unsure what to do next. Fortunately, the silence was broken by the appearance of three Tattoo People, who slipped out of the surrounding thicket with uncanny stealth.

Nolondi walked purposefully toward them, removing the metallic cap from his head. The four faced off, with the humans wondering what communication was going on between them. Someone could have turned on a translator, but no one took the initiative. They just waited in respectful silence.

Finally, Nolondi bowed to the three Tattoo People. This was a good sign. He then turned back to Admiral Chase, switching on his translator.

"They agreed to talk to us," came Nolondi's report. "Tomorrow."

Later, Elsenia sat alone in the camp light. Fires were forbidden owing to the risks they posed to the vine, but Elsenia gazed into the incandescent light of the lamp as if it were a flickering flame. Someone came and sat next to her. She knew it was the Admiral.

"I missed you," he said.

Elsenia was confused. Did he mean 'missed' as in not arriving someplace where she'd been recently, or 'missed' as in feeling unfulfilled by virtue of someone's absence?

"I'm sorry," she said, which seemed like the right response in either case.

"I wish I'd known that Deneb was going to Aurora. I would have followed him there."

"It's not your fault," Elsenia said quickly. "It's mine. Druix told me he had a premonition. It's difficult to explain, but I should have trusted his word."

"I feel like I've failed Benjamin. I promised I'd take care of you."

"You have taken care of me, Admiral Chase—Julian. Had you not given me Stella's EMP weapon I'm sure I wouldn't be here now."

"I couldn't have lived with that."

Elsenia looked at the tan skin of his face, reflecting the glow from the camp light. She put her hand on his. Hers looked remarkably small in comparison.

"We live strange lives, Elsenia."

Elsenia leaned closer and rested her head on his shoulder. It was one of those moments neither wanted to end, and so they stayed still. The camp light glowed, the stars moved silently across the night sky, and the alien vine surrounded them, wrapping them in organic luxury, but the night turned too quickly to day.

THE NEXT MORNING, the Tattoo People returned, this time bringing with them a fourth member of their party.

"This is Larimar. He will speak for us. He knows no more than any of our people, but we together trust him to decide what knowledge to convey to you."

In appearance, Larimar was no different than any of the rest of the Tattoo People, but he carried himself with more self-assurance. In many ways, Larimar reminded Elsenia of the Tattoo People of Happiness, who'd been honest and forthright in their dealings with the humans on that planet. Larimar had an air about him that comforted her, even before he started to speak.

"Please, come with me. You will all be more comfortable in another place." Larimar's words emanated from the translating medallions each of the humans wore on their necks. The Tattoo People on Happiness had manufactured their own medallions to facilitate communication with their human friends. Here on Lumina, the Tattoo People had little use for the device.

They followed Larimar into the forest of vines, walking single file through the narrow corridors the Tattoo People created. Elsenia, Vega, and Ilsa were familiar with the route, but Admiral Chase and those accompanying him moved slowly and cautiously through the dimly lit tunnels.

After some time, they turned into a narrow opening in the corridor and found themselves in a well-lit room with vine benches. The light came from above, where the vegetation had been trained back to reveal a patch of sunlit sky. Elsenia surmised that the space was designed to be a classroom. The low benches would easily accommodate thirty Tattoo children, but the eight human visitors all but filled the space. They took seats and waited respectfully for Larimar to begin.

"We come from a planet with a very unusual history that has shaped our destiny," he began. He moved about the room as he spoke. His lips didn't move, but he gesticulated with his arms and hands. The electronic rendition of his voice emanated from the translating devices worn by the humans. Admiral Chase stood and approached Larimar.

"Please, it would be better for us if you wear this." He removed his own medallion and offered it to Larimar. Turning to the other humans, Admiral Chase said, "You may all turn your speakers off. It will be less disorienting if the sound of Larimar's voice is coming only from him."

They did as the Admiral advised. Larimar proudly donned the medallion and resumed his lecture.

"Our ancestors were from a planet close to the black hole at the center of the galaxy, so close it orbited the galactic center in the equivalent of twelve Earth years. Being that close meant that our planet was continuously bathed in extremely strong radio emissions, produced by the material falling into the black hole. With such powerful radio waves impinging upon our planet, our species evolved senses able to detect reflected radio waves. Remember that the eyes of humans and Tattoo People work by detecting reflected light from objects. On our planet, the ancient home of our people, we developed the ability to detect objects both by reflected light and reflected radio signals. It never would have happened in organisms evolving on Earth as your planet is too far away from a radio source strong enough to produce detectable signals reflected from objects. But on our planet, we were blessed with a sun that allowed us to see optically, and a source of radio waves that allowed us to 'see' in another way. Imagine a world that has two days and two nights, one produced by the rising and setting of the sun, the other produced by the rising and setting of the galactic center. And because the planet orbited the sun more rapidly than it orbited the galactic center, during some parts of the year the two days and nights coincided, while at other times radio day occurred during optical night.

"Wonderful as this sounds, the ability to detect objects by reflected radio waves was not favored by evolution. It's very inexact for locating objects, and doesn't provide the kind of detail an organism needs to sense the surrounding environment. But this phase in our evolutionary development had a secondary effect. It helped us develop the complimentary ability to transmit radio waves, in the same way animals on Earth developed the ability to speak, as a compliment to their ability to hear. As you have seen, our ability to communicate via radio waves gives us the capacity to think and act as a single organism and allowed our ancestors near the center of the galaxy to develop a highly advanced technology. It played the same role in our development as the appearance of an opposable thumb had for humans."

Larimar stopped his circuit of the room and scanned his audience. Satisfied with their interest, he continued.

"Inevitably, an advanced civilization will have thoughts about expanding into space. Our ancestors were no different, but they were very careful and deliberate in their approach. First, they developed a genetically engineered plant that could be introduced on lifeless planets and establish itself, eventually spreading and proliferating. The vine would introduce the right chemicals into the planetary atmosphere to fix and stabilize the environment, making it suitable for habitation. Fortunately for you humans, the same conditions that are right for our people are also right for yours. Our ancestors were very diligent and careful though. To be sure the planet could sustain life, they also genetically engineered a process where the plant produced a population of their own people, what you call Tattoo People. They would live on the planet first, caring for the vine and making sure conditions were just right for the actual colonization. We, the Tattoo People, are smaller versions of the ancient race that evolved near the center of the galaxy."

"So it was this ancient race that deployed the asteroids carrying the seeds of your vine?" Rashera asked the question.

"Yes," Larimar answered. "The ancients launched hundreds

of them into space, all in a direction away from the center of the galaxy. They mastered the technology of harnessing asteroids and applying propulsion to them in such a way as to direct them to any destination. The vehicles were as technically sophisticated as the seeds they carried. They knew the odds of striking a planet randomly were very small, so they equipped the vehicles with sensors that would detect planets and navigate automatically to impact them. After impact, the seeds of the vine would sprout. Once the vine began to grow, it initiated the biological and chemical processes necessary to transition the atmosphere into one conducive to our species. You have seen how successful this scheme has been. Virtually every planet upon which the vehicles impacted has seen the rise of a civilization. In some cases it took more time, but sooner or later the end result was achieved."

"And what about the other type of asteroid?" Rashera asked.

Larimar turned abruptly and looked at his audience. "Who asks this question?"

Although the Tattoo People could detect the radio waves produced by the translators, it was difficult for them to locate the person from whom the signals originated. Rashera waved her hand. Larimar approached her. Admiral Chase moved toward Rashera protectively.

"How do you know of this?" Larimar asked.

Admiral Chase answered. "We found one. We destroyed it because it was threatening one of our planets."

Larimar looked about, an expression of concern forming on his face. "There may be more then."

"What are they?" persisted Rashera.

"I will explain."

Larimar moved away and resumed his pacing of the room.

"For the most part, the Tattoo People are peaceful, but there is something I have not told you about our sensitivity to radio waves. The behavior Nolondi tells me is manifested in the Tattoo People of the planet you call Carbonia is caused by exposure to random, intense radio noise that creates chaos in our mental processes. We hear strange voices, have hallucinations, and become violent and aggressive, producing irrational and uncontrollable paranoia."

"How can that be if your race evolved in the presence of radio waves?" Elsenia asked.

"Consider this," Larimar began. "Have you ever wondered why the light sensitivity of your human eyes is maximum for green colors? It has nothing to do with the color of Earth's sun. One would think evolution would conspire to develop eyes most sensitive to the part of the sun's light with the most energy. If your eyes are supposed to detect reflected light from objects, wouldn't it be best to maximize optical sensitivity to the same wavelengths that are strongest in the light from your sun? Maximum sensitivity, however, is not the only factor that influences one's ability to perceive the external world. Another is consistency. Human eyes are sensitive to light in the part of the solar spectrum that is most constant with time—that suffers least from interference and variability due to other sources. When there is too much variability or unpredictability in a signal, the brain turns off that signal."

"On Earth a long time ago, there was a disease of the eye called strabismus," said Ilsa. Everyone looked at her. She'd hardly said a word until that moment. "With strabismus, the two eyes don't work together. After a long time with that condition, the brain becomes confused by the conflicting signals, and it turns the offending signal off—ignores it. The one eye becomes blind, even though it is functioning normally."

"Exactly," said Larimar. "The ancient ones knew that once they expanded into other parts of the galaxy, they'd be exposed to other sources of radio waves. The radio emissions from the galactic center are stable over many millions of years, but those produced by other civilizations represent random and chaotic interference to the primary means by which we communicate with each other. The ancient ones knew that our species could only survive on a planet sufficiently far from the source of intense radio waves that disrupt our ability to communicate."

"But how does that explain the behavior of the Tattoo People on Carbonia?" Elsenia asked. "It's far from any sources of radio waves. The radio wave interference there should be very limited, certainly no more than it is on Lumina or Happiness."

"True, except for one additional factor, which I fear may be significant. There are now many more planets where humans have settled, and on each of these they have constructed large radio transmitters to communicate with each other. In addition, there are fairly powerful transmitters on the Union supply ships, and many more less powerful transmitters on the space exploration vehicles. All together, they represent a continuous barrage of radio noise, which will eventually have deleterious effects on our species. I believe that is what has affected the Tattoo People of Carbonia. Remember that Carbonia was one of the first planets to produce a civilization of Tattoo People. They have been exposed to human-created radio waves longer than others."

"You mean to say, we humans are making Tattoo People crazy?" asked Rashera.

"I am almost certain of it."

"If that's true, there are ways we can help. We're extremely inefficient in the way we broadcast radio waves into space. We transmit haphazardly, in all directions. It's wasteful to do that, but the technology becomes increasingly complex if we don't."

"A change would help, but it may take thousands of years for humans to make these changes. There will be more violence and destruction until that time, which is why the other asteroids created by our ancestors are larger than the ones carrying the vine. They are designed to detect extraneous sources of radio noise and destroy them. Thousands of these were launched many millions of years ago. The galaxy is filled with them. They do nothing until they detect radio emissions. Then they move toward their target. There is no telling how many civilizations have been destroyed by these devices since their launch."

Larimar paused. He stood looking at the humans, all with their own thoughts. Elsenia broke the silence. "What is happening on Aurora?" She raised her hand to make the Tattoo man see her.

"The launch of the two types of asteroids represents only the preparation for the expansion of our race. The next phase was impossible at first. The ancients knew how to launch asteroids, but did not develop the means to move their civilization. Tattoo People are just custodians of the vine, genetically engineered to perform one function—similar to what you humans call robots, only we are living beings. But the ancient ones didn't know how to launch themselves into space. Like humans, they only live for very short times on galactic scales, and we need food and air to survive. Long space voyages were an impossibility until..."

"Until what?" asked Rashera, but the sharp tone of her voice hinted that she knew the answer.

"Until the Tattoo People encountered humans—humans able to freeze themselves and travel thousands of light-years from one place in the galaxy to another, all within their limited lifespan. Once our ancestors learned of that technology, the remaining obstacle to expansion was removed. Huge space vehicles have been produced with the same type of freezing chambers. These left thousands of years ago and are on their way. There are millions of them, preparing to land and inhabit the planets conditioned by the vine."

"And they've reached Aurora," said Elsenia.

"Yes. They're using the planet as a staging area for the next leg of their voyage."

"And the vine is helping them?" said Vega.

"Who says this?" said Larimar.

Vega raised her hand. Larimar approached her. He rested a slender blue-green hand on her shoulder.

"Yes, Vega, except the vine is not conscious of all that's taking place. The vine's senses are limited. It only knows the information it's given by us, and them."

"The vine is more than that," said Vega.

Larimar nodded. "Yes, it's more than that. It's the way the invaders know everything. Everything that happens on a planet with the vine is communicated back—immediately. All linked to the original vine, which the invaders carry with them. They protect and nurture it and, in exchange, it tells them all they need to know for their galactic expansion."

Vega only nodded.

"You should make sure your brother understands that."

"Yes, I will."

"That's all I have to tell you right now," said Larimar. "I'll escort you back to your camp."

"Wait," said Elsenia. She stood and walked to Larimar. "Perhaps you can explain what this means." She raised her two hands and formed the crossed V sign she'd seen on Carbonia.

"Where have you seen that?" asked Larimar quickly.

"On Carbonia. And on Aril."

There was a long pause. Elsenia knew when Tattoo People paused in a conversation, it meant they were communicating with others. Larimar could be having a long discussion with his fellow Tattoo People on Lumina before answering her question.

Finally, he said, "It's the sign of the ancient ones. It's a secret symbol that few know about. It carries great authority. We're surprised humans know of it. How did you come upon it?"

Elsenia held back the full answer. She told Larimar only of the twisted piece of metal found in the debris of the meteor that struck Aril. Satisfied with her answer, Larimar led the humans out of the room, back to their camp.

Later, they talked long into the night about what Larimar had told them.

"I don't believe the vine is as innocent as Larimar wants us to think" said Rashera. "As the means of communication and information for the invaders, it must be complicit in some way."

"But the vine saved my life on Carbonia," said Elsenia. "Then, before I left, it showed me the crossed-V sign. That demonstrates some measure of good will."

"True, but that was just the vine on one planet, a severely stressed planet that needs help, even human help."

"What about the vine here on Lumina that Deneb and I communicated with? Clearly, it was sending us a warning."

"Perhaps it's a kind of symbiosis," said Elsenia. "The vine is helping us in exchange for getting our help in dealing with the crisis on Carbonia."

"Or maybe endosymbiosis?" added Rashera.

Elsenia shook her head. "Endosymbiosis is a specialized form of symbiosis, when one organism acts inside another to the mutual benefit of both. The endosymbiotic theory speculates that certain organelles in living cells started out as invasive bacteria, but eventually became integral to the survival of the cell. Mitochondria and chloroplasts are believed to have originated that way."

"Right," agreed Rashera. "That's what I meant. My mother, your grandmother, had strange ideas. She believed the expansion of humans to other planets, combined with the communication network that keeps us linked, constitutes one gigantic organism. Looking at it from her point of view, the invasion of the vine, which may've started out as a destructive force, is resulting in interdependence between us and them."

"That certainly explains the efforts to help us," said Vega.

"Alphons was fascinated by the vine," said Elsenia. "Vega, you must have seen his three-dimensional image."

"Yes, he spent hours with it. It frustrated him that he could only see the image. He wanted to understand it fully, especially the tendrils that dropped from the branches into the ground. The Tattoo People protect those tendrils more than any other part of the plant."

"Aren't they just to bring nourishment and moisture into the plant?" asked Rashera.

"That's what I thought," answered Elsenia, "but the vine has many major trunks rooted in the ground. The tendrils seem redundant."

"I think I know."

This came from Nolondi's translating medallion.

"Tell us," said Rashera.

Nolondi seemed pleased to be part of the discussion. "We are told the tendrils must be protected or the vine will forget."

264

"Of course," Rashera said, "The vine stores its information underground. The tendrils connect to its memory banks."

"Incredible," said Vega. "Imagine how much data is stored if each tendril connects to a chemical strand that stores information as efficiently as DNA. Every piece of knowledge the vine acquires from above is collected and saved."

"The vine is a planet-sized brain," mused Elsenia, thinking of the bizarre messages received by the ultra-sensitive radio telescopes of Nuterra. She suddenly realized that the transmissions were not from the Tattoo People, but from the vines themselves.

Admiral Chase had been listening quietly. "This is good news," he said. "It means we may have an ally."

"Right," said Rashera. "But we still have to deal with the invaders, the ancestors. According to Larimar, they're on Aurora preparing."

"Yes, and Druix and Deneb are there," said Elsenia.

"We have to help them," put in Vega.

"What can we do?" asked Elsenia, desperation in her voice.

"I can help," said Nolondi.

"How, Nolondi?" asked Rashera.

"In Elsenia's report of her visit to the UV-60 planet, the Tattoo People there tried to calm the children with a melody. Do you remember it, Elsenia?" Nolondi said.

"I think so. Why?"

"If the radio waves that produced the melody calm the children, we may be able to produce a melody with the equivalent effect on adults."

Rashera rose from her seat with excitement. "Do you mean we might actually reprogram the minds of Tattoo People?"

"It's not so easy, but I believe it can be done. It will take some experimentation. You can practice on me. I've been the subject of such experiments before," Nolondi said.

"Let's get started," said Admiral Chase.

Admiral Chase and his men, along with Rashera and Nolondi, left Ilsa, Elsenia, and Vega at their camp. Elsenia watched the Admiral disappear into the thicket remembering what he'd told her on Lumina many thousands of years ago. He'd only played a superficial role in the history-making events of the Galactic Garden. Now, he felt guilty, not having gone to Aurora to confront the   invaders with Druix and Deneb. Was he being given another chance? For many reasons, Elsenia hoped Admiral Chase wouldn't be disappointed again.

CHAPTER 37

— Century 2200 —

THE CAPSULES CARRYING DENEB AND DRUIX entered an orbit forty thousand kilometers above Aurora, sufficiently far from the planet that they could make observations without being detected. From that vantage point, they saw Aurora surrounded by thousands of spacecraft. Though they were too far away to see individual ships, the combined effect of so many orbiting objects streaking across the field of their telescopes created a hazy shroud encompassing the planet, more highly concentrated about its equatorial regions.

"I can't believe this is the same planet Xyla and I left so long ago. It was a frozen, dying planet, with no technology to speak of and certainly no satellites," remarked Druix.

"That was a long time ago—long enough that any number of fates might have befallen the planet after your departure. It's just puzzling that word of this civilization hasn't reached Earth or the Union. We need to get closer in."

"It may not be safe," said Druix.

"It's almost certainly not safe, but we can't stay here and we can't turn back without knowing more."

There was truth in Deneb's words, and little to be gained by delaying. They fired the retrorockets of their capsules, reducing orbital velocities and causing the vehicles to spiral inward toward the planet. Barely six hours later, they were close enough to see the true extent of the constellation of orbiting spacecraft. Not only were there thousands of ships, but each was massive—like ocean liners in space. Perhaps this was how the inhabitants had escaped the icy grip of the planet, by constructing orbiting cities, finding the harsh conditions of space more favorable than the frozen surface of the planet. How could so many people live in space, isolated from the planet's land and seas, the sources of food, water, and other necessities life depended on?

Deneb and Druix had little time to explore the question.

Alarms went off in their capsules, indicating the detection of a Union tracking beacon, directing them to dock at an orbiting stations. Paralyzed with awe and incredulity, Druix and Deneb followed instructions, navigating their capsules into a landing port. When the airlocks closed and they'd exited their vehicles, they realized their mistake. The beings approaching were not humans at all. They were Tattoo People—a dozen of them—but unlike those Druix was familiar with, these were twice as tall, towering over their human visitors, surrounding them, and examining them with expressions of annoyance and contempt.

Druix removed his backpack and extracted one of the Arilian translating devices. With trembling hands, he switched it on and spoke.

"My name is Druix. We're humans from the planet Aril."

One of the aliens stepped forward. His hands reached out for the translator. Druix surrendered it. Then, from the device came the chilling words in an electric voice:

"You will not need this. You will be dead soon."

And with that, the alien crushed the instrument in his hands. The sound of the collapsing metal, which was undetectable to the Tattoo People, shocked the humans. These aliens were much stronger than others of their kind. Even they had possessed surprising strength for their size, but the power of these creatures left little doubt as to how quickly they could kill.

One reached out and grabbed Deneb's head, the huge hands completely encompassing the young man's skull. Druix reacted without thinking. Delay would've meant instant death to his son. He propelled his body into the alien, enough to interrupt the deadly grip on Deneb's skull. The alien stumbled only slightly at the impact. Recovering, he brought his arm around in a wide arc and caught Druix on the side of the head, a blow that knocked him to the floor and left him semi-conscious, ears ringing and blood spouting from his nose. His eyes were open though. He saw the alien resume his attack on Deneb. He couldn't watch, but his eyes refused to close.

VEGA woke with a start.

"Deneb's in danger," she cried out loud.

"What's wrong?" Elsenia said with alarm.

They'd been sleeping on air mattresses in the clearing next to the space capsules. Admiral Chase and his men were on the other side of the landing area.

"My God!" exclaimed Vega, an epithet rarely used in their family. Ilsa, who'd grown up in 22nd Century Earth, still held the vestiges of belief in a higher deity, which understandably manifested itself during times of stress. The habit had been passed to her children.

"Vega, tell me what's happening."

"No time. It's the Tattoo People. How can we stop them?"

"Stop them..." Elsenia repeated, confused. "Stop them from what?"

"Quick. We have to do something!" Vega was a child again, frightened and hysterical. Elsenia thought perhaps her sister was dreaming, as she was terrified, sitting up with her hands clutching her head and her eyes wide with fear. Elsenia jumped from the bed and grabbed Vega by the shoulders, shaking her.

"My head hurts. Make him stop!" cried Vega.

"Make who stop?"

Vega was crying now, her hands still gripping her head.

Elsenia had a thought. It was a vision—an image—that presented itself in the panic of the moment. What had put the image in her head now, when her sister was in anguish and pain? Elsenia raised her left hand in the sign of a "V", and with her right index finger crossed the upper part of the "V" and held the symbol in front of Vega's terror-filled eyes.

Vega stared at the sign. Then, still sobbing and shaking, with trembling hands, duplicated the symbol that Elsenia had given her.

DAZED and barely conscious, Druix watched what would probably be his son's last moments of life. Remarkably, Deneb's expression held no fear. With the alien's hands gripping his head, Deneb

269

calmly raised his own hands, positioning them in front of the alien's eyes and formed the sign of a "V" with a horizontal bar across the top. The instant the alien saw the sign, he released the grip on Deneb's head and stepped away.

Deneb ran to his father, who was attempting to rise. The aliens stood back, all now wearing blank expressions.

"What happened?" Druix asked his son.

"I'll tell you later. Are you okay?"

"Getting there. Just shaken up. What do we do now?"

As if in answer, another alien pushed his way through the group and approached Deneb, looking down upon him. Deneb turned his head upward and met the alien's stare.

"Dad, get the other translator from my backpack."

"Are you sure? Remember what they did to the last one?"

"It's okay. They won't break this one."

Druix removed the device and handed it to Deneb. The aliens stood watching the exchange. Deneb turned the instrument on and spoke.

"We want to see the vine. Take us to the vine."

Communicating with a group of Tattoo People required recalibrating the pace of a conversation. The silence, after speaking to them, meant almost certainly a group discussion in the space of a few seconds.

When the reply to Deneb's command came, it was impossible to tell who had spoken, but Druix guessed it was the one standing before Deneb.

"How do you know of the vine?"

"I speak only to the vine," said Deneb into the translator.

The alien crouched, leveling his head with Deneb, peering into his eyes as if he could read the young human's thoughts.

"There is another of you," the electric voice said.

"Take us to the vine," Deneb repeated.

"Where is your other?"

Deneb refused to answer.

"Where is your other?" The translator altered the loudness and tone to communicate anger and impatience.

"My other is somewhere else. It's of no concern to you."

The giant Tattoo man raised an enormous hand. It would be instant death if it fell upon Deneb's head, but the young man stood his ground. Nonchalantly, he formed the sign of the crossed V again. The alien paused and lowered his arm.

"Abnaxes will speak with you. Come."

Deneb and Druix followed the alien through a series of corridors that wound around the circumference of the spacecraft, through the interior shell of a rotating cylinder that produced an artificial gravitational field, in a design like those of Union ships. Was it coincidence, Druix wondered, that both species devised the same solution for creating artificial gravity, or had the aliens learned the technology from humans?

They passed through a door, opening onto an elevated platform cantilevered above a large room where two dozen aliens sat at computer consoles with display monitors containing unrecognizable images and characters. On the platform was a single alien, watching over the scene below him. The alien turned as Deneb and Druix approached. The absence of any humanity in the eyes of the alien chilled Druix. It was unusual among the Tattoo People for one of them to be designated a leader. Because of their unity of purpose and efficiency of communication, they were all equally leaders and followers. Typically, one would act as the point of contact, but this was just for expediency.

But this alien was different. Even before he'd transmitted his first thought through Deneb's translating device, he projected an air of pride, arrogance, and contempt that was unique among the Tattoo People. He moved with a purposeful strut, maintaining an erect posture that pronounced his dominance over those about him. Standing before Deneb and Druix, he loomed over them, forcing the humans to look upward at him. His head was framed by red-tinted overhead lighting, giving his silhouette a demonic aura.

"I am called Abnaxes. Why are you here?"

"We came to find out why you're here." answered Deneb.

"To eliminate the human interlopers and populate the

galaxy with our people." Abnaxes motioned to the room below, where every monitor now displayed images of alien spacecraft. "Each of these ships carries thousands of our kind. They will soon begin their journey to the habitable planets of the galaxy. They will land and overcome humans or other species that interfere."

There was something about the electronic rendition of Abnaxes' words that made them colder and more frightening, as if it was the ether itself that delivered the curse.

"And what of the Tattoo People?" Druix asked. "What will happen to them when your people arrive?"

Abnaxes turned his head, lowering it to eye level with Druix. "You speak of the little ones. They are only caretakers of the vine. They are expendable. They will be destroyed."

"You would destroy your own people?"

"They are not our people. They are manufactured beings. Their lives are meaningless."

Deneb and Druix were stunned into silence. They stared at the alien. Finally, Deneb said, "We will speak with the vine."

"How do you know of the vine?" the alien asked.

"That's of no concern to you."

Druix was amazed at the strength and confidence in his son's voice.

Abnaxes looked again at Druix. As if reading the alien's mind, Deneb said, "If you harm either one of us, you'll never know why we're here."

"How is it you know the sign of the ancient ones?" It was unusual for Tattoo People to ask questions. Abnaxes had just asked two.

"Ask the vine," answered Deneb.

At this, Abnaxes swung his arm and caught Deneb fully across the rib cage. He fell sideways coughing violently, Druix rushing to help him.

"Take them away!" Druix heard Abnaxes shout through the translator.

The large Tattoo People surrounded Deneb and Druix and dragged them from the room, back to the area where the capsules had docked. They were thrown into suspended hammocks made of metal mesh, which folded about each of them separately and sealed. Confined to metallic cocoons, offering little room to move and no means of escape, Deneb and Druix struggled for some time and then gave up.

"What now?" said Druix.

"Now nothing," said Deneb in resignation.

"Why didn't they just kill us?"

"Abnaxes wants to know who sent us and what we know. The V symbol alarmed him. He won't kill us until he understands what the implications might be."

"Does Vega know what's happened to us?" Druix asked his son.

"Maybe not yet. I need to rest. You should too."

It seemed impossible to rest in the restricted confines of the hammocks, but soon both Deneb and Druix were fast asleep.

VEGA shivered violently. Elsenia held her.

"Vega, what happened?"

"They were attacked. Dad was hurt, but I think he's okay."

"You said it was the Tattoo People. Did the Tattoo People attack them?"

"Yes, but these were much bigger."

"Those must be the ones that Larimar spoke of. He said that the Tattoo People produced by the vine are smaller versions of those from their home planet."

"Yes," said Vega, still trembling. "They're larger, and they're cruel and aggressive."

"But you think Deneb and Druix are okay now?"

"I'm not sure they're out of danger. They're sleeping."

"What should we do?"

"I need to talk to Nolondi. He'll have a much better understanding of the aliens."

SOMETHING POKING at Druix through the mesh of the hammock woke him.

"Wake up," a voice said.

The shock of hearing a human voice not Deneb's shocked Druix into instant wakefulness. He tried to remember where he was and why he couldn't move his arms and legs. He struggled, but his efforts only fueled his rising panic more.

"Don't bother struggling. You can't escape," the voice said.

Druix peered out through the mesh of the hammock to see a man, wearing the uniform of a Union supply ship custodian.

"Who are you?" Druix asked.

"My name is Max."

Druix searched his memory trying to recall the name.

"I was custodian of Union Supply Ship 2. Do you know what that is?"

Although Druix was a historian, Deneb's memory of names and dates was far superior. He was awake now.

"You're the custodian whose supply ship was hijacked by Stella and her pirates."

"Right. Who are you two, and why are you here?"

Druix answered. "My name's Druix. This is my son Deneb. We're here on Union business. Can you get us out of these?"

"No, I can't. But don't worry. The aliens will let you out when it suits them."

"Are you with them?" Druix asked.

"No, I'm not with them. They've been holding me and my wife captive for a long time."

"Why?" asked Deneb.

"To learn from us. They're copying our space technology."

"You help them?" Druix couldn't disguise the reproof in his voice.

"Yes. And you will, too, when they threaten to kill your son."

"Is Abnaxes their leader?" asked Deneb.

"He is, but Abnaxes isn't one person. Every time they unfreeze me, usually after thousands of years, I speak to Abnaxes, but never the same one. These aliens are super efficient at sharing information—thoughts, attitudes, experiences, emotions—it really doesn't matter whether you're dealing with one or the other."

"Could Abnaxes be freezing himself? Maybe there is only one of him."

"No. That'd mean he'd be out of control for the thousands of years he's frozen. Abnaxes would never tolerate that."

"What about other people? Are they frozen?"

"Some of them are—the ones who'll eventually colonize the new planets. The rest of them live and die on those orbiting spaceships they're on. I think even the ones that are frozen don't last long enough. They can't. Too much thermal exposure. When they spoil, Abnaxes just replaces them with new colonists."

"It sounds barbaric," said Druix.

"It is. They're barbarians, but a still better analogy is that they're ants. They all live with a single-minded determination to propagate their species. It doesn't matter how many of them die in the process. They just keep multiplying and propagating, eliminating anything that gets in their way."

"Very smart ants."

"Yes and no," said Max. "They're smart in how quickly they learn, alright, but they exhibit little creativity. They were stalled indefinitely on their own planet, because they couldn't find a way to travel across the galaxy, until we came along and they figured it out. They suffer a lack of inventiveness and imagination."

"You have to help us. We have to get to Aurora."

"What's on Aurora?"

"Don't tell him, Deneb."

"Abnaxes sent you to question us. Right?" said Deneb.

Max sighed. "Yes, he did. He wanted me to find out why you're here."

"Where is your wife?" asked Deneb.

"She's orbiting Aurora's star, at the outskirts of the planetary system. I insisted on that to ensure she'd remain in absolute zero conditions."

"As soon as Abnaxes has what he needs from you, you'll

both be killed. You must know that. Help us. We'll help you."

As young as he was, Deneb's voice conveyed confidence and certainty. Max moved closer to the metallic cocoon.

"You have a plan. Don't you, Max? You've thought about escaping, haven't you? It's time, Max. All of us can escape from Abnaxes. Tell us how."

Max looked behind him, to ensure they were alone. His breathing was heavy. "Do you have a radio transmitter?" he asked in a whisper.

"In our capsules—unless they were removed. Weapons too."

"Your weapons are useless against these creatures. But your transmitters might give us an edge."

Max paced about the two hammocks, muttering to himself. He passed a nervous hand through his graying hair. Finally, he crouched next to Deneb's hammock, his face inches away.

"They'll come to get you. Go with them. I'll make sure your capsule entry hatches are open. When you see your chance, run as fast as you can to them. Get in and close the doors. You'll have to manually pilot your way out of the spaceport when the airlock doors open."

Druix listened to the instructions. "How can we outrun the aliens? They'll be all over us. Why would they let us board our space capsules?"

"Have you ever stuck a stick into a nest of ants? They'll converge to the location of the disturbance to protect the nest. We're going to do the same thing, except instead of a stick, we'll use the radio transmitters. I'll activate them in a far-off spot on the space station. The aliens will forget you and everything else to find those transmitters. You'll know when that happens. When it does, run to your vehicles."

"The aliens will figure out what's happened," said Druix. "Won't they chase us?"

"I'm sure they'll want to, but they really have no way to. Humans use radars to locate objects. These aliens won't use technology that transmits radio waves. If they lose visual sighting of us, they'll have no idea where we are. You two can land on Aurora if you want. I'm going to rescue Sadie and put as many light-years as possible between us and this planet."

With that, Max hurried away.

"How do we know we can trust him?" Druix asked.

"Because he left without finding out why we're here."

"Maybe he'll arrange for us to be followed after we escape. That's one way to find out what we're up to."

"That might be the case, but I'd still rather be in my space capsule being chased by aliens than trapped inside this hammock."

"Good point," agreed Druix.

For the next six hours, Druix and Deneb could do nothing but wait. They'd both slept after their initial confinement. Neither could sleep any longer. They twisted and turned within the metal sleeves, trying to find comfort, and whispered wild speculations and unanswerable questions to each other. If their captors had been human, it'd be much easier to imagine what fate awaited them, but at the mercy of aliens with advanced intellects and no moral conscience, even the unimaginable was possible. The minutes passed with agonizing slowness.

ELSENIA AND VEGA sat with Nolondi and Admiral Chase. The sun hadn't yet risen. In the damp cool air, Vega was sweating profusely.

Elsenia felt her forehead. "Are you okay? Do you have a fever?"

"It's Deneb," Vega answered. "He's confined somewhere. He can't move."

"Nolondi, can you help? Do you know what might have happened to them?"

Nolondi shook his head. Through the translating medallion around his neck, he said, "I know nothing about the people of which Larimar spoke."

Vega covered her face with her hands. "I wish there was something we could do to help."

"We're still working on the tones to reconfigure the neural pathways in the brains of my people. We will test them soon, but we have no way of knowing if this will work."

"I don't understand," said the Admiral, "Even if you come up with a sequence of sounds to transmit, how will that help Deneb and Druix?"

Nolondi looked to Vega, but she seemed too distraught to answer the question. "I imagine that once Vega has learned the notes, then Deneb will know them as well," Nolondi said.

Vega rocked back and forth, with her arms now folded around her as if she were too cold.

"I'll get back to the Tattoo People to resume testing of the notes," said Nolondi. He rushed off into the predawn darkness.

CHAPTER 38

— Century 2200 —

TRY AS HE MIGHT to avoid horrible thoughts, Druix couldn't coax his mind in any direction that didn't circle back to the same depressing question: how long would it take to die within the metal cocoons in which he and Deneb were imprisoned? It was difficult to imagine a more torturous way to spend the last hours of his life, yet he feared he'd succumb to the lethality of his own imagination. He wondered, too, which moment would contain his last conscious thought, but in so doing he perpetuated his consciousness. Like the paradox that prevented the condemned man from dying as long as he couldn't know the moment of his death, Druix remained in a suspended state of existence.

It would have driven him insane, but Max's words proved correct. After several hours, four aliens appeared. The seams of the hammocks separated and he and Deneb tumbled to the floor. Druix doubted his ability to move his arms and legs again, but he was lifted and carried through the corridors of the alien ship in the illumination of the muted, pale red lighting from above. This time, he tried to memorize the route, searching for objects and fixtures that would guide them back toward the docking area. He hoped Deneb was doing the same. If Max successfully executed his plan, they'd have to run back through these corridors with no time for hesitation or delay.

When they stood before Abnaxes again, the alien leaned toward them menacingly.

"I will ask you again. Why have you come here?"

Deneb touched Druix's arm, indicating that he'd speak for them.

"My father is from this planet. He wishes to visit the place of his birth."

Druix was impressed by his son. He'd said the words least likely to incur the alien's wrath, but interesting enough to keep the discussion going—while waiting for Max to execute his plan.

"Why do you seek the vine on this planet?"

"Our scientists studied the vine and asked questions that can only be answered by examining the plant on Aurora."

Abnaxes hesitated. It was possible he didn't know the human name for the planet they were orbiting.

"That planet belongs to us now. The humans there work for us."

Deneb and Druix exchanged glances. "There are humans on the planet?" Druix asked.

"Yes. We let them live there as long as they give us what we need."

"We want to visit them. They're my people, our ancestors."

"They are nothing," returned Abnaxes. "You may not visit."

There was no response to Abnaxes' statement. The two humans stood there, mute before the towering form of the alien. Abnaxes turned to Deneb. "How came you to know the sign of the ancient ones?"

"I don't know."

"You refuse to tell me?"

"I don't know. The sign came to me." Deneb touched a finger to his temple. "It was sent to me by my other."

"Who is your other? Where is he?"

These were questions Deneb wouldn't answer. He waited.

"You will tell me who your other is and where he is!" Abnaxes repeated. The translator made the words louder in response to the force behind them.

Suddenly Abnaxes twitched, as if reacting to an electric shock. His face contorted into a painful grimace. With a single sweeping motion of one arm, he pushed Deneb and Druix aside and rushed to the door of the room. The four guards who'd been standing behind them followed him out. The aliens seated below in the control room rose together and moved toward the stairs that led to the catwalk where Abnaxes had stood to observe them.

"Hurry!" shouted Deneb, bolting toward the door and through it, just ahead of the aliens. Once in the corridor, they ran back in the direction of the landing dock. To their relief, Abnaxes and the other aliens were moving in the opposite direction. Whatever Max had done made the aliens completely forget their human prisoners. How long would it take before they realized their mistake?

The care Deneb and Druix had taken in memorizing the route from the landing dock served them well. They negotiated the red-lit passageways without error, and quickly found themselves standing before their space capsules, but the outer doors to the landing area were closed. What now? How were they supposed to get the capsules off the alien ship?

"Board your capsules!" It was Max. "Strap in, start the engines, be ready to steer out of here."

"But the landing doors are closed," Druix objected.

"Use your weapons. All of them. Just blast your way out."

Druix's heart sank. Max was crazy after all. His whole plan hinged on their ability to forcefully open a hole in the door of the landing area.

Seeing the doubt on Druix's face, Max said, "I'd do it myself, but they stripped the weapons from my capsule."

"Take my capsule," said Deneb. "I'll take yours."

Deneb ran to Max's capsule. Druix watched his son disappear into the vehicle, then boarded his own capsule.

Max lost no time in firing up the engines and initiating a slow rotation so that the weapons systems, normally used to protect the capsule from incoming objects and space debris, now faced the landing doors.

Deneb and Druix watched on their video monitors as Max activated the lasers and methodically cut into the door of the landing port. The deafening roar and thick clouds of vapor from the rockets of the three capsules filled the room. It would certainly alert the aliens. Druix, seeing what Max was doing, also rotated his capsule, and activated his laser weapon to help. Before long, a large, rectangular-shaped outline of glowing hot metal sizzled before them. Max turned off the laser and fired his ballistic weapon, a single shot that hit squarely in the middle of the rectangle. Druix did the same. The second missile broke the section out. It flew into space, the rush of air from the alien space station providing additional impulse to its flight.

Max maneuvered his capsule smoothly through the opening. Druix waited until Deneb was also out, then followed.

All three capsules, free of the space station, raced rapidly away. Druix kept an eye on the video monitor as Max rotated his capsule. Now, with the weapons pointing back toward the landing port with its gaping hole, Max launched an EMP pulse that entered through the opening. Lightning-like discharges crackled about the hull of the ship, and the entire vehicle went dark. The alien space station was completely disabled—for how long, they couldn't say, but it was definitely enough time for Deneb and Druix to land on the surface of Aurora and try to find the alien vine.

Max's capsule disappeared from view as he set a course to rescue Sadie and start the long journey back to the realm of humans.

CHAPTER 39

— Century 2200 —

THE FIRST THING Deneb and Druix noticed on Aurora was the orange haze that hung in the sky. It was difficult to believe this was the same world Druix and his mother had fled from. Even thousands of years couldn't make such a difference in the environment of a planet. Or could it?

Max had advised them to land at a spaceport near one of the industrial complexes. The site was no more than a large expanse of broken concrete surrounded by a crude fence made of irregularly shaped metal bars. To one side was a squat, windowless structure. Druix and Deneb walked toward it, as it was the only place in view that looked like it might have human occupants.

Before they'd covered the distance, a voice called out to them. They turned to see a thin man in overalls, limping toward them. Where had he come from? With his slender profile and drab clothing, he blended into the gloom.

Druix and Deneb met him and the three shook hands. He spoke rapidly in a language the visitors couldn't understand. Druix held up his hand.

"Union English. Do you speak Union English?"

The man just shook his head. Then he stepped toward Druix, examining him closely. In broken English, he pronounced the words, "You from here." And he pointed to the ground.

"Yes. My mother was Malanite," said Druix.

This response seemed to make the thin man happy. He smiled and started limping away, beckoning them to follow.

The fence surrounding the area was not as solid as it appeared. Deneb and Druix followed through an opening, beyond which was a small vehicle, uncovered and with seats for four.

They rode along the streets of the city, an endless series of manufacturing plants. Smoke billowed from stacks on every one, and all were connected by a disordered array of pipes, cables, and wires. There were few people in the streets. Every now and then, through opened freight doors, they caught a glimpse of the interior of the buildings. The dimly lit spaces within were smoke-filled and murky, revealing shadowy figures working, carrying impossibly heavy loads, or sitting in rows at machines, all in the presence of ear-shattering noises and sickening chemical odors.

Their escort stopped the cart. Druix and Deneb jumped off and followed him into the gloomy interior of the building, where red-hot furnaces, issuing jets of crimson-tinged smoke were being used to form metal. Men worked at stone tables, banging out shapes in glowing sheets with tremendous hammer blows that produced fiery sprays of luminescent sparks.

The thin man gestured for them to wait by the door. Deneb and Druix stood awkwardly conspicuous amidst the gloom in their shiny Union jump suits and backpacks. One of the workmen approached and studied them curiously. He ran his fingers across the smooth exterior of Deneb's backpack, as if unable to comprehend the skill and technology behind its flawless construction. Another man joined him. The new arrival was short, but he may have once been tall. His pronounced stoop gave the impression that his back was hunched, but it was impossible to tell because his coveralls so loosely fitted his frame.

"You are Malanite?" the man said, looking at Druix.

The language was strange, but Druix understood the man's question. Then he remembered, he'd spoken the Malanite language as a child. Though he hadn't used it for many years, he still understood it.

"Half Malanite," he answered, and his lips formed the words as easily as if he'd just left the planet.

"My name is Ka-pong."

"I am Druix." Druix recalled that his name in the Malanite language meant he was of mixed parentage.

Ka-Pong nodded. "Come with me."

The man led them to a small room, which meant to serve as an office, though there were no papers, computers or phones —only a few chairs, storage cabinets, and a small desk cluttered with bits of metal.

"Sit. If you're hungry, I can have some food brought in."

Druix translated for Deneb, who shook his head.

"No, thank you. We're fine."

Ka-pong fell into a chair behind the desk.

"What are you doing here?"

"We came to see the vine."

Ka-pong's eyes narrowed. "What do you know about it?"

Druix started to answer, but Deneb touched his father's arm. "Dad, can you translate for me?"

Ka-pong must've wondered why Druix, clearly the elder of the two visitors, needed his son's approval before answering. He gave Druix a questioning look.

"My son's a scientist," Druix lied. "He's studied the vine on other planets. It's because of him that we're here."

"Other planets?" Ka-pong asked.

Druix translated for Deneb, then answered. "These aliens have planted the vine throughout the galaxy. The vine grows and takes over, killing all preexisting vegetation."

Druix wasn't sure how much Ka-pong understood. The man stared blankly back at him.

"Can you tell us what you know about the aliens?"

Ka-pong snorted. "There's not much to know. They came to Aurora a long time ago. They've exploited the planet and the humans who live here to build spaceships. All mines, refineries, foundries, and chemical plants are under their control. Aurora has become a foul, polluted world where hundreds of millions of humans barely survive, suffering from disease, poverty, famine, and crime."

"Humans make everything the aliens need?" Druix could not conceal his surprise, disappointment, and disapproval. "Why?"

"Why?" Ka-pong repeated. "Why?"

"Yes. What do they give you in return?"

Druix remembered that when he lived on Aurora, the Malanites and the town people lived apart, but traded with each other. The Malanites provided fish to the towns in exchange for fruits and vegetables grown in climate-controlled domes.

"What do they give us?" Ka-pong repeated with a sneer. "They give us nothing. They take. In exchange, they let us live."

Druix translated the man's response for Deneb.

"They're slaves," Deneb said quietly.

"The aliens threaten you?" Druix asked.

"They don't threaten us. They kill us. If we don't do what they ask, they kill us. Have you seen the aliens kill?"

"No," answered Druix quietly, although he almost had.

"They kill us as if we're no more than insects. They're merciless, indiscriminate, and extremely effective at killing humans. And you two are curious about the vine? It's not the vine you should be concerned with."

Druix translated this. Deneb listened intently. "Ask him again," Deneb said. "We need to find the vine."

"Does the vine grow on Aurora?" Druix thought about the smoky pall that suffused the atmosphere. He couldn't imagine any plant growing in the poisonous vapor.

"The vine only grows in one place that I know of—in the big valley. Nowhere else."

"Can you take us there?"

"No. It's prohibited. It's guarded."

"Guarded by whom?"

"The aliens, of course."

"Aliens are here? We thought they stayed in space."

"They're here alright. They've been here for as long as we know. They live within the vine. They don't let anyone get close. When they need parts for their spaceships, a group will come out of the valley. They'll go to whatever manufacturing plant they need parts from and show us what they want and how many they want. We've been providing all the parts and equipment for them for thousands of years. That's all we do. Every factory, every power plant, every mine you see is working for them. They let us do only a minimal amount for our own survival. They take what they need to support whatever it is they do in space, and they leave next to nothing for us."

"That's crazy," Druix said. "Haven't the humans tried to

fight them—defeat them and take back the planet?"

"Not in my lifetime, but ages ago there were revolutions and wars—long bloody ones. We lost them all. Now we just give them what they want."

"How close can they get us to the valley?" Deneb asked.

Druix put the question to Ka-pong, who shook his head. "All approaches are heavily guarded. If you're determined to go there, we'll give you a vehicle and point the way. They'll kill you both as soon as they see you."

Druix translated this for Deneb, who expressed not a trace of fear or hesitation.

"We'll need poison—weed killer."

Druix relayed the request to Ka-pong. The man laughed, then started coughing, until he expectorated a watery phlegm onto the floor. "We don't have weed killer because we don't have weeds. We don't have any plants at all—except that vine. We manufacture our food, such as it is, from chemicals. No, we have no use for weed killer, but we can give you poison. We have plenty of poison. The whole planet is filled with poison."

CHAPTER 40

— Century 2200 —

DENEB AND DRUIX SPENT THE NIGHT sleeping on the floor of Ka-Pong's factory. The next day, he gave them the small car they'd ridden in the previous day.

"This is as much as we can help," Ka-pong said. "The valley is that way. I haven't been on that road for years." He pointed into the distance where the land rose, climbing toward low hills, beyond which were mountains, barely visible in the yellow haze. "When you reach the vine—if you reach the vine—the Tattoo People will be there to greet you. They'll kill you both."

Druix translated for Deneb, "Just tell him 'thank you'."

They shook Ka-Pong's hand and boarded the little car, watching the crippled human return to the gloom of his factory.

"I know the valley," Druix told Deneb, as they drove the car along the rutted roads that wound through the manufacturing plants. Occasionally, they passed the residential areas, which were only a collection of ramshackle shelters pieced together from metal scrap, slag, broken concrete, and other by-products of their sordid industry. Children were nowhere to be seen, leading Deneb and Druix to conclude that they too worked in the factories.

"In the years I lived here, your grandmother sent me to schools in town. I still remember my geography lessons. Aurora has one very fertile valley, created by a large river that separates two mountain chains. Before the planet began to freeze, the valley was the source of most of the fruits and vegetables grown here."

"It makes sense that the aliens would pick a fertile valley to plant the vine," Deneb said.

"But I don't understand how the planet warmed up. When your grandmother and I left, Aurora was dying. Its sun was fading out, the temperatures were dropping, and the surface was covered with ice and snow. What saved it?"

"My guess is that the vine saved it. Or, ironically enough, the aliens saved it. The vine is genetically engineered to transform the atmosphere of a planet in whatever direction it needs to go to sustain life. For Aurora, when the vine took over, it introduced huge amounts of carbon dioxide into the air, creating a super greenhouse effect that offset the influence of the fading sun. You said it yourself. Even when the planet was frozen, the people of the towns grew plants under domes designed to retain as much of the failing light as possible. The vine transformed the entire planet into a greenhouse. The surface temperature increased, and then stabilized."

Druix considered this. "If that's true, then if we destroy the vine, we'll destroy the planet, too."

"Who said we were going to destroy the vine?"

"The poison."

Deneb smiled. "I'm hoping we won't have to use it. Even if we do, I'm sure there's not enough poison here to kill the vine on this planet entirely."

"Then what are we going to do?"

"I don't know yet. I'm just following instructions," Deneb answered.

They drove several hours until they reached a summit of the foothills. The haze cleared somewhat and they saw a band of green vegetation beginning on the mountain slope. It was the alien vine. Tattoo People there would easily see approaching humans.

"We'll walk the rest of the way," said Deneb.

They abandoned the car and trudged along a road that might have been the route to a mine or quarry. There were deep holes and ruts, exposing jagged pieces of cement and occasionally twisted metal, perhaps the tracks of an ancient rail system. Abandoned buildings flanked the road. A heavy layer of soot blanketed the area, mustard colored, filtering weak sunlight scattering off particles of dust and ash, wafting into the air by chaotic gusts of wind, twisting about the structures like ghostly vipers.

Deneb and Druix climbed steadily uphill now, panting with exhaustion, and in doing so inhaled large amounts of the foul air. They stopped to rest, leaning against a slab of concrete threaded with ribs of rusted rebar.

They said nothing. Deneb and Druix knew each other's thoughts. Driven by fear, doubt, and uncertainty, they considered all possible outcomes. Few of them were good. If they could reach the vine, they had a chance, but they almost certainly would encounter aliens before that happened. Deneb and Druix carried EMP weapons, but they knew from their experience on the alien spaceport that the weapons were of limited use against the huge creatures.

They climbed steadily for an hour before nearing the forest. With the higher elevation, the air became clearer. As they approached, the band of green resolved itself into a wall of vegetation. Before long, they saw the tangled branches and leaves of the vine, tightly woven into an impenetrable barrier ten meters high. The space between the branches was so restricted, they'd have difficulty fitting even a fist into the mass.

"What happens now?" Druix asked.

"We climb."

Druix looked dubiously at the wall, craning his neck to see where it ended and the sky began.

"We learned a trick when playing with the Tattoo children on Lumina. When moving by way of the labyrinth of paths to find their teammates proved impossible, the little imps scampered up and ran along the thick canopy above."

"Doesn't seem fair," said Druix.

"Strictly, it wasn't allowed, but they all did it, and no one complained. The real problem was how unreliable and dangerous it was. There might be openings in unexpected places—easy to fall through, but no one did."

"Is it strong enough to hold our weight?"

"Barely. We'll have to be very careful. This vine looks denser than the one on Lumina. It's probably been growing for many thousands of years. I think we'll be okay."

Druix shook his head, then said to his son, "You first."

Deneb found handholds and footholds and started up the wall. Druix, comforted by the ease with which the youth climbed, followed.

The wall was vertical where they'd started, but as they neared the top it rounded out, becoming horizontal, and they soon found themselves standing upright on the dense canopy. The view took their breath away. The surface stretched into the distance as far as the eye could see. It was mostly flat, but gentle mounds and protrusions were visible. Atop the thicket, Druix felt as if he were standing on clouds in a celestial dream of heavenly serenity. The reality was starkly different. He had to remind himself that beneath the rolling surface were fierce aliens. The aliens could be only meters away below his feet.

"Won't they know that we're up here?" Druix asked.

"They can't see us. Our movement will cause vibrations, which they're sensitive to, but hopefully they'll believe other aliens are nearby. We have the advantage that it's likely no other human has ventured to climb on top of the forest."

"There's probably a reason for that."

"You said this was a valley with a river running through it. The river will orient us, once we find it."

"I still don't understand. How will we know the source of the vine?"

"Vega will help. She's communicating with a vine in a different part of the galaxy. It's not like Vega will tell me where to go, or which direction to travel, but when we're closer, I'll feel it. Believe me."

Druix looked doubtful. "Deneb, this is too risky. Those aliens are deadly. They almost killed us once."

"I know, Dad, but we've got to do this. The key to overcoming the aliens is in finding the source of the vine."

Druix sighed, looking out again at the rolling green surface before them. He glanced up at the same sun he was born to. It was a sun that was slowly fading, losing radiance at a rate that should have produced a frigid ice age. Somehow, the vine had reversed that deadly trend and transformed Aurora into a place warm enough to sustain life. It was tragic that most of the planet had been turned into an industrial morass to support the aliens. Aurora had been raped for its metals, fuels, chemicals, and labor force. The humans on Aurora were now a race of slaves, their lives stripped of meaning, toiling at the mercy of savage and cruel taskmasters, who killed with frightening detachment. Deneb was right. They had to try.

"If you want to find the river, I think it's in that direction." Druix pointed to a slight depression in the sea of vegetation. "It ran generally from east to west. If we move north, we'll cross it."

"Okay. Follow me, and try to step where I step. I've done this before. It will be tricky at first, but you'll get the hang of it."

Deneb had overestimated his father's ability to learn how to negotiate the jagged and twisted surface. Though the branches were strong enough, they'd been brushed smooth by wind and rain. Druix slipped often, his feet falling through openings in the vegetation, and he'd have to drop to his knees to steady himself with his hands.

Deneb was patient with him, helping him up whenever he fell, instructing him on what he'd done wrong.

"You have to turn your foot on every step according to the orientation of the branch. You don't want your foot parallel to a branch. That's how you slip off."

Druix found that if he held Deneb's hand, he felt more confident. Rather than following his son, they walked side by side. After a while, he let go and they made better progress.

The slight depression they'd seen from afar became more pronounced. Soon they could make out a narrow bulge running through the center of the depression in a snake-like pattern along its length.

"It should be the river. The bulge must be where the vine comes together to cover it. The river water would nourish the vine well."

Deneb nodded in agreement. His face showed concern. "We need to be more careful. I've the feeling most of the aliens are here."

They moved slowly across the valley. Druix worried about nightfall. With darkness, they'd truly be at the mercy of the aliens.

They were making steady progress toward the center bulge when Druix slipped. His right leg fell through an opening in the canopy up to his knee. Deneb helped him extricate his leg. Druix assured him that he wasn't hurt. They moved on.

Moments later, they felt a quiver in the thicket just below them. A powerful bluish-green arm punched its way through the branches just a meter from where they stood. Deneb grabbed his father's hand and pulled him.

"Run! Run!"

In the next instant, another arm broke through, even closer. The alien hands, failing to catch their prey, began tearing away the surrounding vegetation, breaking the surface of the canopy. Tattoo People had always shown great respect for the vine, but this alien showed little regard for the plant. His powerful hands savagely ripped away branches as if they were twigs.

Druix and Deneb moved as fast as possible across the river, but now both tripped often. They had no time to think about the placement of their panic-driven steps.

Soon, other terrifying blue-green arms penetrated the surface. It was a scene from the most horrible of nightmares: the two humans stumbling across the uneven surface, now in fluid motion, as clutching hands tried to grab them, like demons reaching up from a merciless hell.

They managed to reach the edge of the bulge when an alien broke through, climbed out, and came at them. Unable to stand on the branches, the creature crawled on all fours, quickly closing the distance to the fleeing humans. It was about to grab Deneb's leg, when Druix fired his EMP weapon directly at the alien's head. Druix knew the weapon wouldn't kill the creature, but hoped to slow the attack long enough to let them escape. It did. The alien went into spasmodic contortions, glowing electric blue with the energy of the weapon. It slumped onto the canopy surface, twitching violently, but still, terrifyingly, trying to reach the humans with limbs that wouldn't obey.

Other aliens now broke through to the surface. Deneb and

Druix scrambled up the bulge covering the river center, hoping to put distance between them and their pursuers, but one after another the aliens broke through the canopy, crawling out, joining the chase.

It was hopeless now, Druix knew. Panting heavily, his face showing fear and defeat, he held his EMP weapon, ready to fire in one last desperate stand against the alien force. Deneb, with courage that gave Druix a fleeting sense of pride, stood next to his father, also aiming his weapon.

Before either had a chance to fire, the vine beneath their feet opened, and they both disappeared, falling in a gut-wrenching descent into the rapidly flowing river below.

CHAPTER 41

— Century 2200 —

Druix was well acquainted with the feeling of weightlessness, having experienced it on many occasions in his space capsule. He was used to the frightening, exhilarating sensation accompanying the acceleration and deceleration of the capsule during launches and landings. Yet he'd never felt anything so terrifying as the free-fall he suffered when the vine under his feet parted and he dropped suddenly a hundred meters into the river below.

He struck the water feet first, but the shock of the impact reverberated through his entire body, stunning him into an electrified state of semi-consciousness. Had it not been for the frigidity of the churning water that engulfed him simultaneously, he would have succumbed to the false comfort of oblivion. While struggling to breathe, assess the danger, and remain coherent, he worried about Deneb. He forced his eyes open to search for his son in the foaming turbulence surrounding him. It was hopeless. He flailed his arms about in a futile attempt to find something to grab hold of, a hand or a foot or a length of hair, anything that would offer him hope of saving Deneb. Only after several long seconds had passed did he kick his feet to arrest his descent and start the arduous climb to the surface where there was light and air and life.

Union jumpsuits were designed to be naturally buoyant, so that even with his boots on, Druix made steady progress upward. However, as he rose, he was forced rapidly sideways by the power of the river. It was senseless to fight the current. He let himself be swept along with the single purpose now of breaking the surface and drawing air into his aching lungs.

When he finally did, it only lasted an instant—enough time for him to see the shore, distant, a thin line of green, as slim and tenuous as his hope of ever reaching it, especially with the current now keeping him in the center of the river where the water was swiftest.

Then he was forced below the surface again, gulping in

great quantities of water. Now his desperation was no longer to save his son, but to save himself. The river about him grew more turbulent, whipping his limbs first one direction, then the other, making him long for the predictable feeling of free fall that had brought him here.

Life became distant to Druix—as if it'd never been more than a fantasy. He felt himself become part of another reality, where fear turns into acceptance, pain becomes an abstraction, light becomes dark, and end becomes beginning. It was an inescapable sensation of transition, transformation, and ultimately termination.

A tug on his jumpsuit startled him. It felt different from other chaotic forces the water delivered, as it was from one direction, and it was constant. He was being pulled slowly away from the turbulence, toward the shore, slowly. He kicked his feet to help, rising to the surface for an instant, long enough to see that the line of vegetation was now closer.

Nearing the shore, he was overcome by exhaustion, and let himself be pulled the remaining distance, concentrating on not swallowing more water in his desperation to breathe. When his feet finally touched solid ground, he scrambled up the shore and collapsed onto a spit of sand, coughing up water and gasping the life-restoring air. He felt his rescuer sit down beside him and take his hand.

"Dad, are you okay?"

Druix looked up, eyes blurred with water and tears.

He saw Vega.

Too tired to speak, Druix looked in panic at the river. "Where's Deneb?" he gasped.

"He's okay. He's not here. He's safe."

"But…"

"I'll explain later. Can you walk? We shouldn't stay here."

Druix ached all over, but knew it'd be easy for the aliens to find them if they remained. "Where?" he asked.

"Follow me."

Vega helped him to his feet and held his hand, drawing

him behind her to where the vine's tangled branches presented an impenetrable barrier. In dazed confusion, Druix saw that Vega was wearing Deneb's jumpsuit, with the same backpack, EMP weapon, and canister of poison that his son had been carrying.

"What happened to Deneb?" he asked again.

"We traded places. I swim better," Vega said.

Ignoring the answer, Druix said, "How are we going to get through the vine?"

"Just follow me."

Vega stopped short of the thicket and raised her hands, creating the same crossed "V" sign Deneb had used on the spaceport of Aurora. Nothing happened until Vega's hands came in contact with a branch. Immediately, the foliage began to move, rearranging itself to produce a passageway, barely large enough for Vega and Druix to pass through.

The vine closed behind them, while simultaneously opening up ahead. Barely enough light filtered through the branches for them to see, but it didn't matter. There was only one way to go, in the direction dictated by the alien vine. Vega kept her arms raised before her, maintaining the sign of the crossed "V" that seemed to be their passport to a destination unknown.

They were descending, first gradually, then more steeply. Druix heard the roar of the river close by and understood that had Vega not pulled him to shore, he would've been caught in a tremendous cascade. He felt incredibly fragile, flesh and bones surrounded by an alien vine that could easily crush him and his daughter, and flanked by a mighty torrent that meant instant death were they to slip into its grasp.

Where was Deneb? How could he've escaped the peril so ubiquitous on the ill-fated planet where Druix was born?.

The path slanted laterally as the ground became more sloped, but now the roar of the river diminished, giving Druix a slight sense of relief. He wondered where they were being led. Did Vega know? She seemed unhesitant. Did she have any idea how dangerous the tall Tattoo People of Aurora were?

It grew darker. Their descent separated them from the sky

with an ever thickening layer of branches and leaves. Penetrating deeper into the bosom of the plant as it enfolded them within its woody embrace, Druix kept one hand on Vega's backpack, puzzling over how she and her brother could have traded places. If it was true, how long had they been doing that? It had always been eerie and inexplicable how much the twins shared.

Vega took an abrupt turn. Now they were on level ground, moving more quickly. It surprised Druix how rapidly the vine could reconfigure its branches to allow their passage. Had it been an animal and not a plant, perhaps Druix wouldn't have been so astonished, but he was unaccustomed to a plant having such mobility and flexibility. Was it a simple response to a stimulus? Were he and Vega just some irritant that the vine was disposing of by channeling them to some waste heap, a pile of debris and dead matter it had to shed? Or was there some intelligence behind the route being formed for them, with some ultimate intent, whether it be good or evil?

They finally emerged in a temple or chamber that Druix surmised could only be a place of worship. It was dome-shaped, like Petyuba's undersea home, except larger. The floor was a dense weave of branches from the vine, packed tightly together and polished to a glossy, chestnut veneer as smooth as glass. The dome, in contrast to the rectilinear weave of the floor, was composed of swirls and eddies, nested tightly together. Not a ray of light could penetrate from the sky above. In horror, Druix realized the only light came from the blue-green iridescent glow of six Tattoo People standing at attention in the center of the dome-shaped space. They stood in two groups of three on each side of a "V"-shaped object, a conical shaped container with a ring around its circumference. From the conical container grew a single plant, a miniaturized version of the alien vine.

Druix and Vega took several steps into the chamber, and the vine closed behind them, blocking any possibility of escape. Vega swung off the backpack and opened it. When she withdrew the translating medallion, two Tattoo People stepped forward.

"Stop!" cried Druix. "Don't turn it on. They don't like it."

Vega took the translator in both hands, her finger on the power switch. She held it up to the approaching Tattoo People, as if offering the device to them. The two hesitated, then began to move forward again, now more rapidly. Vega switched on the translator and started to sing. It was a haunting melody of no more than sixteen bars. She repeated it. Druix watched in amazement as the Tattoo People halted their attack. They stood transfixed, not moving, with mixed expressions of confusion and tranquility. Their four companions kept their positions next to the plant, also looking dazed and helpless.

Vega, still singing, walked forward holding the medallion close to the two who were nearest. One by one, each fell to the floor, their legs buckling, their tall frames collapsing into a paralyzed stupor. She passed them and approached the remaining four. They tried to flee, but went limp. In less than thirty seconds, Vega had rendered the fierce Tattoo People harmless and defenseless.

"Dad, do you have your EMP weapon?"

"Yes," Druix said, fumbling to unhook it from his belt.

"Shoot any of them if they start to move."

Druix looked at the six in turn. All seemed incapable of motion of any kind.

Vega withdrew the canister of poison from Deneb's backpack. She opened it and stepped up to the plant, helpless now without protection from its sentries.

"Stop!"

The shout erupted from the translating medallion. Druix looked to see if more Tattoo People were about. There were none.

"How is it you know the chords of tranquility?"

Vega looked confused at first, wondering about the source of the radio waves that were being converted to words in Union English by the medallion she wore.

"It is I. The plant before you."

Vega stepped closer to the "V"-shaped container that held the shrub.

"I am Vega. This is my father, Druix. Who are you?"

"I have no name. I am also a father, and a mother, and the

origin of that which you call the alien vine."

Vega nodded. "Yes, I know. I've come to destroy you."

"Very well," said the plant. "But first tell me how you came to learn the chords of tranquility."

"We learned it from your people, the ones we call Tattoo People."

"Why? They are forbidden to reveal the chord to any."

"My people, the human race, helped the Tattoo People. And the Tattoo People help us."

"This is true?" said the plant.

"How can you ask that?" said Vega. "You know what's happening on every planet the vine has grown. The vine, the Tattoo People, and humans have become friends."

"I know that humans destroyed an entire planet where my vine had grown. I know that humans fill the galaxy with polluting radio waves, disrupting the life spirit that unites the Tattoo People and keeps them attentive to the health of my vines."

"The destruction of the vine on planet Alpha was a crime committed by despicable humans who have been dealt with justly," Vega said. "The pollution of the galaxy with radio waves has been inadvertent, because humans were not aware of the damage it caused to your people."

"Nevertheless, the race of humans is not a benign race."

"And the race that now strives to destroy all humans, as well as the little Tattoo People, beings created by your vines? Is that a benign race, when it conspires to eliminate all other competing races? Is the galaxy not large enough for more than one race? How arrogant and presumptuous for you to believe the galaxy should be home to only one kind of being."

There was a long pause. Only a faint crackling came from the translator. Druix surveyed the temple where the six Tattoo People lay in silent repose. The phosphorescent glow from their bodies that had provided dim light to the room before was fading. He could barely see Vega, standing before the V-shaped container, still holding the poison. He considered getting a lantern from his backpack, but was afraid to let go of his EMP weapon.

At that moment, Vega staggered, as if all the strength had been expelled from the muscles that sustained her posture. She crumbled to the ground, her eyes wide with fear and confusion. Forgetting the Tattoo People, Druix dropped his EMP weapon and ran to her.

"Vega, what's wrong?"

"It's Deneb," she said weakly. "He's in pain."

GROANS WOKE ELSENIA. They came from where Vega slept in her air mattress.

"Vega, what's wrong?"

Elsenia heard only more groans and feeble coughing. She jumped from her bed and rushed to her sister's side.

Pulling back the thermal blanket, Elsenia saw Deneb, lying prone and looking at her, panic-stricken, trying to speak.

"Deneb!" Elsenia cried in alarm and surprise.

Deneb coughed convulsively, interrupted only by quick agonizing moans.

Elsenia looked about helplessly. It was still dark in camp, only a single lantern shone in the distance.

"Julian!" Elsenia cried. "Admiral Chase, we need help. Help us! Please!"

She held Deneb's hand as his body jerked and twisted.

She heard the sounds of others rising from their beds. Lights went on, illuminating the campground. Admiral Chase appeared first, followed by Rashera and Nolondi. They looked down to see Deneb no longer coughing. His body had stiffened into a horrifying and unnatural arch, as if being pushed up from below.

"Where's Vega?" Admiral Chase asked.

"She's gone," answered Elsenia. "She took Deneb's place. I'll explain later. We have to help Deneb. If he dies, so will Vega."

"I'll bring a medical kit," said Rashera, hurrying away.

Elsenia cried in panic, "Hurry!"

"He's drowning," said a voice from nearby. It was Ilsa. She pushed her way through and knelt next to Deneb. She turned him over on his stomach. After gently rotating his head to the side, she pushed down forcefully on his back. It only took one push. Deneb's lungs expelled a gush of yellow fluid. He coughed several times more, his body shaking with each paroxysm. He took a deep breath, then seemed to relax, breathing more easily. Tears filled his eyes.

"I can't feel my legs," he gasped.

Ilsa held one hand on his back. "Don't try to move. Lay still." She turned to the others. "I need to cut open his jumpsuit."

Nolondi produced a knife from his utility belt and handed it to her. Ilsa carefully sliced through the rugged fabric from neck to waist in a line following Deneb's spine. She parted the cloth revealing her son's pale skin.

"I need more light."

Under the illumination of four lamps, Ilsa ran her two hands along Deneb's spine, her hands gently probing the bones through the skin. She applied pressure at various points, squeezing and manipulating the cervical disks through the surrounding dermis and cartilage. At one point, a shutter ran through Deneb's entire frame. Ilsa concentrated on that spot, moving her hands rhythmically in ever widening circles, then reversing the maneuver and spiraling inward again. With the conclusion of each circuit, Deneb's arms and legs twitched. After several minutes, he was wiggling his toes and bending his legs at the knees.

"Don't move," said Ilsa. "Let the healing process work."

She continued her treatment, with the others gazing on in wonder and relief. With the hypnotic motion of Ilsa's skilled hands, Deneb slowly got stronger.

"Thanks, Mom," he said weakly.

"Is Vega okay," Ilsa asked.

Deneb closed his eyes. "I think so. I'm not sure."

Ilsa turned to Elsenia. "Bring me my backpack."

Elsenia disappeared into the surrounding darkness.

DRUIX HELD HIS DAUGHTER, unsure what to do. He noticed with hopeless resignation that the six Tattoo People were beginning to

302

move. He looked at his EMP weapon, several meters away. Vega still had her weapon, but Druix didn't want to move her to retrieve it from her jumpsuit.

"Dad," Vega said, gasping the word.

"Vega, what happened?"

"Not sure." She tried to move. "You have to kill the plant. Pour the poison over it. Without the plant they'll abort their invasion plans."

Druix took the canister of poison from where it lay next to Vega. She was sitting up now, but unable to stand. She reached for her EMP weapon and aimed it at the nearest of the Tattoo People as he rose to his feet.

"Quick," she said with urgency.

Druix removed the lid of the canister and went to the plant, sitting defenselessly in its V-shaped container. Ready to pour the contents into the surrounding soil, he wondered how he and Vega would then escape. Even if the walls dissolved with the death of the plant, he'd still face an army of deadly Tattoo People. He doubted if the melody Vega had sung could ward off a full attack by so many. In any case, she seemed too weak to repeat the song she'd used to overcome the sentries.

Druix capped the canister and with the boldness of someone who has nothing else to lose, jumped onto the container that held the plant. Placing his two feet on its rim, he reached down and in one motion pulled the plant from the soil. Holding it under his arm, he jumped to the floor and returned to Vega.

"Can you walk?" he asked her.

"I think so."

She struggled to her feet. Druix took her arm and pulled her toward the wall. "Use the V sign. See if the vine will show us the way out."

But before they'd reached the wall, the sentries stood and came at them, stumbling clumsily on limbs just beginning to work. Vega turned on her translating medallion and was about to sing, but one of the Tattoo men snatched it from her and threw it clattering to the floor. Druix moved between Vega and the aliens and stood with the plant in one hand and the canister of poison in the other, turned so that even the slightest movement would spill the liquid over the bare roots of the vine.

The sentries stopped with both hands raised, each ready to deliver instant death to the two human intruders. But they held back. Vega turned to the wall and raised her hands in the V sign. The foliage parted instantly. She entered the opening. Druix, still holding the plant, recovered the translating medallion and followed Vega. Once through, the foliage closed behind them, preventing the Tattoo People from pursuing.

DENEB WAS LYING face down on a cot, bare from the waist up. In the light from the surrounding lanterns, Ilsa applied a green paste down the length of his back.

"What did you put on him?" asked Elsenia.

"It's an ointment the Tattoo People gave me. They make it from the residue of the vine. They use it to heal injuries and illnesses."

"But his back may be broken."

Ilsa smiled. It was a familiar smile. "I don't think we fully know all there is to know about the vine and its powers."

"I landed on my back in the water," said Deneb. "I'm sure it was broken."

"How did you manage to trade places with Vega?" Elsenia asked. "I thought the two of you had to be in your magnetocryogenic chambers to make the switch."

"That was Alphons' way to do it, but after having done it once, Vega and I realized that we didn't have to wait until the switch occurred randomly. We could make it happen. I'm not sure I understand, but it worked. Probably another example of Malanite weirdness passed on through Dad."

"However you did it, it was excellent timing," put in the Admiral.

"Vega was always the stronger swimmer. Even if I hadn't broken my back, she would have had an advantage over me in the river. It's fortunate that I lost consciousness. Otherwise, my pain would've crippled her, too. She didn't succumb to it until I started to regain consciousness."

"Is she okay now? Can you tell us what's happening?"

"I just know she's alive and in no danger. I feel a sense of urgency, but not peril."

"You should rest," interrupted Ilsa. "Vega may want your help later. You need to be strong."

With that, Ilsa rose and retreated into the darkness of the camp.

"Mom's different," remarked Deneb, after she left.

"Yes, she is," said Elsenia. "The ship of Theseus."

"What?"

"I'll explain later."

Deneb nodded and asked no more questions. He lay back and closed his eyes, thinking of his sister.

CHAPTER 42

— Century 2200 —

VEGA WAS STRUGGLING. Even though the vine cleared the way ahead of them, they were climbing out of the valley, ascending a slope getting steadily steeper.

"Slow down," called Druix. "If they're waiting for us when we leave the forest, it won't matter whether we get there sooner or later. We just have to hope having the plant with us will keep them from harming us."

"We have to keep moving through the openings the vine is making before they close up."

"The vine's been kind to us so far," said Druix. "We can hope that doesn't change."

"It's a good thing you showed the plant mercy. It's helping us."

To their astonishment and relief, there were no aliens to be seen when they finally broke through and exited the forest. Druix looked about and saw familiar landmarks from the earlier journey with Deneb. In the fading afternoon light, he and Vega returned along the path to the place where Ka-Pong's car was parked. Druix placed the plant in the back and they sped over the same rutted road. In the distance, they saw the outlines of the human factories belching smoke into the twilight sky.

They'd just rounded a curve in the road when they saw, standing before them, Abnaxes and several dozen aliens. Druix immediately swerved the car to the side, barely missing a slab of concrete partially embedded in a low mound that flanked the road. The car was propelled into the air, landing in a great cloud of dust on the far side of the berm. Once behind the obstruction, they were temporarily hidden. With little further thought, Druix accelerated away from the road, twisting and curving among the rocks, debris, metal, and concrete along improbable paths, any one of which could be a dead end.

DENEB RECOVERED QUICKLY and told Admiral Chase about encountering Abnaxes on the alien space station and being rescued by Max. The Admiral lost no time in transmitting the account to his troops on the command ship. Every galactic space vehicle would soon be alerted to watch for Max and Sadie, as well as of the impending threat by alien invaders from the planet Aurora. Now, Deneb sat alone with Elsenia, drinking a tea that Ilsa had prepared for him.

"It's made from the vine," Elsenia said.

"It's good. The vine is remarkable. The aliens managed to incorporate a multitude of life-sustaining properties in one plant. It conditions the atmosphere, eliminates competing plant species, and provides food, medicine, and building material for an emerging civilization. And, the vine offers aliens a means to communicate instantaneously all over the galaxy."

"It's hard to believe anything so inherently beneficial is being used by Abnaxes for destructive purposes."

Deneb shook his head. "The aliens made one mistake, not realizing that in creating the vine, by designing it to communicate, experience, and remember, it acquired a soul, so to speak, and formed its own opinions about right and wrong, good and bad. Whatever self-serving motives these inclinations might've been based on, the vine soon came to realize the role it was playing in the ruthless and indiscriminate expansion of the alien civilization."

Elsenia said, "If these aliens depended so much on the network of vines throughout the galaxy, why didn't the vine just stop communicating the information back to them?"

"Because it's a living thing and above all will protect itself. If the vine didn't report to Abnaxes, it wouldn't be needed. Also, the vine wasn't entirely sure human civilization was any better than the aliens."

"But the vine trusted you and Vega," said Elsenia.

"Yes, it did. And now other humans as well."

"What'll Abnaxes do? Are Druix and Vega still in danger?"

"Yes," said Deneb. "That's why I have to go back."

"What!" cried Elsenia. "But you're hurt. You're in no condition to go back."

"I'll be better soon, with Mom working her magic. In the meantime, I need your help."

"What?" asked Elsenia.

"I need to go back to where Vega and I first communicated with the vine."

"Why?"

"Because if there's a way to overcome the aliens, the vine will know it."

"Back to where it all began," said Elsenia, wistfully.

Deneb smiled. "Do you really think that's where it began, Elsenia?"

"That's when you and Vega first got involved."

"Not quite. Do you remember the stories you used to tell us about the planets?"

"Yes, the Family. How could I forget?"

"You may find this hard to believe, but those stories had a tremendous influence on Vega and me."

"How so?"

"Typically, children get completely absorbed with the task of understanding the world around them, family, environment, and friends closest to them. It's only later in life that young people are able to grasp the larger context of life and the universe."

"That's true."

"Except that your stories reversed that for Vega and me. We started out very young, understanding that ours was only one of many worlds in the galaxy. Our father was from one planet, our mother from another, our sister from a third. This changed our view of the universe indelibly. You didn't tell us stories about people. You told us about entire planets, interacting with each other, fighting with each other, even loving each other. The stories helped shape who we are, how we think, and what we wanted to do. When we were approached by Tattoo People on Lumina, we saw it as an opportunity to be part of the larger universe that you, Mom, and Dad had prepared us for from the very beginning."

Tears were streaming down Elsenia's cheeks. She bit her lip. "I'm sorry. I had no idea. I didn't mean…"

Deneb took her hand. "Elsenia, there's nothing to be sorry about. Everyone knows risks come with expanded awareness of the universe. It's a scary place. But Vega and I would choose this over any other form of existence. Maybe it's in our blood, but one way or the other, we're living the life we were destined for."

Elsenia wiped the tears from her cheek with the back of her hand.

"I'll let the Tattoo People know that you want to communicate with the vine," she said.

"We should hurry," said Deneb.

An hour later, Elsenia watched Deneb limp slowly into the temple-like enclosure where he and Vega had been brought by the Tattoo People during their first visit to Lumina.

DRUIX careened among the fallen buildings and upturned avenues of a city, long since abandoned. Not one structure was left intact by whatever forces had wreaked the devastation. A plume of dust rose behind the car as Druix steered it among the debris. He dared to turn to glance behind them, certain that Abnaxes and the alien horde would be closing the distance rapidly. Though difficult to make out through the trailing dust cloud, he saw several aliens. They were as nimble as the Tattoo People but much stronger. With a sinking feeling of hopelessness, he saw the aliens running on all fours, negotiating turns and obstructions in the road with frightening ease and agility. Ka-pong's car wasn't built for speed. Druix considered abandoning the vehicle and taking a chance on hiding from their pursuers, but he worried that Vega was still too weak. The only advantage they had was that the ground was sloped. He kept the vehicle moving downhill, building speed where nothing interrupted their way.

Just when he thought they were moving fast enough to escape, two aliens leaped into the road in front of the car. Druix swerved, barely squeezing through the space separating two concrete buildings. It led to an adjacent street ahead. He resisted the temptation to turn onto it, choosing instead to continue finding his way between the broken buildings. How long could he delay their inevitable capture? The plant rattled about in the back of the car with the canister of poison. Would the threat of killing the plant deter Abnaxes and his troops?

He must've reached the edge of the city. Exiting from the narrow space between two buildings, he came upon an open area with no road or obstructions. The downhill slope was even steeper here and the vehicle gained speed. In the distance, Druix saw puffs of factory smoke. He was leading the alien horde to where the humans lived and worked, but what could he do? He only hoped that whatever vengeance Abnaxes exacted against him and Vega wouldn't spill over to Ka-pong and the other humans.

Druix continued his course. Then, before he knew it, he found they were driving along a narrow track, with flanking walls growing higher. The road curved and opened up above a tremendous excavation pit, a kilometer across. He'd inadvertently turned onto a road spiraling around the circumference of an abandoned mine. His momentum kept him spiraling downward. To his dismay, he saw the aliens were not on the road, but scaling straight down the rocky slopes of the walls. Several were already waiting for the car on the bottom of the mine. He stopped the car, jumped out, and circled to the rear of the vehicle. He extracted the plant with one hand and found the canister of poison with the other.

A group of four aliens broke off their descent and raced toward the car with incredible ease. Druix saw no sign of fatigue in their movement, even after the long chase. At the head of the group, the form of Abnaxes was unmistakable. Druix watched the formidable alien and opened the canister of poison, prepared to pour it over the alien plant. He'd no reason to spare the vine any longer.

Then, remarkably, along the rim of the mine pit, humans appeared. They emerged by the hundreds, completely lining the circumference of the pit, holding the high ground above the aliens below. Here was a new force, an unexpected one, and Abnaxes looked up at them, his expression unreadable. Though humans outnumbered the aliens, there was no doubt that many would perish at the merciless hands of the giants. The conflict wouldn't end well for either side.

Ever the historian, Druix took advantage of the moment to analyze the tableau before him, to place it in the context of broader human history. He and Vega were on a planet established by emigrants from Earth in the 200th Century, confronting aliens who'd arrived later and enslaved the resident population. If someone was writing the history of civilization thousands of years in the future, would this event even be included? Would it be a paragraph, a chapter, an entire book? Or would it merit no more than a footnote? Would the writer be human or alien? From the aliens' point of view, it would be a brief uprising by humans, making a feeble attempt to disrupt the inevitable expansion of their species in the galaxy. A human historian might report that the spread of an alien species briefly threatened the human population of the galaxy, but was stopped by two descendants from Aurora, who returned to the planet, mobilized the enslaved humans, and defeated a much more powerful force. Druix admitted to himself that the first of the two scenarios seemed more likely.

He looked to where Vega sat, unmoving, in the front seat of the car. "I don't suppose your song will work right now?"

"It might if Vega sang it," came the reply. It was Deneb.

"Deneb?" Druix's jaw dropped. The twins had changed places again. When had it happened?

"I couldn't miss the opportunity of seeing my old friend Abnaxes again."

Deneb stepped out of the car. He moved slowly and carefully, not quite able to stand fully erect. In his right hand, he held an EMP weapon.

"Deneb, what are you doing?"

Nonchalantly, Deneb raised the weapon and fired it squarely into Abnaxes' chest. The alien stopped short, as if confused, then took another step forward. Deneb fired the weapon once more. Again and again, Deneb fired at Abnaxes. The other aliens looked on, not moving from their leader's side, as if they were also being shot by Deneb.

Druix wondered how many times an EMP weapon could fire before its power supply failed. He'd never seen it happen, but now Deneb seemed intent on firing the device until it was spent, each shot aimed directly and mercilessly at Abnaxes, who staggered backward and fell. Deneb walked to the alien leader and with his foot pushed the inanimate body off the road edge. It fell lifeless to the bottom of the excavation pit, a jumble of rocks and boulders accompanying the descent. Much as he was relieved to see Abnaxes destroyed, Druix was amazed at the detachment with which his son dispatched the corpse. He stood transfixed by the scene, still holding the plant and the canister of poison, the absurdity of the situation still working its way into his thoughts.

"What now?" he asked.

"It's over," answered Deneb.

Druix scanned the aliens standing about in confusion. "What about them?"

"They're lost," said Deneb. "Without Abnaxes, the aliens are harmless." He climbed into the passenger seat of the car. "You'll have to drive to the bottom to turn this thing around."

Druix placed the plant in the back again and covered the poison. Taking the driver's seat, he started slowly down the road. To his amazement, the aliens parted and let him pass. Druix glanced at Deneb and noticed his son was shaking. "It's okay," he told him.

Deneb sighed and shook his head. "It was the only way."

"You did what you had to do."

"Yeah," agreed Druix. "Better me than Vega."

Humans surrounded them when they reached the top of the pit again. Ka-pong broke from the crowd and approached. He shook their hands and climbed into the back of the car. Cradling the plant, he said, "Let's get out of here. I'll show you the way."

They returned to Ka-pong's factory. The other humans dispersed, but not before producing an oil drum, filling it with soil, and planting the alien vine in it.

Deneb, Druix, and Ka-pong sat together in the murky

light of the factory.

"How'd you know the aliens wouldn't attack with Abnaxes dead?" Druix asked.

"The vine knew. The whole alien expansion was fueled by the ambition of Abnaxes—all of the Abnaxes throughout time—passing along their legacy of evil, generation after generation. All it took to sustain the aggression was a single destructive idea strong enough to overwhelm the moral conscience of an entire population. In that way, the aliens are very much like humans, except they communicate among themselves much more efficiently. It was a sort of mass hypnosis. But Abnaxes was a single-point failure. Without him, the mentality of aggression couldn't be sustained."

"How can we be sure the remaining aliens will remain peaceful?" Ka-pong asked.

Deneb grabbed a slender metal rod lying on the floor of the factory. In the grease-covered surface, he etched a drawing.

"You need to build a monument—a huge V-shaped container. Fill it with the best earth you can find and put the plant in it. The angle of the V-shaped walls will make it difficult for anyone to scale them, even the aliens. Don't worry. The plant will survive. It takes care of itself."

Ka-pong shook his head. "It won't stop the aliens. I've seen them swarm like ants when they want something. They'll kill each other just to have something to stand on to reach what they're after."

"Right," said Deneb. "That's why you'll also have to build a powerful radio transmitter. Do you know how to do that?"

"We've never built one before. The aliens wouldn't allow it. But we can build anything."

"Good," said Deneb. "We'll stay until it's done. Then I'll tell you what to transmit."

ELSENIA WASN'T SURPRISED when Vega emerged from the temple that Deneb had entered just minutes before. They embraced.

"Deneb and Druix?" Elsenia asked through sobs.

"They're okay. It's over."

A group of Tattoo People emerged from the forest. They surrounded the two humans, forming a protective circle about them. Then they linked arms with Elsenia and Vega and guided them back to the camp, where Ilsa, Rashera, Nolondi, and Admiral Chase waited expectantly.

THE MONUMENT the humans of Aurora eventually built was far grander than Deneb had imagined. It stood the equivalent of thirty stories high, and the metal ring that ran around its circumference near the top was a kilometer in length. Constructed with guard rails, future visitors would be able to safely walk the perimeter of the monument and enjoy the uninterrupted view of the surrounding land. The plant thrived in the huge container, and grew proportionately larger. In a few years, it could be seen from many miles away.

The humans held nothing back in the design of the radio transmitter, making use of the monument's size to deploy thousands of units to line the walls, each transmitting continuously the sequence of frequencies that kept the aliens docile and peaceful. Even though the audible version of Vega's song wasn't needed to produce the chords of tranquility, the humans also added a sound system to the monument, and every hour on the hour, the song played, sending its message of peace.

Vega's song, and its radio wave equivalent, spread across the human population centers of Aurora and were broadcast into space. It became a hymn of peace, tranquility, hope, and resurrection for the people of the planet, as well as for the aliens who'd conquered it. The pattern of radio transmissions created twenty thousand light-years away with Nolondi's help reprogrammed the circuitry in the minds of the aliens, stripping them of whatever hostile, aggressive tendencies remained after Abnaxes' death. The ethics of this mental reprogramming were never questioned.

Ultimately, it had been the vine and all its connected vines throughout the galaxy that had decided what was right and what was wrong. No one contested this.

Eventually, Vega's song was no longer necessary because successive generations of aliens forgot the reasons for aggressive behavior by their ancestors. Vega's song was still sung by humans, and the aliens enjoyed the pattern of radio waves that the melody produced, long after the origin of the music was forgotten.

EPILOG

— Century 2458 —

ELSENIA'S FAMILY FINALLY had its reunion, but this time it took place on Supply Ship 6. It was a strange gathering, appropriately held on the supply ship once commanded by Benjamin Mizello's father, Arthur, and his partner Krystal Charbeau. The reunion was hosted by their daughter, Rashera, and included Benjamin's first wife, Ilsa, Benjamin's daughter, Elsenia, his son, Druix, and his grandchildren, Vega and Deneb. Admiral Chase was there, wearing a ceremonial uniform he'd carried with him from Earth and never worn till that day. Nolondi was also there, in uniform, but even dressed as a member of the Earth Fleet it was easy to tell he was one of the Tattoo People. Nolondi wore the outfit with the combination of humility and pride characteristic of his species. He no longer needed the metal helmet, as humans had created new rules prohibiting the transmission of radio waves randomly into space. All planets with alien populations were now protected from such communications.

Druix and Ilsa were getting along again. Druix recognized that Ilsa was now two people, both of whom he'd known intimately. It was not that difficult for him to accept the new person in Ilsa's body. After all, like the people of Magnetonia, Druix had led many different lives.

Admiral Chase and Elsenia finally came to understand the feeling they shared for each other. Many thousands of years ago on Earth, there was a word that described this emotion. The word had been the basis for unions of every type imaginable. Once the word became obsolete, each couple had to rediscover on their own the feeling, the attachment, and the complications that went with it. The act of rediscovery made these unions unbreakable.

Also present was Risto, who'd returned from Earth healthier than ever, all thoughts of retiring from the galactic explorer force given up for good. With the help of Rashera's computer calculations, Risto had found another asteroid in interstellar space.

This time it was easy to disable the weapon. He just had to destroy the antennas on its surface, rendering it unable to detect the radio waves it used for targeting planets. The asteroid would remain in a stable location forever, its arsenal of magnetic cylinders made useless without the accompanying control system. The galactic explorer fleet continued its vigil to find other such weapons in interstellar space.

Risto was slightly inebriated from drinking wine made on the planet Lumina from the berries of the alien vine. The year was 220,243, a very good year for alien-vine wine.

He'd been trying to get Druix's attention for some time. When he finally succeeded, the two of them moved into the corridor outside the galley, where the festivities were taking place.

"There is something I have to tell you about my visit to Earth," he said, his words slightly slurred.

"What is it, Risto?"

"It's about Petyuba."

Druix looked around to confirm Ilsa wasn't nearby. "You mean the Petyuba of Earth?"

"Yes. My report about her life on Earth after you and Ilsa left was not quite complete."

"Go ahead," encouraged Druix.

"There was a child."

"A child?" Druix repeated. Before the words were out, he already anticipated the response.

"Yes. Petyuba conceived a child seven months after you departed Earth."

Druix stared at Risto, unable to speak. The impact of an event so many thousands of years ago shouldn't have any consequence now. Still, it was a shock to him. Was it possible he had fathered a child on Earth during his visit there with Ilsa? "That was a long time ago," he said weakly.

Risto smiled. "Yes, it was. And it was only one child, but..."

"But?"

"There was a family," Risto began again, choosing his words carefully. 'A clan—all descendants from Petyuba's child.

Earthlings are very careful about tracing lineage. Those who were descended from the child—your child—were said to be blessed with special powers, able to transform their genetic qualities from one generation to the next, in response to social, political, and physiological stresses. Naturally, the members of the clan became great leaders. Even when I was there, Petyuba's clan wielded great power."

Druix took a long swallow from the glass of vine wine he'd been holding. "In a good way?" he asked.

"Yes, in a good way. The clan was largely admired and even respected by everyone on Earth. Not surprisingly, many of them were physicians, gifted through their descendence from Petyuba."

Druix nodded. "It'd be interesting to visit Earth. I wonder what the Petyuba clan is up to now."

"Yes. Perhaps you should, but don't be surprised if you see many people who look remarkably like yourself."

With that, Risto patted Druix on the arm and produced a deep-throated chuckle. "I will refill my glass now," he said, and strode back into the galley.

There were two other honored guests at the reunion—Max and Sadie. If there was any couple who appreciated a good party it was the two previous custodians of Supply Ship 2. They made sure music played. Before long there was dancing as well. Sadie missed dressing up in her 21st Century vintage clothing, all of which had been stolen by Stella, the space pirate. But she made the best of it, affixing a variety of accessories to her Union jump-suit, thereby transforming the drab outfit into a garment of inter-galactic elegance. She and Max waltzed about the galley to the delight of all the others. Their spirit, grace, and rhythm were up-lifting and infectious. Before long, Supply Ship 6 was vibrating with music and merriment, an anomaly and a singularity amidst the cold, emptiness of space.

At Max's insistence, Elsenia joined him for a dance. Her abilities were confined to tapping her toes to Arilian chants, but Max moved slowly in deference to her limited skills. He chewed a chunk of the alien vine Nolondi had given him. Max had bad teeth. Nolondi assured him the medicinal properties of the vine would help.

"Those two are formidable," he said, nodding toward Vega and Deneb.

"Yes, they are," agreed Elsenia. "but I still see them as my little brother and sister."

"So where's Altair?" Max asked.

"Altair?"

"Yeah, the third one."

"There is no third one. They're twins."

"Hmm." Max shrugged.

"Why do you ask?"

"I just figured. Back on Earth, there were three bright stars that appeared in the summer sky: Vega, Deneb, and Altair. The Summer Triangle. I just thought that since your parents named them Vega and Deneb, there might be an Altair out there somewhere."

"Well, there isn't," said Elsenia.

The song ended. Max bowed slightly to Elsenia and returned to Sadie.

Elsenia joined Vega and Deneb. It was good to see them together again, though all understood the twins could be so much more when they were apart. The connection they had with each other, and now with the alien vine and the Tattoo People, made them virtually lords of the galaxy, but neither of them acted any differently. They laughed with all the rest, and when they smiled they both looked like Benjamin.

Not present at the reunion, but very much a part of the conversation, was Alphons Demetriano, whose bothersome meddling had once again made its mark on the Mizello family. It was hard to hold a grudge against the ancient physicist, however, as his wild experiments had proven useful in the end.

"If only Benjamin could be here," Admiral Chase remarked.

"Yes, and Arthur and Krystal," said Elsenia.

"And Xyla," thought Druix, who perhaps more than any-one understood that the universe allowed for many different ways to 'be there'.

CPSIA information can be obtained at www.ICGtesting.com
Printed in the USA
BVOW08*0118110516

447538BV00001B/1/P